The DRAMATIC LIFE of JONAH PENROSE

The Dramatic Life of Jonah Penrose

A NOVEL

ROBYN GREEN

HARPER ◐ PERENNIAL

NEW YORK • LONDON • TORONTO • SYDNEY • NEW DELHI • AUCKLAND

HARPER PERENNIAL

Without limiting the exclusive rights of any author, contributor or the publisher of this publication, any unauthorized use of this publication to train generative artificial intelligence (AI) technologies is expressly prohibited. HarperCollins also exercise their rights under Article 4(3) of the Digital Single Market Directive 2019/790 and expressly reserve this publication from the text and data mining exception.

This is a work of fiction. Names, characters, places, and incidents are products of the author's imagination or are used fictitiously and are not to be construed as real. Any resemblance to actual events, locales, organizations, or persons, living or dead, is entirely coincidental.

THE DRAMATIC LIFE OF JONAH PENROSE. Copyright © 2025 by Abigail Green. All rights reserved. Printed in the United States of America. No part of this book may be used or reproduced in any manner whatsoever without written permission except in the case of brief quotations embodied in critical articles and reviews. For information, address HarperCollins Publishers, 195 Broadway, New York, NY 10007. In Europe, HarperCollins Publishers, Macken House, 39/40 Mayor Street Upper, Dublin 1, D01 C9W8, Ireland.

HarperCollins books may be purchased for educational, business, or sales promotional use. For information, please email the Special Markets Department at SPsales@harpercollins.com.

harpercollins.com

FIRST EDITION

Designed by Jen Overstreet
Stage light artwork © Pankina/Shutterstock
Theatrical icon artwork © Shorena Tedliashvili/Shutterstock

Library of Congress Cataloging-in-Publication Data has been applied for.

ISBN 978-0-06-345367-8 (pbk.)

25 26 27 28 29 LBC 5 4 3 2 1

*To everyone who believes in the magic of the theatre,
and to those who make the magic real.*

THE WOODEN HORSE

ACT ONE

"To Troy"
"The Road to Paradise"
"Helen"
"Agamemnon's Rally"
"What Do We Fight For?"
"My Soul Is Lost"
"The Battle"
"I Pray the Gods Forgive Me"
"The Melody of Achilles and Patroclus"
"In the Light of the Morning"

ACT TWO

"The Road to Paradise (Reprise)"
"Priam"
"Come with Me"
"The Song of the Dead"
"Achilles Waits"
"Answer Me"
"We Build"
"The Horse"
"Eternity"
"The Reprise"

ONE

"And then our bodies, woven as one, shall lie together in golden fields. The bounds of Troy, the destructions of war and wrath of the Gods, lover, we can forget it all. Come with me, across the sea, come with me, come with me."

—"Come with Me," *The Wooden Horse*, Act Two

The glittering champagne kisses of New Year's Eve slowly turned into cotton candy blossoms and buttercream tulips. London thrived in the spring; the buildings blushed at the rays of sun, which allowed the greenery of its parks to flourish once again. Sugarcoated pecans and mulled wine gradually morphed into cherry sweet cocktails and chocolate eggs. Jonah lived for the spring; the long dark days and even longer nights faded away, and duller skies held a promise of sunshine behind dusky clouds. Everything became far less serious as soon as April hit. An infectious sense of childhood seemed to grasp the population and transformed down-turned lips into coy smiles. The flirtation of the sun with its rays of warmth bubbled behind seductive glances and lingering touches. Even the throbbing pain at the front of Jonah's head caused by a copious amount of alcohol from the previous evening seemed somewhat less devastating now blossoms lined the trees.

God, how much drink passed his lips the night before? The evening came to him in fragments, a puzzle with far too many pieces, and he didn't have the energy to find the edges, let alone complete it.

An award show.

No, not just any award show, the fucking *Oliviers*, the thing he'd watched on TV year after year back home nestled between his parents. He remembered observing the glitz and glamour of it, the stars of British theatre coming together for a night celebrating the arts all under one roof. And, like some divine miracle, he'd been allowed to stand with the pinnacle of talent in the industry at the Royal Albert Hall and it wasn't a dream, he wasn't sitting at home imagining himself on the screen; he'd finally made it. For the first time in his life, he didn't feel like a spectator. He, Jonah Penrose, had been *invited*.

He rubbed his hand across his forehead and groaned as he turned toward his window, bedsheets tangling between his limbs as he tried to gauge the time. The movement churned his stomach, and he balked, bile singeing the back of his throat, which he swallowed down with a grimace. The unmistakable taste of tequila burned his gums, and he swore at himself for drinking the vile stuff yet again. Tequila, with its seductive voice and voluptuous curves, told him he could do anything; it provided an outrageous sense of confidence and said he should absolutely buy more shots.

Salt. Tequila. Lime. And repeat.

He should have stuck to the champagne. The flutes didn't allow him to drink to excess; they made him stand tall and sip politely, not throw the drink back then suck on a lime for dear life. If only he hadn't spent his late teens drinking shots the color of drain cleaner and not caring about refining his palate, then maybe champagne might have been more seductive. Golden bubbles. Long slim stem to wrap his hand around. No, he needed to stop sexualizing drinks to excuse his hangover. He didn't even need an excuse last night because he knew, as soon as his name echoed throughout the theatre, champagne simply wouldn't cut it.

He'd won.

The moment still didn't register in his mind. *His* name sounding out, followed by a deafening round of applause and hands grasping him, launching him to his feet as he gawped in complete bewilderment. Despite the thumping haze of pain echoing inside his skull, he could still see the inside of the hall as clear as day. Shining black stage, walls of gold and plush red velvet chairs. Jonah always knew his soul belonged in the theatre; it flourished from a tiny seed nestled between the floorboards and grew into something brimming with decadent petals and vibrant colors. But last night, in the Royal Albert Hall, he saw he belonged to an entire garden full of outstanding flora. For a few seconds, the world slowed down; the noise dulled, and he fully took in the scene surrounding him. Bodies, hundreds of them, stretched out and circled up, up, up into the balconies. The people glittered, they shone in freshly pressed suits and silk dresses dipped in moondust with smiling faces kissed by glimmering stage lights. The same lights shone on him.

He'd allowed himself to dream of it happening, winning an award, of course he had. He even wrote out an acceptance speech in the notes app on his phone while steaming rice the week before. But the reality he found himself in didn't seem to compute with real life. The sheer talent surrounding him—actors, directors, costume designers, musicians, technicians, choreographers—took his breath away. The love of theatre drummed through them, it created an electric wave of joy Jonah could honestly say he'd never experienced before. Gratitude, respect, and passion. And every single person in the vast auditorium looked directly at him.

The memory was enough to make his stomach turn. He recalled he seemed to forget how to walk properly. His feet lifting and landing at an unnatural pace, knees bending too much, an impression of a drunk person stumbling out of a taxi in the middle of the night. Bambi on ice. He worried his suit didn't fit right, too big, too small, and oh shit, what if he tripped, what if his mouth stopped working and no words came to him when he stepped onto the stage and in front of the microphone? His suit, picked out by Sherrie, the most fashion-forward person he knew, fit him like a glove, and he needed to just bloody relax, but in the moment, his mind looped the sound of internal screaming and, inexplicably, the song from the Coco Pops advert he hadn't thought about since he was five.

A blur of color swarmed around Jonah as he neared the stage—hands clapping, clothing fluttering, someone from the back of the hall hollering his name, Sherrie, no doubt—and he forced himself to think about walking more so he could actually get on the stage. Out of the corner of his eye, just to his left, he saw a flash of blond hair and a face he recognized, but it quickly faded into the rest of the noise only to leave a foot jutting out into the aisle. Were they trying to trip him? He shook his head, no, no one would trip him, not while on his way to get his award, not on purpose, and he glanced at the body the foot belonged to just in time to see them shift in their seat, taking their wayward foot with them.

When he finally made it up the six stairs to the presenters and background of cheers, a bronze statue of Laurence Olivier found its way to his hands, the bust more weighty than he expected, and there he stood, looking out at a sea of faces, all smiling, some more than others, and he fought back the urge to cry. He'd been chosen, out of all the amazing people in his category, people he'd admired for so long whose careers were stunning and filled with success, and he'd been chosen as the winner.

He remembered, for the briefest of moments, he tried to find his father's face in the crowd. Broad nose, wispy gray hair, and soft blue eyes reminiscent of the sea back home. He could picture his smile, warm, the smile he looked for constantly as a child, consistent and safe, but it couldn't be found; his father wasn't there. Silly, really, for him to even try to look for him, but he became a boy again, searching for his dad in a crowd, the familiar comfort of knowing he wasn't far.

Words caught in his throat, the tears that had threatened to fall seconds before inching closer and closer until he shook his head and took a deep breath and spoke, the obligatory thank-yous spilling from his lips at such a pace he couldn't keep up. He didn't know if he'd thanked everyone. He tried, he waved his hand to the company sitting in the stalls and the others sitting higher in the balcony, trying to encompass them all, probably failing miserably, but his brain and body were no longer his. He was just a puppet in an expensive suit who didn't know how to walk without looking like he'd just shit himself. The minutes he spent on the stage didn't lodge themselves in his memory; they didn't happen, not really, not to him, his body moved him without thought, a dance created by invisible strings. However, his lack of memory of those important moments didn't take away from the fact he *had* won an Olivier Award. Jonah Penrose. Best actor in a musical.

Holy shit.

Jonah moved from his bed, feet skimming along the wooden floor, one sock still on, the other somewhere in the crumpled suit beside the bed, and he lurched toward the bathroom. His knees smacked against the tiles as his hands gripped the rim of the toilet seat and he vomited. Tequila. Tequila. Tequila. A terrible idea, such a stupid idea, though ingenious at the time. He remembered the bar, The Roundhouse, the place the cast and crew often congregated after a show, and the chosen after-party spot once the photos and niceties wore off at the award ceremony. The air clung to his skin, the night unnaturally warm, though the heat may have come from the permanent flush on his cheeks after clutching his award and beaming at cameras for over an hour. Bodies pressed against him, the cast, front of house, strangers, and he didn't care, they all showered each other with words of eternal love spurred on by the tequila shots floating across the bar. He thought of Bastien, Sherrie and Omari, their arms wrapped around him, lips pressed to his cheeks as they danced happily at the bar. The evening a celebration for them all.

The Wooden Horse won seven awards. The nominations were overwhelming in themselves, but winning? They could now add those accolades to the five-star reviews and sold-out performances. Jonah felt the doubt in the pit of his stomach beginning to lessen. He'd proven himself. Achilles, the role of a lifetime, one he'd poured his heart and soul into, one he'd molded and nurtured, truly belonged to him now no matter what anyone else said.

The floor tiles felt cool against his back as he lay down on them, his chest heaving as he wiped the back of his hand across his mouth. Sun streamed in through the bathroom window, and the sounds of Camden Town spilled into the room, took one look at him on the floor, and left again. A laugh escaped his lips, a thing of pure joy as little sparks of the night before pushed their way to the forefront of his mind. He wanted to scream, to fling the front door open and run down Castle Road to alert all the residents that their house valuations had increased as they now lived on the same street as an Olivier winner. His skewed perception of the win and the impact it might have on the unsuspecting residents on Castle Road didn't matter. He wanted the world to know; he needed to tell everyone, his mum, the woman who walked her dog past his window every morning, even the grumpy man in the corner shop near the tube station.

His laughter stopped abruptly as he recalled the first person he called once he'd downed a few shots at The Roundhouse. He should have called his mum. Did he even thank her in his speech? God, she would kill him if he didn't. Either way, he didn't call her; he called Edward instead. He could remember his hands shaking as he pulled his phone from his pocket, a mixture of too much alcohol and the bitter chill of the night air working its way over his body as he stood outside of the building where the joyous noise from inside became dulled. The desire to hear Edward's voice, the need to revel in his praise was greater than any happy tears his mum may shed over his triumphant win.

Jonah sat up, his stomach turning over itself, and he swallowed down another mouthful of vomit as the floor tilted beneath him. Something didn't feel right; not just his head or the perpetual sensation of being in motion, something else, something awful, something his brain desperately wanted to scrub away.

Edward.

His voice sounded strange on the phone the night before, far away, like he'd submerged himself in water. Edward listened to Jonah speak, he let him talk and talk and talk until he stopped and a vacuous silence lingered between them. Did Edward say anything? Did he offer congratulations? Jonah couldn't remember, all he could recall was the taste of tequila on his lips and the promise of more alcohol on the horizon.

Jonah tentatively rose to his feet; he braced himself against the wall and caught a glimpse of his reflection in the mirror above the sink. His unruly curly brown hair clung to his forehead, his skin a deathly shade of ivory, so pale he could have been masquerading as a ghost, and a rather hideous one at that. He averted his gaze, the devastation of his appearance sickening in itself, and clambered back to his bedroom, the walls morphing in an entirely unhelpful way. As he reached for his phone on the nightstand, his fingers missed it, and he acknowledged the fact he wasn't hungover but actually still drunk and forced himself to grab it like a toddler reaching for a wooden train. Chubby mitts, his dad would say, clumsy chubby mitts.

A plethora of messages awaited him along with three missed calls from his mother, who'd apparently stayed up late to watch the awards on TV the night before. But nothing from Edward. Jonah looked at the vacant space in the bed. The side wasn't technically Edward's, since they didn't live together. But it belonged to him, regardless. A fluttering feeling wormed its way into the center of his chest, an unnerving sensation akin to the final moments before a drop on a roller coaster. Edward should have been there. He should have joined him at The Roundhouse and downed shots of tequila with him. They should have woken up together and complained about how much they drank and vowed never to do it again before having lazy hungover sex in the shower. Jonah stared at the screen of his phone, then clicked the green dial icon, his breath frozen in his throat as he listened to it ring and ring and ring until—

"Jonah?"

"I won an Olivier Award, did I tell you?" The words came before his brain clicked into motion. "Best actor in a musical."

Edward cleared his throat. "Um, yeah, I know, you told me. It's amazing, Jonah, well done, again."

Jonah blinked, his brain still not working with the tequila still swimming through his bloodstream. He expected more, a little enthusiasm at least; Edward sounded like he'd rather grate his ears off than talk with him. "I thought you might want to . . . did you want to get lunch later? To celebrate?"

"Jonah." Edward sighed. "We talked about this last night."

They did? Of course they did, or Edward at least spoke to the hyped-up and incoherent Jonah who was definitely not the hungover and filled-with-regret present Jonah. "Yeah, I mean, yeah of course we did."

"You don't remember."

Jonah pinched the skin between his eyes and sucked in a sharp breath. "I do, yeah, of course I do."

"Then why are you calling asking me to go to lunch?"

Silence.

"Fuck," Jonah murmured. "I'm sorry. We all went out afterward, and drinking ensued. Last night was a complete blur, and I promise you I'm paying for it now."

"So, you don't remember?"

Jonah groaned and flung himself onto the bed, a poor choice given the movement made the taste of tequila work its way up his throat again. "Did you tell me you have a sudden aversion to eating lunch?"

"No," Edward said, his voice far away again, underwater, out of reach. "Jonah. I've met someone else."

The bed creaked as the ceiling spun above him. Someone else. He must have misheard him. *Someone else* didn't compute. There could be nobody else.

"What?"

"I'm sorry."

"No. Wait. What? Someone else? What do you mean by *someone else*? As in, what, a person?"

"Yes, Jonah, a person."

"When would you . . . how did you . . . wait, no, Edward, come on, let's talk about this. You can't . . . we can't, Edward, please, we can figure this out."

"There's nothing to figure out, Jonah." His voice lacked even an ounce of empathy. "I've met someone else. Don't make this harder than it needs to be, okay? I will come over this afternoon to pick up my stuff and leave my key. Relationships end, Jonah. We had a good run."

Jonah bit down on his lip, the taste of blood kissing his tongue and mingling with the remnants of alcohol from the night before. Tears caught in his throat, and the only words he could muster were, "But I'm an Olivier Award–winning actor." The protest came out weak, a pathetic plea mixed with a poor attempt at something resembling indignation. The spring outside the window lost its romance, it lost the taste of bubble gum and lemon curd as the sky turned from powder blue to smoldering ash. Edward said nothing else and hung up the phone, leaving Jonah with a never-ending dead dial tone to haunt him for the rest of the day.

Someone else. It was always someone else.

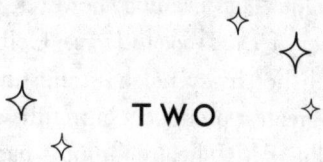

TWO

"In silence we wait, we wait, we wait, for the gates to open and for them to let in their fate."

—"The Horse," *The Wooden Horse*, Act Two

The email came through ten minutes before curtain call. In those precious moments before the theatre turned dark and the audience fell into an excited hush, Jonah usually found himself in the wings just offstage, readying himself for the opening number. However, for the first time since he'd stepped foot in the stunning Persephone Theatre, he didn't want to leave his dressing room. Flowers were positioned in varying vases on every surface available, interspersed by cards filled with congratulations and the odd box of chocolates. He imagined himself to be a starlet plucked from a film, a bevy of admirers lining up outside his dressing room with gifts. Despite the breakdown of his relationship, he'd never felt so loved, so appreciated. Edward found someone else, he turned his back on Jonah and the romance they'd found with each other, but it didn't mean the theatre would do the same. He'd glanced at his phone to see another message from his mum, who he eventually spoke to Monday night once he'd successfully nursed his hangover, and three emails waiting to be read.

Jonah's inbox more often than not became plagued with spam mail and offers from the pizza place down the road from where he lived, a place he frequented far too often but would never admit to. Cheese caused mucus buildup, bad for the vocal cords, apparently, but remarkably good for his soul. Now and then he opened an email from the National Theatre, or an update from one of the many petitions he put his name to when he couldn't sleep at night. That evening, however, at seven twenty, an email from the producer of *The Wooden Horse*, Colbie Paris, consumed his screen. Colbie, with her frizzy red hair and unnatural height, was considered one of the greatest producers currently working in the West End. Her CPTG—Colbie Paris Theatre Group—had worked on numerous productions, all of them beautiful, her creative vision something to be admired. And it couldn't be ignored that her money also did a lot of the talking. She sank incomprehensible amounts of money into her shows and expected a return on her investment, which maybe explained the bitter expression always pasted on her face. Colbie seemed to have a rain cloud looming over her at all times, and she wore it like a cloak. Yet, despite her often-frosty demeanor and a pile of awards from her other shows, Jonah assumed her message would contain a plethora of congratulations for the company; seven Olivier Awards were to be celebrated, but so far she had encased herself in silence.

He opened the email and smiled to himself, awaiting the inevitable applause from within. The celebrations never came. Instead, he faced the list of new cast members for the next year, admittedly a small one given most of the company extended their contracts and were staying in their roles. Colbie offered Jonah a contract renewal months ago, his position safe, the rent on his home paid for another year; but knowing auditions took place a few months ago to replace some of the others left him with a deep sense of unease. He ran his finger down the list, pausing on the new names, knowing some of them and recalling their faces, and made a mental note to look up the ones he didn't recognize. Then he stopped on a name so closely associated with his own he forced himself to read it six times to ensure his brain wasn't malfunctioning. But no. The name displayed on his screen in miniscule pixels was not a figment of his imagination.

Dexter Ellis.

The heartthrob of the West End. Known for being a super swing before landing his first major role as Fiyero in *Wicked*. He became an overnight star, going from one massive role to the next, until his name was always listed first on show announcements. Some marketing decision saw him named the king of the West End, a pretty big accolade, one Jonah supposed he kind of deserved; the guy seemed to be everywhere. A vocal powerhouse. A dance veteran. He simply oozed talent, and his tireless work ethic clearly paid off with a string of high-profile shows all with his name attached to them. He somehow managed to balance working all hours of the day with a thriving social media career, too, his ridiculous number of followers a testament to his video-editing skills and ability to always look flawless in his photos. But, most importantly, he was the actor who originated the role of Achilles in *The Wooden Horse* four years ago. He took on the role for the Edinburgh Fringe Festival and on the pre–West End tour, and for years spouted about how originating Achilles was his proudest achievement. Something tickled the back of Jonah's throat, the same enclosed feeling he experienced when he discovered his allergy to soy milk during his brief foray into veganism, and he swallowed down the electric ball of anxiety working its way up his esophagus.

He remembered the comments beneath the West End cast-announcement posts for *The Wooden Horse* on social media, the ones announcing him as the lead a little over a year ago, and he recalled the rampant assumptions of him tearing the role of Achilles from Dexter's perfectly formed hands written in screeching capital letters and unhappy emojis. Jonah never stole the role from anyone. If only people knew the string of intense auditions followed by months of silence before finally getting the news he'd been cast, they might understand Dexter bloody Ellis never planned to see the role into the West End.

Perhaps he was still drunk from the ceremony on Sunday, and his eyes were playing tricks on him. He spent most of Monday fumbling around his house in tears made worse by the tequila still lingering in his bloodstream, then ate an entire loaf of bread after Edward made a swift visit and collected the small amount of stuff he'd left there. His key still sat on the kitchen table. Jonah didn't want to touch it; if he did then it would make the breakup real. For as long as the key sat undisturbed by the fruit bowl, he could pretend Edward just forgot it. He'd return and slip it back into his pocket, then they'd find their way to bed and Jonah wouldn't have to wake alone. Several hours were consumed on Monday with cycles of vomiting and self-deprecation until he forced himself to his evening yoga class, looking just short of death as he shuffled into the studio. He then returned home and cried over the phone to Sherrie while he consumed a bunch of bananas.

Yet there Dexter's name sat now, perfect pixels on a screen, a ghost of Achilles past come to haunt him. Was Dexter going to come in and steal the show?

Jonah tried to think of the departing cast members and the roles they were leaving to be picked up by others. Priam, no, way too old for Dexter. Odysseus, maybe, but the role seemed too small, no major solos, not something the great Dexter Ellis would deem worthy of his time. Which left Hector. But why would he want to play Hector after playing Achilles? Oh God, what if he was coming in to be Jonah's alternate? The comparisons between them would not be able to be ignored. Jonah would never be able to take a holiday again or be ill and risk Dexter going on his place, he would have to be onstage forever until the day he died, he would—

Fuck. The final stage call sounded from the speakers in the dressing room and a hurried knock reverberated from Jonah's door throughout the room. He turned to see Evie, the stage manager, standing there, headset on, clipboard in hand, face the color of beetroot. She took her role seriously, overseeing every aspect of the production with a permanent flush to the face and endless sighs that echoed throughout the dressing rooms. Jonah sometimes wondered why she didn't delegate more, but the woman seemed intent on giving herself a stress-induced heart attack.

"Jonah fucking Penrose what are you still doing in here?" she seethed, dark brown eyes burrowing into Jonah's core. "Are you a diva now that you've won an Olivier? Lounging in your dressing room full of flowers?" Despite the apparent anger in her words and tone Jonah could sense a warmth there too.

"Just one sec." He smiled at her as Evie rolled her eyes and stormed away.

Jonah placed his phone back onto the table in front of his illuminated mirror. He studied his reflection; his body glistened beneath deep-blue cotton and soft folds of material the color of seaweed. His skin, pale as always, contrasted with his brown curls, and he thought of Dexter Ellis standing in front of a mirror preparing himself to take down the city of Troy. He'd done it first, after all. He'd recorded the mixtape and he'd sung Achilles's sweeping melodies to audiences long before Jonah ever did. Dexter introduced the world of theatre to the tragic hero and his heartbreaking romance with Patroclus. Jonah may have won the award, but Dexter paved the way for him, and now he was returning to the show, a return which would no doubt shine even more scrutiny on Jonah and the role he still believed was never meant for him. No. Dexter wouldn't be coming to be an understudy; he was too big for that, his name far too important. He was going to take the stage and Jonah would have to stand idly by and watch him steal *The Wooden Horse* right from under his feet.

An electricity ran through the audience. They held their gaze on the company, on Jonah, and every move he made. He could feel the tears they struggled to hold back as he held Bastien, his Patroclus, in his arms, his death the most pivotal moment in the production, and they suspended their breaths as he sang to him of his regrets. The phrase "you could hear a pin drop" never seemed more fitting. As the stage revolved and the middle ring lowered, slowly taking both him and Bastien down below it, away from the sight of the audience, he sucked in a breath and tried to hold back his own tears. Bastien looked at him, moving again now he no longer needed to be seen as dead, and frowned, but no words could be spoken, not when the epic story above them continued to unfold.

He moved then, from the lowered platform to the steps leading back up to the stage where his next entrance awaited him. Bastien watched him move, then reached out his hand to touch his shoulder, a simple show of support despite not having the words to convey anything further. Sometimes Jonah wished he could love Bastien the same way Achilles loved Patroclus; they played out their love night after night, the end always the same, always horribly tragic for them both, but their bond lived on long after their deaths. Bastien sang like a nightingale; he spoke with a lyrical flair and always brushed his teeth before a show, something his first cover, Lucian, never did. Offstage, Bastien always brightened a room, he illuminated it with his smile alone, and more than once Jonah hung onto his every word like a puppy dog, only to snap himself out of it to remind himself Bastien had a rather lovely boyfriend who he'd been with for six years. Which is why, when Jonah met Edward, he hoped he might find the love he felt he needed in him. Maybe he, too, could have what Bastien had.

He didn't want to admit to himself the ache in his chest came not from Edward leaving, but more the reason behind it. *For someone else.* He thought of the comment section beneath his headshot announcing his casting as Achilles and recalled the words written there:

> Who is he?
>
> He's fucking ugly, he can't be Achilles.
>
> Why isn't Dexter Ellis playing Achilles?
>
> He looks like a twat.
>
> Bet he can't sing.

The social media manager turned off the comments. They tried to protect him from the keyboard warriors and members of the Dexter Ellis fan club, and when previews started, he showed them he was worthy of the role. But now, even with the Olivier Award with his name on it and the six other awards spread across the company, the familiar stirrings of inadequacy reared their ugly head again.

He'd been chosen to play Achilles. The casting team picked him out of God only knew how many other actors and handed him the leading role on a silver platter. No one mentioned Dexter or the stunning reviews he received before the show found its way to the West End. But Edward offered himself to Jonah, too, or, more accurately, Jonah laid himself out bare to him, told him about his life back home and the anxiety that liked to knock at his door in the middle of the night. Edward didn't run back then, he wrapped Jonah in his arms and kissed him and made him believe they could be something. A quiet and safe corner in the loud and intrusive city of London. But now he'd thrown Jonah out into the cold without giving him so much as an inkling their relationship was crumbling. So why wouldn't Colbie do the same? She ruled the production with an iron fist, her words cutting with a stone-turning stare. If she believed Jonah was being upstaged, she would pull Achilles out from under him once his contract ended and lock the theatre door.

As the cast took their final bows, Omari to his left, Bastien to his right, Jonah looked out to the audience and forced himself to smile. A standing ovation, something they received often, cheered in front of him, and for a moment he allowed the applause to take over his senses; it numbed the anxiety and all thoughts of Edward and Dexter. As they left the stage, the roar of the audience continued, an overwhelming show of support for them all, and Bastien took Jonah's hand into his as they walked to their dressing rooms.

"What's wrong?" he asked, always the empath, always sensing the slightest change in Jonah's demeanor, the complete opposite to Omari, who would notice his mood then talk about skin peels.

"They released the new cast names by email earlier," Jonah said, as they stopped in front of their dressing room doors. He saw Bastien's expression fall, the usual dimples in his cheeks fading to leave behind an expression not usually worn by the man.

"Oh shit, really? Anyone we know?"

"A few I recognize. Dexter Ellis's name sticks out the most, though."

Bastien's eyebrows shot up at the mention of the name. "What? Really? He didn't mention it when I bumped into him at the Olivier Awards."

"He was at the Oliviers?"

Bastien shrugged slightly. "Yeah, came over and introduced himself to me. Didn't mention he'd been working on the production again. Did the email say the roles?"

"Are you talking about the email from Colbie?" Omari asked, seemingly appearing out of nowhere to insert himself into the conversation.

"Yeah," Bastien said, smiling at Omari, who looked as fresh as someone who'd just come from a spa day despite performing onstage for two and a half hours.

"We're getting Dexter Ellis!" Omari grinned. "I can't wait to see that man stretching before me in warm-ups."

Jonah couldn't help the scowl pulling at the edge of his lips. "We don't need to know about your stretching desires, Omari."

"Hey," the taller man said seriously. "I'm dance captain, I take stretching *very* seriously." He emphasized his words by reaching his hands up above his head, exposing his biceps from his costume almost intimidatingly. "I will see you babes later," he said as he dropped his arms and yawned. "Need to get myself changed and home for my beauty sleep." He kissed them both on the cheeks then left them in the corridor after disappearing into the dressing room he shared with other members of the ensemble.

"You don't think Dexter's going to cover Achilles, do you? What if they want to give him Achilles once my contract ends?" Jonah asked Bastien when they were alone once again.

Bastien shook his head and smiled at Jonah fondly. "No, Jonah, come on. Lennon's still here, and he's still covering our roles. Dexter's probably going to be Hector. Stop worrying, you'll give yourself wrinkles." A fond silence settled between them before Bastien rolled his eyes and ruffled Jonah's curls. "Right," he said, breaking the silence to push open his door. "I'm going to check out the email myself then head for stage door to meet all of my adoring fans." He fluttered his eyelashes and framed his face between his hands with a smirk. "See you out there, darling."

THREE

"On, keep going on, on, on, keep going on."

—"The Road to Paradise," *The Wooden Horse*, Act One

The announcement went out at 10 a.m.

Photos of the new cast alongside the cast remaining in their roles were posted across all the social media channels along with a press release sent to various outlets and theatre bloggers. Jonah told himself not to look, to keep his eyes off the comments and reposts, but the temptation to self-sabotage overwhelmed him. He couldn't resist the torment. The first thing to truly irk him was Dexter's headshot; he looked at least five years younger than Jonah, and for a man who just turned thirty the year before and was absolutely having a sort of inner quarter-life crisis, a youthful, blemish-free face was the last thing he wanted to see. He stared at Dexter's features for a while, a frown on his face that would no doubt give him wrinkles, so fuck Dexter Ellis for ruining his skin.

He eventually tore his eyes away from Dexter's face and allowed himself to dive into the comment section. A dangerous mission, one he rarely undertook, but he needed to see the scathing words condemning him even further now that Dexter was going to claim his throne. However, the condemnations never came. While some of the comments held sad goodbyes for some of the old cast, most expressed excitement at the revelation of the fresh faces and surprise at who they would be playing.

Dexter Ellis had been called back to the city of Troy not as an alternate for Achilles, but as Hector, just as Bastien said. The Trojan prince. Son of Priam and Hecuba. Killed by Achilles. Which really was rather fabulous, as Jonah couldn't wait to stab him every night, no matter how violent it sounded.

So, despite looking for words of hate within the hundreds of replies to the posts, Jonah couldn't find any. There were a few remarks about how the casting announcement overshadowed the Olivier wins, and how the timing seemed a little off, which he agreed with, but overall, the negativity he expected to see simply didn't materialize. Which meant the emotional breakdown simmering at the edge of Jonah's aura couldn't be blamed on Dexter Ellis. No. The inevitable breakdown came from Edward's nail clippers neatly tucked away in the cupboard in the bathroom.

As a child, Jonah never imagined cradling clippers in his palm while wailing on his bathroom floor; it simply wasn't a future he hoped for, and certainly not one he ever thought might play out. He also didn't imagine eating a block of cheese for breakfast. Reality, however, proved both scenarios could be real and also happen on the same Godforsaken day. It only took a week for the breakdown to happen, Jonah's mind consumed with performances Tuesday to Saturday, not giving him time to actually sit and contemplate the fact he was miserably single. Again. But as the sun rose on Sunday, the nail clippers came out to play and the cheese offered a comforting hug from the confines of the fridge. He imagined Omari standing before him, his six-foot-five frame taking up most of the kitchen, brow creased with concern. *Mucus. Cheese gives you mucus, Jonah. Think of the mucus, for God's sake.*

He contemplated calling Edward, begging him to dump the other guy and take him back. He missed having to explain over and over to him the difference between a swing and an understudy, because no, Edward, a swing learns multiple roles, an understudy covers principal roles, but he never remembered. He missed Edward's voice and the way he always burned toast in the mornings without fail. He missed his weird-smelling banana shampoo and the way he folded his underwear when they undressed for bed. And he missed the way he kissed him, his lips pressed against his with an intense heat reminiscent of scorching summer days spent back home in Cornwall. Why couldn't he stop thinking about him and his stupidly handsome face? Tears fell down Jonah's cheeks in steady streams as he pushed the last piece of cheese into his mouth, ignoring how sick he felt and the apparition of Omari chiming on about stupid mucus, and let out a muffled cry as he tried to remember the last night they spent together.

He hadn't considered what "meeting someone else" really meant until that moment. Questions buzzed through his brain, too many to consider all at once, but the main one burning at the forefront of his mind was: Did Edward cheat on him? Jonah looked at the empty cheese packaging on the kitchen countertop, then over at Edward's key on the table. The country was going through a cost-of-living crisis, and he just consumed an entire block of cheese over a man who couldn't even be faithful to him. He wiped his sleeve across his eyes, then tapped his fingers over his cheeks to lure himself back to reality. *Fuck.*

His phone vibrated from within his pocket, and he pulled it out to see his mum's face sparkling across the screen. A quick glance at the clock, ten-thirty, told him it wasn't her usual calling time, and his finger hovered over the answer button until the ringing stopped. She would hear the tears in his voice. She'd be able to sense his heartbreak even from hundreds of miles away. When he first moved to London, when the salty spray of the sea still clung to his clothes and grains of sand could be found nestled in the creases of his palms, he called home every week. His parents hung onto his stories of London as if he had ventured out of a black-and-white photo and returned with a far-fetched adventure drenched in Technicolor.

The first time they visited, when he performed as Anthony in an off-West End production of *Sweeney Todd*, they looked at the small theatre in awe. They waited for him at the stage door, clutching their programs with a buzz of excitement, and insisted he sign them despite the deep-red flush on his cheeks and cooing from his castmates. His parents, fiercely loyal and immensely proud, were on the other end of the phone when his first boyfriend in London, Rhys, dumped him by text right as he was about to go onstage. His mum helped him nurse the heartache from her settee at home and made him believe she sat beside him in his dressing room, her voice soothing, like the sea. They welcomed him home during his holidays and they walked along the shoreline as the wind kissed their cheeks, his mum's arm linked with his as his dad skimmed stones across the waves and told folktales he remembered from his childhood.

His phone lit up again and his mother's face smiled at him from the screen, her curly hair framing her round face perfectly. She'd lost weight since he took the photo of her. The last time he saw her he couldn't help but notice how drawn her face appeared, cheekbones prominent, wrinkles more severe. Something stirred in the pit of his stomach as a strange sense of unease bloomed in his chest. He answered the call and pressed the phone to his ear, immediately hearing stuttered breaths gasping for air.

"Mum?"

"Jonah, darling," she whispered, voice so far away, frail, tiny. "I hope I'm not bothering you."

The crumpled cheese packaging glanced up at him from the countertop. "No, not at all. What's up?"

"You've been crying," she said, her breath catching in her chest. "Darling, what's wrong?"

"It's just hay fever." He wiped his sleeve over his eyes again. "Are you okay? You . . . you sound out of breath."

She didn't answer right away, and Jonah could almost hear the cogs turning in her head as she thought of the best way to reply. "It's been a little bit of a shoddy morning, love."

"Why?" He knew the answer.

"He had another terrible night last night."

"Did you call the nurse?"

"I didn't want to bother her."

Jonah took a deep breath. "Mum, it's why they're there, if you need help you have to call them. What happened?"

"He fell out of bed. I kept telling him not to get up, but you know he won't listen. He isn't strong enough to walk these days, but up he gets and then he falls. He doesn't let me help him, he just gets angry. He scares me a little."

Silence hung between them. The conversation one they repeated monthly, the words the same, the advice the same, the outcome always the same. Sometimes Jonah wanted to scream at her, her reluctance to do anything to help herself a constant source of anxiety. Yet, he also knew he viewed the situation from a distance, an impartial spectator with advice but no physical help. In reality, he knew full well that if he were back home in St. Ives nothing would change. She would still refuse help and would only push him away if he so much as offered to make her a cup of tea. But he wanted to help, he needed to help; his mother's world crumbled more by the second.

The day Jonah's father looked at him down on the beach with zero recognition behind his eyes would live on in his memory forever. Jonah reached for him and the taller man stepped back, bewildered, frightened. He'd never seen his father appear vulnerable before, and he couldn't help but think he shouldn't have seen him in such a way; he always saw his dad as invincible, a steady presence who never faltered. Yet there he stood, his eyes searching Jonah for answers he simply couldn't find. His father turned from him and ran, feet pounding the stones along the edge of the beach, and he shouted at strangers dotted along the coastline who sat on beach towels and dined on crab sandwiches. He begged them for help, to get him away from the strange man chasing after him, the strange man he simply couldn't believe was his son. The child he once cradled in his arms and sang to sleep. Jonah remembered the awful sinking feeling he experienced in the moment, like treading quicksand, drowning in it, suffocating.

"Where is he now?" Jonah asked.

"Well, the nurse came in for her usual shift at nine, and she helped him back into the bed. He's asleep, I think, or looking at that damn butterfly book again."

"He hadn't hurt himself?"

"He has bruises on his arms and an enormous mark on his right leg, but I'm not sure if he did that in the fall or before. He was so angry, Jonah, screaming like a banshee."

"Mum, if you need me to come home and help sort things for—"

"Actually," she mumbled. "I think it's time for him to go somewhere

where they can look after him. You know my heart breaks at the idea of it, but I don't know what else to do. And that isn't me asking you to come home, you hear? You stay where you are, my little star."

He couldn't help but imagine his mum alone in the winding house on the edge of the cliff in St. Ives. The many staircases and tall ceilings, far too high even for her elaborate extendable feather duster. Shadows loomed in the hallways there, even on the brightest of days, and he swallowed down the fear they might consume her and he would return to find his childhood home empty, with only a line of shoes at the doorway signifying the family who once lived there.

"I can take some time off to help you."

"Jonah Penrose, don't you dare." He could hear his old mother in the tone she used, the fiery woman who once told their neighbor to kick rocks when he complained about her many chickens roaming in the garden. "I will call once I've got everything set up for him. Then next time you visit, you can go see him. Dad wouldn't want you worrying over him, you know that."

"It's more you I'm worried about, Mum."

He heard a tremble as she breathed. "Well, love, we can't be having you worrying about little old me, can we?" There were tears clouding her eyes, he could tell. Even from his home on Castle Road, he could see the tears gathering against the high tide in Cornwall. If he were there, he would pull her into his arms and she could cry into his shoulder, something she only did once before, back when his dad received his diagnosis, the day Alzheimer's moved into their home without invitation. A collection of heavy rain clouds found their way to their house and hung themselves in the sky just above the chimney to pour misery into the foundations of the bricks. His dad, the man who hugged him so incredibly tightly and kissed his forehead the day he told him he was gay and said he loved him more than anything in the world, would be lost, and all he could do was cling onto the memories he left and hope small parts of him remained behind the darkening of his mind.

"I love you, Mum."

"I love you, too, sausage."

"Are you sure you're okay?"

"I'm all right. I've got a couple of friends coming over tonight to keep me company once Dad's in bed. Might pop open a bottle of wine, it will be good to relax."

"You'll call me if you need me?"

"Of course, love."

Dexter Ellis suddenly didn't seem like such a looming threat. Edward leaving him for another man didn't either. They said their goodbyes, and Jonah placed the empty cheese packet into the bin then picked up the key he gave to Edward months ago, the one Edward dropped off when he picked up his things, the key he no longer needed now that he didn't want Jonah in his life. Jonah turned it in his palm and let his fingers run along the cool metal ridges. Tears threatened to fall again, but he blinked them back and stuffed the key into the designated kitchen junk drawer and silently vowed not to think about Edward Wordsworth ever again.

FOUR

"I love him, this side of him no one else gets to see. Gone are the days we danced between the mountains and trees. But I love him, and his heart belongs with me."

—"The Melody of Achilles and Patroclus,"
The Wooden Horse, Act One

A sparkling curtain of warm orange light shone through the window to the back of the yoga studio as the sun stretched into the early evening. Jonah watched as it danced across the beech wood floorboards and ran its fingertips across the various yoga mats dotted about the room. The moments before the class started, when the students picked their space and lined up their water bottles while talking quietly among themselves, were when he felt most relaxed.

Monday nights were the time he reserved each week to clear his head, to allow the swirling thoughts and physical and mental strain of performing every night to be placed in a neat box even if only for an hour. He never considered himself someone who might get really into yoga and be able to find something calming about measured breaths, but Omari practically forced him to a class and made him go until he found he couldn't be without it. Eventually, Jonah found a studio closer to home, removing himself from Omari and his perfect posture so he could flail about on the mat without his friend's judgmental frown.

Jonah's body thanked him for the relaxation during the week, when things became too much and the thought of his parents back home turned into a treacherous cliff edge. He could mentally place himself back in the studio and force himself to breathe. Breathe. He placed his hands flat on the yoga mat he always chose, the one nearest the wall opposite the door in the last row, where the mirrors at the front didn't quite catch his entire body. He'd found out early on not to sit front and center; he didn't need an unobscured view to observe his sweaty face and ridiculous expressions as he twisted his body into pretzel-like poses and tried to hold them while looking graceful.

As the balmy rays of sun slowly burned into a shade usually found caressing the leaves in autumn, a shadow loomed over Jonah as he sat on his mat fiddling with the lid from his water bottle. He looked up, half expecting to see the woman with bleached-blond hair and purple money piece who usually set up beside him, only to be greeted with someone else entirely. They were still blond, though darker, almost sandy, natural, and they focused solely on readjusting the mat then placing their own water down before kicking off the whitest of white trainers Jonah ever laid his eyes upon. Jonah blinked as he took in the figure. Slender, tall, ridiculously tall, with high cheekbones and fluttering lashes framing hazel eyes reminiscent of the fields back home when they were kissed by the cooler shades of fall. Then he looked at their lips, pouting, pink, as if they'd swiped a bubble gum lip gloss over them before stepping into the room. They were utterly sinful. And then, and without warning, Jonah's mind kicked back into gear and he realized who it was he was not-so-subtly checking out.

Dexter Ellis.

Jonah scrambled to his feet, his breath catching in his chest as he tried to think of something—anything—to say. Dexter's eyes flicked to him, and his eyebrow quirked as a small smile danced across his absolutely ludicrous lips.

"Hey!" Jonah said. Not too bad for someone in complete social free fall. "I didn't know you liked yoga, such a small world, huh?"

Dexter paused slightly as he bent down, his hand reaching for his water, before he grasped it and stood straight again, his height impressive even against Jonah's tall frame. He smiled again before taking a sip of his drink then wiped his mouth with the back of his hand.

"Small world? Do you vet everyone who comes to this class to see if they like yoga?" he asked. His voice was deeper than Jonah expected; he'd only ever heard him sing before, his range on par with Jonah's, though Jonah often opted up in places Dexter could only dream of.

Jonah shook his head. "No, I just . . . I come here every week and I've never seen you."

"Are new students not allowed or something?"

"I mean, yeah, of course, I was just . . . I guess it's just a surprise to see you here, like, what are the chances?" Jonah rubbed the back of his neck as the words fell from his mouth. Rotten words. Rubbish littering the gleaming floorboards.

Dexter looked around the room, his eyes clearly searching for someone or something to remove him from the situation he'd found himself in.

"You *are* Dexter Ellis, right?" Jonah pressed, suddenly fearing he'd mistaken this poor man for his theatrical nemesis. It wasn't like they'd ever met before, after all, but surely this guy was Dexter, unless the man had a twin. Two of him. Great. "Shit, I'm sorry, you just look so much like him."

"Oh," he said with a laugh, the smile returning to his face. "I mean, yes, that's me, sorry, I forget sometimes that people recognize me. The theatre world can feel so insular sometimes." He rubbed his hand over his face, then blew a strand of blond hair away from his eyes. "Do you like the theatre?"

Jonah laughed, somewhat confused, but mostly dumbfounded. "Would be weird if I didn't, wouldn't it?"

"I don't know, would it? Do you work in the industry?"

Holy shit. Dexter didn't know who he was. The dramatic and frankly outraged part of him wanted to tell him that yes he worked in the bloody industry—not only that, he'd won an Olivier Award only a month ago and was the lead in the show Dexter was about to perform in. But the calmer, more mature side of him that was only present because of the lavender air humidifier in the room bit his tongue and forced the smile to remain on his face.

"Yes," he said simply, and reminded himself to relax his eyes as he tried his hardest not to let them twitch.

"Okay, can everyone get onto their mats, please? We will begin," the instructor, Shan, said from the front of the class. Jonah looked over at her as she tied her braids back into a loose ponytail, a couple of them still hanging around the front of her face, elongating her slender neck in the process. She turned on the speaker on the wall beside her spot at the front and a tranquil melody floated throughout the room, a melody Jonah couldn't focus on because Dexter fucking Ellis stood right beside him and had the audacity to imply he didn't know who he was.

It must have been impossible, a strange power play Jonah didn't understand. How could Dexter not know Jonah, the guy who took the role he originated and molded it into something else entirely in the West End? How could he not have seen his face on the posters dotted around the Underground, or the gorgeous trailers playing on the large screens at the end of Regent Street? Or had he gone for a toilet break during Jonah's win at the Oliviers? More importantly, had Dexter really not been to see the show he apparently loved so much (if his social media posts waxing lyrical about it were to be believed?). The guy had been rehearsing in a studio somewhere for the past three weeks, and would have absolutely been shown pictures of Jonah, even recordings of him performing, yet he had apparently erased him from his memory entirely. Jonah took position on his mat, feet firm in the center, and turned his head slightly to see Dexter doing the same thing but staring ahead, as if Jonah didn't exist.

The bastard.

They all inhaled deeply and turned to face the wall with the door before leaning forward and into the downward dog position. Jonah held his breath as Dexter bent in front of him, his arse clad in too-tight joggers as he did the most fabulous downward dog the world ever witnessed. He couldn't look at him, not from that angle. He couldn't look at his bare arms bracing his stance or his remarkably unflushed face hanging between them, eyes closed, pouty lips inhaling and exhaling visible breaths. Jonah couldn't decide if he wanted to kiss or punch him, but the thought of kissing him made his stomach turn and he did his best not to gag as he tried to hold his composure.

No one could deny the sheer beauty of the man; he radiated like the sun, his skin tanned, far too tanned for London in the spring. Seeing him in real life instead of pixels on a screen or frozen in a photograph pulled at something in Jonah's chest; the man he'd heard about for so long painfully real, and there he stood, arse in the air, while Jonah did his best not to look at it. His mind flitted to an image of Edward, of him standing in the living room, hands wrapped around his waist as he doubled over with laughter while Jonah tried to get him to learn yoga with him at home. No. He couldn't think of him, he needed to keep him stuffed away in the kitchen drawer with his key.

"Brilliant, well done everyone. We will do some partner work now. Try to work with someone who is a similar build to you," Shan said, straightening her posture and falling effortlessly into the mountain pose. Strong. Sturdy. "I know we haven't done partner poses before, and this is more to help with your stretches," she explained as Jonah followed her lead and stood only to find Dexter already standing as tall as Mount Everest beside him.

"Would you mind if we—" Dexter looked at him and pointed at Jonah then at himself with a smile. "Similar builds? Both work in the theatre industry? We're the perfect match."

Before Jonah could protest, and protest he would, Shan took the hands of a woman from the front row and guided her to her mat.

"Everyone, please watch me and the lovely Linda here." She smiled at the woman as they both sat down and faced each other. Shan inhaled deeply, her chest expanding as her shoulders relaxed. "Keep your backs straight, then stretch out your legs. Keep them wide apart," she said as she performed the move and Linda mirrored her. "Place the soles of your feet against your partner's and hold hands, then one person slowly relaxes and lets the other person pull them forward." The women moved effortlessly together, Linda's body slumping slightly as Shan carefully pulled her closer. "Take deep breaths then straighten and swap. You will feel a stretch in your hamstrings." Shan nodded at the rest of the group, and within seconds everyone took their positions on the floor.

Jonah didn't have an issue with feet. He didn't have a strange fetish for them, but they didn't repulse him either. Touching his soles against someone else's, however, seemed oddly intimate. Edward had lovely feet. No, God, he needed to stop thinking of Edward with his perfectly formed toes and beautiful ankles. He shook his head slightly as he got to the floor and did his best not to blush as Dexter spread his legs in front of him and Jonah reluctantly did the same. Dexter held no reservations as he pressed the soles of his feet against Jonah's, his toes poking higher, his feet bigger. Of course. His hands reached out to him, his fingers slender, like that of a pianist, and Jonah held them in his and hoped Dexter wouldn't notice just how sweaty his palms were. A tension settled between their arms and Jonah could already feel the pull in his hamstrings before they'd even begun stretching.

"You go first," Dexter said with an encouraging nod. Jonah swallowed thickly and let his body relax. Breathe in. And out. And in again. Then he felt Dexter pulling him, his arms stretching, his legs even more so.

"How's that?" Dexter asked. "I can do it harder, if you like."

"No," Jonah said far too quickly to sound even remotely normal. "It's fine." He sat himself back only to see Dexter with a shit-eating grin plastered across his face. "Your turn."

The blond folded in on himself like a flower closing its petals as the sun hid from the sky. Jonah waited a moment before pulling him forward. As he did, Dexter's body shifted and his right foot slipped from Jonah's and slid rapidly down the inside of Jonah's leg right to his crotch. The pain took a moment to register.

Foot. Penis. Pain.

An inhuman squeak escaped Jonah's mouth, a high-pitched thing that made Shan's head snap over to them. Dexter moved quickly to his knees, hands flying out to grasp Jonah's shoulders and apologies spilling out of his stupidly pink lips.

"Oh my God, I'm so sorry, are you okay?"

Jonah didn't want Dexter's hands on him, their proximity dizzying and ridiculously painful. He'd been kicked in the balls before, but not since primary school when girls thought it funny to run up to the boys in the playground and casually assault them. No such attacks happened in adulthood; Jonah did a good job of not offending anyone enough to warrant an attack on his private parts. Though Bastien once elbowed him dangerously close to his balls during the show and apologized profusely afterward. Heck, he'd even forgive Bastien if he were the one to harm him now, but it wasn't Bastien. It was Dexter bloody Ellis: penis killer.

Jonah shifted from him, finding his way to his feet somehow so he could turn from the class. He hoped the corner of the room would swallow him whole so he wouldn't have to look at the people now worried about his dick and whether he was still capable of fathering children.

"Oh Christ," Shan said, coming to his side as she gestured for the others to carry on with the exercise. "Want me to get some ice?" she murmured, her voice filled with the same lightness that danced with the lavender in the air. "Remember to breathe."

"I am breathing," Jonah said through gritted teeth, his world spinning, the pain mixing with an overwhelming sense of embarrassment. "I'm just . . . I'm just gonna finish there I think." He marveled at how well he stood, the pain should have doubled him over, but his body pushed it aside so he could flee. He quickly bent to pick up his water and shoes and kept his head down as he made his way out of the class, knowing the next time he went there everyone would think about his dick, if only for a split second, but they would absolutely think about it. Dexter somehow ridiculed him by squashing his penis with his stupidly enormous foot all while remaining oblivious to their rivalry; he didn't know Jonah from a stranger on the street. The nemesis who not only bruised his ego but also his balls in the space of an hour.

He hated him.

FIVE

"And now I know, he waits for me beyond the city doors, pacing back and forth, the drums hounding me in my sleep. We cannot escape, we have no tears to weep. Andromache, promise to cover your eyes. For this is it, my final outing, the Gods have planned my demise."

—"Achilles Waits," The Wooden Horse, Act Two

Bastien covered his mouth while biting down on the inside of his cheek as Omari turned away from them, a wry smile twitching at the corner of his lips. Bastien sucked in a breath, seeming to compose himself, and let his hand fall to reveal a remarkably grim-looking frown.

"Sorry, I think you might have to repeat that. What happened?"

"His foot kicked me right in the dick."

Bastien gave a solemn nod, a smile appearing despite his best efforts. "Who knew Dexter Ellis would take aim at your sex life by wounding your little soldier?"

Jonah rolled his eyes and turned his attention to his reflection in the dressing room mirror. "Little soldier? Also, a pointless attack given I have no sex life to speak of."

"You need to get yourself out there," Omari said, leaning over Jonah's shoulder to inspect his remarkably perfect umber-colored skin in the mirror. The skin peels were clearly working.

"You've not found any noble young steeds to ride since Edward?" Bastien asked.

"There are a million things wrong with that question, Bastien."

Bastien reached forward and adjusted a couple of Jonah's curls at the back of his head. "You know what they say, the best way to get over someone is to get under someone else."

Jonah batted his hand away. "Who? Who says that?"

Bastien shrugged. "People. Me. I say that. Go out and sow your wild oats." He went to the clothing rack at the back of the room and thumbed through the costumes Jonah wore throughout the show.

"Sow my oats? Little soldier? What old lady has possessed you, and how do I get rid of her?" Jonah looked over his shoulder at him then pointed to the costume on the far right, the deep-blue and teal cotton ensemble he wore at the end of the first act. Bastien pulled it from the hanger and handed it to him.

"Old ladies are full of wisdom. Besides, sowing your oats wouldn't be a bad thing. I know Lucian has a thing for you."

Omari scowled slightly. "Lucian? He has a thing for everyone, no? Pretty sure he was hooking up with one of the front-of-house girls last week. The little ginger one, Enid, I think? Anyway, I slept with him way back during our previews, I wouldn't recommend."

"Even if he wasn't trying to fuck every person in this theatre, Lucian eats mackerel sandwiches before going onstage, even when he's covering you, Bash, and I have to kiss him repeatedly for most of the first act. Mackerel. Every time," Jonah said seriously.

Bastien scrunched up his nose. "Is that what it is? I always thought he smelled of cabbage." He went to the second rack in the room, the one not usually there but that had been wheeled in early that morning to make space for the extra bodies changing in the building. "Fuck, I'm nervous," he murmured, taking his own first costume off the rack before looking at Jonah. "They got the same photographer again even though I begged them to choose someone else."

"Your ex? Bennie with the bad lens?" Omari asked, going over to another rack with his costumes hung neatly on it.

"The one and only. And I bet he will take as many shots from beneath my chin as he can just to make me look like I have saggy jowls. I mean, it's been eight years since we've been together. You would think he'd be over the petty shit he pulls." Bastien tutted as he removed his clothing. "Though, I am now looking forward to you coming face-to-face with Dexter penis-destroyer Ellis." He pulled his light-green tunic on over his head, then grinned at Jonah. "I don't for a second believe he didn't know who you were."

"No, me neither. Which makes the foot slip even more painful. I mean . . . what's he going to say to me today? Oh, you're that guy whose dick I kicked at yoga yesterday? Or will he pretend it never happened?"

"Money on pretending it never happened," Omari practically sang as he slipped his shirt off.

A light knock on the door interrupted them before it cracked open and the familiar face of Sherrie peered round it. She smirked at them as she stepped inside and gently closed the door behind her. Her cheeks, rounded, flushed with a rose and gold swipe of color finished with a glitter dust settling between her freckles, complimenting the cotton candy pink of her hair. Jonah always found her endlessly refreshing. A rainbow caught in a droplet of water.

"Darlings," she said, waving her hands in the air with a flourish before curtseying to them. "How are my favorite people getting on?"

"Fabulously," Bastien said, adjusting the sleeve of his tunic while trying to get a glimpse of himself in the mirror over Jonah's shoulder. "Have you come to tame my hair? Look at it, it looks like a bird nested in it overnight. I need you, Shez."

"Sherrie, can you get the steamer from my room, please? I think my sinuses are getting blocked." Omari pinched the skin between his eyes lightly. "I'm aging as we speak."

"Your hair looks fine, Bash," Sherrie said, moving toward him despite her words to work her fingers through his brown hair. "Nothing that a bit of my magic can't fix. And, Omari, you can get it yourself." She ignored the glare he sent her way. "Colbie wants full makeup, she said no half-arsing it today, she wants the photos to be perfect. Apparently the new program is going to be A4 and glossy, to hell with the environmentally friendly recycled paper ones from before."

Jonah shifted himself from the mirror, allowing Bastien to take a seat so Sherrie could fix his hair and help apply the minimal makeup he needed. He clutched the blue material of his costume in his hands and frowned; he didn't feel prepared for new photographs. The old ones were beautiful; they captured gut-wrenching moments in the show, and despite Bastien's apparently enormous jowls, they looked dazzling. In those images, Jonah could believe he truly was Achilles, his body on loan to the Greek legend while he took over and performed each night. Edward gushed over those pictures. He asked Jonah to sign his program in bed the night he brought it home to show him, then they had sex and basked in each other until the early hours of the morning. On the other end of the scale, his dad called him after he mailed the program to him, his mind still lucid only a year ago, and expressed an unrestrained pride as he swallowed down tears of happiness.

Who would see the evolution of Achilles now? Edward was nothing but a ghost who lived in his kitchen drawer. His father didn't know who Jonah was, let alone Achilles, and his mum, well, she had bigger things on her plate than new production images to think about. He knew how selfish he seemed; the situation with his parents should bear no reflection on his self-esteem, but his father's approval, his pride and words of encouragement, meant everything. He wished he could go back and relive the moments they shared, the times when it was just the two of them walking along the beach near the house. Or the afternoons lounging in the garden while his mum peeled carrots in her garden chair while listening to music from her earphones on the Walkman she refused to upgrade.

"You're special, Jonah, and I'm not just saying that because you're my son. Though, I'm damn proud to be your dad."

"You going to get changed, Jonah, babe?" Sherrie asked around a hairpin she'd wedged between her lips.

"Yeah, sorry, my mind ran away with me." He pulled off his T-shirt and replaced it with Achilles's first costume. Blue. Like the sea. "Is my hair okay?"

Sherrie sprayed an obscene amount of fixing spray over Bastien's head before narrowing her eyes at Jonah. "For the first time ever, yes." She plucked the pin from her mouth and smiled. "You're pale as fuck, though, babe, let's give you a bit of color, yeah? You're not meant to look dead until the end of the show." She whipped a makeup brush from the bum bag strapped around her waist, then got to work on his face. "I met Dexter earlier," she said, her face so close to Jonah's he could practically count her eyelashes. "Absolutely fabulous arse on him."

Photo shoots for programs were a strange affair. They varied from production to production, but Colbie liked to select a few scenes or songs and have her cast perform them while being photographed by Bennie-with-the-bad-lens. It created a gorgeous illusion of the show, everyone in full costume, acting out the scene as if in front of a full audience. There were occasions, for other shows, where photography happened during a performance, but Jonah preferred this approach; it took away some of the anxiety and allowed the photographer to get in among the cast and gather the best images possible.

The stage had been set for the closing number of the first act: "In the Light of the Morning," a gorgeous piece weaving the melodies of previous songs to reach a stunning climax to entice the audience into the second half. Jonah adored performing it, the staging and ensemble around him creating a work of sheer perfection. It ended with a passionate kiss between Achilles and Patroclus as Hector wrapped his arms around his wife, Andromache, both couples drenched in white light. The song resembled the calm before the storm, the characters in civilian clothing, no armor to be seen. A stark contrast to the bloodbath of act two.

Jonah made his way to the stage, Bastien by his side, Omari nowhere to be seen, and he readied himself to be blinded by the dazzling beauty of Dexter once again. He didn't look the same as the night before. His hair, slicked back away from his face, seemed darker, and his eyes lacked the spirit of autumn they held in the yoga studio. Dressed as Hector, in deep shades of red and orange, he appeared to be an entirely different person, as if the Trojan prince took to the stage instead of him.

Before Bennie called them into positions, Jonah made the rounds and introduced himself to the new cast members, all of them charming, all of them beaming in their costumes for the first time. They spoke with enthusiasm for the show, a genuine passion for the production, and Jonah felt a buzz drumming through his skin at the excitement of working with them. He forgot how easily a theatre family came together, how bonds formed so seamlessly; the company became a rock, a solid foundation who supported one another without question or consequence. As he moved he saw Sherrie to the side of the stage, needle and thread in hand, multitalented, as she knelt beside a woman with long black hair, adjusting the hem of her dress. Sherrie laughed happily, dark eyes glancing up behind even darker lashes and a slight blush decorating her cheeks. Sherrie Cimino, serial flirt.

Despite donning his social butterfly cape to make the best possible impression on the new people in the theatre, Jonah knew his attention wasn't fully on them. He couldn't stop himself from repeatedly glancing over at Dexter. Dexter moved around the cast as if they were there for him and him alone. His hands touched elbows and pulled others into warm embraces, all while smiling and pouting with his ludicrous lips. When he finally came to Jonah and Bastien, his face appeared flushed from excitement, forehead damp, a tragedy given he would be photographed and each bead of perspiration would be there in ultrahigh definition for all to see, but he didn't seem to care.

"Bastien Andrews!" he exclaimed and clapped Bastien jovially on the shoulder. "It is *so* good to see you again, everyone here talks so highly of you."

Bastien absently raised his hand to rub the skin Dexter touched. "Really? Most people think I'm a diva," he said with a smile.

"I doubt that." Dexter smiled back at him, his teeth glistening, white, far too white. He then looked at Jonah, finally, and his smile faltered for a flash of a second before fixing itself back into place. "And you must be Jonah Penrose?" Instead of the friendly slap or hug he offered everyone else, Dexter held out his hand for Jonah to shake. Jonah took his hand into his, and yet again prayed his palms refrained from sweating profusely all over him.

"Yeah. We've met before," Jonah said, daring himself to look Dexter directly in the eyes. He showed no sign of recognition.

"We have?" His smile dropped again, something akin to concern creeping across his face in its place.

Jonah narrowed his eyes at him. "Yesterday. At yoga?"

Dexter shook his head slowly. "I don't recall—"

"You kicked me in the dick?"

Bastien turned away from them both with a snort then inserted himself into another conversation to remove himself from the interaction entirely. The traitor.

"You were at the yoga class?" Dexter's expression remained neutral, and Jonah couldn't help but wonder if he was going fucking insane and he imagined the guy at yoga the night before. But no, the pain he experienced when Dexter's heel connected with his crotch was undeniably real.

"We paired up. You seriously have a mind-blank on that?"

A small smirk found its way to Dexter's face as something clicked into place in his head. "You know it really is amazing how different a bit of photo editing can make someone look." He let his eyes wander up and down Jonah's body. "I didn't know it was you last night! You should have said something, I'm so excited to perform with an Olivier winner. And it's going to be interesting to see how you've taken the role, given I know it like the back of my hand. Achilles is a dream, isn't he?"

Jonah didn't know what to say; Dexter was toying with him, he'd gained the upper hand by simply dismissing their encounter the day before as something totally flippant and turned it into a not-so-thinly veiled insult regarding Jonah's appearance.

"An award-winning dream," he settled on saying in a tone far more spiteful than he intended.

Dexter nodded and swiped his tongue over his bottom lip as he glanced down at his feet. "It's a shame, really, that I'm here to show that an Olivier really doesn't mean all that much."

"What do you mean by that?"

"You'll see." He raised his eyes to Jonah's again then turned from him, any words Jonah could say in response ignored as he made his way over to Colbie, who stood with Bennie-with-the-bad-lens and Sherrie by the other side of the stage.

Dexter might just have well screamed "Macbeth" in his face. His words a threat, a curse, a promise of a takedown. Jonah could feel his hands trembling as he watched him, the words they spoke to each other tumbling together in his head repeatedly until distaste burned at the back of his tongue.

For Dexter was the Trojan horse, and any hope of salvation would be futile.

SIX

"When he holds me, I beg the Gods to let me keep him. Paris, my love, my soul is his, I'll die by his side, our journey then to the underworld, where Hades will greet us and we will drink to our demise."

—"Helen," *The Wooden Horse*, Act One

Tottenham Court Road tube station swelled as bodies funneled into it from above. Jonah adjusted his headphones and kept his head down as people jostled into him from all sides. Tourists stopped mid-walk with their phones out, faces creased in confusion as they peered at the maps on the walls, disorientated from leaving the theatres on Shaftesbury Avenue and having to face the grueling reality of the London Underground. Jonah knew the feeling; he had been one of those bewildered people stuck standing in complete confusion as he tried to find out how to get from one place to another back when he first moved to London. Now he just weaved between them. An oiled cog in the grand machine of the capital.

Cornwall seemed so sleepy in comparison.

He allowed the mass of bodies to heave him through the barriers, his phone beeping against the fare readers, the little gates opening to grant him access to the even busier platforms where crowds surged even at the late hour of the evening. London never slept, and neither did the scorching hot tracks of the Underground. Sometimes Edward used to meet him after a show at the entrance to the Tottenham Court station, opposite Soho Place and the little coffee shop that sold the cinnamon buns Jonah liked. He worked late, always holed up in his office on Hanway Street as the theatres surrounding him told tales of sweeping romances and tragic deaths.

Jonah loved the nights when his body felt exhausted yet sated from performing and he saw Edward waiting for him at the station. Their hands would meet, palms pressed against each other, and they faced the crowds together while Edward pointed out the posters featuring Jonah's face battle ready or prepared to press his lips against Bastien's, lining various spots on their journey.

"Doesn't it make you jealous?" Jonah asked him once, their bodies pressed together in bed, breaths lost in each other's lungs. "That I have to kiss another man multiple times each night?"

"The only time I will get jealous is the day you kiss him the same way you kiss me." The answer seemed so simple, without animosity or conditions, so *grown-up*. Rhys, who he dated before Edward, got his pants in a twist when he went to watch Jonah in *Cabaret* when he was playing Cliff and he kissed the actress playing Sally because it was in the bloody script for him to do so. It didn't matter that Sally and Cliff were doomed, their romance somewhat a farce, or totally a farce depending on the production and interpretation of the characters. And it certainly didn't matter that Jonah was gay and had been sucking Rhys's cock that very morning. Their relationship crumbled due to an onstage kiss, and, if Jonah were to be truthful, a rather unconvincing one at that. Rhys, who at the time just turned thirty, stamped his feet like a child and left.

When Edward came into his life things changed. Edward didn't act like a sullen teenager just out of high school. He wore suits and polished his shoes every morning after shaving and doused himself with cologne. He didn't check his bank account before buying stuff and never went overdrawn. And he always kissed Jonah with a lingering, simmering passion that made Jonah feel completely weightless. Floating. Desired.

Jonah sniffed as he meandered through the Underground, hating himself for thinking of Edward *again* but being mentally incapable of putting him back in his kitchen drawer. He missed him. He missed Edward's hands on his body, the way he knew exactly how to run his fingertips along the inside of Jonah's thigh to make his breath hitch in this throat.

He missed the feel of Edward's lips against his and his stubble pricking Jonah's skin as he worked his kisses down his chest. Or maybe, just maybe, Jonah didn't miss him at all. Perhaps he just needed to get laid.

He could go on a date. Or, maybe not even a date. It didn't need to be that deep. Sherrie put FullStack on his phone, "The best queer dating app, babe," and stood over him as he made a profile despite his groaning protests. He'd looked at the app twice since downloading it and opened eight messages, five of which were dick pics. And they weren't even very good, not enough to entice him out of his house to go investigate, at least. Pride in one's photography seemed like a lost cause on FullStack. The weirder the camera angle the better, and, despite thinking he should just have meaningless sex to dull the empty void inside of him, he wanted to at least do it with someone who could take a *nice* picture of their dick.

As the train rolled in for the Northern Line, Jonah decided once and for all he needed to get Edward out of his head and buckle down on finding someone who could do more than send flaccid pictures of their penis. He'd settle for a nice butt shot. Or no nudity at all. Where were the guys cuddling puppies and eating ice cream or the ones who were nice to their mums? There had to be at least one man in London who was kind to animals and also good at sex. Jonah just needed to find him. He could be anywhere, behind him or standing farther down the platform. He scanned the bodies on the train when he finally stepped into the carriage, at first looking for someone hot before silently begging to see a vacant seat, but of course there were none. He shuffled to the corner of the carriage and held onto the metal bar beside the door to stop himself from falling as the train lurched forward. He fished his phone out of his pocket to check the time—seventeen minutes past eleven—then looked back up to see Edward standing by the next door along the carriage.

Jonah suddenly felt like he might vomit. Bile worked its way up his throat, burning and sickly sweet, and he swallowed it down; he couldn't throw up on the bloody Northern Line. Edward busied himself by talking with a man slightly shorter than himself with striking blue eyes and jet-black hair. Although he would rather look at four hundred lumpy, misshapen dick pics, Jonah allowed himself to study the two of them, the ease with which they conversed with each other, and Edward's subtle hand pressed against the other man's lower back to support him as the train moved. He used to support Jonah in the same way. The man flung his head back in a laugh, dimples forming in his cheeks as Edward chuckled beside him. And there, where the collar of his shirt shifted with his movement, Jonah saw a hickey blemishing the man's skin on his neck.

Jonah turned from them, his face flushed with something—anger, devastation, a mixture of the two—and came face to face with an even more sickening sight. Dexter *fucking* Ellis. He looked at Jonah with momentary surprise before his expression turned into a scowl. His lips moved, words coming from them, but Jonah couldn't hear, the music in his headphones drowning out his voice. He slipped them from his head and frowned as he looked at the taller man.

"What? I couldn't hear you?"

"I said, what are you doing down here?" Dexter asked with an incredulous tone.

Jonah's eyes fell across his body; he'd not seen him outside of the theatre except at yoga where he wore the too-tight joggers and T-shirt, but here, out in the wild, he didn't dress how Jonah imagined. Dark navy chinos cut off above his ankles to reveal sockless feet in gray canvas deck shoes, not unlike the ones Jonah's dad wore even at the height of winter. The collar of a white shirt peeked out from beneath a deep-emerald jumper, and there, on the left-hand side, right where a breast pocket might usually sit, was an embroidered teddy bear wearing a yellow bow tie. The entire ensemble screamed "rich kid sails Daddy's yacht." and Jonah couldn't help but feel slightly grubby in comparison.

"Sorry, do you own the Northern Line?" Jonah asked, the teddy bear looking at him with the same aloof expression as its owner.

Dexter opened his mouth to say something as the train ground itself to a stop. Only darkness lay outside the windows; they had not pulled in at the next station, but stopped in the middle of one of the tunnels. Without his headphones on, Jonah could hear Edward's all-too-familiar voice, the man painfully close, and he wondered if Edward could sense his presence or if he'd wiped everything about Jonah from his mind.

Dexter leaned against the wall at the end of the carriage, angling himself away from Jonah. The tendons in his neck were tense; they jutted out from beneath his skin and made his jaw appear rigid. Several minutes passed without the train moving again, and Jonah waited to hear a voice over the speakers announcing some kind of delay, but none came. He reminded himself this wasn't the Elizabeth Line with all its shiny new bells and whistles and delicious air conditioning in the summer. No, the Northern Line was a drunk aunt, always stumbling about, often late, and with nothing useful to say, but he held a fondness for it, regardless.

"I hate the Underground," Dexter said, though he still didn't look at Jonah. "I should've got the bus."

"Buses are the worst," Jonah said. "Never on time, always full, and they smell like piss."

"No different to the tube, then."

Jonah didn't reply, and instead snuck a look over his shoulder at Edward, who still spoke happily with the man Jonah refused to believe might be the one he left him for. Until then, he hadn't given the mystery person who took his place in Edward's life much thought. He'd shown some kindness to himself and not let any images of imaginary men resembling underwear models work their way into the narrative of his breakup. But now . . . now he could see Edward's life and how he'd been since the split. He didn't seem sad, no sense of regret or longing for the person whose heart he broke. Jonah saw only happiness written over his face.

"You were a beat behind most of the dance numbers tonight."

Jonah turned his attention back to Dexter, who was looking at him again.

"You should probably work on that," Dexter continued.

"You were watching the show?"

Dexter nodded. "I've been trying to go as much as possible. It's all very well practicing in a studio, but seeing it is different. And you fumbled your lines toward the end of act one."

"No, I didn't."

"You did, actually. You said 'And he expects us to fight for him. We won't go, Patroclus.' And the line is 'And he expects us to go to battle for him, Patroclus. We will not go.' There's a difference."

The train whined as it slowly moved again, the air inside stifling hot as they crawled into the next station. As the doors opened, a poster for *The Wooden Horse* greeted them on the platform, the one where Jonah and Bastien were about to kiss, their faces painted in shades of blue against a dark red background. Dexter clicked his tongue against the roof of his mouth, his lips pouting.

"Did you see the show at the fringe or when we did the tour?" Dexter asked. "The tone was different then. Achilles was more playful with Patroclus. I think the character lacks some of that heart now."

"Thank you for the glowing review."

"I didn't say it was your fault, it's all in the direction." He narrowed his eyes at Jonah. "You look like you're going to throw up."

Jonah shook his head as more people stuffed themselves into the carriage, pushing on and on even when space no longer existed. Bodies moved down the carriage, Edward so close he could almost touch him now, and as the doors closed and the train pulled away Jonah could feel tears pricking at the corners of his eyes. He sucked in a deep breath and tried to make himself as small as possible. An animal hiding from a predator, stuck between two dangers, and he didn't know which one he'd rather tear him apart.

"Jonah?" Edward. No. Why did God hate him? "Jonah, hi," Edward said softly, his shoulder knocking against Jonah's as the train fumbled along the tracks.

"Hey," Jonah said, voice clipped, awkward, terribly awkward. He could feel Dexter watching the exchange, his hazel eyes eating up the interaction and no doubt keeping note of how Jonah could have handled it better to report back to him later.

"How are you?" The words were so simple. Kind, even, or an illusion of kindness; Edward didn't actually care how he'd been, Jonah knew that.

"Fine."

"Just finished work?"

Jonah nodded. The dark-haired man standing beside Edward nudged him with his elbow, a bright smile on his face, bright enough to rival the Christmas lights on Oxford Street in the winter.

"Well, Ed, aren't you going to introduce me?" Ed? He hated being called Ed.

Edward ran his finger along the inside of his shirt collar, apparently wanting to loosen it, his jaw set tight. "Wes, this is Jonah."

Wes let out a laugh, slightly strained, though Jonah could sense some genuine joy behind it. He grabbed Jonah's hand and squeezed in his own in a poor attempt of a handshake. "I'm assuming you're *the* Jonah Penrose? Ed's talented friend?"

He wanted the ground to split open and drag him down into whatever lay beneath it. Hell, molten lava, eternal darkness, he would take any of it if it meant he didn't have to be part of this conversation anymore.

"Ed's told me a lot about you," Wes continued. "I keep saying he should take me to see your show, but he's dragging his feet getting tickets."

Jonah wished he could take his eyes away from the way Wes wrapped his arm around Edward's waist, the movement so casual but filled with intimacy. He felt Dexter shuffle closer beside him, forcing himself into the narrative, of course, and he debated pressing the emergency alarm by the door just to make the complete debacle stop.

"You should go. The show is amazing, and Jonah's outstanding," Dexter said, causing Jonah to raise an eyebrow at the compliment. "They don't just hand Oliviers out to anyone."

"Of course!" Wes smiled, and God, his teeth were whiter than Dexter's. "Sorry, I didn't catch your name?" he asked, directing his words to Dexter.

"I didn't say it," he replied, though he spoke with a smile on his lips. "Dexter Ellis."

Jonah noted how Edward's expression changed slightly, the name one he'd heard from Jonah dozens of times, the myth, the legend, finally real in front of him. He shot Jonah a look, one full of questions and a fair amount of confusion thrown in too.

"How do you two know each other?" Jonah asked, looking away from Edward to focus on Wes. "Your name has never come up in conversation before."

Wes rolled his eyes, then glanced at Edward with a fond warmth in his eyes. "Why don't you tell anyone about me? Am I your dirty little secret?" Though his tone came out as playful, there was something accusing laced within his words. When Edward gave an awkward laugh as a response, Wes tutted. "We work together," he said. "And started dating about . . . God, how long, about seven months ago?"

Jonah wanted the carriage to go up in flames. Edward couldn't look at him, his eyes fixed on the floor as Wes continued to speak, but his words were eaten by the drumming sound in Jonah's ears. Seven months. *Seven months.*

"I'm sorry, I can't do this," Jonah said, his body deciding his fight-or-flight mode needed to kick in and concluding flight would be the best course of action. As soon as they stopped at the next station he got off, not caring that he wasn't where he needed to be or about the hundreds of people swarming all around him. The last seven months of his relationship with Edward had been a lie.

Jonah wanted London to swallow him, to smother him in darkness so he wouldn't have to ever bump into Edward or Wes again with their smiling faces and pristine suits. He didn't want the next awkward exchange with Dexter to happen, where he would know he witnessed something deeply personal and no doubt use it in his takedown plans. Fuck. Fuck. Fuck.

It wasn't until Jonah worked his way out of the station and inhaled the night air that he realized tears were falling down his cheeks. He hailed the first taxi he saw, not caring about how much it would cost him. He needed Castle Road. He needed home. He needed to learn how to breathe again and pretend his heart wasn't shattering into pieces he could never put back together.

SEVEN

"His blood, my blood, our bodies are as one, I still feel his kiss, his lips as sure as the morning, but he's gone, the oceans rise, and the winter calls without him."

—"The Song of the Dead," *The Wooden Horse*, Act Two

Jonah didn't hesitate before answering his phone. When his mum's face lit up the screen and sent vibrations skittering across his dressing table, his hands were around it within seconds. He'd been waiting for her calls, eager to get them instead of dreading her lovely round face appearing on his screen like usual, expecting bad news. A little over a month had passed since their conversation in the kitchen and he could still hear her chest sucking in painful breaths as tears created rivers around her home back in Cornwall. Weeks of her not finding a home for Dad. Weeks of excuses and empty promises. He sent her links to nursing homes he found himself, nice places overlooking the sea where Dad could sit out in well-maintained gardens and still hear the waves crashing against the edges of cliffs, but she found fault with them all.

The research, however, helped him take his mind off Edward and the seven months he spent fucking Wes while still fucking him. He never thought dementia homes would quell the burning rage and heartache he could feel brimming in his core at all hours of the day, but desperate times called for unusual desperate measures.

"Mum?"

"Sausage!" Her voice sounded surprisingly jovial. "I've got the girls round, and we were just talking about something totally outrageous that happened yesterday, and I just *had* to tell you."

Jonah eyed the clock on the wall in his dressing room. He needed to be onstage for warm-up in five minutes, but he could hear a slight slur in her words and his chest constricted as he thought of her and her friends sipping wine while Dad sat unaided somewhere in the house.

"I'm at work. Mum, can it wait?"

"Why answer the phone if you can't talk to me?"

Jonah bit down on the inside of his cheek before answering. "I always answer when I can in case it's important, you know, something up with you or dad. Did you look at the new homes I sent you links to?"

"Well, no, Jonah, I didn't, because something rather awful happened yesterday."

"What happened? I thought you said it was outrageous and now it's awful? Are you both okay?"

The phone rustled and Jonah could picture her propping it against her ear with her shoulder while she busied herself with something else as another woman laughed in the background. "There was a flasher down on the beach." The sound of a cork being popped from a bottle of wine interrupted her sentence. "Showed his willy to all the people down there trying to eat their sandwiches."

"Blimey," Jonah said with a slight laugh.

"It's not funny, Jonah. Agatha, you remember Agatha, don't you? The woman who grows the broad beans? Well, she hadn't seen a penis in a decade, nearly gave her a heart attack. She choked on her scone, the poor thing."

"Is she okay now?"

"A bit shaken. She had to give a police statement. Can you imagine going down the station and having to tell an officer about the willy you saw on the beach?" He could hear the wine being poured into a glass. "When was the last time you saw a penis, dear?"

Jonah made a strangled noise from the back of his throat. "Is that your way of asking me how my love life is? I told you Edward broke up with me. No penis viewings for me. And, Mum, seriously, I need to go, I've got to do warm-ups then get ready."

"I just want to know why you can't hold down a boyfriend, Jonah. You work in the theatre, it's the prime place to meet someone. Isn't that where all the gays are?"

Jonah looked to the ceiling and let out a slow breath. " 'All the gays'?"

"Darling, I knew you were gay the moment you came down the stairs draped in my sequin cardigan and made me and your father watch you perform 'Don't Rain on My Parade' for us in the living room. You were seven. You're telling me you're the only gay in the theatre?"

"It's true, no homosexual can deny the call of Barbra Streisand."

"Who?"

"I will not dignify that question with an answer. Look, Mum, you need to get back to me once you've looked at those places I sent you—" The door to his dressing room opened and Sherrie's usually smiling face frowned at him from the hallway. He waved his hand at her, then pointed to his phone. "Mum, look I've got to go."

"Fine," she snapped, the wine-induced playfulness gone. "Go play pretend. It's far more important than talking to me, isn't it?"

"Mum, don't be like that. It's my job, please—" She hung up. Jonah looked at his phone, momentarily bewildered, then placed it down on his dresser.

"Parents, huh?" Sherrie said, pushing the door open more to let him out into the hallway.

His eyes fell on Bastien's closed door, and he went to knock before Sherrie stopped him. "What? He didn't wait for me?"

"The fact you two have to walk everywhere together around here is slightly concerning," Sherrie quipped. "But, no, Bastien's sick."

"He is? He didn't tell me."

"He's got the flu, his boyfriend had to call in for him, apparently he's, like, really ill with it." Jonah hesitated; the thought of going back to get his phone to shoot him a text passed through his mind, but Sherrie linked her arm with his and guided them both forward. "And, well, it's not just Bastien who's ill either. We've got seven cast members off."

"Seven?" Jonah's attention was suddenly piqued. "Seriously? Who?"

"Bastien, Lucie, Nate, Lucian, Elliott, Luca, and Toby," Sherrie said, counting off the names on her fingers.

Jonah tried to piece the names together in his head. Three main cast members, three ensembles, and one swing. His mind started trying to work out who would cover who, and within seconds he'd run around in circles and looped a rope around himself only to trip over his thoughts.

"They haven't canceled the performance?" he asked, though the fact he was on his way to warm-ups answered the question for him. "We don't have enough cast to cover the leads."

"You've got Lennon stepping in," Sherrie said, her voice careful, restrained. "And Sarah covering Lucie."

Jonah gave a nod. Lennon and Sarah were two of the best swings he'd ever worked with, falling seamlessly into whatever track they were given, even on a minute's notice. He didn't know how they did it; they were the unspoken heroes of the theatre, brave, immensely talented, and with memories capable of absorbing countless roles.

"So, just a small ensemble tonight, then?" Jonah said. "Is Lennon on as Patroclus?"

Sherrie shook her head. "No. Odysseus."

They moved through the wings to the stage where Evie, their stage manager, stood with her hands on her hips, overseeing her cast as they stretched in front of her. She glanced at Jonah and waved him over, her movements choppy, as if she couldn't shake off the tension building in her muscles. As he approached, Sherrie went to Sarah and spoke quietly with her, their words light and friendly, and Jonah wished he could be with them rather than with the clearly frazzled Evie.

"Slight issue," she said as Jonah reached her, and he noted just how frizzy and large her usually neat dark hair had become. "You might not have a Patroclus tonight."

Jonah laughed, not knowing how else to respond, but when her pinched expression didn't change the joy seeped from his tone. "But we can't do the show without him."

"I know," she said with a roll of her eyes. "I called Colbie, and she's made some calls. I'm just waiting on a response and hopefully we can go ahead, but I need you to be on your A game tonight because you will have to carry someone who is unfamiliar with the track."

"Oh, yeah. I mean, of course."

"Fabulous." She forced a smile. "Now warm up with the others, we're going to make this happen, I'll be damned if we have to cancel the show tonight." She waved Jonah away with a small, dismissive jerk of her hand.

Jonah took his space on the stage and moved with the others, all of them watching Omari as he led the stretches. Jonah marveled at the man, the way he moved, so fluid, effortless, never breaking a single bead of sweat, and it pissed Jonah off to no end that someone could be so frustratingly perfect. But despite Omari's best efforts to energize the cast the mood became subdued. They knew the likelihood of a performance tonight was slim; there would be no show without a Patroclus. Evie's voice kept interrupting them as she spoke on her phone, becoming more of a distraction when they were running their vocal warm-ups, her tone shrill, desperate, until finally she stuffed her mobile into her pocket and clapped her hands together loudly.

"Because I am the best person in the entire world, I have a cover coming in for Patroclus. Please continue to get ready and, Sherrie, I need you and the wardrobe team ready to make some adjustments to the first cover costume and make sure he's looking fabulous for stage." She then let out an uncharacteristic squeal. "Tonight is going to be huge!"

"Who is our hero, then? Who stepped in to save us last minute?" Sarah asked, crossing her arms over her chest with a smile. "Don't leave us hanging."

Evie smirked. "Dexter Ellis."

Jonah hadn't seen Dexter since the incident on the tube. He'd expected him to show up for yoga, but he didn't, and he kept an eye out for him during and after the shows in case he popped up to tell Jonah about all the mistakes he made again. He *might* have spent a couple of hours scrolling through Dexter's Instagram, and God, the man was a bore. He posted photos from rehearsals and gushed about his excitement at taking on the role of Hector. There was a worrying amount of photos of salads he'd eaten and even more photos of himself pouting in mirrors. Yet people ate his content up. His followers were nearing one hundred thousand, an obscene amount given how utterly mundane he was, but it only solidified his position as the darling of the West End. True theatre royalty.

Jonah adjusted the collar of his costume, then fiddled with the microphone poking out of his hairline. He had not really allowed himself to ponder the reality of performing with Dexter; the cast change still wouldn't happen for five weeks, and even then his scenes with him were limited, save for the fight scene, and he couldn't deny feeling slightly excited at murdering him onstage. Dexter covering Bastien meant their rivalry now faced a different turn. There would be no besting him in a sword fight; he had to make out with him instead. At least he wouldn't taste of mackerel like Lucian did. Or, Jonah hoped he wouldn't taste of mackerel, anyway.

A loud knock on his dressing room door jostled Jonah from his thoughts. Before he could answer, Dexter made his way into the room and closed the door behind him. He looked . . . undeniably handsome in the costume Bastien usually wore, though the tunic sat higher on his thighs, the man's height his downfall. His hair looked tousled and playful and made Jonah want to run his fingers through it. No. No. The guy was a giant dick, and Jonah hated him.

"So, I thought we should quickly talk about the sex scene?" Dexter said bluntly. "Normally Achilles disrobes Patroclus then lays him down on the bed, but I think we should switch it."

Jonah blinked slowly at him. "So, you want to take my clothes off and get me onto the bed instead?"

"I just think our dynamic is clearly different from the one you have with Bastien, and it would work better if Patroclus takes the lead in the sex scene. I don't think the audience will believe you could be dominant in a sexual situation with me."

"Are you for fucking real?" Jonah scoffed. "You've never played Patroclus, you've never acted with me, and it shouldn't matter what you think our dynamic should be because we have directions and lines to say and don't have any choice in what our characters do onstage."

Dexter clicked his tongue against his teeth then smirked. "You are so wildly unprofessional."

"*I'm* unprofessional?"

"Yes. You've been a total twat to me for absolutely no reason from the moment I stepped foot in this theatre for the photo shoot. And now you won't even discuss a way to make our performance stand out and be the best it can be."

"I've hardly had time to be a twat to you, have I? We've spent . . . what, twenty minutes together? And even if I have been a twat, I've only been mirroring the way you've been with me," Jonah said. "You pretend like you didn't know who I was at yoga, then you come here and threaten me and then—"

Dexter raised his hand to hush him with a laugh. "Wait a minute, threaten you? When the hell did I threaten you?"

"When you said I'll see how an Olivier really doesn't mean that much?"

"Why would you think that's a threat?"

"Because it is one?"

Dexter continued to laugh and shook his head. "Wow. You're even more insecure than I first thought." He took a deep breath and let his laughter subside. "Look, Jonah, let's be professional here."

"I am being professional!" His protest sounded whiny, desperate, like a child. "You can't go changing scenes half an hour before going onstage without talking to the creative team first. I don't know who you think you are, but you can't waltz in here and expect everything to change for you."

Dexter's posture changed from cocky to somewhat vulnerable, his shoulders turned in, his height seemed to shrink. "Why don't you like me, Jonah?"

Jonah opened his mouth to answer, then closed it again, any words he might muster running away from him.

"I stood up for you on the tube with those guys, just so you know," Dexter said. "I tried to make it better. I could see the situation was proper shit for you so I tried to help and you still have a problem with me."

"You didn't need to say anything because it was nothing to do with you." Jonah knew he sounded spiteful, his tone sharp, set out to harm, but he couldn't stop himself. "And don't talk to me about 'not liking you' when you're the one who has come here and caused problems. Like, no one's asked for your opinion, Dexter. I don't care if you think I messed up a line or was behind a couple of beats, it's none of your concern."

Dexter appeared to be carefully considering his next words before frowning and taking a deep breath. Jonah readied himself for more criticism or an explanation for why it *was* Dexter's concern, but the reasoning never came. "We're switching the bit in the sex scene. I will take the lead," he said, turning to open the door. "Break a leg, Jonah."

EIGHT

*"He wore your armor. He moved just like you.
I thought I'd defeated the mighty Achilles."*

—"Answer Me," *The Wooden Horse*, Act Two

Dexter didn't kiss like Bastien; he kissed like a long-lost lover starved of affection for thousands of years. His lips, soft, ridiculously soft, pressed against Jonah's and it seemed as if Dexter were trying to devour the air from his lungs. He let Dexter turn him, Patroclus taking the lead, even though his mind should have been screaming at the change of blocking, something they should never do, something Colbie would scream at them for later if she ever found out, and felt Dexter's fingers sneak below the shoulder of his tunic. Dexter didn't disrobe him, not like Achilles usually did to Patroclus; he only showed a glimmer of Jonah's skin, enough to tantalize, enough to tell the audience more would be revealed, but in private, a moment for the characters and the characters alone.

He'd been so used to kissing Bastien, to the stubble lining his jaw no matter how freshly he shaved, and the way his body moved against his. They'd established a delicate balance where they could create a romance onstage and not allow it to leak out past the stage door, but Dexter? Jonah didn't have any rules in place with him, unspoken or not. It left an unsettled feeling in the pit of his stomach, one he didn't know how to navigate or place. Of course, professionalism came into play. Jonah knew full well a kiss between actors meant nothing. But Dexter kissed him like they'd known each other forever, their lips as familiar as the rising sun, a promise of summer after a harsh winter. And when Dexter sung to him, his voice reverberating off Jonah's skin, the moment became absurdly intimate, despite being viewed by hundreds of people.

As Dexter lowered him down onto the bed where Achilles and Patroclus made love, he pressed his lips to Jonah's again, the second kiss not in the script, but Jonah cupped his cheeks as the lights dimmed on their scene. His skin felt surprisingly cool beneath his palms. As the world turned dark Dexter's lips remained on his, and just as Jonah attempted to pull away Dexter seized his bottom lip between his teeth and bit him. He fucking bit him. Jonah's hand immediately covered his mouth as Dexter parted from him and exited the stage. Jonah drew his fingers back expecting to see blood. They were clean, but the pain still lingered.

The precious twelve minutes until Jonah needed to be onstage again were spent in his dressing room, changing from Achilles's casual wear into his armor as Sherrie fussed around him. He stood, looking at himself in the mirror, his bottom lip slightly redder, plump, and he wondered why the idiot bit him. Normally, he wouldn't mind a bit of nipping and teeth grazing, but that would be in the bedroom, not onstage in front of six hundred people, especially when it wasn't even in the bloody script. Did Dexter bite in the bedroom? Did he like to scratch and nip at exposed skin while fucking? No. *No.* Jonah did not want to think about Dexter having sex. He could imagine his stupid lips pouting as he gasped and groaned, and really, the thought should have repulsed him. But it didn't. He really needed to find a date to get the stupid horny images out of his system; even thinking about Dexter in an intimate position was crossing a line he didn't know he would ever even get close to.

Dexter behaved himself for the rest of the show, and Jonah didn't want to admit it but he did a bloody good job given he'd never performed Patroclus before and only knew his track from observations and his knowledge from before *The Wooden Horse* took to the West End. He died beautifully in Jonah's arms, his death surprisingly realistic, his body turning into a dead weight as Jonah held him. As the middle part of the stage lowered, taking them out of sight, he didn't look at Jonah, he simply walked away, back to his dressing room—no, *Bastien's* dressing room—and then waited for his call back onstage for the bows. Bastien would usually stand by Jonah's side at the end of the show, the cast clutching hands as they bowed for their audience and basked in the applause. But Dexter stood three bodies down from him, a snub if Jonah ever saw one, and completely reveled in the fact he got the biggest cheer of the night. The audience propelled themselves to their feet the moment he came onstage, the sound deafening, only to fall slightly when Jonah walked on right after him. He gathered the remaining applause and ran with it.

Dexter's return to *The Wooden Horse* could be seen as nothing other than a success. He'd saved the day, ran to the theatre at a moment's notice, and took on a role he'd never played before. As they left the stage, he saw Colbie standing there with a gigantic bouquet of orange and red flowers, an unsettling surprise given he didn't have a clue their producer was lurking in the building. She handed the flowers to Dexter and pulled him into a hug then gushed about just how good he'd been, how proud he'd made her, and just how excited she was for him to come back as Hector. She said nothing to Jonah as he passed, not even a scolding for allowing Dexter to change the details in the sex scene.

"You should give me your phone number," Dexter said as they shrugged their coats over their shoulders after getting changed before heading out of the stage door to the inevitable crowd waiting to fawn over Dexter. "Chances are I'm going to be on for Bastien again tomorrow unless he makes a miraculous recovery overnight." He adjusted the collar of his coat, then picked up his flowers from Colbie. Jonah looked at the man's coat, long, tan and . . . was it cashmere? The thing must have cost a fortune. "I would like to hear if you have any notes for me," Dexter said, his tone serious.

Jonah zipped up his own coat, the black thing he picked up in a thrift shop back home, and raised an eyebrow at him. "You want my opinion on your performance tonight?" After their exchange before the show, Jonah was a little surprised Dexter was even talking to him.

"Yes," Dexter said quickly, as if it were the most obvious answer in the world. "Is that a problem?" He produced his phone from his pocket and unlocked it before passing it to Jonah. "Give me your number and I will text you later. I'm assuming you don't want my notes on your performance?"

Jonah knew how pathetic he was being for not wanting to give Dexter his number. He didn't want to text him; he didn't want to have any more contact with the man than absolutely necessary, but he put his number into his phone anyway and handed it back to him.

"Your assumption is correct."

"Right, well, thanks for giving me your number at least," Dexter said, a small, genuine-looking smile on his face. "Right, um, see you later." He opened the stage door and his little smile turned into a huge one as he saw the crowd of people waiting there to greet him.

Jonah followed out after him, taken aback by just how many people were there. He hadn't seen so many people outside of the Persephone before, and part of him felt a little vulnerable as a few of them jostled forward to talk to them. He'd heard about sizable crowds waiting at stage doors for other shows, usually one-night-only concerts where a big name had flown over from Broadway to perform. There were often small crowds gathered at the Persephone, but nothing like this, bodies everywhere with beaming faces and programs stretched out to be signed. He could see Omari farther down working his way along the line, sharpie in hand. Clearly no one else in the company seemed remotely bothered by Dexter joining the cast; the problem lay with Jonah alone. He needed to pull himself together.

"You were amazing," a woman said, clutching her program before holding it out to Jonah. "Would you mind signing this, please?" He took a sharpie out of his back pocket, the cast now well versed in keeping a good stash of them on hand at all times, and scrawled his signature across the front of it.

"Would it be okay to get a picture?"

"You were *so* good, oh my God, like so good."

"When you sang 'The Melody of Achilles and Patroclus' I cried."

"Would it be okay to get a picture of both of you, please?"

Jonah noticed Dexter beside him, only to see him nodding enthusiastically. The girl who asked nestled between them while her friend took a photo, then they switched places so another photo could be taken.

"Thank you," the first girl said. "And, I hope it's okay to say, but this is my ninth time coming and tonight was my favorite. You guys as Achilles and Patroclus were absolutely perfect."

"That's so kind of you," Jonah said, as Dexter allowed a blush to spread over his cheeks. "Dexter did a great job, didn't he? Hardly any mistakes." He felt Dexter's eyes burning into the back of his head. "You'll come back and see him as Hector, right?"

"We've got tickets for the first performance," she replied enthusiastically before moving aside to let them sign more programs.

Other cast members were filtering through the crowd as Jonah finally reached the end of the line, and he saw Omari waiting for him. The taller man pulled Jonah into a one-armed hug, then lightly kissed his cheek.

"Fabulous tonight as always, my love," he said. "I'm going to a dance workshop tomorrow morning if you fancy it?"

"Where do you get the energy?" Jonah smiled at him.

"If you took the vitamins I told you about and ate the food from that list I sent you, you would have more energy to be like me," he replied seriously.

"I wasn't expecting you to actually have an answer for that, you know."

"I have an answer for everything."

"I know."

Omari smirked at him. "See you tomorrow. Don't stay up late eating ice cream and crying, okay?"

Jonah narrowed his eyes at him. "I don't stay up late eating ice cream and crying."

Omari cocked his head to the side then patted Jonah condescendingly on the head. "Good. Ice cream gives you mucus."

Jonah watched as Omari lost himself in the crowd, and when Jonah could no longer see him, he pulled his headphones out of his bag and placed them over his head. Usually fans, if he could call them that without sounding terribly pretentious, respected their space when it came to the stage door. If an actor skirted away quickly, they left them alone, and the unspoken rule of someone wearing headphones meant they no longer wanted to be disturbed. That night, however, a man grabbed

Jonah's shoulder as he tried to walk away, the soothing sounds of Efterklang already floating in his ears, and pulled him back hard enough for Jonah to stumble slightly. The man's fingers dug into his shoulder blade, possessive, righteous, as if Jonah owed him something.

"Hey!" the man said, voice so loud Jonah could hear it over his music. "Let's have a photo, mate!" He wrapped his arm around Jonah's shoulder and held his phone out to take a selfie as Jonah blinked in confusion. He didn't smile; he didn't have a chance to even register what was happening, let alone slap on a look of happiness.

"Thanks, man," the stranger said, clapping him on the shoulder as he let him go then lost himself in the crowds of Shaftesbury Avenue. Jonah watched after him, unsure of what exactly just happened and why he couldn't help but feel slightly taken for granted in the situation. He stood dumbfounded, his heart racing at being caught off guard. Sherrie made her way toward him, pushing through the crowd by the theatre, pink crimped hair bouncing as she walked.

"You okay?" she asked as he took his headphones off. "I saw that, what a dick. Some people have no respect for others, huh?"

"I'm fine," he said, but the way his knuckles were turning white from how tightly he gripped the headphones told another story.

"You sure?" Her eyes scanned his face, looking for signs of distress, but she found none. When Jonah nodded, she cleared her throat and her lips stretched into a smile. "Um, while I've caught you, it's my birthday Sunday, so I'm arranging drinks for after the show Saturday. You in?"

"Oh, yeah, of course, sounds good."

"I've invited the new cast." A shy smile tugged at her lips. "Including Romana."

"Oh?" Jonah thought back to the day he met the cast for the new photos and recalled the woman with the long hair Sherrie was blushing at while adjusting her hemline.

"I might have . . . you know . . . been slowly seducing her."

"Of course you have."

"You know me, babe, can't be waiting around for love to come my way." She paused. "I've also invited Dexter," she said. "I hope that's okay.

I'm getting the impression you two aren't fond of each other despite the rather hot making out onstage tonight."

Jonah shrugged. "No, it's fine. I mean, he's fine, we're fine. Um, yeah, Saturday night, sounds good." He forced a smile. "See you later, yeah?"

Sherrie leaned forward and pressed a cotton candy pink kiss to his cheek. "Love you, darling, get home safe!"

Shaftesbury Avenue took him into its arms and sheltered him from the rain falling lazily from the sky. He'd been grabbed before, it was no big deal; he kept repeating it to himself as he walked to the tube station, keenly aware of anyone who looked like Edward or Wes, but to his relief he only saw unfamiliar faces who all blurred into each other and paid him no attention. As he boarded the train on the Northern Line, he saw a flash of orange and red flowers on the platform, only for them to vanish as the carriage doors closed and Castle Road called him home.

Jonah kept glancing at his phone as he brushed his teeth. The incoming message from Dexter loomed over him, an axe waiting to fall. The time inched closer to midnight, and he expected him to have been texting Jonah eager for feedback the moment he left stage door, but the message never came. Instead, as he peeled off his clothes and pulled the T-shirt he wore for bed over his head his phone lit up with a message from Bastien.

> Omari told me you made out with the penis destroyer tonight?

Jonah glared at the message. Fuck off.

The little dots signaling Bastien replying kept disappearing then reappearing on the screen, and Jonah could only imagine how much his friend was likely enjoying how traumatizing the evening had been for him.

> Heard it looked rather steamy on stage. Did he get you all hot under the collar?

Jonah scowled.

> Leave me alone. Traitor.

How am I a traitor?

> Getting the flu and leaving me to perform with the devil is traitorous behavior.

But I'm a faithful, Jonah!

> Don't make me call Claudia Winkleman to escort you from the theatre next time you come in.

Seriously, though, I hope it was okay?

> He bit me.

Bastien took a moment to respond.

No, he didn't.

> Yeah, he did.

What the fuck?

> My thoughts exactly. Please say you'll be back tomorrow? Don't make me kiss him again.

Probably not, I'm on my deathbed.

> I hate you.

Love you too.

NINE

> *"The blood of the city pollutes the sea and angers Poseidon who dwells beneath the surface of the waves. If we torment the Gods, they will retaliate."*
>
> —"Agamemnon's Rally," *The Wooden Horse*, Act One

> I have hands down never felt such a range of emotions at the theatre. Joy and despair mixed flawlessly. Dexter Ellis was sheer perfection.
> #Thewoodenhorse #Dexterellis

> Holy shiiiit Dexter Ellis and Jonah Penrose last night were SO amazing. I literally can't stop thinking about them.
> #Thewoodenhorselondon #Jonahpenrose #Dexterellis #Dexah

> Dexter Ellis made his long-awaited return to The Wooden Horse last night and stole the show. His Patroclus will go down as one of the best in history. Five well-deserved stars.
> #Thewoodenhorse #Theatrereviews #Dexterellis

> Um, does anyone else think Jonah Penrose and Dexter Ellis are actually in love because that kiss on stage last night was a bit too convincing to not be real. Right?
> #Jonahpenrose #Dexterellis #Dexah

They had a bloody ship name. Jonah woke to hundreds of mentions on social media and a flurry of new followers. For the briefest of moments, he forgot about the night before and Dexter Ellis with his stupid teeth sinking into his lip, and wondered what on earth he'd done to garner such attention. His name alongside Dexter's online seemed strange, a call back to the year before when he'd been announced as playing Achilles and the theatre circles went into meltdown. These posts, however, were a lot nicer than the ones from the previous year. They not only praised Dexter, but praised him as well, all while dragging poor Bastien in the process. He hoped Bastien hadn't seen the posts slamming his portrayal of Patroclus; he didn't deserve to be compared to Dexter, especially when being ill meant he could do nothing about it. Besides, Bastien was incredible in the role, and it was only the fans with permanent hard-ons for Dexter who thought otherwise.

The ship name, however, left him with a sour taste on the back of his tongue. Fucking Dexah. It sounded like an antibiotic or something you might wash contact lenses in. The posts kept piling in, comments upon comments and photographs upon photographs tagging both him and Dexter at the stage door. Dexter looked overwhelmed in the photos, his cheeks flushed, forehead damp from sweat as he clutched his bouquet close to his chest and smiled brightly at the cameras. He looked as if he'd never done stage door before, his eyes slightly too wide, almost scared; but then again, the pictures of Jonah were no better. The skin below his eyes appeared abnormally dark against his pale complexion, like he hadn't slept for a month then crawled out of a cave to put on a sickly performance. He wiped his hand across his nose and grimaced at the shining trail of snot left on his skin and groaned.

His throat chafed like sandpaper against flesh.

Nope. No. No way. He couldn't be sick. He dumped his phone into his bedsheets and forced himself to get up and go to the bathroom. His reflection in the mirror looked at him solemnly; if he didn't know better, he would assume he'd been on a bender and still hadn't gone to sleep. He should have used one of the rehydrating face masks Omari and Sherrie kept not-so-subtly leaving in his dressing room. Maybe then he wouldn't look like a Victorian child wasting away.

Jonah forced himself into the shower, the hot water cascading across his skin already healing him, and the raw feeling in his throat subsided slightly. It wasn't the flu; he was just tired, and still slightly unnerved by the man grabbing him the night before. It shouldn't have surprised him. He'd been grabbed before, pulled about, arms thrown around him, and even wandering hands working their way down his back to his arse, and for some reason he just stood there and took it. He never complained, never said a word to the security staff at the theatre, Evie, or the other cast members; if he kicked up a fuss, people might think of him as ungrateful, and he couldn't be seen as anything other than bloody happy about his role and the attention that came with it. There were nights he skipped the stage door altogether, opting to slip out with his hood up and headphones already on so no one expected anything from him. He'd always inevitably receive a bevy of aggressive messages from random people who didn't know him complaining he'd ruined their night by not stopping to take photos afterward.

Once out of the shower, he wrapped his towel around his waist and wandered back to his bedroom, where his bed looked at him and whispered intricate words of seduction to get him back in it. He contemplated the offer; he needed to go for a run then head to the dance studio for the class Omari was hounding him about on every form of social media possible, but the bed, God, the bed looked so bloody good. His phone peered at him from the blankets, the screen lit up with an unrecognized number, and he stared at it for a good few seconds before realizing someone was calling him. He grabbed it and held it to his face as droplets of water from his curls dripped across the screen. The number must belong to Dexter; who else would have the gumption to call at eight in the morning and expect someone to answer?

"Hello?"

"Yeah, hi, it's Dexter."

Jonah's lip stung at the name. "It's so early."

"Is it? I always go for a run at five, then do Pilates. I've been up for hours."

"You're insane."

Dexter scoffed. "A healthy mind and body are the first steps to success."

Great. Another Omari. "But you don't have to do those things at five in the morning, you absolute weirdo." Dexter didn't respond. "I thought you were going to text for your . . . feedback? Do you really want me to give you feedback?"

"Yes."

"Don't bite people when you kiss them."

Silence. Jonah waited, not willing to say more, not allowing him to worm his way out of the confrontation by simply not responding. They played phone-chicken with each other, both waiting patiently for the other to make a move until Dexter finally cracked.

"I went to a bar after the show last night and saw one of the guys you talked to on the tube the other week."

Out of all the responses he could have given, Jonah couldn't have guessed he would come out with that. "Okay? And you're telling me that because?"

"He came up to me and just started talking shit about you. Thought you might want to know."

Jonah paused. Edward surely wouldn't have anything bad to say about him; Jonah had been a great boyfriend, obviously not great enough to not let Edward's hands wander, but still pretty good by normal standards.

"What did he say?"

"That you were having an affair with his boyfriend. Apparently, the night you saw them on the tube it all came out. I knew something weird was going on there. Never pegged you as a home-wrecker, though."

"Wait." Jonah let out a disbelieving laugh. It couldn't have been Edward, it must have been Wes who spoke to Dexter. "I wasn't having an affair with anyone. Edward was *my* boyfriend, that guy was the 'other man,' not me."

"Tomatoes, to-mah-toes." As he spoke, Jonah could hear another voice in the background, and Dexter gave a laugh. "Anyway, I've got to go. Was that all the feedback you had for me? No biting? Nothing about my actual performance?"

"I mean, that technically is a note on your performance, I just—"

"Okay, Jonah, cool, speak to you later." He hung up. Dexter Ellis hung up on him. Jonah gawped at the phone, his hands trembling. He hated the feelings the man conjured inside of him. Glinda and Elphaba described it best: unadulterated loathing. Only Jonah didn't know if he was the green witch or the one floating about in a bubble. He wished he could place his anger somewhere other than the center of his chest. Back home when he felt this way he would go to the beach, near the little cove only he seemed to know about, where he could skim rocks and scream at the top of his lungs and it didn't matter because no one could hear. London couldn't offer him the privacy he craved. It simply sat back with a bag of popcorn and watched as his personal life went up in flames.

He'd been called in for a meeting with Colbie. The dreaded summons came from Evie asking him to come in an hour early. "An emergency," she said, "Colbie needs to see you," the words no actor ever wants to hear about their producer. On his way to the theatre, he convinced himself this was it. He was going to be told his contact wasn't going to be renewed again; Colbie saw how amazing Dexter performed the night before and now Jonah could kiss Achilles goodbye and go back home to Cornwall next year with his tail between his legs. It didn't matter how many times he tried to tell himself how ridiculous his prophecy of self-doom seemed, he couldn't stop the thoughts from growing. As the Northern Line pulled him closer to the theatre, he could feel a weight pushing down on his shoulders. He debated texting Bastien, but his messages to him from the morning still went unanswered, and he guessed Bastien really was as sick as he made out if his phone wasn't permanently attached to his hand like usual. He could reach out to Omari, but he was likely using his treasured steam-inhaler cup to cleanse his vocal cords somewhere. And Sherrie—well, Sherrie would probably only add fuel to the fire, even if she didn't mean to.

The Persephone looked glumly at Jonah as he approached. The stage door whined as he opened it, crying out for him to leave, to turn back while his name could still be up in lights and Colbie couldn't dump a rain shower of bad news onto his parade. Still, his feet moved him forward; he passed his dressing room and walked up the ridiculous number of stairs all the way to Evie's office, where Colbie would be lurking. He could feel her presence as he readied himself to knock on the door, hear her voice speaking animatedly as Evie cackled, and he shuddered.

"Come in, come in," Evie said once he'd worked up the confidence to knock and peeked his head around the door. Colbie sat behind the desk, laptop open in front of her, light illuminating her sharp features and constellation of freckles. She flicked her eyes up to look at him, glasses perched on the end of her nose much like his dad's used to be when he was completing a crossword. He took the seat on the opposite side of the desk and prepared himself for the bollocking he thought he was going to receive the night before.

"I'm going to start doing the rounds for tonight," Evie said, swiping her phone from the desk while heading to the door. Jonah wanted to reach for her, to pull on her sleeve and beg her to not leave him alone with possibly the most terrifying person he'd ever encountered, but his hands stayed firmly in his lap and all he could do was listen as she left the room. The door clicked shut behind her.

Colbie tapped her nails on the top of her laptop as she looked at him, a grin on her lips as something devious brewed behind her eyes. "So, last night was rather interesting. Can't say I was thrilled about the change of blocking in act one, but the risk paid off," she said. "You know not to do something like that again without running it by someone first, right?"

Jonah nodded. "Sorry."

Colbie waved the apology away like a cloud of cigarette smoke. "It's fine, but it is one of the reasons I called you in here. Do you think that choreography would work with you and Bastien? I've been keeping a close eye on social media today and people really liked it. They're excited about coming to see the change."

"Sure, I think it could work."

"Great." She smiled, and for the briefest of moments Jonah allowed himself to relax. "Have you had a look at your socials today? It seems like the whole of the West End is talking about you and Dexter."

Jonah nodded. "Yeah, I saw some stuff. I try to keep away from it, though."

"Sensible," she said with a hum. "But I'm going to capitalize on this. I'm going to introduce you and Dexter to Niamh, she manages our marketing. She thinks we could get you both onto some podcasts and some guest-takeover spots on various social media sites. It will drum up excitement for the cast change and also cash in on this fascination people seem to have with the two of you."

"The fascination comes from people thinking I stole the role of Achilles from him, nothing more."

"Maybe at first, but now they *love* you two together, after only one performance!" She turned the screen of her laptop around to show Jonah some posts she'd bookmarked. "The only issue we have is the fact that you two don't like each other."

"Oh," Jonah said quickly. "No, it's not—that's not the case at all."

"The audience may not notice any animosity between the two of you, but I picked up on it straight away. And here we have people speculating that you two might actually be in love." She laughed then, a noise not usually associated with Colbie. "A theatre romance is better than a theatre rivalry."

"Romance?"

"It either ends in blissful marriage or devastating heartbreak, and people love it. It's good publicity, and I don't want there to be any whispers of you two not getting along. Dexter will be on for Bastien until he's better, and it's the perfect marketing opportunity for us."

Jonah narrowed his eyes at her. "I'm a bit confused about what you're wanting me to do here. Pretend we are together?"

"No, Jonah, this isn't a rom-com. Look, I'm not asking you to suck his dick or anything, that would be totally unethical and clearly the last thing either of you want to do. Just make people think you're sucking his dick, praise him, and he will praise you. I spoke to Dexter, and he's fine with it."

Jonah stared at her, unable to compute that he was actually discussing the topic of sucking dick with the producer of the show. "So, you're asking us to be nice to each other? I haven't been . . . I mean I haven't been *not* nice to him."

"That's not what Dexter said."

Jonah rolled his eyes. "Whatever. Fine. I can be nice, I can say nice things, I'm not a monster, Colbie. But I'm not implying anything when it comes to my private life," he said, hands clenching into fists in his lap. "If people want to speculate about some totally made-up romance, I can't stop that. But I'm not fueling the fire."

"Do you want our ticket sales to plummet, Jonah?" Colbie asked bluntly. "We are in a cost-of-living crisis, and theatre is a luxury many people can't afford. But after the show last night, we had a surge of people booking. If you want to get extended, then we need to keep it up. You can either help with that or watch everyone lose their jobs. Trust me when I say that animosity behind the scenes can destroy a production."

"I'm sure we can be professional with each other. We have been so far."

Colbie threw her hands in the air with an exasperated sigh. "Jonah. I don't know what to tell you. I want this show to be one of the long-standing ones. We need to be up there with *Les Mis* and *Phantom*. We can't ride the high then allow ourselves to crash and burn. My reputation is on the line."

"So, you think by pushing a narrative that me and Dexter are . . . what? Dating? That will help?"

"It won't hurt. And you don't have to even *do* anything. Just do the press stuff and be nice to each other, post a few photos, social media will do the rest." She took a deep breath. "You're actors, for God's sake, pretend, at least for a few months until the new cast is settled. Then you can channel the dislike into killing him each night, okay?"

Well. Fuck. He found himself between a rock and a hard place, smacking against both with no means of crawling his way out of it. He didn't want anyone to fabricate romantic ties between him and the West End suck-up, but if they were going to do it anyway, he could at least make sure tickets were sold because of it. And he couldn't say no to Colbie, not now, not when so much could be taken from him. Only now his rivalry came with its own ship name, and it seemed he would drown with it.

TEN

> *"King of walls, king of beauty, the king favored by the Gods. He sits on his throne, looking out on a sea of blood, of bodies, of destruction, and he hides her from view. He allows the world to crumble for the beauty of one, the desire of his son."*
>
> —"Priam," *The Wooden Horse*, Act Two

"**W**e need to talk."

Jonah stopped in his tracks and looked over his shoulder to see Dexter standing behind him. He'd hoped he could escape the theatre and grab a coffee before having to head back for warm-ups so he could digest everything he'd discussed with Colbie, but no. Not when Dexter Ellis was around. He looked at the other man, strands of blond hair kissing his forehead, another embroidered monstrosity on his jumper, a kite, perhaps, though Jonah couldn't be sure. He stood with his shoulders back, posture impeccable, and nodded toward the stage door.

"Come on, let's go for a walk," he said, a statement rather than a question.

A million excuses bubbled on the end of Jonah's tongue, but his mouth betrayed him and the only word that escaped his lips was, "Okay."

They walked together in silence, away from Shaftesbury Avenue, through the busy London crowds until they walked farther past the Playhouse Theatre and came out on the embankments of the Thames. Jonah expected the other man to speak, to assert himself as they walked, but he didn't. He kept his head down, hands in his pockets, and chewed on his bottom lip, seemingly lost in thought. Jonah heard snippets of conversations from people they passed, arguments, gossip, plans for dinner, and he wondered if anyone paid any attention to them as they walked, two ghouls who knew no words and wouldn't even look at each other. A cool breeze lifted from the river, and Jonah peered at the water as they moved along the pavement and danced his fingers along the stone wall separating them from the river below. The Thames, gray, reminiscent of soot, did little to ease the pining in his heart for Cornish seas. But the sounds of the water lapping against the banks soothed him. It almost called him home.

"So, Colbie spoke to you?" Dexter finally broke the silence. "About the whole being nice to each other thing?"

"Yeah."

"And about people thinking we are, I don't know, a thing?"

"Yup." Jonah nodded.

"I don't know why people would think I'm remotely interested in you," Dexter quipped, and Jonah looked at him with a scowl. "But then again, I know how good I've been performing as Patroclus, so I suppose I can understand why they might think the romance has carried off the stage."

"You really are the most arrogant person I've ever met." Jonah shook his head slightly as he walked.

"I don't care what you think of me."

Jonah rolled his eyes. "No. Of course you don't."

"And, unlike you, I want to ensure everything I do is a success. Which is why I told Colbie I'm willing to go along with whatever I need to do to make this work. I can be nice. I can post some photos. But your social media needs some work."

Jonah contemplated hauling him over the wall and into the river. He somehow restrained himself. "I'm sorry, I don't feel the need to post pictures of lettuce every five minutes."

Dexter huffed. "No, you like to post pictures of pavements and trees."

Jonah knew this was an admission from them both at having checked out each other's social media, but neither of them acknowledged it.

Dexter gradually came to a stop as they walked, Jonah falling in beside him naturally, and he watched as Dexter rested his arms against the stone balustrade and looked out over the Thames. "As you're awful at social media, I will handle it," the blond said. "I can tag you and it will come up on your profile too. But you could at least post some stories or something, or comment on my stuff every now and then."

"Why the hell would I do that?" Jonah took up a similar position beside him and looked down into the murky water. "What would I even say?"

"I don't know, just be nice or whatever."

"Fine."

"Fine."

Dexter cocked his head slightly to look at him. "I'm guessing from your disastrous love life this isn't going to cause any problems with any relationships you have?"

Jonah paused. He hadn't considered how this would look to people he knew or if it might impact his *actual* love life, or lack of it. "No," he mumbled.

"Me neither." He continued to peer at Jonah. "You look tired. We should head back to the theatre so someone can sort your face out."

Jonah forced himself to bite his tongue. Retaliation would be futile; the guy was an absolute arsehole, and even Dexter's delicious-looking lips did nothing to soothe the rage burning in Jonah's chest. For, what good were kissable lips if they belonged to a bell end?

Jonah found himself engulfed by the whirlwind created by Dexter. The man knew how to work a crowd; he devoured the applause and charmed his fans at stage door. People queued up to speak with him and showered him with gifts while the other cast looked on, slightly jealous, but more relieved they could sneak off to get the earlier train home with little blowback. Onstage, Dexter kissed Jonah softly, like he'd been sculpted out of glass, and moved during the bows to stand beside him, their palms pressed together, fingers intertwined. Outside the theatre, Dexter wrapped his arm around him and together they smiled for photos and gushed to the fans about each other, nothing but praise and the fakest of smiles.

They hadn't talked again about Colbie's insistence on kindness. In fact, Dexter said very little to Jonah when they weren't masquerading outside the theatre or reciting their lines onstage. Jonah expected him and his gigantic head to saunter into his dressing room spouting off all the times Jonah didn't hit his mark at the very millisecond he should have, or coming up with a convoluted plan to ensure that Dexter's takeover as Hector would be as extravagant as possible. But Dexter shrouded himself in silence. Not that Jonah made any attempt to communicate with him either. Though he pondered texting him several times; he felt like a fish out of water, unsure of how he should act or what he should say. Their weird relationship had no lines, no blocking.

Despite their lack of communication, they saw a rise in social media interactions and general buzz surrounding the show. The charade dragged on for three more performances, and though they did nothing to suggest anything other than admiration and a respect for each other, the spark of a romance between them turned into a wildfire on the internet. Jonah knew the theatre community could be dedicated, but this was on a completely different level. It took less than a week for Dexah to become part of West End history, and Jonah wanted to scream; he wanted to be remembered for his work, not his suspected romance with the biggest dickhead he'd ever met. Dexter became borderline insufferable, literally pushing his way past Jonah on the way to the stage, talking over him whenever he saw the chance, and doing the loudest vocal warm-ups known to man outside of Jonah's dressing room.

Even now, sitting beside him on a bright orange sofa in front of a microphone in some strange little makeshift recording studio in a room above a bar, Dexter annoyed him in ways he'd never experienced before. He tapped his fingers across his knees constantly and always licked his bottom lip like he needed to seduce whoever so much as glanced at him. He touched Jonah too much, always a hand on his arm as they talked with others or tapping him on the shoulder like a child in need of attention. Even his breathing pissed Jonah off. Too loud, too intrusive. He needed to do it for survival, of course, but Jonah wished he could be more subtle about how well his lungs worked.

"So, how has it been, returning to a show so close to your heart this week?" Jay, the host of the *West End Wonders* podcast, asked as she smiled over at Dexter, clearly caught in his flytrap charms.

Dexter placed his hand over his heart and let out a breathy sigh. "Amazing. Totally amazing. The show's changed, obviously, since I last worked on it, but all for the better. And the cast, wow, incomparable. I can't wait to work with them when I start properly."

"Stepping in for Bastien Andrews last minute must have been nerve-racking. How did you manage taking on a role you've never performed before?"

"Oh, it was terrifying." Dexter laughed. "But I was lucky to work so closely with Jonah, he totally held my hand through everything and made me feel relaxed the whole time. Patroclus was never a role I thought I would play, so it's been fun stepping into his shoes for a few days."

"Dexter took to it like he'd always played the role," Jonah said, remembering he needed to praise the compliment vacuum beside him. "We were lucky he was available. The flu wiped out a huge number of our cast, and the show wouldn't have been able to go on without him."

Jay tucked a strand of black hair behind her ear and smiled at Dexter coyly. "Bastien is due to be on this evening. Will you miss being onstage?"

"I'm going to be at the show tonight watching and cheering Bastien on, then I'm back in a few weeks to be Hector, so, no, I don't think so. I'm going to take the time to relax between rehearsals, to be honest. I don't think people appreciate how intense it is being in such a well-loved show night after night."

"And how has it been with the two of you?" she asked. "There used to be a lot of speculation within the theatre circles online that there may be some animosity between you over the role of Achilles?"

"I'm really not sure where people got that idea," Jonah said. "The first time we met was for the photo shoot for *The Wooden Horse*'s new program. Obviously, I knew of Dexter—I'd listened to him on the original-cast recording of the songs—but I didn't know him personally. There was certainly no animosity from my side."

"Well, there wouldn't be from your side, would there?" Jay's smile faltered slightly. "Because you got the role Dexter originated."

"There was no animosity on my side either," Dexter said, somewhat sternly. "People think there was this big competition between the two of us, but that wasn't the case. I auditioned for *Tick, Tick . . . Boom!* and got the role, so that's what I did. There were never any plans for me to play Achilles on the West End."

"It's good to clear that up, especially as you now seem so close. I think everyone who considers themselves a theatre fan has seen the photos of you outside of the Persephone. It's lovely to see cast members bond in such a way. Do you think you will be friends for life now?"

"Friends?" Dexter gave a laugh. "Sure, *friends* for life, right, Jonah?" He looked at him, his hazel eyes warm, something brewing there beneath them, but for what reason Jonah didn't know. The podcast wasn't filmed, his fond glances were for no audience.

"Sure, friends," Jonah said, with a smile back at him.

Jay cocked her head as she took in their interaction. "So, I've had some listener questions, if you're okay to go through them?"

"Sure!" Dexter beamed. "Throw them at us."

"What is your favorite song to perform?"

"Oh, well, as Patroclus this week, 'The Melody of Achilles and Patroclus.' It's a gorgeous song and captures the characters beautifully. As Hector, it has to be 'Answer Me.' It's his big number after all."

"I like 'The Song of the Dead,'" Jonah said. "I remember hearing it for the first time and it made me cry, and I wasn't sure how I could perform it without bawling my eyes out each night. Luckily, it's an emotional number, so it doesn't matter if I get teary singing it."

"'Answer Me' is my favorite," Jay said, which didn't surprise Jonah at all. "Next up, have you ever had any major mishaps onstage?"

Dexter nodded earnestly. "Back when we took *The Wooden Horse* on tour, I had a major wardrobe malfunction during the song at the end of the first act. Everyone saw my arse, and I had to pretend everything was okay."

Jonah gave a genuine laugh. "The audience certainly got their money's worth for that performance." Dexter offered him a smile in return. "I wouldn't say I've had any major mishaps. I once called Bastien by his name rather than Patroclus and the way he looked at me made me want to laugh, but it was during a really serious scene, so it was hard to keep going without cracking a smile. We managed it somehow."

"Last question," Jay said, looking at the laptop screen in front of her. "I've not had the pleasure of seeing you this week, Dexter, but word is you two have the most amazing chemistry onstage. Is it easy to turn off that intense relationship once you leave the stage?"

Dexter sucked in a breath and clasped his hands together in his lap as he spoke. "Hearing we have a good chemistry is honestly the highest compliment. It shows we are doing our job as actors in showing the love between those characters. I can only speak for myself here, but I get caught up in the show, you feel these intense emotions and portray them all while singing these outstanding songs to each other. It's really strange to then walk off the stage and just be yourself again. It takes a while for me to wind down."

"You certainly become close when acting out those scenes," Jonah said. "Even after only a few days you establish a bond, which is necessary to make sure you're doing your characters justice. I think, now I've played Achilles for a while, I can leave him behind when the costume comes off and the audience leaves. But, yeah, the bonds you create with your theatre family go beyond costumes and makeup. I wouldn't want to turn off those relationships."

"That was a very diplomatic answer from you both." Jay laughed. "But, seriously, I'm gutted I didn't get to see you as Patroclus this week, Dexter. I'm so excited to see you as Hector. And the other new cast members too."

Jay wrapped up the podcast with more niceties before a string of sponsors spilled from her lips, leaving Jonah and Dexter to sit there silently while she reeled off the business names. When she finally finished, she stopped recording and smiled at them both, but her eyes settled on Dexter, and Jonah couldn't help but feel slightly snubbed by her.

"Thank you both for coming in so early today," she said, cheeks flushing as she let her eyes wander across Dexter's face. "I know it's a double show day for you."

"Well, for Jonah, at least," Dexter said as he smiled sweetly back at her before turning his attention to Jonah. "Though, I hope you don't mind me saying, you've looked exhausted this week. Aren't you due some time off? It might help with some slipups you've been making."

If Jonah's look could kill, Dexter would be six feet underground. He didn't understand the man's motivation; had Colbie not explicitly told them they needed to put on a show? How was putting him down in front of a podcast host going to help?

"Thanks for that," Jonah said, trying his hardest not to let the smile on his face falter. "Good to know you think I look like shit."

"I didn't say you looked like shit."

"You might as well have done."

Dexter's smile widened, and before Jonah could register what was happening, Dexter reached over to him and ruffled Jonah's curls between his fingers like he was fussing over a dog. "Jonah isn't good at taking criticism. Are you, sweetheart?"

Jonah wanted to pluck the sickening "sweetheart" from his lips and set fire to each syllable. He could feel Jay watching them, breathing in every moment of their interaction, affectionate hair mussing, *sweethearts*, and all.

Jonah scrunched his nose and maintained his forced smile. "Oh, I don't mind. At least I can get those high notes easily, unlike you, Dex."

Dexter made a fond-sounding hum from the back of his throat. "High notes aren't everything though, are they?"

"No, but Olivier Awards are."

Jay cleared her throat, and they turned their heads to look at her. "So," she said, clapping her hands together. "If it's okay, I will just get a couple of photos of you both for the podcast announcement then get this thing edited." She wanted them to leave. Dexter nodded and wrapped his arm around Jonah's shoulder, his cologne so strong it took Jonah's breath away as he pressed himself against his side. Jay took a couple of photos of them both, their smiles as real as they could be, reminding Jonah the role of liking Dexter wasn't one he could play with ease.

ELEVEN

"The drumming of the waves against my skin, enough to form a fire within."

—"To Troy," *The Wooden Horse*, Act One

Sherrie threw back a bright green shot of unidentified alcohol, then let out a screech as she slammed the empty glass down onto the table. Her hair shone under the disco ball twirling above their heads, the glitter spray she'd doused herself in picking up every ounce of light. She licked her deep-purple lips, the color staying put despite the amount of times they'd been swiped against a glass already, then she reached across her chair for Jonah and pulled him close to her face. For the briefest of moments, he thought she might kiss him.

"You know," she slurred, placing her finger over his lips to stop him from speaking. "It's your turn to get a round in." It wasn't his turn. In fact, he'd got the last two drinks for her. But he didn't have the energy to complain, especially as they were celebrating her birthday.

"What can I get you?"

Sherrie hummed, then slumped in her chair, her arm falling from Jonah. "Just a bottle of gin, darling."

Bastien, who seemed determined to sniff every two seconds, making Jonah believe he still wasn't over the flu, shook his head and placed his hand on her shoulder. "Sherrie," he said, voice light, joyful, as if speaking to a child. "I think you might have to go home soon, don't you?"

Sherrie sat up abruptly, like a puppet whose strings were pulled, and smacked his hand away from her. "Don't give me the sad-drunk-girl voice," she said, her words blending into each other. "I'm here to get pissed, and if you're not gonna support me in that, then *you* can go home, Bastien."

"Drinks?" Omari said, returning from the bar with a black tray in hand filled with shots. He placed it down on the table, and the unmistakable scent of aniseed invaded Jonah's nostrils. Sherrie reached for a glass, her hand missing it so her fingers dipped into the top of the alcohol, before getting it the second time and throwing it down her throat with ease.

Bastien narrowed his eyes at Omari, who gave a nonchalant shrug in response. "It's her birthday," he said and took a shot himself. "And they're from Dexter, not me." He nodded his head toward the bar, where Jonah saw Dexter standing and talking with a woman he didn't recognize.

He hadn't shown himself after the evening show; Jonah didn't see him lurking around backstage or continuing to lap up praise from stage door despite not being part of the performance. Jonah relaxed, thinking Dexter might skip Sherrie's birthday drinks, but of course he showed up, ordering a tray of sambuca no less. The podcast they did kept replaying in Jonah's mind. The falseness of it turned his stomach, and Dexter's overly friendly gestures and the pet names falling from his lips only made his mood curdle.

Dexter finished up his conversation at the bar, then made his way over to their table. Other members of the production greeted him as he went, but his attention seemed fixed on Sherrie as he approached. Jonah couldn't stop himself from looking him up and down, not checking him out, definitely not checking him out, but rather not-so-subtly judging his attire. Like usual, he wore something a mother might dress her child in if they were ludicrously rich and called Cyril or Cuthbert. Chinos, cream, cut off at the ankle again, but this time white socks poked out of ugly brown shoes that went into points at the toe. Yet again a white shirt covered his torso, hidden beneath another jumper, and Jonah stared at it as the man drew closer. Instead of a small bear with a bowtie on the breast pocket, or an abstract kite, this stunning piece of couture bore the face of an embroidered Golden Labrador. It was the single most hideous thing Jonah ever had the displeasure of seeing. Even worse than some of the questionably infected dick pics clogging up his FullStack inbox.

"Fucking hell," Bastien said under his breath as he leaned close to Jonah. "He looks like a knockoff Prince Harry."

"Don't be mean. Prince Harry would never wear something so rancid," Jonah said, reaching for a shot to down before Dexter got to the table.

"Happy birthday, Sherrie," Dexter said, a wide smile across his lips that didn't look pink like usual, but red, deep red, as if stained by the petals of a rose. "Thank you for inviting me." He took the vacant seat next to Jonah.

"Nice jumper." Jonah spoke without thinking, the sambuca giving him a momentary rush of confidence.

Dexter narrowed his eyes at him, then wiped his hand across the front of the dog's face. "Yes. It's Piniquo."

"Piniquo?"

"Yes." Dexter frowned. "Very high-end designer, I'm not surprised you haven't heard of it. This piece was a limited run for the fall collection last year."

Jonah raised an eyebrow and allowed a smirk to form on his lips. "Piece? It's a jumper, Dexter. And you mean to tell me you paid for this? It wasn't forced on to you by relative?"

Dexter picked up a shot and drank it before grimacing slightly. Of course he couldn't handle sambuca. The absolute wet wipe. "That's rich coming from someone who looks like they've raided their grandfather's wardrobe."

Jonah looked down at his own clothes. Black cotton trousers, oversized, nice, they made his arse look great, and a black shirt buttoned to his navel to reveal a black T-shirt underneath. Then, to finish his rather perfect ensemble, a beige cardigan that, yes, perhaps a grandad might enjoy, but who in their right mind didn't like a good cardigan?

"You both look abso-bloody-amazing," Sherrie gushed, empty shot glass in her hand, and Jonah couldn't tell if it was the one from earlier or if she'd drank another. "I should know, I'm a fashion queen."

"I don't know if those are fashionable," Bastien said, and gestured to the pink jelly shoes on her feet. "My sister used to wear those when we were kids."

Sherrie swallowed thickly and gave a sambuca-filled gurgle. "Then she was bloody cool, Bash. Anyway," she said as she narrowed her eyes at Dexter. "Romana has been at rehearsals, right? You've seen her? Has she said anything about me?"

"Oh, give it a rest, Sherrie," Omari groaned before taking a sip of a glass of water. Apparently one shot was enough for him. "She's clearly not interested."

"That's not true," she whined. "She was interested when I had my head between her legs."

"Sherrie!" Omari screeched, raising his hands defense. "I do *not* need to know where your head has been."

"Champagne?" The welcome distraction came courtesy of the sound technicians, who, after bringing three bottles to the table and taking up the rest of the chairs, admitted it wasn't champagne but some cheap knockoff that tasted the same. Sherrie didn't seem to care, and she swayed in her seat, champagne flute in hand and a glazed-over expression on her face. Gold-colored bubbles danced across their tongues as the music got heavier, the beat louder and louder until Bastien pulled them to their feet and dragged whoever he could onto the dance floor.

At some point, Dexter took his jumper off and tied it round his waist and loosened three of the buttons on his shirt, his blond hair sticking to his forehead as he danced with Sherrie, their bodies flickering beneath the disco ball. Jonah wasn't watching him. He certainly wasn't watching the way his hips moved and didn't marvel at how big his hands looked splayed across the small of Sherrie's back. And Jonah certainly wasn't looking at the flash of exposed skin on his chest, because, actually, wait, no, he totally was. Jonah drank more, deciding that if he must socialize with Dexter, then he needed to be completely smashed to do so, and if he were drunk, he wouldn't remember feeling a weird sense of attraction to him in the morning. He leaned against the bar and watched as his cocktail pitcher was mixed before him. Vodka. Peach schnapps. Cranberry juice. Bloody delightful.

"You're so fucking gay." Bastien laughed as he sidled up beside him.

Jonah laughed before placing a hand over his heart and gasping, feigning shock. "No way? Am I?"

"We are drowning in beer and shots and you're over here ordering a pitcher of... what is that? Woo Woo?"

Jonah nodded, impressed. "It *is* a Woo Woo."

"You're getting two glasses, right? We're gonna share?"

"No, babe," Jonah said, taking the pitcher from the bartender then grabbing a straw to dunk in it. "This big gay drink is all for me." He ignored Bastien's pout and hugged the glass pitcher to his chest as he sucked on the straw. A man from across the bar looked over at him—neatly trimmed beard, long hair tied back into a bun—and Jonah could feel the stirrings of attraction brewing, an attraction he hadn't experienced since Edward dumped him.

"Hello?" Bastien shouted in his face, waving his hand to get his attention. "Don't zone out on me just because there's a hot guy. You promised you would dance with me."

"Dexter's dancing," Jonah said, nodding toward the tall blond surrounded by the rest of the cast on the dance floor. "Go dance with him."

Bastien made a retching sound from the back of his throat. "Oh, get the hell over it. He's fine. A bit... standoffish, but totally fine. Plus... God, he's hot, isn't he?"

Jonah scowled as he looked at his friend. "Stop it. You're practically drooling. The guy wears embroidered dog jumpers out of choice. And you have a boyfriend."

"Doesn't stop me from looking, though, does it?" Bastien grinned and shimmied his shoulders in what Jonah could only assume he meant to be a seductive move. When Jonah didn't give him the praise he clearly felt he deserved after his impromptu dance, Bastien shuffled his way back to the others, and Sherrie draped herself over him as she swayed to the music.

It didn't take long for Jonah to finish the cocktail, his paper straw soggy as the ice cubes melted sadly at the bottom of the empty pitcher. It also didn't take long for the man with the delicious beard and outrageously shiny hair to work his way over to him and even less time for him to shove his tongue down Jonah's throat. His hands cupped Jonah's cheeks as they kissed in the corner, the glittering light from the disco ball illuminating them in small bursts, their encounter private aside from those passing to use the toilets. He hadn't made out with someone in a bar in years. In fact, he hadn't made out with anyone in a bar in London. Back home in Cornwall he kissed a boy the night he turned eighteen when he got blindingly drunk and thought it might be a good idea to kiss whoever showed him attention. He ended up vomiting on his yellow trainers.

There would be no vomiting on his man, however. Jonah might have consumed an entire cocktail pitcher all by himself, but he could still walk in a straight line and so far hadn't needed to pee every five minutes. They kissed for what could have been hours. Jonah didn't care, he was more than happy to lose himself in a handsome stranger who kept guiding Jonah's hands to his waist. Their bodies were flush against the wall, and Jonah could feel the man's erection against his thigh, and, fuck, he was hard too; how long had it been since someone turned him on like this? Perhaps it was the thrill of grinding against a stranger in a public place that was driving Jonah totally wild, though he couldn't say he ever experienced a desire for performative public sexual exploits before. Or maybe it was that he could feel himself finally unwinding, the tension in his shoulders giving way to something hot and burning in the pit of his stomach. He wanted this man to fuck him; he wanted to take him home and get on his knees for him and make the dirtiest sounds escape his lips. He wanted—

"Jonah," someone whined, their voice high-pitched and intrusive. He ignored it, deciding to kiss the stranger with more passion, their tongues exploring each other's mouths, desperate, hot, and rudely interrupted by someone pulling at his shoulder.

"Jonah." Bastien lunged at him, his limbs moving wildly, as if controlled by someone else. "I'm gonna go home." He slurred his words and tripped over his own feet as he tried to turn Jonah to look at him. "I love you," he cooed. "I love your nose and your hair and I love your eyes. You're so pretty." Bastien managed to narrow his eyes at the man who still had his hands on Jonah's waist. "You better make him have an orgasm tonight."

"Okay, Bash," Jonah said, reluctantly removing himself from the man, who groaned in response. "Have you called a taxi?" The making out seemed to have sobered him up. His body trembled from the adrenaline of what might come later, the pleasure he would receive if he went home with the stranger.

"Yeah," Bastien said through hiccups. "I'm going with Sherrie. She's wankered."

Jonah laughed. "Okay, well, be safe, yeah?"

Bastien swayed slightly and tried to step away, but slumped against Jonah's shoulder instead. "Take me to my chariot."

Jonah glanced at the Man Bun guy. "Sorry, I'll be back."

"Yeah, sure," he said somewhat awkwardly as he adjusted the waistline of his jeans. Jonah hooked his arm around Bastien's waist and allowed the smaller man to put his weight on him as he guided him through the dancing bodies and out of the bar.

Outside, the air made Jonah's head swirl, and he acknowledged he might have been more drunk than he first suspected. The busy sounds of London closed in on him, the car horns honking, the revelers tumbling out of bars while pedal bikes with carriages attached to the back of them pounded loud music and tourists rode around with huge grins on their faces. It must have been nearly 2 a.m., but London seemed as alive as it did during the day, and Jonah couldn't help the swell of affection in his chest thinking of how he got to live in such a vibrant place. Sherrie sat in the back of a red Volvo, the door open, her long legs spilling out as she called out to Bastien. Jonah helped him to the other side of the car and placed him down in the seat while Bastien mumbled words of affection through his champagne-fueled haze.

"Where's Omari?" Jonah asked him once he'd safely deposited Bastien into the car.

"Went with Lucian ages ago," Bastien said, trying to stroke Jonah's face before slumping against the seat.

"If Romana shows her stupid face," Sherrie said aggressively as Jonah tried to haul her legs into the car once he finished helping Bastien with his seat belt. "Tell her I hate her." There were a dozen questions about what was going on with Sherrie's love life brimming on the tip of Jonah's tongue, but the drunk and angry version of Sherrie was not the version he needed to direct the questions to.

"Just get home safe, yeah?" Jonah said as he closed the door and Sherrie pressed her lips against the window, leaving behind a smear of purple lipstick. Jonah watched as the driver pulled away, and he debated for a moment if he should leave, too, but hot Man Bun was waiting for him with his calloused hands and a tongue that had already worked wonders.

"You." A hand found its way to Jonah's shoulder and roughly turned him around to face whoever the voice belonged to. Dexter stood behind him, his fingers far too close to Jonah's collarbone for comfort. "You took my jumper." His accusation was shrouded in indignation. "Give it back." He didn't speak like he usually did; his words were a little too soft, the vowels elongated and without definition. Drunk.

"I didn't take your ugly jumper," Jonah said, pushing past him, only for Dexter to grab his arm. "Let go of me."

"No. Give it back."

Jonah looked at Dexter's waist, the last place he saw the questionable piece of attire, only to see it truly was missing. "Dexter, I didn't take it. I've not been near you."

Dexter's face crumpled, his lips turning into such a dramatic frown he could double as a sad clown. "Why do you always take things from me? This is why you're a massive prick."

Jonah shook his arm from Dexter's grip. "I've not taken anything from you, Dexter."

"I'm gonna be sick." Dexter covered his mouth as he retched and swallowed down what Jonah could only assume was a mouthful of vomit.

"You should go home."

"Right, yeah." Dexter turned from him and took a couple of steps off the path and into the road. He lifted his hand at a car coming toward him, and it beeped its horn aggressively. Jonah pulled him back onto the path and to safety.

"What the hell are you doing?" Jonah asked, his voice shrill, louder than it really needed to be, but he could blame his volume on the alcohol he had consumed.

"Are you thick? I'm hailing a taxi."

"You're not hailing anything." Jonah looked at the taller man as he swayed on his feet and stumbled a few steps away so he could lean against the wall outside the bar. "Where do you live? I'll get you an Uber."

"I'm not telling you where I live."

"Fine, then walk into the road and get run over."

Dexter seemed to consider his words for a moment, his face pale, hair a mess. "Camden."

"What?"

"I live in Camden," he said incredibly slowly, words beyond slurred as he waved his hands in front of him for no reason. He looked as if he might take a step closer to Jonah, but instead he twisted on his heel and fell to the ground. Jonah looked at him and waited for him to stand, but he didn't; he just lay there, back flat against the pavement as he looked up at the night sky. A horrible realization dawned on Jonah: He was going to have to get the idiot home.

"I live in Camden too," Jonah said, pulling his phone out of his pocket to open the Uber app. "We can get a ride together. What road are you on?"

"Lawford."

Jonah paused and shuddered at just how close they lived to one another. "Get up."

"No."

"Get up or I will drag you up."

"You can't drag me anywhere."

Jonah put his phone away and gazed down at him. "Okay, stay there until the car comes."

"Don't tell me what to do."

He should have been back in the bar with Man Bun. But no. Yet again, whatever divine being looked down on the world decided they hated Jonah and cursed him with the eternal plague that was Dexter Ellis.

TWELVE

> *"And when we die our bodies will create a constellation. We will live forever."*
>
> —"The Melody of Achilles and Patroclus,"
> *The Wooden Horse*, Act One

"Carlos," Dexter said, leaning forward in his seat to tap the driver on the shoulder. "Take us to The World's End."

"Don't listen to him, Carlos," Jonah mumbled, trying to focus on the screen on his phone rather than the drunk imbecile beside him in the back of the car.

"I want to go to the pub," Dexter said, continuing his pestering of poor Carlos. "The World's End."

"Sure thing," Carlos said, coming to a junction and signaling left, the opposite direction from the home address Jonah gave him.

Jonah lowered his phone. "It's closed," he said. "Carlos, keep going to Lawford Road." Carlos signaled right.

"Carlos!" Dexter whined. "Carlos, old buddy, old pal. Please, don't listen to this absolute swine. He knows nothing." God, drunk Dexter was insufferable. Carlos hesitated.

"Lawford Road, Carlos. I'm paying for this, not him."

Dexter scoffed and folded his arms across his chest. "I can pay for myself. I will give you a tip too. The World's End. Go! Ahead! God's speed!"

"One star, Carlos," Jonah warned. "I swear I will give you one star." The debate ended and Carlos swiftly headed toward Lawford Road. Dexter groaned and knocked his head against the window, leaving a sweat mark where his skin touched the glass. His cheeks were flushed against his pale skin, his tan from a few weeks ago faded, and Jonah wondered if he'd been on holiday to have had such a color. He could ask him; Dexter might even indulge Jonah in his drunken state, but Jonah couldn't help the burning rage inside of his chest at the blond having cock-blocked him by being such a messy drunk, so any small talk questions fizzled out on his tongue.

"I can't believe I lost my jumper," Dexter pouted as he pressed a finger to the car window. "I lose everything."

"Don't be so dramatic."

"I do, though." His eyes glazed over as he watched London pass beyond the glass, bright lights fading as they neared Camden and the town became sleepy. "You wouldn't understand. You get everything you want. Bet you don't lose your clothes."

Edward came to Jonah's mind. Again. God, he wanted him to disintegrate into specks of dust so tiny he wouldn't be able to recognize him anymore. He wished he'd stayed at the bar, even if just to make out with Man Bun for a little longer, even if it went no further. He needed the attention, he needed to forget. More than anything, he needed to rectify the fact that the last hands to touch him intimately were Edward's. He looked down at his phone and opened FullStack to see eight new matches, and only three of them started the conversation with pictures of their penises. He lingered on one photo, the angle actually quite flattering, before Dexter swiped the phone from his hand.

"You dirty little pervert." He laughed and stretched his arm away from Jonah as he tried to snatch it back. "Mate, you can't be looking at pictures of dicks in Carlos's car!"

"Fuck off, Dexter." He grabbed the phone and wrestled it from Dexter's grip. "I can't help getting unsolicited dick pics, and it's none of your damn business what I do on my phone." By pulling the phone away from him, he inadvertently caused Dexter to shift in his seat, their legs pressed together, but neither of them moved. Jonah didn't want to think about how nice it was to have someone pressing against him, and he blamed the alcohol for not minding it was Dexter's leg against his.

"Why are you so mean to me?" The question came out as pathetic as it sounded, and Jonah rolled his eyes at him. "What?" Dexter pouted, those stupid lips of his so full. "At least I've got a reason to be angry with you."

"Yeah? And what's that?"

"You took Achilles from me."

Jonah stared at him. "No. I didn't."

"Yeah. You did." His speech suddenly sounded more coherent. "You took him from me. It should have been me. It should have been me taking it to the West End and winning the fucking Olivier Award, but they gave it to you, and I still can't understand why."

A numbness crept over Jonah's skin. "I auditioned," he conceded. "It took months. I . . . I actually asked if you were taking the role and they said no, you were cast in something else, so I've got no idea what you're talking about."

"That's a bloody lie. I saw that role from the workshops all the way to the tour. Then they had me audition for the West End and told me they were giving it to someone else. You. You got it. And I had to pretend it was fine and that I always had something else lined up, but I didn't. My agent got me an audition last minute for *Tick, Tick . . . Boom!* And thank God, I got it."

If Jonah didn't feel sober before, he certainly did now. "Really?" he asked quietly.

Dexter nodded. "And I loved the way people tore you apart online," he said, though there seemed to be no malice in his tone. "And how people wanted me. But then . . . then they loved you. And I went to see the show and of course you were amazing and it . . . it *hurt*. Then the Olivier and WhatsOnStage awards came around and the nominations alone made me want to set fire to everything, but I had to just grin and be, like, fine with it." He spoke quickly before tapering off into a whisper. "Achilles is mine." He sounded broken, his voice quivering, on the verge of tears, and for the first time Jonah saw a side of him he never thought he would be privy to: he was vulnerable.

"I'm sorry you're upset," Jonah said. "But I'm not sorry for auditioning and getting the role. It's how it works, we audition, some stuff we get, some we don't. You can't blame me for that. Blame the casting team. Blame Colbie. Blame yourself for returning to a production that's clearly hurt you."

Dexter looked at him then, his eyes glistening as he blinked back tears. "It's the biggest show in the West End right now. I would've been stupid to turn down a role in it, even one I didn't want. It's just . . . your life is perfect, and it pisses me right off."

Jonah sucked in a deep breath. "My life isn't perfect," he said. "You don't know me."

"And you don't know me."

They descended into an awkward silence as Carlos pulled up on Lawford Road. Dexter sat motionless, his eyes trained on his hands as his head lolled slightly, still clearly drunk, and a shadow of the cocky persona he usually portrayed.

"You're home," Jonah said after four excruciating minutes.

"Yeah." Dexter nodded. "Thanks." He didn't look at Jonah as he got out of the car and wandered down the road before stopping at a door and fumbling about with a key. Carlos seemed to have the same concern as Jonah, because he didn't drive away and instead watched as Dexter tried time and time again to insert the key into the lock.

"You should help him, man," Carlos said, looking over his shoulder at Jonah in the back of the car. "He's gonna end up asleep on his doormat."

Dexter shouldn't have been Jonah's problem. Yet there he was. A bloody problem.

"Fine, wait here," Jonah snapped and got out of the car and crossed the road to where Dexter still struggled with his door. "Let me," he said, whispering so as not to disturb Dexter's neighbors. He took the key from him, and Dexter blinked in bewilderment. The key didn't fit the door. "Dexter, is this your house?"

Dexter took a wobbly step back and peered at the building. "Huh. No."

"What number are you?"

"Eight."

"Dexter," Jonah hissed. "You told me you lived at forty-eight. Eight's all the way down there!" Jonah tried his hardest not to raise his voice as he gestured toward the end of the road. "Come on." He allowed Dexter to cling to his arm like a lost child as they walked farther down until they finally came to number eight. Jonah left Dexter standing by the curb fiddling with his shirt buttons as he unlocked the door for him.

"Thanks," Dexter said, stumbling forward. He stood face-to-face with Jonah, the flush of his cheeks even redder than before. He opened his mouth and Jonah expected a snide remark to come from it, but instead Dexter doubled over and threw up all over the front of Jonah's trousers. The vomiting seemed to go on forever, and Jonah just stood there, not making any attempt to move, the shock clearly having paralyzed him until Dexter stood back up and wiped his sleeve across his mouth. "Fuck. Sorry," he said and took the key from Jonah's hand and stepped through the threshold. "See ya, Jonah." He closed the door.

Jonah could feel his heart pounding in his chest. He looked down at himself, vomit seeping through his trousers and covering his shoes, the smell utterly rancid, and he kept his hands above his waist as he trudged back to Carlos, unsure of what to do or how to function.

Carlos unwound his window and leaned out to look at Jonah before locking his doors. "No, sorry, mate, not driving you anywhere like that."

Jonah stared at him. He imagined he looked like Carrie after they poured the bucket of blood over her at prom, his limbs stiff, eyes wide. "Carlos. Help me."

Carlos shook his head. "Sorry, man." He shut his window and drove off without another word, leaving Jonah standing in the middle of the road trying his hardest not to throw up himself.

The streetlights were off, drenching the roads in the pitch-black darkness of the night, a blessing in that no one would see him covered in sick. He began to walk, Castle Road only ten minutes away, and he could feel a dampness in his socks, the vomit having worked its way down the ankle of his shoes. This wasn't how his night should have ended. It should have been full of blow jobs and orgasms. But instead of having sex he was walking home covered in someone else's regurgitated dinner.

Castle Road turned its nose up at him as he walked down it, his house unhappy to see him as he stepped inside and undressed in the kitchen. He stood naked in front of the sink and rinsed his clothes off before stuffing them in the washing machine. His shoes looked at him sadly as he placed them in the bin, beyond saving, and he walked stiffly to the bathroom. The tiles on the wall felt cool beneath his palms as he stood beneath the steady stream of water from the shower, more sober now than he'd ever been in his life, and he scrubbed his skin with such force it turned red beneath his sponge. He dried himself roughly with the towel, not caring if his skin remained damp, simply thankful he'd washed away the vomit, and collapsed onto his bed completely naked with a groan.

"Fuck," he said to himself as he reached for his phone and looked at the screen, wanting to text Bastien but knowing full well he would be passed out by now at home in his bed with his perfect boyfriend. The FullStack app remained opened, the photo of the penis still in full glory, and he grimaced before deleting the message. Was this his life now? Dick pics and vomit? And did he seriously have a seed of guilt about getting the role of Achilles over Dexter? He did what any actor would do. His agent arranged an audition, he went to it, he did his best and got the job. He rarely thought about the other people also vying for the role; he couldn't, the industry moved so fast, and everyone seemed to know they had to roll with the punches. But he never expected Dexter Ellis to be sitting somewhere heartbroken at the role he originated being given away to someone else. Jesus Christ. He did feel guilty. The realization weighed heavily on him; it pressed him down into the mattress and turned his limbs to concrete.

He tried to swipe on FullStack, tried to distract himself with nearby men and promises of a life where he wouldn't die alone surrounded by microwave meals and blocks of cheese. He kept his phone in his grasp as he allowed his eyelids to droop. Sleep so close, with the promise of clearing his mind. The room turned fuzzy, the alcohol still lingering in his bloodstream dulling his senses until his phone vibrated in his palm. He blinked at it, the screen far too bright against the darkness shrouding the room, and he squinted as he tried to get his head around what he was looking at. Because there, in the stark contrast of the night, was a message illuminated in blinding white from Edward. Three little words.

I miss you.

And Jonah fell asleep in the knowledge his life was officially a complete and utter joke.

THIRTEEN

"Lie down in our wedding bed, let the flowers touch your skin and my hands show you how a garden can bloom."

—"Helen," The Wooden Horse, Act One

Dexter sipped at his bottle of water, lips wrapping around the rim, throat bobbing as he swallowed down the liquid. The sight just so happened to be the first thing Jonah saw when he stepped into the rehearsal studio. He'd been waiting for Tuesday the eleventh of June to come around, the date circled in his planner with red ink. Stage combat blocking with Dexter. Their bodies would be close, movements intricately planned, and he half expected Dexter to challenge Peter, their fight captain, with the choreography. Dexter at least dressed suitably for the occasion, no embroidered jumpers in sight, but he had on his tight joggers from yoga and an equally tight white T-shirt clinging to his body. Somehow, he made Jonah feel underdressed as he stood in the doorway, tote bag slung over his shoulder, baggy black T-shirt hanging from his torso and wearing the scruffiest gray joggers in the universe.

"Oh, hi," Dexter said when he saw him, placing his water bottle down on the little table beside the mirrored wall. "Peter isn't here yet."

"I can see that," Jonah replied, walking over to the table to dump his bag down on it. He pulled his phone out of his pocket to see two missed calls from his mum and one from his aunt, then sighed. "Fuck," he said under his breath. "I need to step out and make a call. If Peter arrives, can you tell him I won't be long?"

As Jonah turned to leave, Dexter reached for him, his touch gentle as his fingertips brushed against Jonah's elbow. "Um," he said, cheeks reddening. "Did I throw up on you Saturday night?"

"Oh. Yeah. You did." Images of Dexter in the back of the car flooded Jonah's mind. How vulnerable he seemed, how honest the alcohol made him, and how, right now, Jonah didn't feel the animosity he once felt for him. He couldn't waste his life hating someone who was clearly just as insecure as himself; where would it get him? Covered in vomit again, maybe, but at least he could try not to wake with a bitter taste in the back of his mouth each morning.

"Shit. I'm so sorry." He sounded genuinely remorseful. "I had this hazy image of doing it, but I wasn't sure if it was a dream, and I'm so embarrassed."

Jonah could still feel Dexter's fingers ghosting his skin. "It's okay, it happens," he said. The memory still haunted him two days later, but no, he was letting it go. Positive vibes. "I threw up on someone once, so I guess it was finally time for someone to do it to me."

Dexter smiled and dropped his hand, the whisper of his touch still burning Jonah's skin despite the retreat. "Well. Um. Okay, thanks for not being a dick about it. Um, can I ask you something?"

"Sure?"

"Can we totally forget that ever happened? Can we just . . . move on and be civil? We need to work together, after all." So, Dexter maybe had the same idea as Jonah. A new beginning, a line drawn under the weird and frankly ridiculous start they gave to each other.

"It's fine. Forget it." Jonah offered him a smile, but Dexter's words in the back of the car Saturday night still played over in his head. *Achilles is mine.* Forgiveness was all fine and good, but that sentiment wouldn't leave him. Perhaps holding Dexter at arm's length would be the best course of action; though . . . he certainly wouldn't mind if their legs pressed together in the back of a car again. Jonah turned from him, and this time Dexter didn't stop him as he left the studio.

Outside, the sun sat high in the sky, warming the city with its buoyant rays and yellow hues. The studio sat nestled away in the heart of Covent Garden, the pavement mismatched and utterly charming. It reminded

Jonah of the winding streets back in St. Ives, the streets he used to know like the back of his hand as a child, streets that would no doubt welcome him with open arms if he were to return there. Leave London. Perhaps one day when the theatre no longer sang to him, though he doubted that would ever happen. His stomach tried to crawl up his throat as he thought of his mum back by the sea, so far away, and he quickly pressed her number on his phone and waited for her to reply. It barely took one ring.

"Jonah," she said, breathless. God, why did she always sound so breathless these days? "I'm sorry to bother you."

A sinking feeling made his stomach plummet from his throat right back to where it belonged. "Are you okay?"

"No." Her voice cracked as tears made their way across the miles between them. "A fox got the chickens."

Jonah felt slightly bad at the relief he had knowing her chickens were the reason for her tears rather than his dad. "Oh Mum," he said, tone soft, comforting. "I'm so sorry." The sound of a bottle clinked in the background.

"It took them all. Even my lovely Beryl. I didn't hear a peep last night, or I would have gone out to them." Her sobs became hysterical. "I tried to talk to your dad about it, but he said we didn't have any chickens and that made me mad, so then I shouted at him, and I don't want to shout at him." The words tumbled from her mouth. "And then he fell when he tried to get out of the lounge chair without help and he broke my mother's vase, the one with the rabbits on, and he cut his hands all up, and I just can't do this anymore, Jonah."

"Right," he said, deciding he needed to take control of the situation then or he never would. "It's okay. Everything is going to be okay. I'm going to make some calls today. I've got a work thing this morning, but as soon as I'm done, I'm going to look into some homes for him, okay? Then I will call you tomorrow, and we can make a plan."

"I'm not asking you to do that."

"I know. I want to do it. Then, once we've made a plan, I will book some time off work and I will help you."

"Your work is important to you."

"Not as important as you."

He heard her suck in a shaky breath, her tears having subsided. "You're a good boy, aren't you, sausage?"

Jonah laughed lightly and blinked back his own tears. "Um, is Dad okay? His hands? He didn't hurt himself in the fall?"

"The nurse cleaned him up and bandaged them. Poor sod."

"Give him a kiss from me, won't you?"

"Always, love."

"And, Mum?"

"Yes?"

"I'm sorry about the chickens."

She sniffed. "Yes. Me too. Bloody fox. You're lucky you don't get them in London."

"Mum, I've seen more foxes here than what I ever did in Cornwall. My neighbor had one with babies in their garden last year."

"Really?" She sounded genuinely surprised. "Well, I never. Even London isn't safe from the buggers." She paused. "Oh, Jonah?"

"Yeah?"

"Thank you."

Once he said goodbye to her, he sucked in a deep breath and clicked to return the call to his aunt. She never called him, only texted now and then, stupid things about the ugly paintings she'd found in thrift shops and how many tomatoes were growing in her garden. For her to call meant something big happened, but his mum seemed fine on the phone, and she said Dad was okay, so he silently hoped it was nothing but a butt dial as it rang.

"Hello, Jonah, my love." Her voice sounded warm, freshly baked scones with melting butter and raspberry jam.

"Aunt Penny." He matched her tone, genuinely happy to hear her voice. "I had a missed call from you?"

"Yes, well, I wasn't sure if I should call or not, but . . . here I am." A silence hung between them. "I'm worried about your mum, love, she's not been herself." Three years younger than his mum, Aunt Penny lived with a woman called Sally who she referred to as her roommate, but as Jonah got older he realized they lived in a one-bedroom apartment adorned with photos of the two of them looking remarkably loved up. Even when Jonah came out, Penny never hinted at anything other than friendship with Sally. But one time Jonah saw them kiss each other softly in the kitchen when they thought no one was looking, and he was happy to quietly back out and pretend he hadn't seen anything while their backs were turned if that was how they wanted it.

"She just called me in hysterics about her chickens, but that's okay, Pen."

"I had that this morning too. It's not just the chickens, Jonah. I went over there yesterday morning and she just sat there trembling, not from cold, I don't know what it was." Penny sighed.

"She's stressed about Dad," Jonah said, not wanting it to be anything serious; he didn't want to think of the alternative. "I'm going to do some research this afternoon on more homes. Dad needs to be somewhere now. She can't look after him."

"I agree with you there," she conceded. "We are all worried about your dad, but sometimes I think she gets forgotten in all this."

Jonah knew what she meant, though her statement felt like perhaps she was trying to say maybe *he* was forgetting her. "I will call her more often, check in on her. It's hard being so far away."

"Oh, I know, love," Penny said softly. "We will keep an eye on her here for you. I just thought we should maybe talk more, keep each other up-to-date on what's going on so we can support her."

"Of course."

"Well, I will let you get on, you're a big star now, aren't you?" Penny laughed sweetly. "Keep safe, Jonah"

Dexter grimaced and slammed his hands on the floor. Jonah stood over him, panting as Peter meandered to the side, arms crossed over his chest. It was the twelfth time in a row Dexter messed up the tiniest bit of combat choreography. Where he needed to fall to Jonah's right, his sword swiping out in an attempt to strike him, he pivoted his foot to the left, resulting in him stumbling while waving his prop sword redundantly in the air.

"Beyoncé would not be happy with me for saying this, but it's to the *right*, Dexter, to the right, to the right!" Peter clapped his hands together as he spoke, emphasizing each word, turning them into an attack of his own. "If you go to your left, the audience won't see the move, which is what?"

"Pointless," Dexter grumbled from the floor.

"Let's take a break. I'm in desperate need of a vape, and don't either of you two lecture me on the dangers of vaping, because I've had it up to here with it." Peter gestured to his forehead aggressively before turning from them, grabbing his bag, and stomping out of the room.

Jonah placed his hands on his hips and looked at himself in the mirrors lining the walls. His curls were plastered to his face, the room insufferably hot with no windows to allow in any air, and the sweat patches on his T-shirt were rather embarrassing, to say the least. He directed his eyes toward Dexter, who seemed just as sweaty as him, his shirt sticking to his chest in damp patches, and held out a hand to help him off the floor. Dexter hesitated, raising an eyebrow as he looked at Jonah's hand before taking it and allowing him to help him to his feet.

"It's the move before that's throwing me off," Dexter said, running his hand across his forehead before reaching for his water. "It naturally makes me want to step left afterward because you're not close enough."

If Jonah's eyes could roll all the way into the back of his head, they would. "So, it's my fault?"

"No," Dexter replied quickly. "It's me, but, yeah, I don't know."

"Let's try it again." Jonah watched as Dexter finished his water. "From the move before into this one, then we can see exactly where it goes wrong."

Dexter looked at this empty bottle, then gave a nod. "Okay, yeah, thanks."

They moved into position in the middle of the room, weapons in hand, as if to prepare to duel for real. Jonah could feel Dexter's hazel eyes on him, scanning his body, taking in each miniscule movement right down to the tendons in his wrist tensing. Jonah counted them down, and Dexter lunged on the count of one, the move perfect as Jonah maneuvered around him, close, but not close enough for any actual harm to come to either of them. But then, right after Jonah readied himself for the next move, he saw Dexter veering to the left, and, as he momentarily tried to correct himself, he spun on his heel and tumbled onto the floor.

"Okay," Jonah said, as Dexter grimaced on his knees before him. "You need to stop thinking about it and looking at your feet. Use my body as your mark rather than the tape on the floor."

Dexter groaned as he stood up and readied himself to try again. "Okay, sure, let's try that."

They tried the move again. This time Dexter went to the right, but when he swung the sword it missed Jonah completely, sailing through the air as if Dexter had no intention of hitting him in the first place. And he needed to hit him, or at least make the audience believe he did.

"You're not close enough!" Dexter seethed. "You need to be closer."

"Or you just need to learn how to aim."

"No," Dexter snapped and went back to his first mark. "You need to be a step forward than where you usually start." He pointed at the space of flooring in front of him. "Seriously, stand here."

Jonah debated arguing with him, but the morning had long since passed them by and his stomach was rumbling and the calls he promised to make for his mum were sitting there waiting to be made. And of course, the text from Edward from the weekend still went unanswered, dancing around in the back of his mind like it was at a disco. So, he stood where Dexter pointed, too close, he never stood that close to the guy currently playing Hector, and he stared at him, his expression deadpan, without an ounce of enthusiasm.

"Closer," Dexter said, and he placed his free hand on Jonah's waist and gently pulled him forward. The action was strangely intimate, even more so when Dexter kept his hand there and they looked at each other, Dexter's eyes searching his, as if asking permission. "Perfect," he said and left his fingers pressed against Jonah's hip bone for a few more seconds before letting go to hold his sword properly.

"I'm warning you that if you actually hit me with that thing I'm gonna be pissed," Jonah said, nodding toward the sword. "There's a reason they don't normally have us this close."

"I think it will work. Trust me." God, he asked for a lot. But Jonah decided to hell with it and put his trust in the man who had previously kicked him in the crotch. "The same as always, just closer, okay?"

Jonah nodded, and this time Dexter counted them in, and they started out the move, bodies invading each other's space, but it worked. Dexter's hand found its way back to Jonah's waist and used it to maneuver him into the next position with complete ease. Dexter stepped to the right, swung his sword, and Jonah recoiled back, like he'd practiced, as if Dexter struck him across the chest. They stood motionless after the move, both of them staring at the other with wide eyes before Dexter broke out into the brightest smile Jonah had ever seen. He reminded Jonah of a dog being shown the biggest stick in the park only to be told it was all for him and he could take it home.

"We did it!" he exclaimed, and Jonah bit his tongue to stop himself from saying that, actually, Jonah had always been doing it, so he smiled warmly at him instead.

"Only the killing part left to do," Jonah pointed out. "But yeah, amazing. Want to try it again?"

"Can we go from the start?" Dexter asked, moving away from Jonah and shaking out his shoulders as he went to his first position. "I want to make sure I've got everything locked in here." He tapped his forehead. "Did you know there was never a fight scene between Hector and Achilles during workshops?"

"Really?" Jonah said in surprise. "But it's a huge part of the story, why didn't they include it?"

"They sang instead." Dexter twirled the sword in his hand as he spoke. "A battle through words, I guess? This is much better." He stopped speaking and looked at Jonah before darting his tongue along his bottom lip, eyes focused, as if he intended to devour him. "Let's go."

Dexter somehow hit every single step without fault, and as they came to the part he had fumbled on he pulled Jonah close again, such a minute movement, barely noticeable, but it worked, and he stepped to the right and finished with a slightly harder blow to Jonah's chest. He seemed pumped, an excitement behind his eyes, and Jonah didn't know if it was adrenaline from finally mastering the move or the thought of getting to smack Jonah repeatedly in the ribs.

A slow clap came from the doorway, where Peter stood with a satisfied smirk on his lips. "Finally!" he said. "Though, don't think I haven't noticed the little change you've put in there. I'll allow it if only to get us to move past this and finish, so I don't go insane."

"Do you think we should add some more choreo in?" Dexter asked, and honestly, Jonah could kill him for real. He had stuff to do and a show to perform later in the evening; he didn't have time to play with Dexter for longer than needed. "Because I think the battle is one-sided."

Peter cocked his head as he took Dexter in. "You want to change the choreography put together by professional choreographers because you think it's one-sided? Hector's literally fighting a demigod. Of course it's going to look that way."

"Can we just finish, please?" Jonah asked, whining more than he hoped to but not regretting a moment of it.

"Fine," Dexter said, pouting.

Peter stood by Dexter's side as they worked through the rest of the moves, demonstrating them first with Jonah before allowing Dexter to take his place, the pacing fast, maybe a little too fast, but Jonah wasn't about to complain. He could see sweat beading across Dexter's forehead, his shirt flush with his skin, wet through, and Jonah liked how hot and bothered he seemed.

"Right," Peter said, sweating himself as he glanced at his watch and groaned. "Let's finish the last move, then we can do full run-throughs next week."

The fight ended with Achilles straddling Hector, dagger raised above his head before plunging it into Hector's throat. Apparently, in the original myth Achilles killed him with a spear, but spears were cumbersome onstage so a dagger came into play instead. During performances, a blood pack would burst when the tip of the prop weapon touched it, ghastly realism that often earned several gasps from the audience and was a nightmare to scrub off your skin at the end of the night.

Dexter got into position on the floor, and Jonah crouched beside him before slinging one leg over his hip so he sat atop of him, holding his weight up slightly so as not to cause Dexter any discomfort. Peter spoke, his voice aimed at Dexter; Jonah did this multiple times a week, his hand clasped above his head around the dagger before plunging it down to kill the Hector beneath him. Only this time, Dexter threw his hands up and gripped Jonah's wrists, his breathing heavy beneath Jonah's thighs, and he resisted Jonah's movement to bring the dagger down.

"Dexter. What are you doing?" Peter asked, lips in a thin line, foot tapping impatiently on the floor. "Let him kill you, for fuck's sake."

"Hector would fight until the last minute," Dexter said, looking at Jonah, eyes wide, as if he were performing in front of thousands of people. "Let me try." Jonah let him, allowing the show of last-minute strength to play out until Dexter faltered and he let Jonah plunge the dagger down to the left of his neck, the side the audience couldn't see.

"How truly method of you," Peter quipped. "But fine. Whatever. It works. Just make sure you don't overrun the music. We can practice with it next week." He picked up his things from the table and looked at them both on the floor. "That's enough for today. I need some food." He narrowed his eyes at them. "You can get up now, you know."

Jonah fumbled off of Dexter's lap and stumbled to his feet, brushing off his knees before dumping the dagger onto the table. Dexter sat up but didn't remove himself from the floor. Jonah rummaged through his bag and pulled out his phone, relieved to see no calls from his mum, but his stomach flipped seeing a new unread message from Edward.

"I've got to go," he said, sweat dripping from his curls. "See you next week."

"Yeah," Dexter said quickly, still not moving, his body hunched over a little awkwardly. "Bye."

"Do you need help getting up?"

"No! I mean, no, I'm fine, I just need a minute."

Jonah hesitated, clutching his phone as Dexter angled his body away from him. "Okay. Bye." He didn't turn back as he left, the phone in his hand burning his palms, the reality of his life beyond the doors screaming at him to get outside.

FOURTEEN

"Hera. Poseidon. Athena. We feel your feet behind us. We move with your army. You spread our arms and raise our weapons."

—"We Build," *The Wooden Horse*, Act Two

The messages came in from Edward each day, and then on Sunday Jonah finally replied. Each text said the same thing: he missed him; he wanted to chat; he regretted the way things turned out. They came between calls to nursing homes and endless scrolling online to find out every single little detail he could about the place his father might end up living, and, despite the heartbreak Jonah experienced from Edward leaving, the communication became an annoyance. Even more so when Jonah allowed himself to scope out his ex's Instagram only to see he'd posted a photo of him and Wes an hour after sending his last message begging Jonah to talk to him. The bastard.

> You have a boyfriend, Edward. Go talk to him and leave me alone.

Sending it terrified him. His hands trembled so much his phone practically shook out of his grip as he typed out the words and pressed send. He knew he should block Edward's number, but the self-destructive devil sitting on his shoulder told him not to; the messages, no matter how inappropriate, boosted his almost nonexistent self-esteem. And he needed self-esteem. Now more than ever. He didn't have time to dwell on Edward and his stupid infidelity. His life was more than full with work and combat rehearsals where he definitely wasn't enjoying straddling Dexter each day and certainly not thinking about him at random moments and wondering why he liked it when Dexter's skin touched his.

He tried to busy his mind with other things. He listened to Sherrie talk about Romana and their topsy-turvy relationship, if they could even call it that. Sherrie told him about the birthmark on the inside of Romana's thigh and how she liked her toast slightly burnt in the mornings. She also told him how much she *didn't* actually like Romana and was totally fine when she didn't text her back or stood her up on dates. Jonah listened and nodded at the appropriate times and showed outrage when required. But, it didn't matter how much he tried to focus on the confusing love life of his friend, his mind constantly went back to Dexter Ellis and his toned arms and gorgeously defined cheekbones.

And he couldn't help but think about how nice it was when, during certain moves at rehearsals, Dexter's breath tickled his neck, the sensation dizzying, and Jonah half wondered if he should go back to completely disliking the guy rather than feeling sorry for him so he could fold away the unwanted and unwarranted attraction he was slowly beginning to feel for him. The messages didn't help either. They'd somehow settled into casually messaging throughout the day, to the point where Jonah found himself texting back and forth with Dexter more than he did with Bastien. The texts were nothing important, of no real substance, but Jonah still found ways to look at them and wonder if Dexter *did* hide a meaning behind his playful words, or if this was just their friendship now, sarcasm and slightly fond insults galore.

The Penis Destroyer: Saw a dog today. It looked like you.

Jonah: What a coincidence. Saw a pigeon today that looked like you.

The Penis Destroyer: You've totally made me realize who you remind me of. The old pigeon lady in Mary Poppins.

Jonah: I'm quite the tourist attraction out there with all my pigeons.

The Penis Destroyer: And so very attractive.

Jonah: Stop flirting with me.

If anything, Jonah felt as if he were in some kind of Dexter Ellis montage, where his mind played clips of him on repeat intercepted by stupid texts. Then there were the social media posts. Dexter snapped pictures of them during combat rehearsals then incessantly posted them online and tagged Jonah in every single one, which he made him repost while looming over his shoulder. It was mildly infuriating because he never thought he would let Dexter take up so much of his time, and he let him do it willingly. In fact, he rather enjoyed it. But he would never admit to anyone that he liked it when Dexter's shirt, drenched in sweat, clung to his arms, and he certainly wouldn't tell anyone that sometimes, when Dexter was beneath him, he thought about what might happen if he were to lean down and kiss—

"Your harmony was off," Dexter said, turning to Jonah when they'd finished rehearsing. "You made me question my last note, but it was you, not me."

Jonah offered a condescending smile. "If you weren't hollering in my ear, then maybe I could hear what notes I'm hitting." Their vocal rehearsals often turned into a tit-for-tat exploration of annoyances. It was always only a matter of time before one of them found an issue with the other.

"I do not holler."

"Yes. You do."

"If I do, it's only to drown out your nasal tone."

"Oh, fuck off with the nasal tone." Jonah nudged him with his elbow in the ribs as Omari shuffled about behind them, guzzling yet another bottle of water.

"You need to be softer," Dexter said, rubbing his side where Jonah touched him. "Maybe I should give you some one-on-one vocal sessions. I bet I could make you sound better."

"That sounds very erotic," Omari said from behind them, and, really, thank God he was there, otherwise Jonah might have not been able to resist the urge to flick Dexter in the eye after the suggestion.

"There is nothing erotic about vocal sessions," Dexter tutted and grabbed his own bottle of water but offered Omari a smile as he did so. "Unless Jonah wants them to be?" He looked back over his shoulder at Jonah, who could feel his cheeks turning a deep shade of red.

"Not with you," he managed to say, keeping a shred of whatever dignity he had left.

"No?" Dexter smirked, and God, how Jonah despised the smirk. Oddly seductive. Far too attractive.

"Stop flirting," Omari complained as he shrugged his coat over his shoulders. "Sickening, the both of you."

"We're not flirting," Jonah protested, just as Dexter said the same thing.

Omari looked between them, an amused look on his permanently refreshed-looking face. "Is this where I say, suuuure, and we all know you're both talking crap?"

Jonah opened his mouth to speak, but Omari raised a finger, hushing him. "I'm going to go, but if I hear you two have been having sex in the rehearsal studio, I will not be pleased. Think of the germs." He didn't wait for either of them to answer before turning on his heel and flicking his wrist dramatically as he left the room.

Jonah could feel Dexter's eyes on him, and he slowly turned his head to meet his gaze.

"I can't think of anything worse than having sex with you," Dexter said.

"Me neither. I'm repulsed."

"Totally repulsed."

The roar of the crowd from West End LIVE boomed across the theatre district, jolting Jonah from his forbidden Dexter thoughts and reminding him that a looming army of theatre fans braving the stuffy June heat in the middle of Trafalgar Square were just beyond the safety barrier. The event, spread across two days, saw performances from a plethora of shows to an audience of thousands, all for free. Sparkling costumes found their way out of the theatres, and backstage casts brimmed with excitement. The event was a brilliant source of promotion, even for the longest-running shows. A red flag currently waved around on the stage, the cast of *Les Mis* rallying the crowd in a moving rendition of "Do You Hear the People Sing?" and Jonah smiled from the sidelines as he watched in his Grecian armor.

Dexter stood in the wings, stage left, a microphone in his hand because of course he was hosting the event, alongside Penelope Crossings, another darling of the West End. They made a strange double act, bouncing off each other effortlessly, but there was also an obvious tension between them with false smiles and overly friendly touches. Jonah decided not to pay attention to Dexter and instead looked at Bastien, who paced beside him as they waited for their time onstage. Sherrie stood to the side, staring down at her phone.

"What's wrong?" Jonah asked, noticing the way the other man chewed his thumbnails absently.

"I'm nervous."

"Why? You're fabulous."

Bastien stopped pacing to look at Jonah. "I know I'm fabulous, but I read that over the course of the weekend last year over four hundred thousand people came to watch this. That's insane."

Jonah hummed, then shrugged. "But there's not that many people out there all at once, is there? Evie said about twenty thousand can fit into Trafalgar Square."

"That's still an insane amount of people!" Bastien exclaimed. "I'm going to watch cat videos to calm myself down." He produced his phone from somewhere in his costume, and Jonah cocked an eyebrow as he watched him.

"Where were you keeping that?"

"I have my secrets, Jonah." Jonah shook his head and grinned fondly at him. He could see the sound technicians by the side of the stage, setting up the next performers who would be on before him and Bastien, adjusting their microphones and talking to the cast with precise instructions. Jonah could barely contain his excitement; he'd always wanted to perform at West End LIVE. The event was one of the most important in the theatre social calendar, so to be there, backstage, readying himself to go on, felt completely surreal.

"Oh shit," Bastien murmured and shot a quick, guilt-ridden look at Jonah. "Um, Jonah, my darling, have you seen the video circulating online... about you and Mr. Ellis?" As he spoke, Sherrie glanced up from her phone, interest piqued.

Jonah let out a breath. "Colbie wants people to be making videos and posting stuff. We are totally best friends, didn't you know that?"

Bastien slowly shook his head with a frown. "Well, your best friend may have tried to humiliate you at the Oliviers."

"What?"

Bastien tapped his phone screen a couple of times as he worked his bottom lip between his teeth. "I don't know if I should show you this."

"What is it?" Jonah reached for his phone, but Bastien managed to sidestep him and kept it from his grasp. "Bastien, show me."

"I don't want you to get mad."

"I'm gonna get mad if you don't show me. What is it?"

Bastien reluctantly handed the phone over to him, and Jonah pressed play on the video paused on the screen as Sherrie peered over his shoulder. It was the Olivier Awards ceremony, a shot from the crowd as Jonah walked toward the camera, his name having only just been called. Bloody hell, he barely remembered the moment, so seeing himself looking as dazed as he felt seemed strange. But then, there, in the audience, on the aisle seat, sat a familiar head of blond hair on a body who didn't rise to give Jonah a standing ovation. Dexter. Fine, Dexter not wanting to applaud him was totally on-brand for his personality, but then Jonah saw it, the detail the whole video focused on. Dexter looked over his shoulder to watch Jonah getting closer and he extended his foot out into the aisle, right in the way for Jonah to trip over it.

He could see it now in his memory, the flash of movement in the corner of his eye, the sweep of blond hair and body moving as he tried to remember how to walk to the stage. A foot out, moved only at the last second, and Jonah didn't notice at the time, but there it was, in startling detail. Dexter wanted him to fall. He quickly scrolled down to the comment section and scanned the words as quickly as he could:

> OMG he tried to trip him!

> What a prick.

Dexter Ellis totally tried to trip Jonah Penrose. Jealous, much?

So much for #Dexah.

OMFG he's a snake.

At least the comments were on his side. No one tried to explain Dexter's actions away. They all condemned him, his name well and truly dragged through the mud. And he deserved it. Jonah wiped a hand across his eyes as he passed the phone back to Bastien, unable to fathom why watching the clip made his eyes water, because there was no way he would be crying over Dexter Ellis. But Dexter had wanted to humiliate Jonah on the most important night of his life, he wanted to see him fall in front of his peers and God knows how many people watching the ceremony at home. How could he?

"Are you okay?" Bastien asked, reaching out to pull him into a hug. Jonah allowed it, finding comfort in his friend, and he repeated to himself that he would not cry, he would not cry, he would not cry. "He's a massive bell end," Bastien whispered.

Sherrie wrapped her arms around the both of them and pressed her face against Jonah's neck. "He's such a twat."

"It's fine," Jonah said as he pulled away from him. "I don't want to think about him. I just want to get this over and done with, then go home and eat cheese in my bed."

"You've got to stop with the cheese. Omari will kill you."

"It's all I have left." He paused for a moment, then groaned. "What's the betting Colbie will blame this on me somehow? Dexter's her golden boy, and this is fucking terrible publicity. She said we can't have animosity behind the scenes, it's bad for ticket sales."

"Then Colbie is also a bell end," Sherrie said evenly. "We've had a full house every night this week, so she can shove that where the sun doesn't shine."

"Are you guys ready?" A technician asked as he waved them over to him. "Three minutes till you go on. Let's get you set up." Bastien took Jonah's hand into his and gave it a squeeze. Thank goodness he had him and Sherrie by his side.

Dexter bounded over to them after their performance, his hair shining beneath the sun, a Golden Labrador who'd just chewed up every shoe in the house then shit on the floor and was still happy with himself. Jonah handed his microphone off to the technicians, turning away from Dexter and his blossom-pink lips. Bastien spoke to him, his tone clipped. Jonah couldn't make out what they said, but the cadence of Bastien's voice alone told him the conversation wasn't a pleasant one. Bastien, his own little bodyguard, a chihuahua snapping at the dopey retriever.

"Jonah," Dexter said, moving closer to him and out of Bastien's range. "Jonah, I'm so sorry." The smile on his face from moments before was gone. "I'd no idea that video would come out."

"You're apologizing for the video coming out, but not for what you did in the video? Unbelievable." Jonah shook his head and stepped away from him, taking a towel from a backstage member to wipe the sweat from his face.

"Let me explain." Dexter followed after him. "Please, it was a momentary lapse of judgment. I didn't actually trip you, did I? I stopped."

"A round of applause for you, then," Bastien said from behind them, jogging slightly to keep up with Jonah's pace as he worked his way through the backstage madness of the event.

"Can you just stop?" Dexter asked, and Jonah readied himself to feel the man's hands on him to halt him, but he didn't. Dexter let him continue to stomp through the area. "Let me explain, Jonah!"

Jonah turned on him, face red from exertion, eyes flaming with rage. "What is there to explain?" he hissed at him, determined to keep his voice down, given the dozens of people surrounding them and the thousands of theatre fans just beyond the barriers. "I need to get to the theatre and take off this costume so I can go home. I don't want to hear any convoluted explanations from you."

"Jonah, please, let's go somewhere private."

"There isn't anywhere private around here." Jonah saw a stagehand hovering close to them. "And you have a job to do. So go host, Dexter, have fun, and don't trip on your way back to the stage."

Dexter pursed his lips. "Come and speak with me privately." His voice came out stern, authoritative, and Jonah could see why he'd been cast as Hector. He exuded dominance, but there was also a kindness there, something soft behind the way he stood, vulnerable like the night in the Uber.

"Bash?" Jonah directed his words at his friend who stood by his side, loyal, a true Patroclus. "Can we meet back at the theatre?"

"Sure," he said with a nod. "I'll go find Sherrie and go back with her." He turned up his nose as he looked at Dexter. "You're lucky. I wouldn't give you a chance to explain yourself." Dexter opened his mouth to speak, but Bastien shushed him then kissed Jonah on the cheek. "See you in a bit."

Dexter gestured to a beige-looking cabin to the side of a row of Porta-loos. "Come on, I've got ten minutes before I need to be back onstage. No one will bother us."

Jonah could sense the number of eyes on them, averted when they passed but quickly boring holes into the backs of their heads as they made their way to the cabin. They climbed up the couple of plastic steps into a room that looked like it'd been constructed out of cardboard. Inside, a small table was placed against the wall with a tiny circular mirror propped up on top of it.

"Is this your dressing room?" Jonah asked, standing awkwardly in the middle of the room as Dexter closed the door behind them. "It's super fancy."

"Oh fuck off." Dexter sighed. "You can't help making a dig, can you?"

"That's so rich coming from you, Dexter."

"I didn't trip you, did I? Can't we move past this?"

"But you wanted to! You were going to before any form of sense clicked into place! It was the *Oliviers*, Dexter. Why would you want to humiliate me like that? I didn't even know you then, but you wanted to make me look like an idiot on the most important night of my life."

"I'm sorry."

"I don't think you are."

"I am," Dexter conceded. "I shouldn't have done it. I only did it because—"

"You were jealous."

Dexter rubbed the back of his neck and looked down at his feet. "Well, yeah. And it was childish and stupid, I know that. But, just so you know, I wouldn't try anything like that now, not now I know you."

"Oh? Now you know me? You've been awful to me this whole time. It wasn't until you threw up all over me you seemed to change." Jonah laughed bitterly at him. "You hate me."

"I don't hate you."

"Then why are you like this with me?"

"You don't get it, do you?" Dexter asked. "You really don't get it."

"Get what?"

Dexter groaned and dropped his hand from his neck to reach forward and grasp Jonah by the sleeve of his costume and pull him forward. They were too close; Jonah could feel Dexter's breath whispering against his cheeks, his eyes darting across his face, trying to search Jonah for something. Dexter's other hand found its way to Jonah's cheek, and he ran his thumb along his cheekbone. Jonah flinched slightly at the touch before relaxing at the invasion of space. His heart thumped painfully against his chest as they looked at each other, and then, without thinking of the consequences, Jonah closed the gap between them and pressed his lips to Dexter's.

It took a moment for Dexter to respond, the tension in his body dissipating until he let go of Jonah's costume and used his hand to cup his other cheek, kissing him softly, sweetly. Jonah's hands found their way to the other man's waist, pulling him closer by his belt loops so their bodies were flush, not an inch of space between them. He'd kissed Dexter before as Achilles, he knew what his lips felt like, how he moved himself and how his skin felt against his. But this, this was different; he wanted to kiss him this time. When did he start wanting to kiss Dexter Ellis? The penis destroyer—the lip biter and clothes vomiter?

Dexter's tongue swiped across Jonah's lips until they deepened the kiss, Jonah backing up until he hit the wall and Dexter's body covered his, making him feel small despite their similar height. Dexter's fingers worked through Jonah's curls, the small gasps they made devoured by the kiss. Dexter pushed his leg between Jonah's thighs, earning him a moan from Jonah he wanted to take back, but couldn't. Fucking hell, what was he doing moaning in front of him like some idiot being felt up for the first time? But then Dexter moaned back, the sound guttural, needy, and the noise alone made something stir inside of Jonah. He broke the kiss, his hands pressing against Dexter's chest, pushing him away as they both panted heavily, eyes locked on each other.

"Did I do something wrong?" Dexter asked, lips glistening, plump, more red now than pink.

Jonah shook his head. "No. No . . . I just . . ." he trailed off as a knock on the door interrupted them.

"Dexter, you in there?" a male voice sounded. "We need you onstage in two."

"I'll be right out," he called, then turned his attention back to Jonah. "I'm sorry, I have to—"

"No, it's fine, seriously, go."

Dexter nodded. He looked like he might go in for another kiss, but he didn't, his hands clenched into fists as he swallowed thickly. "I'll text you."

And for once, Jonah couldn't wait to see what Dexter would send him.

FIFTEEN

"We are all hollow now."

—"The Reprise," *The Wooden Horse*, Act Two

The week went by without a word from Dexter. He called in sick for their combat rehearsal on Tuesday, and again for vocals on Thursday, and Jonah waited and waited for a message to pop up on his screen, but nothing came. He debated contacting him himself, throwing a casual noncommittal text his way, something along the lines of *Hey, I can't stop thinking about your lips* or the even more casual *I want you to run your hands through my hair again and make me moan*. But he couldn't be the one reaching out; the ball was in Dexter's court, and Jonah wasn't climbing over the net to fetch it. More than anything, he hated how Dexter somehow bewitched him; only a few days ago he couldn't stand the sight of him, and now . . . Well, now he wanted to look at all of him for hours, preferably naked in his bed.

Even now, as Jonah sat on the never-ending train to Cornwall, his head resting against the window, he willed a message to come through. But no, the only thing that happened as he neared new destinations were FullStack notifications telling him single men were nearby. Which, in all fairness, wasn't a bad thing to be aware of. The notifications and thoughts of Dexter were a welcome distraction as the train hurtled him toward home.

It only took a week for him to find somewhere perfect for his dad: a picturesque old manor refurbished into a specialized dementia-care nursing home. The gardens were lush and green, and to its left there was a gorgeous view of the sea. His father had a special affinity for the ocean, a true water sign if there ever was one. Jonah hoped if his father looked at the waves enough small memories might come back in the sea foam and he could collect them up, and for a moment he might be like the old dad Jonah once knew. A fantasy, of course, but one he could easily put his faith in if it meant his father might return from the hazy place he now lived in. Jonah let out a heavy breath as he thought about his dad and how anxious he was at seeing him again. He wasn't due back in the theatre until Tuesday night, which meant he had half of today then all of Monday and Tuesday morning to help his mum settle Dad in at the new home. And honestly, thank God they didn't perform on Sundays and Mondays, or he might never be able to help with this kind of thing. But would him being there really make much of a difference? Would his dad even recognize him? He didn't the last time he saw him, and the pure pain of having his father not recognize him tore Jonah apart. But Jonah needed to face him, face the Alzheimer's and support his mother through it.

His mother was another problem.

He'd kept his promise to Aunt Penny and called his mum more often, just little check-ins to make sure things were okay. But during each call she ended up tearful, not about his dad, but about the bloody chickens. He wasn't sure if she was pushing her grief over effectively losing her husband onto the death of her "babies," as she lovingly referred to them, but her tears each night broke Jonah's heart. He left the calls reluctantly, the speaker at the theatre asking for first positions, something he couldn't ignore, and she seemed to understand, but the disappointment in her voice didn't waver. Which meant he'd felt immeasurably guilty the whole week but knew he would be home with her Sunday—today—and, hopefully, he would head back to London knowing she would be okay.

Bill Penrose once swam in the sea every day without fail. Even when the heavens opened or when snow came down in thick flurries, he made his way to the beach and set off for his fifteen-minute swim, always returning for a mug of Ovaltine and Marmite on toast. He looked out at the sea now from the deck chair in the back garden, his limbs thin and frail, and danced his fingers through the air as if pushing through water, swimming again, in his mind, at least. Jonah sat down in the chair beside him, the green and white stripes of the material faded from the sun, and looked out at the beams of light kissing the skyline.

"Gorgeous day," Jonah said, keeping his eyes on the horizon so he didn't have to look at his father's sunken cheeks. "Bet the sea is warm."

"Yes," his dad said, voice full of rubble and years of nicotine damage. "Went out there this morning on the boat."

"You did?"

"Took my boy with me."

Jonah's heart tugged in his chest. "Bet he loved that."

"He did." He lowered his hand and placed it on the arm of the chair, his knuckles protruding from the skin, little mountains on his hand, extreme dips and highs. His skin seemed blemished, one hand still wrapped in a bandage, the other bare but covered in deep-purple bruises. He didn't recall his dad ever having a boat, but it was okay him having one now, moored on the shores of his mind, and he hoped he did him proud on the boat, manned the sails and . . . whatever else sailors did on boats.

"Where you from, then?" his dad asked, turning his head to look at Jonah, and Jonah dared himself to look back. His father's strands of wispy white hair were thin, his skin pale, eyes still striking blue, the ocean not lost from them.

"Oh, here, St. Ives."

"A local lad, then."

"Born and bred."

"You got a wife?"

Jonah laughed and shook his head. "No. No wife."

His father pondered the answer before asking, "Got a husband?"

Jonah tutted and shook his head again. "Sadly not."

"Hmph," he grumbled and tried to stand from his seat, but Jonah placed a hand on his knee to settle him back down. "I've got a wife. Call her and get her to bring us some tea."

"She's a bit busy at the moment," Jonah said; his mum was inside speaking with the nurses who were going to help get his dad moved on Monday. "I can make you a tea a little later, though."

"You don't look like you would make a good cup of tea."

"Wow, what a cutting insult." Jonah smiled. "You're no good at making tea, either, you know. You never brew it long enough."

"My son can't make tea. He has a habit of stirring it too much, and it bursts the tea bag."

Jonah bit down on his bottom lip to stop himself from crying. His father spoke about him as if he were a ghost, someone far away, the distant tea bag destroyer with no face and no name.

"I still do that, you know."

His father narrowed his eyes at him. "You're a strange one, you are. What's your name?"

"Jonah."

Something registered behind his blue eyes. "Jonah. My boy's called Jonah. We play the piano together . . . he always likes to play the same song . . ." He tapped his finger against his forehead. "Can't for the life of me remember it now."

"'You Win Again' by the Bee Gees," Jonah provided. "It's actually quite an aggressive song when you look at the lyrics."

"A God-awful song if you ask me." His dad laughed. "But my boy liked it. He liked ABBA too. Always with the sequins, that kid."

Jonah didn't like ABBA. When Bastien found out, he threatened to take his gay card from him and called him a disgrace, which only made Jonah become more vocal over his dislike of them.

"It wasn't ABBA," Jonah said. "You're thinking of Girls Aloud. Slightly different era, though."

"Still camp as hell."

Jonah laughed loudly then. "You're not wrong."

His dad raised his hand again, but this time he reached for Jonah's and took it in his. "You remind me of him," he said, his voice full to the brim with sincerity. "My boy. You remind me of him."

Jonah squeezed his hand lightly, careful to not hurt him; he wanted to wrap him in cotton wool. "I love you very much. I want you to know that."

"You do? Why say that? Am I dying?"

"No," Jonah whispered. "But I think it's important to tell people when you love them, don't you?"

"I wish I could tell my son."

"Don't worry. He knows."

Jonah unscrewed the second bottle of red wine and left it open on the kitchen table to breathe. He wasn't sure if you let screw-top wines breathe, but he wanted to pretend he was sophisticated so let it bask in the warm evening air. His mum swirled the dregs of the wine in her glass around, her eyes fixated on the red liquid the same color as the nail polish on her fingernails. Her lips were slightly stained from the drink, her eyes heavy and dark, and Jonah's eyes fell to the line of empty wine bottles by the back door waiting to be taken to the recycling center.

"You have your friends over a lot, Mum?" he asked, trying to sound as casual as possible.

"Yes. And book club."

"I didn't know you did a book club," Jonah said, genuinely pleased to hear she was involving herself in the things she used to enjoy, reading being one of her many passions. He could remember when he was a child, her sitting on the edge of his bed reading him stories, letting him get lost in fantastical worlds where the troubles of the real life didn't exist. "What have you been reading?"

"Something about murder and old people. We don't actually read the books, Jonah, it's just an excuse for a gossip and cake."

He eyed the wine bottles again. "And tea?"

"Sometimes." She waved her hand in the air dismissively, ending the topic of conversation.

"Dad seemed in good spirits today," he said, subtly screwing the lid onto the bottle he opened and sliding it back into the wine rack. "I think tomorrow will go well."

"Maybe," she said, eyes still lost in her glass. Jonah sat down beside her.

"Jonah, have you found a boyfriend yet?" she asked, tearing herself away from the tiny puddle of wine to look at her son. "Why can't you fall in love and make me worry about you less?"

"Why would being in love make you worry about me less?"

"Because then I'd know you wouldn't be lonely in London."

"I'm not lonely."

"You have friends?" She ran her finger around the rim of the glass. "Outside of your job?"

"I'm still friendly with some of the previous casts and crew I've worked with. But it's hard to make friends in London when you work the hours I do."

"And hard to find a boyfriend." She lifted the glass to her lips and finished the last few droplets of red. "Have you tried those dating websites? Cathy's son found his girlfriend on one, and they are getting married next week."

"That's fabulous news for Cathy's son. But, Mum, seriously, when I meet someone I will tell you."

She scoffed and rubbed her hand over her eyes. "Right, well, I won't hold my breath. I'm heading to bed. You staying down here?"

"Yeah, I'll do the washing up."

"You're a good boy, sausage." She ran her hand through his hair, then pressed a kiss to his forehead. He watched as she wrapped her bathrobe tighter around her body, then shuffled out of the kitchen and upstairs to her bedroom.

Jonah stared at the dirty dishes stacked by the edge of the sink, then added the empty wineglasses to the pile and got to cleaning them. The window in the kitchen looked out over the garden, and the moon shone down over the sea, creating a silver mirror from the water, a sight he'd missed since being in London. He pretended he was eighteen again, readying himself to leave his home, imagining all the wonderful things awaiting him in the capital. He had dreamed of being in the West End, something he'd achieved; he even dreamed of an Olivier, and holy shit, he'd actually achieved that too. Where else could he go from there? He'd reached the top level. He could win more awards, sure, but would he be happy? Were awards enough?

His phone vibrated on the kitchen table, and he glanced over his shoulder at it before grabbing a tea towel to dry his hands. He squinted at the screen to see two messages come through together—the signal on the coast of St. Ives leaving something to be desired—and felt his stomach drop as he read the names. The first, Dexter; the second, Edward. He ignored Edward and went straight for the message from Dexter.

The Penis Destroyer: Sorry I've been MIA. Been super ill :(I'm okay now, can we meet for a drink? Dex x

Jonah scowled at the mention of illness and half wondered if Dexter should have told him earlier, given they made out. But he'd been fine, so he reluctantly let it slide, mostly because Dexter had put a kiss at the end of the message.

Jonah: Sorry you've been sick. I'm in Cornwall till Tuesday but can meet when I get back? x

He deleted, then replaced the kiss eight times before settling on sending it.

The Penis Destroyer: Cornwall? Impromptu holiday? I'm free Thursday, can meet after the show or get a coffee in the morning if that works with you? Also, I need to do some social media damage control after the whole tripping thing . . . any ideas before Colbie kills me? x

Jonah: Maybe you shouldn't have tried to trip me in the first place, then you wouldn't be needing to maintain your squeaky clean image? x

The Penis Destroyer: Avoiding holiday and drink question? Fine, I guess I deserve that. Groveling at your feet. x

Jonah: I'm visiting my parents. Thursday morning is good. Don't grovel, it doesn't suit you. x

The Penis Destroyer: Duly noted. Though, I've been thinking about getting on my knees for you since that kiss x

Jonah covered his face with his hand and slipped his phone into his pocket. He couldn't have this type of conversation in his parents' kitchen. He switched off the lights and headed upstairs, where he lingered outside of the room his dad slept in, listening for the soft sounds of his snores, smiling knowing he was asleep and safe. His own bedroom was farther down the hall, the last door on the left, and he opened it to see the bag he had brought with him and dumped on the bed unpacked neatly on the mattress, courtesy of his mum. Unlike some people who spoke about their childhood rooms remaining the same since they left home, Jonah's parents completely overhauled his room and turned it into a cozy guest room. Yellow curtains hung from the rail at the window, and a plush beige carpet stretched across the floorboards, which hosted a king-size bed. It was a far cry from the navy-blue-walled and emerald-green-carpeted room Jonah once called his own.

The Penis Destroyer: Sorry, was that a step too far?

Jonah grinned at the message. He pictured Dexter sitting in his home on Lawford Road, phone in hand, eagerly awaiting Jonah's response.

Jonah: Just recovering from the shock of you thinking about me in a way that doesn't end with me covered in vomit or with your foot in my crotch x

The Penis Destroyer: FYI, I genuinely didn't mean to do that.

Jonah: Sure Jan gif.

The Penis Destroyer: I don't know what that means. x

Jonah: Urgh, stop messaging me and brush yourself up on memes before we can no longer be friends.

The Penis Destroyer: Is that what we are now? Friends? x

Jonah: Depends. I'm still mad at you. x

The Penis Destroyer: Understandable. I'm sorry, again. Seriously. x

Jonah smiled at the message. Truth be told, he still didn't fully trust him; he could forgive the string of unfortunate incidents culminating in the vomiting, but he couldn't yet forget the tripping attempt at the Oliviers. He didn't think he ever would. But he could allow himself to flirt, kiss, maybe more; Dexter was attractive, he could never deny that, and now that he'd experienced a more honest and vulnerable side of him he could see him for more than the massive dickhead he masqueraded as. Jonah put the phone down on his bedside table and ignored the unread message from Edward while also choosing not to reply to Dexter. He could sweat for a response; it was Jonah's turn to hold the cards.

SIXTEEN

"Turning tables, the sun burns on the horizon and we ride to our deaths."

—"The Battle," *The Wooden Horse*, Act One

The wails from Jonah's father haunted him the entire journey home. The image of him slumped on the floor of his new room, body contorted at odd angles as he cried out to Jonah and his mum, replayed over and over again in his head. His father couldn't understand the space, his mind reeling at the change, a change Jonah didn't think he would even notice; but he underestimated the power of the mind and the pitfalls of the disease plaguing his father. The nurses at the home were brilliant. They knew exactly what to do and how to calm his mum, who cried hysterically outside the bedroom door, overcome completely with guilt and remorse.

"It's for the best, Mum," he told her, but even he didn't believe his words. He replayed the day as he stared at the vacant seat opposite him on the train and contemplated the idea that maybe he shouldn't have intervened in his parents' lives; he'd caused an untold amount of distress, something he would never forgive himself for.

When he got back to Castle Road, his body cried out for rest, for a reprieve from the waterfall of guilt, but he couldn't relax. The Persephone Theatre called out to him, the evening performance waiting, an audience ready to be swept up in the tragedy of Troy. He kept his head down as he traveled through London, his phone on silent, all distractions taking up too much of his attention, draining him even further. His dressing room did nothing to comfort him, and neither did Bastien, who barely said a word as he signed in then closed himself into his own room, leaving Sherrie to help Jonah get ready.

"So, I finally saw Romana over the weekend. It was *amazing*, we had the most mind-blowing sex, seriously, but then I've not heard from her since," Sherrie said, swiping a makeup brush over Jonah's face. "She acts like I don't exist, then picks me up when she wants me."

"What do you want out of this . . . thing with her? A relationship? You've never been too fussed before." He was glad Sherrie was in the mood for talking; hearing about her dating life took the spotlight away from his father sobbing on the floor.

"That's because I've never met someone like her before. She's stunning, obviously, and she's funny and does this cute thing with her nose when she laughs. And when I'm with her it's like we've known each other for years, you know? But now . . . well, now I know I'm nothing more than a booty call."

"Well, don't be a booty call. Leave her hanging."

"Coming from the man who is painfully single and seriously needs to get laid."

Jonah scoffed and batted his hand at her. "I do not need to get laid."

"Babe, I've seen how tense you are since you broke up with Edward. Haven't you met with anyone on FullStack?" She went back to inspecting his face before putting her makeup kit away. "You're a cutie, you should have dozens of guys messaging you on there."

"They do message me."

"Then go fuck one of them!" she exclaimed as she helped to fix the microphone wire in his hair. "Get the tension out of your system."

Jonah allowed the image of Dexter on his knees with those beautiful lips of his to cross his mind, then shook it away. "We are talking about your love life, not mine."

"Well, my vagina's going to be as dry as a desert from now on. It's closed, and Romana won't be getting access ever again, so I have nothing further to report."

"Too much information, Sherrie."

"What? Do vaginas scare you, Jonah?"

"No, but I don't want to hear about how dry yours is."

She tutted, then sighed loudly. "I just want Romana to admit she's in love with me so we can get a dozen cats and live in happy lesbian bliss until we die. Why is that so hard?"

A message from Dexter flashed on his phone.

"Bit soon for the L word isn't it?"

"Lesbian?"

"No, *love*, you idiot. Have you tried talking to her about it?" Jonah asked, swiping to read what Dexter had to say.

The Penis Destroyer: Can't do Thursday. Sorry.

No kiss. No explanation. Brilliant.

"She doesn't listen," Sherrie said. "Hey, what's with the frown?"

"Oh, nothing." He placed his phone back on his dresser. "Just . . . family stuff."

"Shit, yeah, sorry, Bastien said you went up to help your dad. How was it?"

"Fine." He lied just as his phone lit up again; this time a notification from Instagram sat on his screen. He reached for it and swiped up to unlock the screen, only to see he'd been tagged in a photo by Dexter. It must have been taken a while ago. Jonah's hair was shorter than it was now, which reminded him he needed to book himself in for a haircut, and he stood onstage, his hands clasped together as the rest of the cast stood behind him. It would have been taken just as he came out for his bow at the end of the show. He wondered when Dexter took it, the faceless person with his phone held up taking photographs, and why Dexter felt the need to keep it and then post it after what must have been weeks.

Jonah looked down to the caption beneath it: *So lucky I get to call this star my friend*. He stared at the words with such intensity the letters ran around on the screen, muddling the meaning entirely, and a rather large part of him wanted to remove the tag while also removing himself from Dexter's apparent damage control. Dexter made out with him, ghosted him for a week, then canceled their drink plans just to post this crap? Jonah groaned and slammed his phone down, causing Sherrie to flinch.

"What's wrong?" she asked, eyeing his phone suspiciously. "More family stuff, or is it Edward?"

"Why would you think it's Edward?"

"Bastien told me he's been texting you, begging to get you back. Kinda romantic, don't you think?"

Jonah stood from the chair in front of the mirror and went to the rack with his costumes. "No. Not really. He left me for the guy he was cheating on me with, and now it seems he wants to see me again while also seeing him." His words came out as bitter as he intended. "I swear to God, I'm done with men. All the good ones are gone."

Sherrie stepped by his side and rested her head on his shoulder. "Maybe we should just marry each other. We could get a dog and a hamster and live happily ever after? A sexless marriage, of course, but sometimes I think sex is overrated."

"I don't." He pulled his first costume from the hanger. "I think that's the problem."

"You need some hanky-panky."

Jonah laughed and moved from her so he could take his top off and drape it over the back of his chair. "Has the old woman who sometimes possesses Bastien moved onto you?"

"Oh, shut up." She smiled. "Let me set you up with someone. Please? I have a friend who is also recently single, and he's cute as fuck and would totally be up for a date."

"Maybe," he said, despite the little voice in his head screaming at him, telling him it was a bad idea, and the even smaller voice whispering Dexter's name that he did his best to stamp out. "Let me think about it."

Edward stood by the wall opposite the stage door. Jonah saw him as soon as he stepped outside, his body tensing, breath staggering in his throat. He looked . . . rugged, a vibe he never really went for before; he needed a shave, the stubble he sometimes had now a full-on beard. It didn't suit him. He locked eyes with Jonah, and Jonah, much to his surprise, didn't feel weak at the knees like he used to whenever Edward's eyes found his. Instead, he gave his undivided attention to the people waiting for autographs and photos, taking longer than he usually would with them, talking with them, listening to them speak about the show and how much it meant to them. The interactions were humbling, and he decided he would try to stay as long as possible in the future; they loved the show as much as he did. Eventually he ran out of programs to sign and he ended up face-to-face with Edward, who smiled at him then pulled out a program from inside his jacket.

"Can I get a signature?" he asked, voice low and quiet. It used to be seductive. "You were amazing tonight."

Jonah gently placed his hand on Edward's arm and guided him away from the line by the door, not wanting to be overheard. "You came to the show?"

"You've been ignoring my texts. I was worried you were sick or something."

"Why are you worrying about me? We aren't anything to each other anymore," Jonah said, looking over his shoulder to see Bastien watching them with a grim expression. "You need to leave me alone."

"I love you, Jonah," Edward said. "I love you. I was an idiot. I didn't know what I had till I messed everything up, and I'm regretting it. Please forgive me? We can make this work. We were good together, weren't we?"

If Edward presented him with this speech a week after their breakup, Jonah would have probably believed every word and gone home with him. Now, though, he saw a man who wanted the world despite not deserving it. The definition of having his cake and eating it too. Whatever that meant.

"We weren't good together, or you wouldn't have cheated on me," Jonah spoke under his breath, knowing a few wandering eyes were caught on the two of them. "I can't believe you thought me ignoring your messages meant you could come to my work. It's out of order, Edward."

"Have you met someone else, is that it?" Edward asked, his voice rising as Jonah's fell.

"You know what, Edward?" Jonah took a step back from him. "If I had met someone else, it's none of your business. You need to stop contacting me, and you can't come here again."

Edward opened his mouth to say something else, but Bastien stepped forward with a member of the security team, Matt, beside him. "Everything all right here?" Matt asked, sounding like he belonged on a long-running daytime TV police drama. "Jonah?"

"Yeah. Thanks, Matt. He's now going." Jonah gave Edward a pointed look, his lips pressed in a firm line.

Edward scoffed and shook his head. "Wow. Security? Really? Don't be like this, Jonah, come with me and get a drink and let's talk about this."

"Actually," Bastien said, stepping between them. "I think I heard him tell you to leave him alone. In what universe does that translate to going to get a drink?"

Edward looked between them and raised an eyebrow before a strange look of recognition passed across his features. "Oh. So, it's him, is it?"

"What?" Jonah asked.

"You're with him?" Edward waved a nonchalant hand toward Bastien. "Well, I hope you're happy. But it's fucking hypocritical of you to get angry with me when clearly something's been going on with you two for months."

Jonah opened his mouth and closed it again several times, doing his best impression of a goldfish before answering. "Fuck off, Edward."

Bastien raised his middle finger as Edward looked at him. His bravery was something Jonah could only marvel at, though it might have come from having the six-foot-five Matt standing behind him. Edward seemed pensive, as if he wanted to say more but thought against it. Jonah watched as he walked away, a churning feeling in the pit of his stomach. Matt placed a sturdy hand on his shoulder.

"Hey, mate, you okay?" he asked.

"Fine," Jonah whispered.

"Come on," Bastien said. "Come stay at mine tonight. Don't go home alone, in case that creep decides to haunt your house or something." He winked at Matt. "My hero," he cooed. "Thanks, babe." Matt shot him a grin then went back over to the stage door.

"You don't have to take me back to yours," Jonah said.

"It's fine. Casey is away for work, so we can put on face masks and watch *Funny Girl*."

"It's two and a half hours long, Bastien."

"Best we hurry back then, huh?" Bash smiled at him and linked his arm with Jonah's, directing him toward the tube. "I kinda need the company too. I've had a shit day."

Jonah allowed himself to be led down Shaftesbury Avenue, Bastien's words clear despite the noise and hundreds of people congregating along the streets.

"You have?"

"Yeah," Bastien said, his eyes ahead, focused. "Casey has been offered a job in New York."

Jonah stopped abruptly, the people walking behind him barging into his back then grumbling as they stepped around him. Bastien looked at him, brows furrowing. "New York?" Jonah asked.

"Yeah. He's asked me to go with him. Actually, he asked me a couple of things last night."

Shaftesbury Avenue seemed to fall into slow motion. The only things in focus were Jonah and Bastien as they stood looking at each other on the road that led down to Chinatown, the huge red lanterns glowing in the night sky.

"What else did he ask you?"

"He proposed."

"Bastien!" Jonah exclaimed, unable to keep the wide smile from taking over his face. "What did you say?"

"I said I needed to think about it." He took Jonah's hand into his to urge him forward, and the street catapulted back into blazing color and motion. "And he left for work this morning and we didn't talk about it and now he's away for three days."

"You don't want to marry him?" They rounded the corner and headed along the road leading to the tube station. "You've been together forever."

"It's not the marrying him I'm not sure about. It's New York." Bastien groaned, then stopped, more people tutting and muttering as they blocked the path yet again. "I'm so sorry, I've just realized I haven't asked how things went in Cornwall."

"What? It was fine. Don't apologize, you've clearly got a lot going on right now." Jonah watched as Bastien wiped a hand across his eyes, tears just beginning to fall. "Come on," Jonah said. "I think Barbra Streisand will make everything better."

"She will, won't she?" Bastien laughed with a sniff. "I love you, you know that, right?"

"Don't get sappy on me," Jonah warned. "Or I will cry, too, and then we will just be two weirdos crying instead of going home."

Bastien nodded. "Right. Okay, I hate you."

"That's more like it."

Bastien choked on a mouthful of ice cream. He pounded his fist against his chest, then grabbed the glass of wine beside him and used it to wash the cold dessert down his throat.

"Don't say something like that when I'm eating, you bloody psychopath," he whined, throwing a cushion from the sofa at Jonah's head.

Jonah batted it away with a smile. "It's not my fault you've been shoveling ice cream into your mouth for the past twenty minutes. I couldn't hold it in anymore."

"Dexter Ellis kissed you?!" He dumped the tub of ice cream onto the coffee table and shuffled closer to Jonah. "Tell me everything."

"We kind of kissed each other."

"But you hate him."

"I don't hate him."

"He hates you."

Jonah rolled his eyes. "Apparently not. And he texted me when I was in Cornwall and was super flirty and asked me to meet him for a drink on Thursday. But he's since canceled, and I think he's just messing with me."

"I knew he liked you," Bastien said, a smug grin plastered on his face as Barbra sang on the TV. "Omari said the same thing. It's a simple case of a boy pulling girls' pigtails in the playground because he likes them."

"But that's shitty, isn't it?" Jonah asked. "Being mean because you like someone? And I don't think that's the case at all."

"No?" Bastien hummed. "What do you think it is, then?"

"I think he genuinely disliked me, then . . . something changed, and he'd established this weird relationship with me and didn't know what to do to get past it. And even then, he's not really done anything overtly unkind. Unwanted feedback, sure, and the lip biting, who knows if he meant to do that?"

"He was going to trip you at the Oliviers."

"Well, yeah, but that was before he knew me."

"So? What now, then? Are you going to rearrange the drinks?"

"I haven't replied to him yet."

Bastien kicked Jonah's foot with an annoyed gasp. "Then do it. I'm going to call Casey, and you can text Dexter, deal?"

Jonah shook his head and finished his glass of wine. "Nope. No deal. You know what you're going to say to Casey, I don't know what to say to Dexter."

"Tell him you want to suck his dick."

"Bastien!"

"What?!" Bastien chuckled. "Don't you?"

"Even if I did, I'm not texting him that."

"Why not?"

"Because I don't want to look desperate."

Bastien sighed and stood from his position on the sofa. "It's not desperate," he said, wandering over to the kitchen to put the ice cream back into the freezer. "But maybe just send something flirty without being overly obvious about what you want to do."

"So, you get to tell Casey you want to marry him and you're going to have a shining career on Broadway in New York with him, and I have to send an embarrassing message that shows how sexually starved I am?"

"Exactly that." Bastien dropped the spoon into the sink. "You sure you don't want to share the bed with me tonight? You're happy out here?"

Jonah patted the duvet Bastien gave him earlier and grinned. "I'm fine."

"Okay." Bastien turned off the TV and yawned. "Well. We can regroup in the morning. I'm gonna make that call, then get my beauty rest. I'm already regretting the wine and ice cream. Omari will smell it on me. I forgot it's double show day tomorrow."

Jonah whined in response. "Don't remind me."

Bastien leaned down to kiss him on the cheek. "Sleep well. And text your archrival, yeah? Something sexy."

"Yes sir." Jonah saluted to him as Bastien shook his head fondly and left the room.

He'd stayed at Bastien's before, usually when they were blindingly drunk and thought it would be a good idea to continue the party after the bars were closed, only to get to Bastien's and fall asleep while microwaving frozen meals. The last time they did it, Jonah woke to find a half-eaten ball of mozzarella in his hand, the thing squashed and smelling like it died. Now, though, he had the warmth of a couple of glasses of wine to relax him but his mind was clear, and as he heard Bastien's muffled voice from the bedroom a sense of contentment washed over him knowing how amazing his friend's life was about to become.

His own life, however, left a lot to be desired.

He looked at Dexter's last text and scowled at the screen for a while, still in disbelief at the shortness of the message and the lack of a kiss. Perhaps Dexter no longer wanted to pursue him, or maybe he was trying to remain professional . . . or maybe he really was just fucking with Jonah just to be cruel.

Jonah: **Shame. Want to rearrange?** x

He locked his phone after taking in the time. Dexter would be asleep, and even though he told himself over and over again Dexter wouldn't reply, he fell asleep with his phone in his hand waiting for it to vibrate.

SEVENTEEN

"Patroclus, my heart belongs to you."
—"Eternity," *The Wooden Horse*, Act Two

So began the week of rehearsals. Jonah looked forward to Thursday when the matinee show meant he wouldn't have to go to the rehearsal studio. He could relax and enjoy himself onstage for the day, not swelter under unforgiving yellow lights in a room with no windows. He also didn't want to see Dexter; he hadn't replied to his message, and Jonah debated messaging him again. He ultimately decided against it. If Dexter didn't have the decency to send him a response when he seemed pretty bloody active on social media, then Jonah wouldn't beg for attention. It didn't matter that the kiss was amazing, or that he'd thought of the idiot every night since it happened. He didn't want to like Dexter. He seemed unstable, emotionally stunted, and incapable of thinking beyond his own nose. Yet Jonah wanted him to want him. He wanted Dexter to yearn for him and want to kiss him and place his hands on his waist then trail his fingers over his thighs. Fuck. Fuck. Fuck. The infatuation needed to stop.

Jonah looked at himself in the mirror above the sink in the tiny toilet tucked away in the studio in Covent Garden. He'd looked better; his skin appeared dull, eyes hollow and hair a downright mess. He hadn't gotten much sleep the night before. His phone rang in the middle of the night, and he answered only to hear his mum rambling on the other end, speaking about chickens and his dad and a car she saw with tinted windows and she wondered if King Charles drove past her house. Because why wouldn't King Charles drive past her house in the middle of nowhere at an ungodly hour? Jonah somehow convinced her to go to bed, her phone still pressed to her ear as she settled beneath the duvet, and he stayed on the line with her until she said she needed to sleep. After she hung up, he called Penny, waking her, and she sighed down the phone and asked if his mum sounded drunk when they talked. She didn't. At least, he didn't think she did. Because she wouldn't have been, because despite the collection of empty wine bottles at the house, he knew she consumed them with friends, not alone. Penny didn't seem convinced and left a tiny seed of doubt in the crevices of Jonah's mind. After they talked, he looked at the vacant space beside him in his bed and tried not to think about how comforting it would be to have someone there to share his worries with.

Dexter. Edward. Someone else. Anyone.

He made his way out of the bathroom in the rehearsal studio where the cast who were staying on mingled with the new cast. Memories of his first time in the space almost two years ago now, when rehearsals for *The Wooden Horse* first started, came flooding back to him. He found the studio charming then, a beautiful space nestled in the heart of Covent Garden, but now it seemed dull almost, as if Dexter Ellis roughed off the shine from it with a Brillo pad. But this was the first rehearsal with the new cast, all of them together for the first time, and Jonah couldn't deny the excitement he felt, even if it meant having to spend more time with the man who seemed intent on ignoring him. The unfamiliar faces of the new cast members didn't seem as strange to him now; he'd seen the amount of content posted on *The Wooden Horse*'s socials, highlighting each of them, celebrating their induction into the family. He saw Romana, long hair tied back, warm ochre skin shining beneath the lights. She looked over at Jonah and smiled, then beckoned him to her side.

"Hey," she said with an accent he couldn't identify, Irish perhaps, with a hint of an Australian twang. "I feel I know everything there is to know about you from Sherrie already."

He desperately wanted to pry, to dig out little nuggets of information about her relationship with Sherrie. He couldn't let on just how much he knew about her, or the fact Sherrie texted him the night before saying how much she hated Romana for standing her up for dinner. "And I've heard a lot about you," he said instead, regretting it immediately when Romana's eyes widened and she tucked a stray strand of hair behind her ear.

"All bad, I'm sure."

"No," he hurried to say. "No. She likes you a lot. But not too much, a normal amount. A totally normal amount." Fuck. Sherrie would kill him.

She narrowed her green eyes at him. "Right."

"I've made this awkward," he said with a grimace. "I'm just gonna . . ." He turned from her, and his eyes fell on Dexter, blond hair kept back from his face with a black elastic band. He seemed as in need of a haircut as Jonah. He wore the stupid tight joggers again, but a tank top covered his upper body, revealing his toned arms, and fucking hell, Jonah wanted to lick his biceps. Dexter's eyes locked onto Jonah as he spoke with Lennon and Omari, and he kept the smile on his face as he conversed, but something strange lay behind the way Dexter gazed at him. Jonah decided to ignore him and went to Bastien, who was showing off his hand to Lilly, the new cast member taking over the role of Helen.

"Isn't it just gorgeous?" he gushed and smirked at Jonah as he approached, then wiggled his fingers in the air, showing off a gold band decorated with six tiny diamonds. "Look what Casey gave me."

Jonah took Bastien's hand into his and gazed down at the ring. "Holy shit, Bash. It's stunning."

"He did so good," Lilly said, smiling brightly with sparkling white teeth and intense blue eyes. "When do you think you will get married?"

"I want an April wedding. He wants December, but I know if we get married in December it will end up being Christmas themed, and don't get me wrong, I love a bit of Santa rocking around with mince pies, but not for my wedding."

"April, then." Jonah laughed. "I hope I'm invited."

"Only if you bring a date." Bastien winked, and Jonah stuck his tongue out at him. "And, talking of dates, a rather handsome bell end is approaching."

Jonah peered over his shoulder to see Dexter coming over to them. By the time he looked back Bastien had ushered himself and Lilly away to another part of the room, leaving Jonah to stand alone as Dexter bit his bottom lip anxiously.

"Jonah," he said, fingers twirling around each other as he fiddled with the hem of his top. "Sorry I've not been in touch."

Jonah did his best nonchalant shrug and tried to keep his face looking as unfazed as possible. "It's fine." He flicked his hand in the air, as if brushing away the apology. "I see your Instagram post got the attention you wanted. You being the theatre villain didn't last long."

"Oh, yeah," Dexter said with a nod. "People think it was just a prank, the Olivier thing, a weird 'bro thing.'" He used air quotes as he spoke. "And the fact you've been silent on the matter seems to have dulled any flames. So . . . thanks for that?"

"Did you think I would hop online and start slagging you off?"

"No, but I don't know. I'm just trying to thank you."

He looked beautiful standing there. Golden hair and hazel eyes singing the song of autumn, with his lips looking absolutely delightful, lips that dripped words of sarcasm and unwanted critiques, lips Jonah kissed not just onstage but for real now, and he craved the way they felt against his own.

"Why didn't you text me back?" He knew he came across as somewhat pathetic, the lonely man clinging to his phone, waiting for a message from the guy he made out with but who was so out of his league that of course he didn't text him back.

Dexter rubbed the back of his neck. "It's complicated."

"Do you have a boyfriend?"

"What?" Dexter's nose crinkled. "No."

"Girlfriend?"

"No, it's not like that. It's . . . family stuff."

Well, Jonah knew enough about "family stuff" to last him a lifetime, which meant he knew he didn't have any right to pry. "Oh. Well. I hope everything's okay."

"Thanks."

Jonah closed his eyes and swallowed down the lump he didn't realize had formed in his throat. "But. You could have sent me a message, right?

Like, I know that sounds super needy or whatever, but you just left me hanging. Again. Which is fine, but I'm not just waiting around for you to pick up whenever you feel like it."

Dexter gave a small, understanding nod. "I guess that's fair." He looked around the room before leaning slightly closer, close enough Jonah could feel his breath on his cheeks. "I kind of like you sounding needy."

Jonah blinked. "You do?"

"Yeah." He delivered his signature Dexter Ellis shit-eating grin. "Shows how much you want me."

"I don't want anyone who wears one of these." Jonah reached for the elastic band keeping back Dexter's hair and pinged it against his scalp. "You're not David Beckham circa 2003."

"Did you . . . did you just make a sports reference?"

"No. I made a fashion reference."

Dexter laughed then and adjusted the band on his head. "Whatever." He deliberately made a show of looking Jonah up and down. "I'm hardly going to take fashion advice from someone so passé."

"You need to shut your face, because I'm not the one who goes to a fucking club wearing an embroidered Labrador on my jumper."

Dexter's face fell. "Shit. I forgot I lost that, thanks for reminding me, you twat. And, I'll have you know, that jumper has got me a lot of attention."

"Sure, you keep telling yourself that." Jonah brushed past him and made his way over to the other side of the studio, where Peter stood talking with a couple of members of the ensemble. Jonah didn't need to look to know Dexter still had his eyes on him.

Dexter squirmed beneath him, hands clasped around Jonah's wrists as he tried to stop the dagger from coming down to deal the final blow. The rest of the cast stood round in rapt attention, the tension Dexter added to the scene enthralling, a completely desperate and believable side of Hector no one had seen before. It worked. The struggle. The last-ditch attempt to save his life. And when Jonah finally plunged the dagger to the side of his neck, some of the cast gasped and covered their mouths in shock. They knew the scene, of course, but seeing it played out so close and with the added hope from Hector meant the experience hit them differently. Jonah had to give it to Dexter; he played the part brilliantly. He wondered what Dexter was like as Achilles. If he put as much of his soul into the role as he clearly was doing with Hector, then he must have been spectacular.

"Amazing," Colbie said from the corner, unlit cigarette between her lips as she clapped, spurring the others on to do the same. "I bloody love it!"

"So, the stage will rotate here as the orchestra start the beginning notes of the next song, and when it gets to the back you guys will be in darkness ready to exit stage left," a stage technician said, gesturing with his hands how the rotation would work as Jonah watched him from his position straddling Dexter's lap.

As the cast for the next scene made their way onto the stage marked out on the flooring, Jonah looked down at Dexter as he felt him shift beneath him. He knew he needed to get up to make way for the others, he didn't want to be the one responsible for holding up a rehearsal, but the look on Dexter's face told him to stay still. Jonah became aware of two important things at the exact same time. Firstly, Dexter looked fucking insatiable with a deep red flush over his cheeks. Secondly, he could feel from where his legs were positioned on either side of the other man, right where his arse was, that Dexter was undeniably hard.

"Oh my God, are you—"

"Shut up," Dexter whispered, his tone as sharp as knives. "You need to get off me and make sure no one looks at us."

Jonah glanced at the bodies congregating along the white line on the floor, all with their backs to them, apart from the people sitting at the front of the room watching. "You've got to move, or we are going to be stuck right in the middle of the scene."

"Just hang on." Dexter placed his hands on Jonah's waist and eased him from his lap, then not so elegantly rolled onto his side to face the back of the studio then shuffled on his bum to the edge and out of the way of the others. Jonah watched him, his own cheeks burning, and stood awkwardly; he'd already taken too long to exit the space, and he could feel Colbie's eyes drilling into the back of his head as he took a seat on the floor beside Dexter.

"That will teach you not to wear such tight joggers," Jonah whispered.

"Shut up."

"Wait, oh my God—" Jonah gawped at Dexter as realization dawned on him. This happened before. Dexter also didn't get up from the floor the first time they did their combat rehearsals. "You got turned on the first time we did this." He was hard then and hard now. All from having Jonah on his lap, riding him like a cowboy. Yee fucking haw.

"Will you keep your voice down?" Dexter cupped a hand over Jonah's mouth. Jonah licked his palm in retaliation, and Dexter scowled at him, dropping his hand. "Seriously, I'm bloody embarrassed."

"Don't be."

"Easy for you to say." He adjusted the crotch of his joggers and pulled his legs up to his chest protectively. "I swear it won't happen onstage."

"I should hope not. Can't have Hector all aroused while being stabbed to death." He nudged his shoulder against Dexter's and leaned in to whisper to him, his breath tickling the skin on the blond's neck. "If you took me for that drink, you might get me on your lap without all these people watching."

Jonah didn't think it was possible for Dexter's face to turn a deeper shade of red, but somehow he managed it. He swallowed thickly and turned his head to look at Jonah, their faces close, close enough for their lips to meet with very little effort if one of them made the move.

"What if," Dexter whispered, "I would rather be on top of you like that?"

It was Jonah's turn to feel the stirrings of something in the pit of his stomach. Butterflies, maybe. Or probably just carnal desire, but butterflies sounded better.

"Take me for a drink and we can find out."

Dexter nodded. "After the show."

"Huh?"

"After my first show as Hector, I'll take you for a drink then."

Jonah's eyes flicked down to Dexter's crotch. Despite the way he sat, being so close to him meant Jonah could still get a good view of him, and he could see the outline of his erection clear as day. "That's in a week," Jonah stated, bringing his eyes to meet Dexter's again. "Why wait a week?"

"It'll be better that way." Dexter cleared his throat as the cast in front of them slowly chanted the next song. He waved to Peter, who still stood at the front beside Colbie, and gestured to the bag on the floor next to him. Peter rolled his eyes and kicked it across the floor to him, where it hit Dexter's shins. He wasted no time in opening the bag to pull out a lavender-colored jumper, and Jonah noticed the embroidered lemons on it right away.

"Piniquo?" Jonah asked, earning him a surprised but delighted smile from Dexter.

"Yes," he said. "Fashionable and also doubles up as a boner protector." He stood and held the jumper loosely at his waist, covering his crotch entirely as he smirked down at Jonah. "Now, leave me alone; I'm incredibly busy and important." He sauntered out of the room to the sound of the cast singing aggressively about the gods and spoils of war.

God. Jonah wanted to touch every inch of his skin and he couldn't believe he was thinking this way about Dexter bloody Ellis. The thought terrified and excited him in equal measures. A drink in a week, seven days. He reminded himself that good things come to those who wait.

EIGHTEEN

> *"Is their blood there for you to take? Or do we stain our souls with the color of the people we are told are our enemies? Who is he to say who we must hate based on one man's inability to keep a wife?"*
>
> —"What Do We Fight For?" *The Wooden Horse*, Act One

The atmosphere in the theatre buzzed with electricity. The Persephone glowed as if filled with rivers of gold, the red velvet of the chairs pristine, the carpets fragrant, like orchids. During warm-up, Jonah stood at the front of the stage and looked out at the auditorium. A deep clean over the weekend seemed excessive, but it totally paid off; the place looked fit for royalty. Which, if rumors were to be believed, would be in the left-hand box for the show tonight. Famous people did come to watch, actors and singers who often were allowed onstage afterward to have photographs with the cast. But royalty? Shit, royalty was a different bag entirely. He didn't even know who it might be; they'd not been allowed the super-secret information, but Jonah knew he wouldn't be able to resist a glance into the box as soon as he stepped onstage.

The nerves, however, at having such a prestigious guest only added to the new cast's anticipation for their first performance. But pressure creates diamonds. And, as much as Jonah adored the original cast, this new group would soar even higher than their predecessors, he just knew it. He'd watched them all week; he'd acted with them, sang with them, moved his body in tandem with theirs. He knew their talent, and together they would take the show to a completely new level.

Despite his excitement at taking the stage with the people surrounding him, he also couldn't stop the anxious turning of his stomach knowing tonight he would go for the long-awaited drink with Dexter. Part of him didn't want it to happen; he'd built it up too much in his head, he'd perfected things to say and ways to sip a cocktail sexily, practicing in the mirror just how to wrap his lips around the straw, because he really was that much of a complete and utter loser. But he wanted to make a good impression. He'd spent so long not giving a toss what Dexter thought of him, so long not even remotely liking him, and now he wanted more than anything to kiss him and touch him and make the most gorgeous sounds leave his mouth. He supposed it made sense, the mutual dislike turning into something sexual. He'd seen it played out in enough films and shows to know physical tension blossomed between rivals. He just never thought his life would turn out like a weird romance film with three dodgy sequels on Netflix.

"And here is Jonah Penrose, our fabulous Achilles. Jonah, say hi to the people watching." Jonah closed his eyes and took in a deep breath before turning to look at Dexter, who stood behind him with his phone lifted to Jonah's face. "We're live!" he exclaimed, pointing to the phone.

"Hey," Jonah said, smiling, not knowing if he should look at Dexter or the device in his hand.

"Can you tell everyone what's happening right now?"

Dexter stepped closer, bringing his phone even closer to Jonah's face. "Well, it's warm-up, so we do our movement warm-ups first, led by Omari, who is our dance captain, then we move on to the vocal ones. Then we get dressed for the show."

Dexter panned the phone around the others, who were busy stretching, as Jonah talked, before quickly swinging back to Jonah. "People have been sending in questions, and this one is for you." He smiled at Jonah from behind the screen. "Apart from *The Wooden Horse*, what would you say is the best show in the West End right now?"

Jonah twisted his lips as he thought for an answer. "You can't beat *Les Misérables*, can you?" he said after a moment. "It was the first West End show I saw."

"Really?"

"Yeah, my dad took me to see it. I didn't have a clue what was going on and the gunshots scared the life out of me, but I loved it."

"Aren't you just adorable?" Dexter tapped his screen then put his phone into his pocket. "Sorry," he blurted. "They want me to keep hopping on to do live updates tonight. I've even got to do them in the interval." He seemed harried, his cheeks carrying a red blemish to them and his hair pushed back with the bloody elastic band he'd been wearing the entire week of rehearsals. "Colbie doesn't seem to care it's my opening night tonight and wants me doing all this social media shit." He glanced around them before leaning slightly closer. "Apparently, I need to do more damage control over trip-gate. At this point, I think she just wants me and you to make a sex tape and post it on *The Wooden Horse* Instagram."

Jonah tutted and shook his head ruefully. "You know, I don't even think a sex tape would cut it. Tripping someone on their way to get an award is pretty low, Dex."

Jonah smiled as Dexter rolled his eyes. "I didn't actually trip you," he said, words he'd repeated multiple times over the rehearsal week as Jonah dug into him over it. "And I've said I'm sorry, what more can I do?"

"Dexter, honestly, I'm over it." Jonah placed a hand on his bicep soothingly. "Seriously. Though, if you don't take me out for that drink tonight, I might change my mind and make your life a living hell."

"I doubt that."

"Oh, you wanna fuck around and find out?" Jonah smirked.

"Are you blackmailing me to take you on a date?"

"A date?" Jonah quirked a brow. "Is that what it is? I don't think we've referred to it as a date, have we?"

Dexter's tongue swiped across his bottom lip as he looked at Jonah's mouth. "Oh, it's a date."

A gagging noise pulled their attention from each other and to their left where Bastien stood, arms crossed over his chest and hip cocked out to the side, watching them. "Will you two get a room?"

"Gladly, but that's for later," Dexter said, clapping Bastien on the shoulder before taking position with the others to do his warm-up.

Bastien's eyes looked like they were ready to burst out of his head as he pulled Jonah to the side with an iron grip. "So, it's actually happening? You and him?"

"Nothing's happened."

"You made out!"

"Shut up!" Jonah hissed as a couple of members of the orchestra peered at them. "But, yes, we are going for drinks after the show."

"Drinks? On a weeknight?" Bastien recoiled slightly. "Jonah Penrose, you dirty stop-out."

"Er, Jonah, Bastien?" Omari snapped his fingers at them from where he was leading the others onstage. "If you two pull a hamstring because you've not warmed up, don't come bitching to me about it."

Bastien pouted his lips and, rather dramatically, tucked a strand of his hair behind his ear before going back over to stretch with the group. Jonah followed behind him and joined in with some of the casual conversations floating about as bodies moved effortlessly across the stage with measured lunges and deep breaths. When the vocal warm-ups started, his eyes found Dexter, and the man looked back at him, a smile on his lips as they climbed the vocal scales with ease, the group surrounding them creating a beautiful harmony, something far too good for a simple practice. And then in a blink he was in his dressing room, Sherrie flittering in and out, makeup brushes floating through the air with hair spray, and needles and thread working through parts of costumes. A glossy program found its way into his hands, and he thumbed through the pages of the photographs, all of them beautiful, even Bastien who didn't have a double chin in any of them. Bennie-with-the-bad-lens did good. He stopped on a picture of Dexter, his Trojan armor exposing his toned arms and the tanned skin he still had all those weeks ago. He stood on one side of the stage while Jonah stood on the other, their eyes intense, a rivalry brimming from the page. Hector vs Achilles. Dexter vs Jonah. Tonight, London would finally get to see the rivalry they'd been waiting for.

The fight was everything. The build of the music, the words sung in breathless agony, the sheer multitude of silence from the audience before the gasp as Jonah plunged the knife into the blood pack on Dexter's neck and the red liquid pumped out over Jonah's hands and cascaded across Dexter's cheeks and collarbones. He died so beautifully. Jonah stood, hands trembling as he threw the dagger down on the floor beside Dexter's motionless body and he glared up at the wall of Troy, just to the left of the box containing royalty, who he didn't recognize at all, a D-list member of the family, and the stage turned to darkness as the revolve changed scenes. As soon as they were out of sight Dexter stood, the stage blood trickling down his arms and dropping from the tips of his fingers, and Jonah blindly followed him into the wings.

It took three steps for them to lose themselves behind a curtain and then Dexter's lips found Jonah's, the movement quick, so fleeting it might have not even happened, the only evidence of it a bloody fingerprint pressed against Jonah's collarbone. All the air in Jonah's lungs halted in his chest then exhaled in a shaky breath as Dexter moved from backstage to the dressing rooms. The desire to follow him pinched at Jonah's soles, his feet telling him to move, to go chase his lips and kiss him until neither of them could remember their names, but his head knew he needed to stay. He had a wooden horse to build, Trojans to kill, and deaths to avenge. Oh, and he needed to die too. All in a good day's work.

When Dexter stepped out onto the stage for the final bows, the audience erupted in the most deafening round of applause Jonah ever heard. And he couldn't blame them; Dexter stole the show. He took a character who was previously played as a villain and turned him into as much of a hero as Achilles. He gave him warmth, with a history and a future he would never get to see. The outpouring of admiration from the audience made tears form in Jonah's eyes, the standing ovation the longest they'd ever received, even longer than the performance after the Olivier wins. But he knew the tears didn't come solely from happiness, he knew they also came from the crippling realization that Colbie could see how the audience adored Dexter; they clapped for the company, but the loudest cheers came only for him. She would realize she'd made a fatal mistake in casting Jonah; she'd witnessed how Dexter commanded the stage, how he entranced hundreds of people and would now do so night after night while Jonah faded into the background.

God, jealously was the most frustrating and unpleasant thing in the world, and Jonah knew just how ugly it made him look.

He needed to shake it off.

Dexter didn't answer the door. Jonah knocked, once, twice, three times before giving up and going back to his own dressing room to grab his bag. He let his eyes linger on his headphones, not knowing if he should put them on and escape from the crowds outside or if he should embrace the love beyond the doors and pretend they wanted to see him as much as they wanted to see Dexter. By the door, three members of the security team were talking with some of the cast, giving them a warning before finally letting them pass. Sherrie stood there with Romana, their fingers laced together, light words spoken beneath coy smiles. Jonah grinned at them and gave Sherrie a thumbs-up behind Romana's back, which only made his friend's cheeks turn the same pink as her hair. As Jonah stepped outside, he was surprised not only to see Dexter already out there but also metal barriers lining the pathway from the door, holding back the many people standing waiting for them to come out. He signed programs and felt more than relieved people were pleased to see him. Dexter pushed him to perform better onstage, he made Jonah's Achilles into something it wasn't before; so instead of being jealous he needed to be thankful. But looking over at Dexter and the absurd amount of roses being handed to him made his eye twitch slightly.

"Need a hand?" he asked, catching up to him as Dexter tried to juggle at least thirty of the flowers while still trying to sign programs.

"Oh," Dexter said airily as Jonah took some from him and freed up one of his hands. "You're great, thanks."

"Is it true you're dating?" one girl asked, smirking at them both before laughing and cupping her mouth with her hand. "Oh my God, I can't believe I just asked that, sorry."

"He wishes." Dexter winked back at her.

"Hey!" Jonah laughed and nudged him with his elbow with a fond smile. He turned from the crowd and leaned in to Dexter to whisper in his ear. "I'm gonna wait over there, I'll look after your flowers, sir." He nodded toward the wall where the barriers tapered off.

He fished his headphones from his pocket, managing not to drop a single rose, and placed them over his head before walking away, smiling at some more fans who were respectful enough to leave him alone as he leaned against the wall. He watched Dexter, his interactions with the audience effortless. The man was the definition of a social butterfly, a genuine star. The green monster bubbling away inside his chest calmed down; Dexter needed this, after the heartbreak of losing a role he so clearly loved. This would help heal him and bring back his shine.

With his eyes on Dexter, Jonah didn't see the figure approaching from his right until they were practically standing in front of him. He opened his mouth, ready to ask whoever it was to politely give him some space, but the words died in the back of his throat as he recognized the man standing before him.

Jet-black hair. Piercing blue eyes. Wes.

"Oh, Wes, hi, I — " The words he managed to find were torn from him. It took Jonah a few seconds to register what happened. The pain shot through his left cheek then circled his eye socket before going numb for several seconds, before bursting into tiny specs of electricity that burned his skin.

Wes had hit him.

Jonah braced himself for another punch, Wes's hand pulling back into a fist again, before movement scurried around them, the sound of radios buzzing in his ears. The security team. Someone pulled him along the barriers, back toward the stage door where people gasped and cried out his name before angrily shouting back at Wes as security guards swarmed him. Jonah's body trembled as hands touched him. He didn't know who was there, who the voices belonged to, the ringing in his head louder than the world swirling beneath his feet. Something hot and wet trickled down his chin, and he raised his fingers to his nose only to pull them back and see they were covered with blood.

His blood.

"Shit, is my nose broken?" His voice sounded shrill, and a cloud of pink embraced him and ushered him back into his dressing room. Bubble gum. Glitter. Sherrie.

"Babe," she said seriously, crouching down in front of him after forcing him to sit in his chair. "Babe, look at me, can you see me?" Her face blurred as he tried to focus. "The first aiders are on their way."

"What the fuck happened?" The next voice came from Colbie, her hair burning fire as she screeched in the hallway. "Has someone called the police? We had royalty here tonight; we can't have a fucking security issue!" Her voice faded as quickly as it arrived.

More hands and more faces appeared, Bastien's face pale, tears tracking his cheeks as he dabbed a tissue carefully at Jonah's nose. Omari and Romana hovered in the corner of the room whispering to each other while glancing anxiously over at Jonah's face. At some point, he thought he saw Evie's blunt haircut out of the corner of his eye, but he couldn't be sure. Then, of course, there was Dexter, with his skin flushed red, hair ruffled, shirt unkempt and speckled with drops of blood, typing something furiously into his phone.

"What a prick!" Dexter paced in the room, rage clearly having taken hold of him, and if Jonah wasn't in so much pain he might have found Dexter's protective side remarkably hot, but his nose hurt and he was pretty sure someone was pressing a million tiny needles into his cheek.

"Jonah." This voice he didn't recognize; the face he knew in passing, but their voice? No. But they sounded kind, and they pressed something cold against his face, and honestly, he could have made out with the fifty-something-year-old woman because her cold pack made him feel like he was in heaven. "He should be fine," she said, talking to the others and not to him. "But someone should stay with him. Jonah, do you live alone?"

"Yeah."

"Is there someone you can stay with? I have a pamphlet about head injuries with signs to look out for, and you need to be with someone." She waved a white booklet in front of his face, then placed it in his lap.

"He can come home with me," Bastien said.

"Or me," Omari chimed in. "He needs some TLC on that face because it is going to look hideous tomorrow. Don't worry, Jonah, I have a cooling mask in the freezer. We can pop it on as soon as we get inside."

"Well, actually." Dexter looked at them both. "I have a spare room at mine, and we are both in Camden. I can get him home to get some clothes then take him back to mine. If . . . if that's okay with you, Jonah?"

He'd never felt so much like a child in all his life. To make matters worse, all he wanted to do was cry and call his mum. Oh, God, he would have to tell his mum about this; she'd find out some way or other if he didn't; but not now, he could wait and worry her in the morning instead. He nodded at Dexter and saw the way Bastien narrowed his eyes at the man, forever his best friend, forever protective of him.

"It's fine, Bash," Jonah said, wrapping his hand around the ice pack and sighing. "I'm fine."

"What about the cold face mask?" Omari asked. "Seriously, Jonah, you need a face mask."

"I'm sure I have something he can use," Dexter said, though he didn't sound entirely convincing.

"Who even was that who hit you?" Sherrie asked. "Some random?"

"No," Dexter said with a shake of his head. "Jonah, was it who I think it was?" Jonah nodded, and Dexter's top lip curled slightly. "I'm actually gonna step out and just chat to Colbie and Evie about who he is."

Jonah started to protest, but a sharp pain in his head told him to shut up. Why, oh, why couldn't whoever planned the trajectory of his life give him a Goddamned break?

NINETEEN

"Do you remember how oranges taste?"

—"What Do We Fight For?" *The Wooden Horse*, Act One

Jonah clicked on the light in his kitchen. The bulb flickered before bursting into a white glow, and he squinted at the intrusion from the darkness. Dexter wasted no time opening cupboard doors, raiding Jonah's belongings, before he found a glass, filled it with water from the tap, and handed it to him. Jonah's face didn't hurt as much now, the painkillers Sherrie stuffed into his mouth before she left the theatre hand in hand with Romana finally taking effect. Dexter watched him, shaking his head each time Jonah tried to put the glass down, insisting he finish every last drop.

"You've got to stay hydrated," he said when Jonah finally drank that last drop. "Omari said if I didn't have a stupid face mask, I needed to at least keep you hydrated. What stuff do you need to take to mine? Pajamas, toothbrush, clothes for tomorrow, anything else?" His words were loud. Their taxi ride to the house had been filled with silence as they passed the gorgeous shadows of London, and now everything, including Dexter, seemed oddly deafening.

"I, um, actually I just want to stay here." Castle Road pulled him into its arms the moment he climbed out of the Uber and it saw the bruising on his face. He didn't want to leave its embrace; he could fall into a dreamless sleep and wake to find the world fuzzy and numb.

"Caroline told me you couldn't be left alone."

Jonah pinched the skin between his eyebrows, grimacing at the slight jolt of pain but breathing through it. "I honestly just want to get into my own bed and forget this night ever happened."

"Well. I could sleep on the sofa, if that's okay?"

Jonah dropped his hand and studied Dexter's face. He knew Dexter wouldn't agree to leave him alone. "Fine. Yeah. I've some clothes you can sleep in."

"Can I ask you something?" Dexter asked, filling the glass up with water again and handing it back to Jonah. "Why did he do that? Wes? Because he still thinks you were sleeping with his boyfriend?"

Jonah gave a one-shouldered shrug. "I guess? Edward won't have admitted the truth; he's a coward. He's been texting me, begging me to meet up with him. He even came to the theatre, all while still posting loved-up photos of him and Wes online."

"Did you tell the police that?"

God. The police. He hadn't wanted to talk to them; he wanted to hide himself away in his dressing room, but Colbie insisted. The officer looked at him with trepidation behind her eyes, which did nothing to calm Jonah's nerves. When she talked to him, he let out a laugh and her brow furrowed, trepidation turning to concern, and he didn't tell her all that was going through his mind was that his mum's friend recently spoke to an officer and had to describe a penis. It would bring up too many unnecessary questions.

"Yeah, of course," Jonah said. "But if Wes thinks there's something going on, then . . . maybe that's why he did it? I don't know. Either way, I'm so done with being involved with Edward. This just put the final nail in the coffin."

"You're trembling," Dexter said, looking at the glass of water in Jonah's hand as the water rippled between his shaking fingers. "It's okay, you know, you're home now. And you know they won't allow that guy anywhere near you or the theatre again."

"I just feel humiliated." He placed the drink down on the counter. "He did that to me in front of all of those people. And . . . fuck this was *your* night, and I've ruined it."

"You've not ruined anything." Dexter took Jonah's hands into his and held them firmly. "This wasn't your fault."

Jonah could barely look at him. "Let's get you those clothes, yeah? Come with me."

He led the way upstairs to his small bedroom and even smaller bathroom. Dexter peered around the space, taking in each little detail, and Jonah wondered if his home was what Dexter imagined, if he'd even imagined what Jonah's bedroom might be like and if the reality lived up to his expectations.

"Here," Jonah said, reaching into his dresser to pull out a T-shirt and shorts. "You can wear these."

Dexter took the clothes from him and balled them up in his hands. "Jonah. I'm so sorry."

"Why?" Jonah asked as Dexter looked to the window. "Jesus Christ, him hitting me wasn't something to do with you, was it?"

"What?" Dexter's head snapped back to him. "No! I'm just sorry it happened to you. I'm sorry you've been hurt. I wish I could make it better."

"You bringing me home is enough, Dex."

"It's not, though, is it? Are you sure you don't want to go to the hospital?"

Jonah shook his head, then sat on the edge of his bed. "No. It's fine. I'm sure it looks worse than it actually is." He fiddled with the duvet as he spoke. "Will you stay in here with me tonight? You don't have to. I just... I really don't want to be alone."

"Of course," Dexter said without hesitation. "I'll be honest. I would rather be here so I can keep an eye on you." He tapped the pamphlet he still held in his hand with the clothes. "Can't see if you're unresponsive if I'm downstairs, can I?"

Jonah smiled, the change of expression painful but fleeting. "Can't see if I'm unresponsive if you're asleep either."

"I can stay up."

"I'm not having you watch me while I sleep."

Dexter took a seat beside him. "Yeah. I guess that's bordering on creepy, isn't it?" He brushed Jonah's hair away from his face, tucking a curl behind his ear carefully. "Even with a bruised and bloodied face you're still hot as fuck, did you know that?"

"Oh, shut up." Jonah smacked a hand against his chest and got up. "I'm going to clean myself up."

His reflection didn't shock him as much as he thought it might. Once he washed the dried blood from around his nose and chin, the bruising beneath his eye and across his cheekbone just looked like someone swiped dark colors across his face. Makeup for Halloween. He changed into his pajamas, then went back into the bedroom to see Dexter already in the clothes he gave him, sitting awkwardly on the end of the bed.

"I didn't know which side was yours," he said, voice nervous.

"Oh." Jonah looked to the side that once belonged to Edward. Tonight, it would no longer be his. "I sleep by the window. That way, if someone breaks in, they'll kill you first because you're closest to the door."

"Charming," Dexter scoffed as he moved to the side Jonah allocated him and pulled back the cover before a look of alarm crept over his face. "Do you mind if I sleep under the covers with you? I can sleep on top, if you like, but I get cold."

"Bloody hell, Dexter, stop being so polite." Jonah got himself into bed and watched as Dexter slid in then pulled the cover up to his chin stiffly. "Wow. Dex. You look comfy."

"I'm sorry. I don't know how to act." Dexter laughed. "I'm lying in Jonah Penrose's bed, and it feels like . . . fuck." He groaned, then pressed the heels of his hands into his eyes. "I've been thinking about tonight and all the things I want to do to you if we ended up in bed together, and now you're hurt and this isn't how I thought our first date would go."

"Hey." Jonah reached across and took his hands away from his eyes. "The date hadn't started, so it doesn't count. And I am *very* interested in finding out what these things you've been thinking of are."

Dexter turned on his side to face him, and Jonah did the same. Their knees touched beneath the covers, skin on skin, and Jonah wished stupid Wes hadn't hit him and made his face totally un-kissable and he wished they hadn't wasted so much time being horrible to each other because they could have been in bed, like this, much sooner.

"Tell me," he whispered as Dexter trailed his fingers down Jonah's bare arm. "Tell me everything."

"I wanted to kiss you." His fingers found their way to his collarbone. "All along here." This thumb caressed the side of his neck. "And here."

Jonah swallowed. "And then?"

Dexter's voice went low in his throat. "I want to kiss every inch of you. Run my tongue along your skin." He dropped his hand to Jonah's leg and ghosted his touch to his inner thigh. "Feel how soft you are here."

Jonah shifted, the pajama shorts he wore suddenly too hot and horrendously uncomfortable as Dexter bit down on his bottom lip, his face close, agonizingly close. "I've wanted to feel you grow hard for me, then taste you by taking you into my mouth while looking at your pretty face and hearing you moan while gripping your thighs." Dexter placed his hand on Jonah's hip and gently urged him closer, their legs intertwined now, breaths tickling into each other's skin.

Jonah let out a quiet moan, his eyes on Dexter's lips, the thought of him taking Jonah's length into his mouth driving him wild. Dexter's touch didn't leave Jonah's skin as he worked his fingers down his thigh again, then hooked Jonah's leg over his waist. Jonah could feel how hard Dexter was, their bodies pressed together, and he wanted him just as bad, his own erection straining from inside his pants, the heat between them intoxicating.

"Please," Jonah murmured, though what he was asking for he couldn't say. He would take anything.

"I don't want to hurt you," Dexter said, the cadence of his voice changing to that of concern. Jonah knew Dexter wanted to kiss him, he could practically feel his lips on his, but he could also feel the dull ache in the side of his face, and he tilted his head to the side.

"You won't," he said, moving from Dexter to lie flat on his back, resting his head on the pillow, exposing his neck, showing him where he could touch without repercussions. "I want you."

"Are you sure?"

Jonah turned his head back to look at him. "I am. Are you?"

Dexter answered in movement. He straddled Jonah with ease, the roles reversed, and leaned down to press his lips against the fluttering pulse point in his neck. "Fuck, yes."

Jonah arched his back as Dexter continued to work his lips against his skin, his hands dipping beneath the hem of his shirt before bringing it up over Jonah's head. Dexter wasted no time in running his tongue along Jonah's collarbone, his teeth just grazing the skin, his left hand cupping the side of Jonah's neck. Jonah's fingers buried themselves into Dexter's blond hair, small noises escaping his mouth as the other man took his time in moving painstakingly slowly down his body. The attention he gave to Jonah's skin seemed almost sinful, his tongue and lips tingling down his chest to his navel. Dexter seemed intent on killing him by acting as if time didn't exist, the moments stretching on for eternity, and Jonah knew they were in no race, but he was needy, his body ready and wanting.

"Dex," he whimpered, and he allowed himself to feel embarrassed at just how desperate the name sounded. "Please."

Dexter looked up at him, hazel eyes dilated, as if high on Jonah, and, fuck, he looked gorgeous. He half expected some cocky reply, a question about what exactly Jonah was begging for, but Dexter didn't say a word. No, instead he sat up and ran his fingers along the waistband of Jonah's pajama shorts, a smug grin on his face as if he knew something Jonah didn't.

"Do you have any idea how long I've wanted to do this?" Without the words to speak, Jonah shook his head in response and Dexter bit down on the side of his bottom lip as he looked at him. "Tell me something about you I don't know."

"Dexter," Jonah moaned, bucking his hips up impatiently. "Why ask me that now?"

Dexter trailed his finger down the center of Jonah's chest. "Tell me something I don't know about you. Something I can't find out online. Go on."

Jonah placed his hand over Dexter's, stilling him, not able to handle his touch if Dexter was in the mood to torment him. "I'm boring. You know everything."

Dexter raised a very unimpressed eyebrow and pouted his lips. "Well, I can't possibly have sex with someone boring."

"I . . . had an imaginary friend as a kid," Jonah said, scrambling around in the recesses of his mind for any kind of fact and for some bizarre reason settling on that.

"Yeah? What was their name?"

"Macbeth."

"As in, *the* Macbeth?" Dexter nudged Jonah's pants farther down his hipbones.

"No, just, his name was Macbeth, and whenever I did something bad and my parents would yell at me, I blamed it on him."

"Naughty Macbeth," Dexter said with a grin.

"Fuck's sake, you're driving me insane." Jonah sat up, shifting Dexter on his lap, hands on his waist, Dexter's thighs either side of his.

"It's what I do," Dexter said, pushing him back down then shuffling down his body, slipping his fingers beneath Jonah's waistband to remove his pants.

Jonah shuddered at the cool rush of air caressing his skin, his body so hot, painfully so, and he felt exposed being completely naked in front of Dexter, but he didn't care, he wanted Dexter to see him; he wanted Dexter to look at him and touch him and do whatever thoughts had crossed his mind when he imagined this moment. And Dexter took him all in, his eyes scanning Jonah's body, bottom lip working between his teeth before he took off his own top, his hair ruffling, making him look delightfully unkempt. He lowered himself down again and pressed light kisses on the inside of Jonah's thighs before taking his length into his mouth.

And. Fuck. Jonah's breath came out ragged. He let Dexter settle between his thighs, his fingers in his hair again, gentle, not urging him to do more, not trying to set a pace; he just wanted to touch him. Dexter moaned around him, the noise insatiable, and Jonah let his head fall back on his pillow as he looked up at the ceiling; if he looked at Dexter with his lips wrapped around him and eyelashes fanned beautifully against his cheeks, he wouldn't last a minute.

A gap in the bedroom curtains allowed the light from the streetlamps outside to filter into the room, the warm orange glow shimmering over Dexter's skin, bathing him in sheets of pure gold. Jonah decided the next time they did this, if there was a next time, and he bloody hoped there would be, then he would light candles beforehand. He wanted to see the light of the fire dance across Dexter's features, illuminating him like a casque of treasure, glistening, each bead of his sweat a diamond pressed into his skin. Outside, Camden faded into a muted silence and all Jonah could hear were the greedy moans coming from the back of Dexter's throat and his own small gasps and needy utterances of pleasure.

The pain in Jonah's face took second place to the tingling in his spine and the tension building deep in his core. He allowed himself to look down at Dexter again, his hazel eyes looking up at him, dark and filled with a cloud of desire. Jonah shuddered as he flicked his tongue around him and arched his back, fingers slipping through the strands of Dexter's hair as he could feel the heat rising inside of him.

"Dex," he panted, his own curls sticking to his forehead. "I can't . . . please, I just—"

"It's okay," Dexter said, taking his mouth off him for a moment. "Come undone for me." He licked his lips, smirk on his face, and fucking hell, Jonah wanted to kiss him, but then Dexter licked a line up Jonah's length and . . . well Dexter's mouth clearly had better things to do. He kept his eyes on Jonah the whole time, hands wrapped around his thighs, lifting them onto his shoulders as he lay between his legs. He looked perfect, so bloody perfect, and as Jonah reached his orgasm Dexter moaned loudly, the sound so utterly sensual Jonah knew nothing could ever compare to how hot he sounded.

Jonah didn't know how many minutes passed. He found himself stuck in a contented haze, his body exhausted, limbs heavy. Dexter kissed his way back up Jonah's chest, then found his neck and groaned as he placed a last kiss just beneath his ear.

"Fucking hell," Jonah murmured, before running a hand down Dexter's left bicep. "I need to make you feel as good as you just made me feel."

Dexter lay down beside him and wound his fingers through Jonah's curls. "You don't have to, you're hurt."

"I'm okay," Jonah said with a laugh, though the movement did, in fact, make the skin around his nose and eye sting. "I have some rather fabulous hands, you know."

"Is that so?"

Jonah hummed and ran his fingers along Dexter's collarbone. "I do. Want to see what I can do with them?" Dexter shivered, goose bumps cascading over his skin, and he nodded, eyes dark, lustful, and Jonah knew their night was far from over.

TWENTY

"Look down, the bodies weave a path to the gates, look down, and build, we ride upon their souls."

—"We Build," *The Wooden Horse*, Act Two

Official Statement from Colbie Paris Theatre Group and The Persephone Theatre

It is with deep regret that tonight's performance of *The Wooden Horse* has been canceled due to a very serious incident that occurred after Tuesday night's performance. We do not tolerate any form of abuse to our hardworking cast and crew, and the safety of our company is our top priority. We are evaluating our security protocols today and hope to resume performances for both the matinee and evening shows on Thursday. However, we've made the tough decision to close the Persephone stage door to the public. We would like to take this opportunity to remind audiences that interactions at stage door have always been at the discretion of the cast or crew member and it never has and never will be an obligation. For ticket holders affected by tonight's cancellation please contact your point of sale to rebook or request a refund.

Jonah stared at the screen of his phone, or, more precisely, the picture of himself displayed on the screen of his phone. Eighteen minutes ago, Dexter posted a photograph of Jonah taken during the rehearsal week, his hair a curled mess, face flushed but smiling as he sat on the floor, cross-legged, with a bottle of water in his hands. He remembered Dexter taking it. His phone constantly out during rehearsals, the man obsessed with taking the most mundane photographs, this being one of them. But it wasn't the photo that caused Jonah to stare; it was the caption beneath it:

> @Itsjonahpenrose I promise to always make you smile like this, even on the days when smiling is the last thing you want to do.

Jonah glanced at the bathroom door. Dexter had been in there a while, the sound of the shower water hitting the tiles on the wall oddly comforting, and something stirred inside him knowing Dexter made the post while naked in his bathroom, his clothes still in a heap on Jonah's floor. Part of him knew the caption came from the agreement with Colbie, to keep up a façade, but after last night, did the façade even exist anymore? Jonah didn't want to ponder the lines between fantasy and reality, but surely things were different now, which meant he could absolutely read into the words. And read into them he would.

The comments beneath the picture were filled with nothing but love. It didn't take long for rumors to spread about what happened the night before, the statement from Colbie and the theatre adding fuel to the fire of wild tales circulating on the internet. Jonah untagged himself from a couple of photos posted of him being ushered back into the theatre, his nose bleeding, head down, with security trying to shield him from the crowd. He knew photos would find their way online, but why someone felt the need to tag him in them was beyond him. Reminders of the night someone punched him in the face were hardly on the top of his wish list.

The comments, however, were welcome. The incident seemed to have sparked a debate about the expectations of actors when it came to leaving theatres, if they should be left to finish work and go home unbothered or if they should always stop to talk to the people waiting. It only took a quick glance online to see the discussion swirling around other cast members from different productions who shared their own positive and horrifically negative experiences at stage doors. The casual sexual groping and intrusive grabbing seemed alarmingly common.

Jonah flinched as the comments on his phone vanished, revealing instead the little phone icon shaking in the center, just below Edward's name. The urge to fling his phone out of his window crossed his mind, though he knew simply blocking him would be the easier option, but Jonah lived for dramatics and his phone shattering on the pavement outside seemed the more fitting option. However, to save himself the hassle and expense of getting a new phone, he answered it, surprising himself at how quickly he came to the decision, and placed the phone against the good, unharmed side of his face.

"What the hell do you want?" Jonah asked, impressed with the authoritative tone in his voice.

"What happened?" Edward sounded tired. Jonah had heard him speak with the same exasperation after endless nights of staying late to work at the office, or, now that he thought about it, more likely staying late to conduct his affair with Wes.

"Your boyfriend thought it would be a good idea to assault me when I left work last night."

Edward groaned. "He went through my phone and saw my messages to you and went off on one. He left, and I didn't know where he went. I assumed to the office or a bar or something. I never . . . I never expected him to go find you . . . Can I come over? I want to make sure you're okay."

Jonah pulled the phone away from his ear and stared at the screen. He could still hear Edward talking, his monotonous tone going on and on and on until Jonah pressed the red phone icon and hung up on him. He swiftly blocked his number than deleted it from his contacts, then proceeded to block him on every form of social media and also went to the effort of blacklisting his email address. He could hear Dexter singing softly from behind the bathroom door, the shower no longer on, his voice quiet but clear. He knew the song—"Goodbye Yellow Brick Road" by Elton John—and Jonah placed his phone down on his bedside table as the song transported him back to the sandy tides of St. Ives.

In the summer months, the large glass doors leading from his father's study opened out onto the back garden. Jonah dug holes in the vegetable patch, his little yellow spade turning over the earth as the sound of his dad's records playing from inside trickled out into the balmy air. He remembered plucking sugar snap peas from where they grew on the trellis beside the green garden shed and crunching them in his mouth as David Bowie, Elton John, and Phil Collins became the soundtrack of his youth. He wondered what his dad would say if he saw the bruises on his face, though he knew he wouldn't have suggested hitting Wes back. No. Bill Penrose prided himself on being an assassin with words, never with physical violence.

"Oh, you're awake," Dexter said as he emerged from the bathroom in a cloud of hot steam, Jonah's towel wrapped around his waist.

"It's all right, just use all my hot water. Help yourself to all the food in the kitchen too. I've got some change in a jar somewhere, might as well take that too."

"You can't take a man to bed, then not let him have a shower in the morning. It's common courtesy. And, yes, I used your shampoo." Dexter ran his hand through his wet hair, rubbing his fingers through it, causing droplets to trickle onto the carpet. "How are you feeling this morning?"

Jonah shrugged and shuffled himself up the bed so he could sit with his back against the headboard. "Fine? My nose hurts."

"I should warn you, it . . . doesn't look great."

"My face?"

"Yeah."

"Thanks for that, Dex." Jonah rolled his eyes as Dexter sat himself on the edge of the bed. "Though I guess I don't have to cake myself in makeup given the performance tonight is canceled."

"Yeah," Dexter said somewhat skeptically. "I saw the post. I messaged a few people, and no one else has heard from Evie or anyone else. It's kinda weird they've not told us directly."

"They will. It's still early." He watched as Dexter took the towel from his lap then slid back under the covers. "I liked your post."

"Oh. Yeah, I probably should have asked before, but you were asleep."

"More trip-gate damage control?"

"No," Dexter said quickly. "No. I wanted to post that."

"It was kinda . . ."

"Shit, you hated it, didn't you? Do you want me to delete it?" He quickly reached for his phone, hands fumbling as he smacked his thumbs against the screen.

"No." Jonah laughed. "I'm just saying . . . promising to always make me smile? That's an awfully big commitment."

The color drained from Dexter's face. "So, I've frightened you off by being too keen?"

Jonah cocked his head as he looked at him. "Did I say that?"

"I'm not asking for commitment, you know that, right? I know this—" he gestured between them "—is just a casual thing."

Jonah felt winded. He hadn't thought about what he might call the relationship with Dexter, but he certainly never thought it would be something just casual. He didn't think Dexter would refer to him as his boyfriend anytime soon, but he also didn't want to think of Dexter flirting with anyone else either. He knew the irony of his thoughts; it wasn't long ago he couldn't stand the guy, his very presence an annoyance, and now, well, now he didn't like the thought of being something unimportant to him.

"Do you want it to be casual?" Jonah asked, his hands gripping the sheet on the bed beneath the duvet.

Dexter tipped his head from side to side, as if the movement helped him consider his options. "I think casual is a good place to start. I mean, I'm not looking for anything more than that. I'm sure you're not, either, right?"

Jonah shrugged then shook his head before nodding slightly, unsure if he was agreeing or simply covering all his bases because it was the only thing he could think of doing.

"So, you won't freak out if I flirt with someone else?" Jonah asked.

"I . . . I don't know. I've never done casual before," Dexter admitted.

"Me neither."

"I just . . . don't want there to be too much pressure? We work together, so we need to be careful about this. From my experience, feelings in the workplace can create complications."

"You've dated someone you worked with before?"

Dexter nodded and looked down at his phone. "Yeah, it all came to a head when I was in *West Side Story*. Henrik Larsson made my life a misery."

"Oh . . ." Jonah knew Henrik; he'd met him at a couple of industry events, and Sherrie sometimes invited him out for drinks with them. He always seemed tired, eyes sunken in his skin, likely exhausted from the phenomenal choreography he'd been performing for the past few years in *West Side*. "I didn't know you were in that."

"I was Riff."

"What?" Jonah frowned. "Isn't that who Henrik plays now? I didn't even know you were in it."

Dexter looked from his phone to Jonah and raised his eyebrows. "I was in it when it first opened. Henrik took over the role from me when I left. He was part of the ensemble before that. And the only reason I didn't look to extend my contract was because he made the atmosphere backstage so toxic I couldn't stand to be there any longer."

"What a bastard."

Dexter smiled. "Exactly."

"Was . . . was Riff a dream role of yours?" Jonah asked somewhat carefully, not wanting to add any salt to the wounds, but also genuinely intrigued.

"No. The role was only meant to be short-term anyway, just a six-month contract because . . . well I thought I would get the Achilles role." He cleared his throat awkwardly. "Riff was great to play, but I have my heart set on another Sondheim character."

"Yeah? Who?"

"George."

Jonah raised his eyebrows and smiled brightly. "From *Sunday in the Park with George*?" Dexter nodded. "I could see you doing that. Maybe when you're older, though?"

"Well, I'm hardly getting any younger. I'm thirty-three."

"No. You're not."

"I think I know how old I am, Jonah."

"Then you're older than me." It made no sense. Dexter's skin glowed with the youth of someone in their twenties, not someone in their thirties. "I'm aging terribly," Jonah groaned and went to wipe his hands over his face, but stopped, feeling the sting on his nose as soon as his fingers brushed his skin.

"You're gorgeous." Dexter took his hands into his. "Tell me. What's your dream role?"

"Emcee."

"From *Cabaret*? Haven't you been in that show before?"

"Yeah. But I played Cliff. I didn't even audition for Emcee, didn't think I could pull it off. But now . . . now I think I could."

"It can be a pretty dark role."

"It's perfect," Jonah said, as Dexter gave his hands an encouraging squeeze. "If you have the right director and production team, you can make that character whatever you want it to be. Playful, sinister, sexual, a mix of all those. And the songs, Emcee has the best songs ever, the opening number alone is one of the best pieces of—" The sound of his phone vibrating cut them off. Jonah reluctantly peered at the device, half expecting to see Edward had somehow bypassed all his blocking, but instead he saw his mum. "Sorry, I better take this." He pried his hands out of Dexter's grasp and went to get out of bed, but stopped, aware of how naked he was, which made Dexter snort from the back of his throat.

"Dude, I literally had your dick in my mouth last night, don't be shy now."

Jonah scowled at him before grabbing his phone and darting into the bathroom while Dexter wolf whistled behind him.

"Mum, hey, you're calling early."

"Gilly from down the road popped down with my milk because the milkman left it at her door again and told me that her daughter Kelsey, you remember her, the one with ginger hair who you used to play hide-and-seek with on the beach when you were kids, you remember, well, she told me Kelsey said it was all over social media that someone was attacked in your show last night. And I said I didn't know about it, and she looked it up on her phone, and there was a photograph of you with blood all over your face." His mum spoke with such speed he could barely keep up. "And I had to stand there looking stupid because of course you haven't told me anything. and then she said oh no it's your son, and then there were loads of other photos of you being escorted by security guards."

"Mum. It happened after the show," Jonah said slowly. "It was late, and I didn't want to worry you. Everything's fine. It isn't as bad as the pictures look, and I was taken care of straight away."

"You're not hurt?"

"Well. I've got a bruise," he said as he looked at his face in the mirror and grimaced. "But nothing serious, Mum. Please, don't worry." He turned his head to the side to see a red mark on his neck left behind by Dexter's mouth. "How are you?"

"I was fine until this morning. No parent should ever have to find out their child was assaulted secondhand like that."

"I was going to call you this morning, I promise. But it's still early and, like I said, I didn't want to wake you up and worry you last night. I was taken care of, there's really nothing for you to be upset over."

"Nicola's son lives in London, and he calls every day to see how she is, and you never call me. You never come and see me. I sometimes think I'm just going to rot here alone. You've abandoned me."

The words hurt. He knew he'd been there, maybe not physically, but he'd done all he could from afar and returned when it mattered most, but now wasn't the time to argue. He recalled the conversation he had with Aunt Penny, her words, asking if his mum sounded drunk when he spoke to her in the middle of the night. She didn't sound tipsy now, thank God given the early hour of the day, but something still played in the back of his mind. A small worry. The seed started to sprout. "Mum. Have you been drinking?"

She laughed, the sound not happy but filled with something different, a sadness Jonah couldn't describe. "Don't be ridiculous."

"Mum," Jonah pleaded. "Tell me what's going on."

"You've let me down."

"Do you really believe that?"

She paused. "No," she said, followed by a heavy sigh. "I'm sorry. I just... I heard what happened, and it scared me. I love you, I love you so much, and you're so far away, Jonah. I can't look after you."

"I love you, too, Mum. You can come here to visit. You know that, right? Or I can come up again soon. Do you think that would help?"

"Maybe getting away from here for a couple of days would do me good... but your dad, what if... what if something happens and I'm not here?" He heard a glass shattering across the floor. "Shit. Sausage, I've got to go. Don't let anyone else hit you, okay? I love you." She hung up before he could say goodbye. He stared at his phone, a dreadful feeling of unease caressing his skin, pushing its way inside of him to wrap around the ache in his chest.

When Jonah went back into the bedroom, Dexter had left. He'd made the bed and folded the clothes he borrowed from Jonah and placed them on top of the dresser neatly, as if he'd never been there. Jonah dressed himself in a pair of loose cotton trousers and pulled on the first T-shirt he could find, then went downstairs to find Dexter pouring out two bowls of cereal.

"You really have a lot of gumption, you know," Jonah said, opening the cutlery drawer to get out two spoons. "Rummaging through my stuff to get food. Did your parents never teach you how to behave in other people's homes?"

"Well, my mum ran off with a man from Spain when I was three and my dad decided the stock market was more important than spending time with me, so I guess not." Dexter handed a bowl of cereal to Jonah with a grin. "That question backfired, didn't it, arsehole?"

Jonah snatched it from him, then slumped down at the table. "Sorry," he mumbled.

"Eh, don't worry." Dexter sat opposite him and shoved in a giant mouthful of cereal. "I have my dad coming to watch the show this Saturday night, actually. Can't wait for him to tell me how disappointed he is in me afterward."

"He doesn't like you working in the theatre industry?"

Dexter waggled his spoon in the air. " 'It's a bloody outrage!' " he said in a croaky voice Jonah could only assume was an impression of his father. "'You should work with numbers, not dance around on the stage like a pansy!'" Dexter laughed, then plonked the spoon back into the bowl. "Imagine how he reacted when I told him I was, actually, also a pansy."

Jonah shook his head with a disbelieving laugh. "Shit. Well. I'm sorry, that really sucks."

"How were your parents when you told them?"

"That I wanted to go into the theatre or that I was gay?"

Dexter laughed. "Both?"

"They were fine, actually, about both things. Maybe not so much the theatre stuff, as I was a typical theatre kid and constantly singing show tunes, which I think made them go a little insane. Unfortunately, the issues are only now cropping up." He forced himself to eat some cereal and grimaced as he chewed. "Not with me liking men, or being in the theatre, just other stuff. My dad's unwell and it's taking a toll on my mum and . . . well, I'm not there and the feeling of guilt is getting pretty overwhelming."

Dexter stirred his spoon around his milk and cereal. "You think they want you to go home and drop the life you have here?"

"No," Jonah said truthfully. "But it doesn't stop the worry. And Cornwall's hardly down the road. I can't just pop in on them."

"Then just do what you can," Dexter said, the solution simple, one Jonah was already doing. But it wasn't enough. "And let's get ice cream today so you can let all the shit that happened in the last twelve hours be forgotten for a while."

"You want to get ice cream with me?"

"Yeah," Dexter said with a smirk. "Or sorbet, if that's more your thing."

"Where do you want to go for ice cream?"

"The shop down the road sells it."

"Oh. Fancy. You do spoil me."

"And we can bring it back here and you can lick it off me."

"Deal." It was the quickest decision Jonah had ever made in his entire life.

TWENTY-ONE

"My body, I can feel it falling, turning to stars. I will be with you there, and no one can tear us apart."

—"Eternity," *The Wooden Horse*, Act Two

Melanie Cowperthwaite holed herself up in a tiny office in Richmond. Jonah hated going there; the minute he stepped off the tube the world changed from shades of gray to shining silver. Richmond exuded wealth, and no matter how nicely Jonah dressed he always knew he didn't belong there. Richmond had no time for boys from the coast who dreamed of sand between their toes. But Melanie called him, her voice filled with passionate concern, and when Melanie called and told him she needed a face-to-face meeting, he went.

Her office, up six flights of stairs with no elevator, welcomed whoever stepped inside with shades of peach and pink. A white fluffy computer chair sat behind a light oak desk, and there, sitting in it, was Melanie, tapping away enthusiastically on her laptop. She looked up as Jonah entered the room, the bright smile on her face fading as soon as she saw the bruises on his face.

"Jonah," she said in her rich Trinidadian accent. "What are we going to do with you?"

"You say that as if I did this to myself." He didn't wait for her to invite him to sit in the luminous pink chair opposite her desk, and instead made himself comfortable and crossed one leg over his lap casually. "And I'm starting to think I'm actually being held responsible for this?" The question came off the back of Melanie's call; not long after, he received a message, not even a call, from Evie telling him to take another day off to "get himself together."

"Colbie Paris is a witch," Melanie said, standing from her seat to go to the little coffee station she'd set up in the corner by the window. "I don't know why that woman thinks she's God's gift to the theatre. Seriously, people need to stop giving her awards. She's not *that* good. She called me late last night on my personal number saying she needed to speak urgently regarding you."

Jonah could feel the ground beneath him slowly sinking. "What did she say?"

"That the assault was because of personal issues in your life and that she is deeply unhappy you brought those troubles to the theatre," Melanie said as she poured them both a cup of tea. "And she wants you to take the rest of the week off and have a social media blackout for at least two weeks to let the drama subside so it doesn't overshadow Dexter Ellis joining the cast."

Jonah couldn't tell if the feeling brewing inside his chest came from rage or despair. "What happened wasn't my fault. I could never have known he would come to the theatre. I mean, I only met the guy once for about two minutes on the tube," he explained as he took the tea from Melanie.

"Like I said, she's a witch." Melanie sat back down and twirled one of her brown curls in her ring-adorned fingers. "I told her she can't control your social media, and the world doesn't revolve around Dexter Ellis. But, I do agree you should take a few days to recover from this." She made a vague gesture toward his face. "I will be honest with you, Jonah, I didn't like the way she spoke. So, it's time for me to ask you: Are you wanting to extend your contract there once this one has ended?"

Jonah hadn't allowed himself to consider life outside of *The Wooden Horse*; the thought of starting over again terrified him almost as much as being unemployed. But then, people didn't stay with shows forever. They moved on, they carved different paths for themselves, and he knew he would one day have to leave Achilles behind. He just didn't expect it to be so soon.

"I love the show. I love the people I work with. If they offered me another year's contract, then I would take it."

Melanie nodded, then sipped her tea. "Okay. If a contract renewal isn't on the table, would you want to take some time out or have something lined up?"

"Is there a chance my contract won't be renewed?" he asked. "Did Colbie imply that?"

"I think there's been a lot going on behind the scenes there since the moment you landed the role," Melanie admitted. "There's been a shit ton of drama surrounding Dexter Ellis and his insufferable agent, and his name being connected with the show again says a lot about what's going on with the big bosses. I think we need to make some smart moves here."

"What kind of smart moves?"

"I've got a few projects you've been invited to audition for," she said, tapping at something on her laptop then making a content noise from the back of her throat. "I think if things come through you are even remotely interested in, we should get you an audition. You know these things take months. Auditioning now would mean you're set up for when your contract ends."

The cup in Jonah's hands burned his palms, but he gripped it tighter as Achilles moved further and further away from him. "Well. What things have I been invited to audition for?"

"They're planning a revival of *Oklahoma*. They were keen to talk to me about you putting yourself forward for that. Then there's *Crazy for You*, which I actually think you'd be perfect for. You'd be a brilliant Bobby."

Jonah raised his tea to his lips and swallowed a mouthful despite the liquid scalding the back of his throat. "Um," he said, grimacing slightly as the drink made its way down his esophagus. "What role are they thinking for *Oklahoma*?"

"Curly."

"Then, no, he's a dick."

Melanie laughed, the sound melodic. "Fair enough. What about *Crazy for You* then?"

"Sure." Jonah nodded, gripping the cup even tighter. "If you think there's a strong possibility I won't get a new contract for *The Wooden Horse*."

Her smile faded, leaving a grim expression in its wake. "She didn't say outright. But, I think their plan is for Dexter Ellis to take over the role. At least, that's what I've heard on the grapevine, and her call this morning seemed to be laying foundations for that decision to be made."

She didn't know her words winded him, and Jonah did the only thing he thought he should do: smile and nod as if he didn't have a care in the world. For who wouldn't be flattered when they were told they had been asked to audition for West End shows? He knew how fickle the industry could be, how quickly someone could be on top, then find themselves without a job and wishing they hadn't turned their backs on the opportunities they once had. He didn't want to say goodbye to the world he loved, to the music and movement, the beautiful stories he could tell. If Achilles no longer belonged to him, then he needed to find someone else to embody. But the thought of leaving, of stepping away from the thing he worked so hard for, the role that put his name into the mouths of important people and won him the Olivier, well, it felt like Edward leaving him all over again. For someone else. Dexter.

"It's dance heavy though, you know that, right?" Melanie said, snapping Jonah out of the twirling vortex of doom he threw himself into. "Big tap numbers."

"Yeah," he said blankly. "I know. That's fine. I can . . . yeah . . . if you can set up an audition that would be great."

Melanie offered him a sad smile. "I know landing Achilles was huge for you, but I don't think it's the role you will be remembered for."

"You think Bobby Child is?"

Melanie tapped the handle of her mug with her nail. "No. I think we've yet to come across the role people will remember you for. Achilles got you your first Olivier, but you can get more. I believe in you." She spoke with such sincerity Jonah believed her. Achilles, his *first* Olivier, but it didn't need to be his last. *The Wooden Horse* was his way in, and now he had the keys to Troy, and he would conquer it.

As Jonah left the office, he took a deep breath and looked up to the sky.

Endlessly blue. It took him back to Cornwall, to the scorching summers and romance of the sea. He fished his phone from his pocket and scrolled through until he got to his mum's number. He could call her. He *should* call her. In so many ways he still felt tethered to her, a child searching for her hand, the umbilical cord stretching but not letting go. She'd been there for him when he scraped his knees, when he failed his stupid art exam, and when he accidentally threw up all over the front doormat after returning home drunk. So why did he feel scared to talk to her?

"Hello, Jonah," she said, answering after five excruciating rings. "How is your face?"

"Not too bad," he said as he moved through Richmond. "How are you?"

"Oh, fine." She seemed distracted, words a little quiet, slightly slurred. "Doctor gave me some new medication. You know, to help with the nerves."

"The nerves?"

"I've been finding it a little difficult to just . . . sit still lately."

"Is the medication helping?" he asked, keeping his tone light.

She hummed before answering. "I've got to go, Jonah. There's a cat outside." He could definitely hear the words slurring together as she spoke and he knew, he just knew, from the calls with Penny with hints of his mum's drinking in their conversations, medication may not have been the cause.

"And that means you have to go because . . . ?"

"Have a nice day, sausage." She didn't wait for him to say goodbye. He looked down at his phone as he stopped in his tracks, the fear he felt before calling her having now multiplied. Shit. He needed to talk to Penny.

Jonah missed the stage. His soles itched for the floorboards and his body cried out for his costume. Social media seemed rife with rumors over his absence, concern over how badly he'd been hurt, if his mental health had also taken a beating, and worry over whether he would even return to the Persephone. Colbie messaged him each day, not to check in on his well-being, but just to enforce the social media blackout, even though Melanie told him to post whatever the hell he wanted. In some ways, he felt guilty that the incident overshadowed the new cast's first week; he knew the spotlight didn't linger around for long and he'd redirected it, stealing it all for himself. But he didn't want it. He just wanted . . . he wanted to be back. He wanted to be laughing with Bash and Sherrie while Dexter annoyed the hell out of him. He wanted—

The Penis Destroyer: Can I come over? x

Jonah: Thought you were having drinks with your dad tonight? x

The Penis Destroyer: Long story xxx

Jonah: Sure. I'm up. Don't think this is me agreeing to a booty call though x

The Penis Destroyer: I wouldn't dream of it x

Jonah got out of bed and pulled a T-shirt on over his head, then made his way downstairs to wait for him. They'd not seen each other since Dexter left the morning after the incident. They'd messaged, of course, but physical contact remained elusive, and Jonah certainly didn't think he'd see him tonight; even if Dexter wasn't seeing his dad, a cast party had been planned for after the show, which he would no doubt go to. Yet, he'd chosen Jonah, and Jonah tried to suppress the warm feeling in his chest as he thought of what that could mean. If it meant something or nothing at all.

For, since he saw Melanie, Jonah's reality didn't feel steady. The floor seemed uneven, crumbling, and his perception of Dexter slightly blurred. If Colbie really wanted Dexter to take over as Achilles, then did he know about it? Was it something he signed on knowing would eventually happen, and if he did, was this whole thing they were playing out together some kind of joke? No. No, he couldn't think like that. Not when Dexter was knocking at his door, reaching out to him and only him after his first full week onstage at the Persephone.

"Wow," Dexter said when Jonah answered the door. "How does your face look worse today than what it did Wednesday? Does it still hurt?"

Jonah very nearly slammed the door in his face. "Well, fuck you," he said instead. "What the hell is wrong with you?" He stepped aside to let Dexter in. "And no, it doesn't hurt much now, but why would you think that's a—" He stopped as Dexter pulled him by the collar of his shirt and pressed a kiss to his lips.

"That's right, get all wound up for me," Dexter whispered against his mouth, then kicked the door with his foot to shut it. "Love it when you get all annoyed like that." He wrapped his hands around Jonah's waist and kissed him again. "Fuck, I've been wanting to do this since the moment I left. Been thinking about you constantly." He backed Jonah up against the wall and trailed his lips down his neck.

"I told you I wasn't your booty call," Jonah said, but let his head tip back to allow Dexter better access to his skin.

"You're not going to let me take you upstairs and fuck you?"

Fuck. Fuck. Fuck. His voice sounded wrecked already, gravelly and low. Jonah couldn't even answer him, his mind repeating Dexter's words like a damn broken record.

"Well, babe?" *Babe*. Jonah never really cared about casual "babe"s flung between him and his friends. But Dexter calling him *babe*? Who knew he could be so completely and utterly simple in the bedroom that a *babe* would make him go weak at the knees?

"What happened to your dad?" he asked, and Dexter pulled away from him abruptly. It was as if Jonah had picked up the sexual tension between them and pissed all over it. "Sorry if I've just killed the mood."

"Yeah, well, bringing up my dad when I said I wanted to fuck you will do that." He wiped his hands on the front of his jeans. Jeans. Jonah had never seen him wear jeans before. He looked at the rest of him then, a black long-sleeved T-shirt with a burgundy shirt opened over the top of it and navy sneakers. Remarkably casual.

"Sorry," Jonah said again as they stood awkwardly in the hallway. "But seriously. Didn't he come?"

"He came." Dexter looked down at his feet. "Sent me a text during the interval to say he was leaving."

"What? Why?"

Dexter fiddled with his fingers, then shrugged uncomfortably. "He said, and I quote, 'I don't want to watch a fucking pansy show.'"

Jonah could feel his mouth hanging open as he looked at Dexter, his impression of a goldfish spot-on. "What the hell?"

"Typical Dad."

"What a wanker."

Dexter shrugged again. "Whatever. Let's not talk about it."

"It hasn't upset you?"

"Do you want it to upset me?" He looked back at Jonah. "Is that what you want?"

"What? No. I just . . . thought you might want to talk about it? Didn't he see you in it when you were at the Fringe or on tour?"

Dexter sucked in a sharp breath. "No. He didn't. And good, too, or he would have seen me making out with another guy onstage. At least tonight he got to live out his fantasy of me being straight for a while. Good old manly Hector with his wife." He shoved his hands into his pockets. "I didn't come here to talk to you about my dad, though, Jonah."

Jonah moved past him to go to the kitchen and flicked the kettle on. "Tea?"

"Jonah," Dexter groaned as he followed him. "I don't want to talk about it."

"I didn't say we had to," Jonah said, grabbing two mugs from the cupboard then plopping a tea bag into each. "I'm just making tea."

"Tea makes people talk." Despite his words, he started opening the kitchen drawers until he came across the cutlery and handed Jonah a teaspoon. "I just can't believe he didn't even have the decency to stay until the end," he said as he watched Jonah pour the boiling water into the mugs. "To get to my dressing room to see that message felt like he'd just come in and kicked me in the balls."

"Is kicking people in the balls something that runs in the family?"

A small ghost of a smile made its way to Dexter's face. "That was a genuine accident."

"Yeah? And not knowing who I was . . . was that genuine?"

"No," Dexter admitted. "I freaked out seeing you there and didn't know what to do, and for some reason pretending I didn't know who you were seemed like the best thing to do."

Jonah raised his eyebrows as he stirred the tea. "So, the comment about how good Photoshop can be was just you being a massive dick?"

"Are you trying to say I'm like my dad?"

Jonah stopped and looked at him. "No, not at all. No offense, but he sounds like a homophobic idiot. That's not you."

"You know, he's never met anyone I've dated," Dexter said. "Even my long-term boyfriend. We lived together, his brother's kids called me Uncle Dex. I really, *really* loved him, and I asked my dad time and time again if he would come meet him, or if we could go to him, whatever he wanted, but he always said no. He once said my sexuality was just a phase like my love for the theatre."

"Jesus Christ, Dexter. Why do you still keep trying with him?" He handed Dexter some tea, and Dexter took it from him gratefully.

"Because he's my dad." He blew out air over the drink, the steam tickling his cheeks, then took a quick sip. "I told you tea makes you talk."

"You started talking before you had any of that."

"But it was in the room. The aroma got to me. It got me talking about my dad and my ex. Good times."

"How sexy," Jonah said with a wink. "Love a bit of dad and ex talk."

"I don't think you're one to talk about things being sexy when you're standing there in the baggiest pajamas and a cup of tea in hand. It's hardly saying 'come to bed,' is it?"

"It's saying exactly what I want it to say." Jonah cupped his tea in his hands and leaned against the counter. "Aren't you exhausted? After a two-show day, all I want to do is sleep for a week."

"I think I'm high on adrenaline."

"Was it a good first week, even with the shit from your dad?"

"It was amazing." He smiled the smile Jonah was so used to seeing, his face as bright as the sun, beautiful, golden. "It would have been better if you were there, though. No one can kill me like you do."

Jonah placed a hand over his heart and grinned. "What a compliment."

"I mean it," Dexter said, tone surprisingly serious. "You're amazing." Jonah could see something in the way Dexter's jaw clenched, something tense, something he couldn't quite understand that made a deep pit of unease settle in his stomach.

"Thank you."

"Will you be back next week?"

"If Colbie lets me."

Instead of answering Dexter nodded and drank his tea. The mere mention of Colbie's name caused a frost to edge into the room.

Dexter let out a yawn and placed his mug down beside the sink. "I should probably head home."

"You're not staying?"

"I don't want to intrude more than I already have. I wasn't like . . . planning on staying the night or anything."

Jonah could feel an unpleasant sinking feeling in his stomach. "I told you I didn't want to be a booty call, Dexter."

"You're not. I thought . . . I thought we were clear about what this was between us?"

"We were?"

"Casual," Dexter stated simply.

Jonah nodded slowly. "Right. Casual. Yeah."

Dexter ran his hands through his hair, his expression slightly pinched, exasperated. "Jonah, if that isn't something you're happy with, then we can . . . I don't know. Forget this?"

"Do you want to forget it?"

"No." He sighed. "No, of course not. I just want us to be on the same page."

Casual still sounded like a rotten word scraping at Jonah's skin. He didn't know how to be casual. He didn't know the lines of it, the blocking, or the stage directions. But he wanted Dexter, he wanted to feel his mouth on him again, he wanted to kiss him, because fuck it, he'd somehow annoyingly grown to like the guy.

Jonah placed down his half-drunk tea and stepped closer to Dexter, running his fingers down his arm slowly. "We are on the same page," he said, lying but knowing he could get to the book Dexter read from. It might just take some time. "And I think it would be rude to leave now when you had the intention of taking me upstairs to fuck me. That is what you said, isn't it?"

Dexter closed his eyes for a moment before looking back at Jonah again. "And you said you weren't a booty call."

"Booty calls never include tea."

Dexter kissed him, the movement quick, hungry, and Jonah kissed him back, hands cupping his cheeks as Dexter wrapped his arms around his waist and pulled him closer. "Thank fuck for tea," Dexter said against his lips, and Jonah would create a river of tea if it meant Dexter would kiss him like that forever. No. Forever and casual didn't mix. For now, casual would have to do.

TWENTY-TWO

"I'm yours, and I always will be."
—"Eternity," *The Wooden Horse*, Act Two

The Oxford dictionary defines *casual* as relaxed and unconcerned, not regular or permanent. Jonah knew because he googled it. He stared at the words and couldn't match any of them to the not-relationship he had with Dexter. The first reason being that *relaxed* and *unconcerned* were foreign words in the theatre industry. Jonah would have liked to think of himself as totally Zen and laid-back, but reality showed he was actually highly-strung and neurotic, and the same went for Dexter, who didn't stop thinking or analyzing everything around him for a single second. The second reason came from the fact that they were having sex whenever they could, which didn't fit in with the *not regular* part of the definition. *Not permanent*, however, seemed to be the only aspect Jonah could agree with. But Dexter fit into his life so seamlessly, and to think he might one day not be there made Jonah's palms sweat in the most unnerving way, because Dexter was still a complete and utter prick.

They sniped at each other often. Little comments here and there, and Jonah couldn't stop the tiny voice in his head telling him that Dexter's relentless performance feedback came not from a gentle ribbing but from a desire to actually get under his skin. The unknown terrified him, and knowing things were happening behind the scenes at the theatre made his stomach tie itself in knots. He couldn't shake the preconceptions he had of Dexter before they knew each other, the idea of him, the rival, and although they lessened with each day, Dexter still somehow added new levels of anxiety to their relationship.

For example, Dexter didn't want anyone to know about them. It came out of nowhere, a casual remark before a show, and it felt to Jonah like Dexter had stabbed him directly in the chest.

"I just think with things being casual, we should keep it between us. I know Bastien knows, but no one else." He didn't ask if Jonah agreed, he simply stated the rule, and Jonah didn't want to say that, actually, Sherrie and Omari both knew they were sleeping together as well.

"I don't want to be a dirty secret, Dex."

"You're not a dirty secret." Dexter's stoic expression changed then. It softened, and he ran his fingers through Jonah's curls. "I just don't want there to be any pressure on us."

Jonah thought of Edward and wondered if he once told Wes he didn't want anyone to know about them, to keep their relationship a secret so Jonah would never find out. Did Wes think he was casual with Edward? Is that how it started between them? What if Dexter was actually seeing someone else?

"Who is putting pressure on us?" Jonah asked, knowing full well he sounded needy, which he didn't want to be. But there in the back of his mind stood Edward, making out with Wes over and over again.

"No one," Dexter conceded. "But they will. People will look at us differently."

"But people already think there's something going on between us. That's exactly what Colbie wanted."

Dexter stepped away from him with a heavy sigh. "I know. But there's a difference, isn't there? People here don't think there's something serious going on, do they?"

"But there isn't something serious going on, Dexter. We're *casual*." He sounded spiteful, and for once he didn't regret the tone. Dexter didn't have an immediate answer to that. Instead, he smiled, which Jonah couldn't understand, and simply shook his head fondly.

"Look. I don't care if people believe what Colbie wants them to believe online. But my actual private life? I don't want everyone knowing."

Jonah couldn't argue with him. He knew Dexter deserved the right to protect his privacy, but it still hurt. He half expected Dexter to act differently around him after the conversation, for him to back away completely to preserve the idea they weren't going home together to give each other totally casual blow jobs before having totally casual sex. But he didn't. Dexter flourished in the theatre, he bloomed like a social butterfly, wings spreading, colors vibrant. He spoke openly with Jonah, gave him hugs before and after the show in front of the others, stayed close to his side during warm-ups. He remained true to his Dexter persona, and on nights Jonah thought he pulled off an absolutely flawless performance, Dexter would send him catapulting back down to earth afterward, lips twitching as he tried and failed to keep in his critique. Only, unlike before, Jonah now knew how to shut him up. A month of getting to know Dexter's intimate needs and desires meant it only took a lingering kiss to his neck in the dressing room afterward to get him to stop talking; he'd stand, mouth slack as Jonah licked a line up from his collarbone to just below his ear. All unwanted feedback would be lost as Jonah stepped away, a satisfied smirk on his face.

However, Dexter was also learning the things he could do to make Jonah melt like butter in the palm of his hand. Before heading onto stage for the start of act two, he always whispered something completely filthy into Jonah's ear, leaving Jonah motionless, his fingers rubbing his palms as he tried to think of something, anything, to stop the stirrings Dexter set off inside of him. He did it so brazenly, in front of the rest of the cast and crew, which only threw his casual and very secretive needs into disarray in Jonah's mind. Dexter, with his insatiable smirking and devilish lips, would be the death of him.

The sex could only be described as mind-blowing, but it wasn't the sex that kept Jonah awake at night thinking of Dexter. No. It was the way, when they left the stage door, Dex walked just in front of him, shoulders tense, broad and undeniably protective. Most people followed the new rule and stayed away, but there were a few who still waited, lingering on the other side of the path after security ushered them away, hoping to talk to them, eager for photographs and signatures. Dexter acted as a shield, eyes scanning anyone in the vicinity who looked their way, and Jonah knew he was keeping an eye out for Wes even though Jonah didn't think Wes would be stupid enough to return and risk getting into even more trouble than he was already in. Bastien always looked over at them when they left, smirking at the way Dexter tried to shield Jonah, and then, when Dexter wasn't looking, he'd make a gesture resembling someone giving a blow job and Jonah would roll his eyes at him and laugh.

The protective side of Dexter turned Jonah on more than he cared to admit. As he lay alone in his bed at night, he often thought of Dexter's body covering his, and his hands may or may not find their way into his pants to help him enjoy the image. And the image often became a reality. Dexter between his legs, tongue mapping his skin while his moans sent shivers down Jonah's spine. The nights they performed they always traveled home together, alternately taking the bus or the tube, Dexter whining each and every time they got on the Northern Line, his lips turned down into the most unattractive frown in the world. They sometimes wordlessly went back to Dexter's place, his house immaculately tidy and horrendously white and sterile, and made out in his bed until they fell asleep. Other nights, they went to Jonah's, where Dexter seemed more relaxed than in his own home, and explored each other's bodies until the early hours before falling into an orgasm-fueled sleep.

The weekends, however, were strange. After Saturday's two-show days, Dexter seemed to vanish off the face of the earth. On Sundays he didn't respond to messages and always avoided Jonah suggesting they make plans for their days off. His elusive nature carried on into Monday, and, despite Jonah practically begging him to come back to yoga, because it would be hot now with the couple poses and he could touch Dexter and make him squirm, he never showed up. When Tuesdays rolled around, Dexter sprang back into life, invading Jonah's space every second with his loud voice and opinions no one asked for.

It brought unwanted thoughts of what Dexter might be doing with his free time. It made Jonah nervous, but he tried to put it aside, needed to put it aside. He needed to be Jonah Penrose, cool as a cucumber, so laid-back he might be asleep, totally not obsessing over Dexter flirting with other people on a Sunday, Monday, or any other day of the week they were apart. He needed to be totally and utterly A-OK with just not knowing where the hell he stood with the man who frustrated him both sexually and professionally. Absolutely fine with it.

Colbie tapped her fingers on Evie's desk, pink nails shimmering in the dim light of the office. Jonah sat opposite her, hands in his lap, palms sweating profusely, and he wondered if this was it, if she was giving him his marching orders. He'd only been back a month since being forced off work for a week because of Wes and his flying fist, and Evie seemed intent on ignoring him up until this very moment where she stood behind Colbie, peering at him intensely. She called him into her office, not mentioning Colbie would be waiting for him; Colbie, whose hair looked brighter than usual, freshly colored, the skin around her nail beds stained the same vibrant red, and who sat with a face pinched like a raisin as she looked at him.

"I need you to do something for me," she said eventually, breaking the silence between them with a voice filled with nicotine. "Niamh has set up an interview for you and Dexter for the *London Theatrical Stage* magazine. They want the total package: interview, photo shoot, the works."

"Okay, wow, that sounds great."

"They will probably ask about what happened at stage door," she said, then clicked her tongue against the back of her teeth. "The whole thing's kicked off some debate about performer safety and, to be honest with you, Jonah, I don't want to be part of that narrative. So you will not answer questions about it."

Jonah bit down on the tip of his tongue to stop himself from saying something he shouldn't. The debate had raised the important issue of boundaries and how production companies needed to put measures in place to protect their cast and crew. But assaults garnered negative publicity, and extra security cost money, both things Colbie clearly hated.

"And I need you to ramp up the act with Dexter too. You've both been, dare I say it, disappointing with the social media stuff. You barely interact online anymore, and the buzz surrounding you two has fizzled out. We need to keep pushing this. We want people interested in you both so they buy tickets and get us all paid." Jonah's eyes flicked to Evie, who crossed her arms over her chest and nodded along to Colbie's words. The loyal lapdog.

"You told my agent you wanted me to not post on social media."

"That was weeks ago."

Jonah deserved an award for managing to not roll his eyes. "Okay. I can do that."

"Good." She smiled, eyes piercing into him. "Now, get out of here and warm up." She waved her hand, dismissing him in quite possibly the rudest way he'd ever experienced.

"Oh, Jonah," Colbie said as he stood. "We think your energy has been lacking the past few performances. Pick it up, yeah? Can't have a weak link. I don't want to make your agent aware of your shortcomings." The spite in her voice couldn't be denied.

He decided against retaliating, knowing full well any challenge to Colbie resulted in a swing being put on in his place and a black mark against his name. It didn't matter if she behaved like a rotten cow; in the theatre world, her name was gold and a bad word from Colbie Paris meant saying goodbye to any dreams of being cast in another production. Instead, he gave her the nicest, most shit-eating smile he could muster, vacated her office, and went straight to Dexter's changing room.

Jonah didn't knock; Dexter never offered him the courtesy of knocking, so Jonah returned the sentiment and allowed himself full access to Dexter's room whenever he felt like it. Dexter stood beside his clothing rack wearing only his boxers and bright green socks, and he fumbled with the costume in his hand for a second before dropping it to the floor.

"You made me jump," he complained, bending down to pick it up as Jonah closed the door behind him.

"Mind if I take a photo of you?" Jonah asked, taking his phone out of his pocket to open the camera, and pointed it toward Dexter. "Colbie wants the world to think we're fucking each other so people buy theatre tickets."

"Don't you dare take a picture of me in my pants, Jonah."

Jonah lowered the phone. "But social media would love it, Dex," Jonah said, imitating Colbie's voice. "You know what she said to me the first time she pushed for us to be nice to each other? She said we don't have to suck each other's dicks, but make people think we are."

"Do you mean I didn't have to give you blow jobs this whole time?" He picked up his costume and pulled it on over his head. "I could have saved myself a lot of jaw ache."

"What's her fascination with wanting people to think we are a thing?" Jonah asked, sitting himself in Dexter's dressing room chair. "Best friends, boyfriends, whatever it is she wants us to be, is bloody weird."

"I know. It's why she hasn't talked to me about it since, because I told my agent it made me uncomfortable."

"What? Really?" Jonah's voice came out higher than intended. "And Colbie backed off? Who the hell is your agent?"

"Stephen Carrington."

Jonah sat up straight in the chair. "As in . . . *the* Stephen Carrington? How did I not know this?"

"He's very discreet. Everyone wants him to be their agent, but he actually has very few clients." Dexter adjusted his costume, then cleared his throat. "He's a dickhead, though."

"But the best dickhead in the business, right?"

"He's highly manipulative and doesn't care about anyone other than himself. He's formidable, sure, and represents some huge names, but I wouldn't call him the best in the business."

Jonah stood up and helped Dexter to fix the back part of the collar on his costume. "He's not done right by you?"

"He's . . . he's actually the ex I told you about, the one who I wanted my dad to meet."

Jonah's hands froze midair as he considered the weight of the admission Dexter made. "You were a couple?"

"Yeah. He signed me and about a year after that we started sleeping together and it went from there."

"That's . . . I don't think that's okay, Dex. He's a lot older than you. Like . . . he's *old*."

Dexter sucked in his bottom lip, then shrugged. "His age didn't bother me."

"But you were young, and he was in a position of power."

Dexter grimaced. "It wasn't like that."

"All right, we'll have to agree to disagree on that," Jonah said. He couldn't see how it wasn't a relationship created around a power imbalance. "Isn't it weird he's still your agent now that you're not together?"

"It was at first. Especially when . . . fuck, I don't want to get into it. Either way, I signed an ironclad contract with him and I couldn't get out of it. I could leave now, but I would be stupid to. It's all in the past, and he gets me work. He got me Hector."

"But not Achilles."

Dexter scowled as he glared at Jonah. "Was there any need for that comment?"

"I'm just saying he didn't get you the role you wanted, so why stay with him?"

"What does it matter? It's nothing to do with you. And this is exactly why I said it's not good to date people you work with. It makes things awkward."

Jonah raised his hands up to his chest in surrender. "Okay. Sorry. I only came in here to get a picture so I could post it and write about how amazing you are." Jonah paused for a moment. "Wait. I thought it was Henrik you were talking about dating when you spoke about it before."

"Henrik? No." The way he scrunched up his nose as he said his name told Jonah there would never be any inkling of romance between Dexter and Henrik. "That's . . . way too complicated, and I can't talk about it right now. Just take your picture, then leave me alone."

Jonah couldn't tell if Dexter was actually pissed with him or if the sullen attitude came as an accessory to the pout on his lips. He encouraged him to smile, then took a picture of him, his face illuminated by the lights surrounding his mirror, costume slightly out of place, eyes still filled with annoyance.

"Is it okay?" Dexter asked, swiping the phone from Jonah's grip to critique himself. "My hair's a mess."

"It's cute."

"Cute?"

"Super cute." Jonah reached up and ran his fingers through the blond strands. "You mad at me?"

"No."

"Can I kiss you?"

Dexter thought for a moment. "Yes."

Jonah closed the gap between them and felt Dexter's lips against his. They fit together perfectly, two halves of a unique shape. He wanted to know more about him, about the secrets he seemed to guard, about the people in his life and the stories connected to them.

"So . . . the whole dating someone you work with thing. Is that because of what happened before? Do you still want us to just be casual? A secret?" Jonah asked, the question caught up between their breaths.

Dexter pulled away, and Jonah felt the heat of his body fade. "Jonah," he groaned. "I don't know, okay?"

"Oh," Jonah mumbled. "I'm sorry. I'm not even sure why I asked that." He cleared his throat, then forced a smile. "You coming to karaoke after the show tonight?"

"Yeah," Dexter said awkwardly, rubbing his hand across the back of his neck. "I love karaoke."

"Yeah. Me too."

Silence hung in the air as they looked at each other. They'd experienced the silence before, but it usually came from built-up tension and ended in them taking each other's clothes off in a heated frenzy. This silence, however, gave Jonah physical pain.

"I . . . um, I should go get ready for the show."

"Yeah," Dexter said with a nod.

"Break a leg and all that," Jonah said, backing up to the door in quite possibly the most uncomfortable and horrendous way someone had ever tried to leave a room.

"The fuck are you doing?" Sherrie asked, seeing Jonah step out of the room like a burglar on a kids' cartoon show.

"I literally have no idea," he said and walked past her, swearing at himself under his breath and praying that the world would implode so he wouldn't have to spend the rest of his life replaying the exchange over and over again in his head.

TWENTY-THREE

> "*The blood of the innocent seeps into the soil and I can hear Demeter weep as the grain drips rubies.*"
>
> —"I Pray the Gods Forgive Me," *The Wooden Horse*, Act One

Dexter stood on the stage in the bar. He wound the microphone wire around his palm, cocky smile plastered on his face as the first few notes of the song he chose drifted through the crowd from the speakers. Jonah laughed to himself and shook his head as Dexter pointed at him, singling him out from the others, then felt a flush spread over his cheeks as he realized what song Dexter had on. "Afternoon Delight" by Starland Vocal Band. Jonah watched as Dexter swayed his hips, the bright yellow T-shirt he wore practically glowing beneath the glitter ball above his head. Jonah already gave him shit for the top before they even left the theatre: one of his Piniquo specials complete with an embroidered cat right in the middle of it, something Jonah would have happily set fire to before Dexter told him how much the hideous thing cost. But, seeing him up there, the most stunning smile on his face as he put just as much energy into singing a song about sex in the afternoon as he gave throughout an entire 150-minute performance at the theatre, made something inside of Jonah tingle, a feeling he hadn't felt in . . . he didn't want to think how long.

The feeling, something he recognized, couldn't be the one he associated with Dexter. He could look at him and feel all levels of lust, his attraction to him couldn't be denied, but this feeling . . . the feeling of floating, of feeling warm even in the midst of the deepest, darkest winter, it couldn't be real. He didn't want it to be real. Yet, there the feeling dwelled. It flourished as he watched him, the goofiness of his performance earning him cheers while Sherrie danced with Bastien happily before him. Was a month all it took? Four simple weeks of finding a strange and unnerving balance between professional criticism and the most mind-blowing orgasms Jonah ever experienced? A month of letting Dexter's name fall from his lips, of feeling his palm pressed against his under the sheets and eking out parts of him he kept undercover, things that made him feel so much more than bloody casual he could scream?

It wasn't love. He wasn't *in love* with Dexter Ellis. Not yet, anyway. But he liked him, he really liked him. He was in like with him, which he knew was a treacherous hill to be on because those two L words could so easily be interchanged. Like. Love. Like. Love . . .

The feeling didn't come in like the tide, steady and reliable. No, his fondness for the man gallivanting about onstage crashed into him like the sea on a stormy night, the same storms that used to scare him as a child when the thunder rolled on the waves outside of his house. It winded him. It reached down his throat and pulled the air out of his lungs then left him with nothing but the overwhelming feeling of wanting, no, needing Dexter, like he'd never breathe again if he wasn't near him. Which, when Jonah really thought about it, was mildly terrifying.

As Dexter finished his song, the crowd in the bar clapped loudly, like fireworks on New Year's Eve. Dexter made his way from the stage, his eyes on Jonah as he moved through the bodies before him. He danced as he moved, smiling and laughing as people spoke with him. Jonah stood back and watched, the smile on his face mirroring Dexter's, and he allowed himself to forget about their awkward exchange in the dressing room earlier. Dexter moved closer and closer until he suddenly stopped, his path blocked by a man taller than himself, and his smile turned from jovial to something far more intent, the same smile he gave Jonah before telling him exactly what he wanted to do with his mouth before going onstage.

The man who stole Dexter's attention rested his hand on Dexter's hip, a small gesture, friendly on the surface, but Jonah could see how firmly his fingers were pressed against Dexter's hip bone, and he wanted to snap each and every one of them in half. The man said something, and Dexter threw his head back with laughter, sweat glistening across his forehead. Then he leaned closer to the man, Dexter's lips so painfully close to his ear, and Jonah wondered what the hell could be so funny to warrant Dexter following it up with a seductive whisper.

"Babe!" Bastien hollered over the crowd, his cheeks red, limbs loose from alcohol. "It's our turn." He grabbed Jonah's hand and pulled him toward the stage, away from Dexter and the man with groping hands and into the spotlight he hoped wouldn't wash out his complexion. Omari already stood there with a microphone, his cheekbones glistening with glitter beneath the sparkling lights, ready to show everyone just how professional karaoke could be. A microphone found its way to Jonah's hand, and Bastien nudged him in the ribs with his elbow, gesturing toward the TV screen displaying the song title and opening lyrics. But Jonah couldn't tear his eyes away from the man whose hand had now made its way to Dexter's forearm.

The crowd cheered as the first notes of the song played. Sherrie's bright-pink hair bobbed beneath the glittering lights as she waved her arms rhythmically, doing her best impersonation of Stevie Nicks. Romana danced beside her, slender warms wrapping around Sherrie's waist as she pressed kisses to the other woman's neck. Bastien started singing and nudged Jonah again, who this time looked away from Dexter and focused on the screen, where the lyrics to "We Built This City" flashed before him. He opened his mouth and assumed noise escaped him, words, hopefully, and not some strangled screech akin to a dying animal. By the sounds of the people in the bar who sang triumphantly along with them, he guessed he wasn't embarrassing Bastien and Omari by wailing and decided that, hey, Dexter could flirt all he wanted, they were *casual* after all. Not only that, but he didn't want to be anything other than casual with someone who attempted to trip him on national television, kicked him in the dick, and accosted his lips for no reason other than jealousy.

Only. Those things didn't matter anymore. Dexter opening up about the relationship with his dad mattered, him standing close to be protective at the stage door mattered, and the way he mumbled in his sleep mattered. The man Jonah knew as the real Dexter Ellis mattered, with his embroidered clothes and obsession with cleaning; he became more real each day, and the green monster Dexter started out as faded as if he were a bad character note scribbled out by a director.

As Jonah continued to sing, Bastien dancing and belting by his side, he searched Dexter out in the crowd again and found him, the man he spoke to leaning in, eyes closed, moving toward Dexter's lips. The room flashed in shades of green and red, Jonah becoming the jealous creature left behind by Dexter, and he shouldn't have cared, he really shouldn't have given it a second thought; Dexter owed him nothing. But it didn't stop the bitter taste from seeping through Jonah's gums, the words he sang suddenly angry and less joyful than they should have been. Omari glared at him, karaoke something he took as seriously as his role onstage, but Jonah didn't care because who gave a fuck about karaoke when Dexter was about to make out with some random guy right in front of him?

But then Dexter stopped the man. He moved his head back and placed a hand on the guy's chest, halting him. The stranger frowned and narrowed his eyes, a look of bemusement on his face that Jonah totally understood; the guy was bloody gorgeous and Dexter had just turned him down. They spoke, the words forever lost in the sea of voices and karaoke background music, his own vocals drowning out whatever they said to each other, and the man shook his head, stepping back as Dexter pointed up to the stage, to Jonah, and the man looked, too, and he saw Jonah looking back at them and something like realization dawned on his face.

Jonah focused his attention back onto the screen and his friends beside him, who didn't have a clue as to what just unfurled before them. Bastien swung his arm around Jonah's shoulder, face too close as he belted into his microphone. Even drunk out of his mind Bastien sang like an angel, his voice pitch-perfect, and Jonah let the idea of Broadway cross his mind for a moment. New York didn't know how lucky it was for Bastien Andrews to cross the sea and spread his talent over there. When Jonah looked back into the crowd, he saw Dexter dancing with Sherrie and Romana, the same smile he had on his face when he sang on the stage himself, and he looked up at Jonah and cheered while singing along. Had he really turned down the advances of someone else because he wanted to be with Jonah? Or was it just politeness, seeing as Jonah was right there and making out with someone else in front of him was low even by Dexter's standards?

The answer came when Jonah left the stage and Dexter pulled him close and kissed him, openly, in front of strangers, in front of their friends, and in front of the rest of the crew who had come out to let down their hair after another full-on week at the theatre. He heard a cheer, Bastien's and Sherrie's voices leading the rally, and Dexter kissed him deeper as he wrapped his arms around his waist and held him close.

"What happened to being secret and casual?" Jonah shouted over the music when Dexter finally released him from the kiss.

"I'm sorry," Dexter said suddenly, and Jonah's eyes widened, expecting him to repel him across the room and pretend he didn't just kiss him in front of everyone. "For being weird in the dressing room earlier. Because, seriously, fuck casual. Fuck secret. We don't need to be those things. We aren't those things. Fuck them."

Jonah tried not to smile too much; he couldn't let Dexter see how happy those two words made him, but he couldn't stop himself, and Dexter smiled right back, and holy hell, Jonah couldn't get over just how beautiful he was.

"Come with me?" Dexter asked, taking Jonah's hand into his, and Jonah let him pull him through the throng of people, ignoring the cooing noises from their castmates while hiding his smile with his free hand.

"Where are you taking me, Mr. Ellis?" he asked as Dexter led them out the front of the bar, where a string of people stood along a wall smoking and vaping, the smell of nicotine mixed with summer berries and bubble gum almost nauseating. "It better not be a back alley."

"I'm taking you home with me."

Jonah stopped and cocked his head to the side, doing his best impression of a pigeon eyeing up a Krispy Kreme wrapper on the floor. "Did I say I wanted to leave?"

"Are we gonna play that game?" Dexter stepped toward him and tucked a curl behind Jonah's ear. "You want to stay, babe? We can stay." He spoke with the voice he knew made Jonah weak at the knees, low, as if he didn't want anyone in the world but Jonah to hear his words. "But I'm sure I can put my mouth to better use than singing karaoke."

"What's brought this on?" Jonah asked with a laugh. "Was all that flirting turning you on?"

"Flirting?"

"With the guy in there. I saw."

Dexter smirked. "The flirting made me realize I didn't want to flirt with anyone other than you." He squeezed Jonah's hand lightly. "Come home with me?"

"So we can fuck casual?"

"So we can fuck casual."

The Northern Line ushered them into a stifling hot carriage, still filled with tired bodies despite the unsociable hour, though Jonah knew it couldn't have been as late as he thought, given the trains were still running. Dexter kept pressing kisses to his forehead as they stood in the carriage. Usually such public displays of affection made Jonah a little nervous; being gay meant still looking over his shoulder for someone who felt the need to throw hate his way. But no one took any notice of them. They looked at their phones or reveled in drunken conversations and didn't bat an eyelid when Dexter took out his phone and snapped a photo of him and Jonah, Jonah's head resting on his shoulder as he pressed a kiss to his cheek.

Jonah half wondered if Dexter was drunk; he'd never been so open with their situation, he'd never kissed him in front of anyone else, and to do so in front of so many people they worked with must have meant something. *Fuck casual.*

"I hate the tube," Dexter said as they came to their stop and the doors opened, allowing them to disembark to the equally stuffy platform.

"I know. You say that every time we get on it."

"Can't break the habit of a lifetime."

Emerging from Camden station finally allowed them a breath of fresh air, and Jonah inhaled deeply as Dexter fiddled with his phone beside him. Jonah glanced at his screen as they walked and saw the photo Dexter took on the tube: them together, the perfect image of a couple, loved up, traveling home together. Then he saw Dexter typing something, a caption, and he realized Dexter was posting the photo.

"Wait. Are you posting that?" Jonah asked as they made their way down Kentish Town Road. "Colbie might—"

"Colbie can't tell us what to do," Dexter said. "But, if you don't want me to . . ."

"No. It's not that I don't want you to. I just . . . your fans can be pretty intense. They're going to jump all over that. I mean, the stuff we've posted before, it's friendly, there to be taken as more if someone looks. But that? That's obvious."

"Is it too much of a *fuck casual* statement to make?" Dexter asked as he turned his phone over in his hand.

"Maybe?" Jonah could see a warring range of emotions spreading across the other man's face. "Earlier today we were a secret. Casual. Now . . . now you want to post that?"

"I thought . . . I thought this was what you wanted?"

"I do," Jonah said quickly and took Dexter's hand into his, reassuring him. "Let's just . . . enjoy this tonight, yeah? Enjoy being no longer casual without posting it on social media?"

"But, Jonah," Dexter said as he allowed a smile to reach his lips again. "Nothing is official unless it's on social media, don't you know that?"

"Should we announce to the world we're officially no longer casual with a TikTok dance?"

"That is a perfect idea. I'll choreograph it. We can wear matching outfits."

Jonah shook his head and pressed a kiss to his cheek. "Can't wait. But for now, let's go and fuck casual, Mr. Ellis."

Dexter closed the social media app on his phone. "Yes. Fuck casual. Casual was a stupid idea, anyway."

"Wow, you're admitting one of your ideas was stupid?"

"You're the stupid one for not protesting it." He slipped his phone back into his pocket and took Jonah's hand into his as they walked.

"Ah, it's my fault, of course."

"Everything is always your fault," Dexter said fondly. "And that's why we work." He smiled before groaning and pulled his phone from his pocket. "Oh fuck, Colbie's calling me."

"It's so late. She shouldn't be calling you. Don't answer it."

"I . . . should, though, right?"

Jonah could see the panic in Dexter's eyes. "She should get a fucking life."

Dexter paused, conflict warring over his features before rejecting the call. "You're right."

"Does she usually call you in the middle of the night?"

Dexter cleared his throat and shook his head. "No. Well. No. It's a bit more complicated."

Jonah waited for him to elaborate, but when he didn't, he decided to push just a bit further. "Complicated how? She's the producer of the show you're in, how can that be complicated?"

"She used to be a friend."

Jonah clicked his tongue against the roof of his mouth as Dexter dropped his hand and looked back at his phone, his thumbs swiping across the screen as he typed something out.

"A friend?" Jonah played on his acting skills to sound as casual as possible.

"She's best friends with Stephen."

Well. Fuck. Goodbye, Achilles.

Dexter put his phone back into his pocket and smiled at Jonah as they walked. A second later Jonah felt his own phone vibrating in his pocket, but he ignored it, fearing it might be a scathing message from Colbie, though he knew it wasn't likely the case.

"Did your phone go off?" Dexter asked, his own acting skills failing terribly as he sounded far from relaxed.

Jonah narrowed his eyes at him. "Are you a fucking bat with sonar hearing?" he asked but got his phone out to see a message from Dexter illuminating his screen. "You're such a loser." Jonah opened the message as Dexter nonchalantly peered at the screen beside him.

The message showed the photo Dexter took of them of them on the tube with a message typed underneath:

> Who knew Achilles and Hector would fall for each other?

"Needed to post it somewhere," Dexter said. "If it's not online then . . . might as well send it directly to you."

"Fall for each other?" Jonah looked from the screen to Dexter as his heart thumped in his chest.

"I know it's too soon for love. I mean, it took Stephen almost a year to tell me he loved me. But I think . . . when you know, you know, right?"

"And this is your way of telling me you're falling for me?"

"Isn't it kinda romantic?"

Jonah wanted to hug him, he wanted to wrap him in his arms and shower him with kisses, but doing that on Kentish Town Road at an ungodly hour didn't seem like the right time to do it. "You're an idiot. You know that, right?" Jonah said, putting the phone back into his pocket. "You could just . . . you know . . . say it?"

"Well, I can't now, can I?"

"Why not?"

"Because it's going to sound weird and unnatural."

Jonah laughed and kissed his cheek. "See? This is why you're an idiot."

"*You* could say it, you know."

"No, I can't." Jonah shook his head. "You've made it into something and now we can't address it for at least seven working days. Who knows, you might change your mind by then. Karaoke can make people feel all kinds of things."

"That's very true. We'll blame the karaoke."

"Splendid idea."

TWENTY-FOUR

"Are we ghosts?"

—"The Song of the Dead," *The Wooden Horse*, Act Two

He fucked up. Jonah knew the moment he stepped to the left instead of the right that his chance at playing Bobby Child was well and truly over. He saw the way the casting director's smile turned into a deep grimace, and no matter how well he read his lines later in the day or how brilliantly he sang he couldn't get the smile to reappear. The hours he spent recording audition tapes suddenly became futile, because in person he couldn't remember the difference between left and right, and now everyone in the room thought he was a complete and utter idiot, and they weren't wrong in thinking it.

To think he could lose a role because of one little misstep might be verging on dramatic, but Jonah knew how picky casting teams could be; they had dozens of people lined up for the role, eager to take it, and things like Olivier wins or the theatre magazine announcing him and Dexter as the West End's golden couple didn't matter. They didn't matter, because Jonah just danced like someone who didn't know how their feet worked. A newborn lamb jittering around a field while its mother looked on in bemusement. Melanie would kill him; she told him time and time again to rehearse the moves until they were burned into the back of his eyes, and he did, but no one could account for nerves on the day. And he would put it down to nerves to save himself from admitting he simply blanked and went in a totally different direction than everyone else.

It didn't help he'd been practicing for the audition and recording his tapes behind Dexter's back. He wanted to tell him, he really did, but Melanie swore him to secrecy and made a pointed note that despite his relationship with Dexter flourishing, he was still a rival when it came to jobs in the West End. For all they knew, Dexter could have been auditioning for the same role; he still vanished on Sundays, and Jonah remained too worried to ask him what he did from Sunday until Tuesday, just in case he admitted to auditioning for all the roles Melanie was throwing Jonah's way. He didn't want to compete with him, and if Melanie's hunch about Dexter taking over the role of Achilles was correct, he didn't want there to be any awkwardness between them either. He needed to be seen as stepping away from the role rather than losing it; that way Dexter could take over with little guilt and they could continue with their domestic bliss bubble Jonah very much didn't want to pop.

Melanie Agent Extraordinaire: Casting director called. What happened?
Jonah: Already? I only just left.
Melanie Agent Extraordinaire: Call me.

"Jonah." She answered on the first ring. "They loved your audition tape. What the hell happened?"

"I went left instead of right."

He heard her exhale a disappointed breath and could picture her pinching the skin between her eyes in frustration. "You'll be the death of me. I sent you the choreography tape a month ago to learn."

"I take it they called to say I didn't get it."

"They want you to go back and do the dance part again next week," she said, much to his surprise. "They really like you but were worried you hadn't committed to learning the choreography. They're willing to give you another shot, so don't you bloody well blow it, Jonah."

"I won't."

"And I have another audition lined up for you. Well, I say audition. They called me to see if you might be interested, and I said I would discuss it with you. They were . . . very keen."

Jonah dodged pedestrians as he made his way to the tube station, keeping his head down as a sudden downpour of late September rain erupted from the sky. "Who?"

"Julianna Orwell."

Upon hearing the name, Jonah stopped and ducked beneath a doorway, sheltering himself while cupping his hand around his phone to hear better, because he was pretty sure Melanie had just said the name Julianna Orwell, and if it were true, then he needed to be standing still to take it in.

"Sorry, I didn't catch that."

"Julianna Orwell."

"Julianna Orwell?"

"The one and only."

Jonah's mind short-circuited. Julianna Orwell. One of the most esteemed directors, famous for her work on Broadway and in the West End. Winner of countless Oliviers and Tony Awards, one of the most respected directors in the entire theatre industry. Holy Jesus Christ on a biscuit.

"You spoke to her?" Jonah asked as he huddled as far beneath the doorway as possible. "Like, actually her?"

Melanie laughed, her beautiful voice rich and lyrical. "Yes. I met her years ago and we've stayed in touch. She's working on a revival and came to see *The Wooden Horse* a couple of weeks ago. She was very impressed with you."

Jonah could feel his hands turning numb, not from the cool chill of the rain but from Julianna Orwell acknowledging he existed. "Wow. Okay. And she's considering me for a role?"

"She's asked if we can meet for lunch sometime next week. Think you can manage that without getting flustered?" He heard her typing on her laptop. "She's proposed next Wednesday at one, over at The Forge in Chelsea."

"Yes," Jonah replied, without a single ounce of hesitation. "Yes."

"You don't want to know what show she's going to be directing?"

"It's *Julianna Orwell*, she could be directing a silent show all about dogs and I would want to be involved."

"Okay, well, it's not a silent show about dogs. It's *Cabaret*. I know you've done it before, but this will be entirely new staging and a completely different theatrical experience, from what I gather."

Cabaret. 1920s Berlin. Sally Bowles. The Kit Kat Club. Frilly knickers and suspenders, gin and gorillas. The leads dancing through the darkness taking over Germany, hands covering their eyes until they have no choice but to open them or continue to dance until their feet bleed. And, of course, the Emcee, the center of the show.

"Did she . . . did she say the role she's interested in me for? Is it Cliff?" He could play Cliff again. Poor gullible Cliff, who tries to view his life through rose-tinted glasses until they shatter, leaving him with the broken shards he flees with, away from Sally, away from Berlin, and away from the horrors that inch closer each moment. Jonah could step back into his shoes, but were Cliff's shoes more comfortable than Achilles's?

"Emcee. I know it's a dream role for you, Jonah. She said your emotional range when performing Achilles really opened her eyes to just what you can bring to a role. It's a complex character, and she already has some ideas about how they will be played in this version she's putting together, but it would be an excellent move for you."

"Better than Bobby?"

"It's certainly different. But given your success in *The Wooden Horse*, now might be the right time to go after something a little different. Besides, you've probably lost Bobby now because you didn't practice, practice, practice." Despite chastising him, her tone remained lighthearted. "Shall I say yes to next Wednesday?"

"Yes. One hundred percent yes."

"Fantastic, but keep this hush-hush, okay? Oh, and Jonah?"

"Yeah?"

"Go home and practice those bloody moves. The more options we have the better."

"I promise I will do nothing else in my spare time."

"Very good."

When Melanie hung up, Jonah wanted to run into the rain and scream at the top of his lungs. Julianna Orwell wanted to meet him. She wanted to talk to him about the role he'd dreamed about for God knows how many years, and Jonah felt overcome with the urge to yell about it to everyone who walked past with their heads bowed beneath umbrellas. Yet somehow he refrained from getting himself arrested for accosting strangers and instead walked with a spring in his step, ignoring the water trickling down the back of his collar. He hummed "Singin' in the Rain" and wished he had worn a suit and tap shoes so he could do his best Gene Kelly impression while twirling around lampposts.

Dexter threw his head back with a moan as he threaded his fingers through Jonah's hair. The sounds coming from his mouth were downright indecent, and Jonah bloody lived for them. He could feel Dexter's thighs trembling beneath his palms as he worked his mouth around his length, and he knew the other man wouldn't last long, not with the way his grip on his curls tightened and his jaw slackened with each needy pant. God, Jonah loved seeing him like this, eyes closed, a pink tint swiped across his cheekbones and body completely prone to every little thing Jonah did. Jonah kissed his thighs afterward, causing Dexter to twitch slightly as his body worked its way through its intense sensitivity before he reached down to tilt Jonah's chin up and guide him to his mouth. They kissed lazily for several minutes, Jonah in Dexter's lap in his dressing room chair, the position not entirely comfortable but neither of them cared.

"Bloody hell," Dexter whispered, his voice sounding wrecked despite needing to be onstage in less than an hour. "I think that was the most enthusiastic blow job I've ever had."

Jonah laughed and removed himself from Dexter's lap, scooping his underwear from the floor and chucking it to him playfully. He could feel how swollen his lips were. They tingled slightly, and he reveled in the sensation. "I've had a good day, and I wanted to show you how much I missed you." Julianna's name was on the tip of his tongue, but he couldn't tell Dexter about the earlier call, not yet, not until he had something concrete to tell him. Hush-hush.

"Missed me? You saw me Saturday."

"Yeah, and then you went off-grid for two days like usual."

Dexter cleared his throat as he reached for the comb on his dressing table to tidy his hair. "I don't go off-grid."

"Yeah you do," Jonah said, throwing caution to the wind by deciding to address the missing-Dexter phenomenon head-on. They'd been not-casual for a month now, and Jonah thought he deserved to know what his boyfriend, if he could call him his boyfriend, did when he didn't answer messages for two days and vanished off the face of the earth.

"I usually spend Sundays in the gym," Dexter said, leaning forward to inspect his face in the mirror, tapping his fingers along his flushed cheeks while pouting at himself. "And I like to step away from my phone for the day, otherwise I end up endlessly scrolling and doing nothing with my day off."

"Well, you could ignore your phone while doing something with me." Jonah leaned against the wall as he watched Dexter admire himself. "We could go to Brighton or something. We wasted the entire summer by not having a beach trip and now it's basically October, and we can't sunbathe in October, Dex."

"You would burn if you even tried to sunbathe."

"I will have you know I go a lovely shade of pink in the sun."

Dexter scoffed as he looked at him. "Ah, yes, pink, the color everyone hopes to achieve when sunbathing." He raised an eyebrow with a smirk. "Anyway, you do get to see me on a Sunday. I was over yours a couple of weeks ago and we had breakfast."

"Yeah, then you ran away the moment you ate all my cereal. I'm just saying it would be nice to see you when we don't have to worry about doing shows."

"What's bought this on?" Dexter asked as he stood from his seat to grab his first costume. He wasted no time in taking his top off, his eyes on Jonah as he did so, and he smiled when he saw the way Jonah's gaze scanned his torso. "Like what you see?"

"You know I do."

"So, you just want me for my body, huh?"

"No," Jonah said, crossing his arms over his chest. "We've never been on a date. Let me take you on a date. This Sunday. Please?" The choreography for Bobby Child flashed into his mind; he promised Melanie he would spend his spare time drumming each tiny movement into his head, but, surely, he could let himself relax for one day to date his maybe boyfriend.

Dexter, however, didn't have a chance to answer, for Jonah's phone rang loudly in his pocket, jolting him from his leaning position against the wall, unsure of when he turned the phone off silent; he didn't even know it had a ringtone. He pulled it from his pocket and glanced down at the screen.

"It's my mum," he said, looking at Dexter. "Do you mind if I—"

"No, go ahead. Don't ignore your mum."

Jonah nodded, and while the phone still rung in his hand he stepped out of the dressing room and into the hallway. "Hey, Mum." He'd spoken to her almost every day since he called her in Richmond. The call back then left an unnerving beat in his veins, one he needed to stamp out. He knew his dad was safe in the home, so he focused on the well-being of his mother.

Her tears were the first thing he heard. She'd been better recently; she sounded more like her old self, less slurred words and full of gossip. He guessed the new medication was settling into her system, giving her a sense of normalcy. Or, that's what he hoped, at least. Dad even seemed happy in his new home. In fact, the last photo his mum sent to him showed his dad looking healthier than he had in years, his cheeks no longer sinking into his skull, a smile on his face while he looked out the window at the sea. For the first time in a very long time, Jonah could feel a weight lifting from him; his love life wasn't a total disaster, things were well back home, and he didn't wake in the middle of the night in a cold sweat brought on by the anticipation of something bad about to happen.

Which is why the tears caught him by surprise. "Mum, what's wrong?"

"I need you," she sobbed, words filled with alcohol; they flowed into each other, indistinct and strange. "Jonah, come home, please come home."

"Mum, I can't," he said and tried to ignore the plummeting feeling in his chest. "What's wrong?"

"I'm all alone." The three words wrapped around his heart and squeezed until he couldn't breathe. Alone. She felt alone, and the miles between them stretched even further.

"Can you go to a friend's house?" Jonah asked. "Or call someone and get them to come to you? How about I call Aunt Penny?"

He heard his mum sniff before letting out another breathless cry. "No. I need you. I need my son."

Jonah looked at the clock on the wall just above the sign-in sheet. He couldn't leave now, not so close to a show, and even if he did, he couldn't get to her for hours. "Mum, what's made you feel like this?"

"I was looking at the photo albums," she said. "And it made me so sad. So sad. Jonah, I miss him, your dad, and I miss you, and I don't know what to do with myself anymore. Sometimes I think about just walking out into the sea and not coming back."

Jonah froze. The words she said, the admission she made, even if she was under the influence of alcohol, chilled him to the core. "Mum, I'm going to call Aunt Penny, okay? I will need to hang up to call her, but then I will call you right back. Do you promise me you'll answer?"

"Yes, sausage."

"I love you."

"I love you too."

Jonah hung up the phone with shaking hands only for bigger, steadier hands to cover his. He looked to his left to see Dexter beside him, Hector ready, with his mouth in a grim line as he searched Jonah's face for an answer to what the call was about.

"Everything okay?" he asked.

"No, I need to call my aunt," Jonah said, gently moving from Dexter so he could scroll through his contacts. "I need to call her quickly because I'm worried my mum's going to hurt herself."

"Shit. Okay. What can I do to help?"

Jonah paused as he found Penny's name. "I don't think I can go on tonight." A lump worked its way to his throat as tears brimmed at the edges of his eyes. "I need to get to her."

"Make the calls you need to make. I'll sort everything else out. Go to your dressing room." Dexter spoke with such confidence Jonah hung onto his every word and did exactly as he said. His dressing room wrapped him in a warm hug and ushered him into his seat, where he finally called Penny and prayed she would answer.

"Jonah?"

"Aunt Penny," he said, trying hard not to let his trembling voice break out into cries. "Can you get to mum?"

"Of course I can. What's wrong?"

"She . . . she was slurring, she's been drinking," he said quickly. "She said something just now that's terrified me, and I don't want anything to happen to her."

"Was it about walking into the sea?"

"Yes, how did you—"

"Jonah?" The voice changed, and this time it was Sally on the other end as Jonah heard rustling in the background. "Penny's getting her coat on and will head over there now."

"Has she said something like this before?"

Sally didn't answer for several seconds before finally letting out a regretful sigh. "We decided not to tell you. We didn't want to worry you."

"Tell me what?"

"Two days ago, she called Pen and said she was going to walk out into the sea and not come back. We drove over there and she wasn't in the house and we went down to the beach and there she was, in the sea. We took her to hospital. Penny stayed there with her, but they came home this morning."

"You should have told me." He was crying freely now, unsure of how else to convey the excruciating pain in his chest. "I'm coming home. I'll get a train tonight and—"

"Jonah, we'll look after her."

"No, I need to be there. Penny's on her way to her now? Is she? I need to call Mum again."

"She just left."

"Okay, thanks, Sally, thank you."

He couldn't stop crying, his eyesight blurring as more tears filled his eyes. New hands found his, Bastien's, and took the phone from his grip.

He turned Jonah to look at him before pulling him into a hug. Jonah tried to talk, but words were lost. He needed to call her, he needed to know she was okay.

"I need to—"

"Who do you need to call?" Bastien asked, picking up Jonah's phone. "Let me help."

"Mum."

"Okay, I'll call her." Jonah would have protested, would have told Bastien he didn't need to get involved if he thought he could pull himself together. But he didn't want her to hear him like this. He couldn't allow himself to show a weakness in front of her; she needed him to be strong, to be there for her, but his own devastation stood in the way. So Bastien called his mum. He paced in the dressing room, dressed as Patroclus, a ridiculous image of a Greek man on a mobile phone, and he talked to her. Jonah listened as he rambled about nothing and everything all at once. He told her about his wedding plans, about how he was moving to New York, and about the white fluffy dog he saw on the way to the theatre that afternoon. Jonah could hear his mum's voice whenever Bastien stepped close to him, and the tears she shed earlier were long gone; she spoke to him with warmth, his voice clearly a comfort to her as she let out a laugh, and the tension in Jonah's shoulders dissipated.

"Jonah?" Bastien said, snapping him out of staring at his red, blotchy face in the mirror. "It's your aunt, she's with your mum and wants to talk to you." He handed the phone to him, and he put it up to his ear, body numb.

"Jonah? I'm here, okay, she's fine. Just . . . had one too many glasses of wine. I've told her to stop drinking with the medication she's taking, but . . . well, she hasn't." She spoke with a high-pitched voice, as if the higher her tone the better it would be for his mum. "I'm going to bring her home with me. I'll look after her, okay? I'll call you in the morning. Please, don't worry. She's fine."

"Okay," he said, his voice still shaking as fat tears rolled down his cheeks. "Tell her I love her."

"I will."

As he hung up the phone, Bastien knelt before him and rested his hand on Jonah's knee. "Everything's okay," he said. "Omari's going to call you an Uber and you're going to go home."

"No. I need to get ready for the show."

"Jonah, you can't go on like this."

"I'm fine." He looked at the clock on his wall. "I've got twenty minutes."

Bastien chewed his bottom lip as he wiped some of Jonah's tears away. "Lennon's already getting ready to go on, don't push yourself."

"No." Jonah jerked his head away from him and rubbed his hands over his skin, removing the tears and the salty tracks they left behind. "I need this. I need my mind to be on something else."

Bastien stood, his demeanor pensive, unsure, but he didn't stop Jonah as he pulled off his clothes to get into his first costume.

"You've not been mic'd up," he said. "Let me go get Sherrie." He left the room quickly as Jonah focused on the costume, dressing himself as quickly as he could before Sherrie came into the room with Dexter following behind her.

"Okay, let's do this," she muttered, pulling a makeup brush out of her bum bag to fix Jonah's face. Her hands were trembling slightly, cheeks flushed an angry red.

"Are you okay?" Jonah asked quietly, his own mind working overtime, but he couldn't ignore her distressed expression.

"Hmm?" She shook her head slightly. "Just Romana, nothing for you to worry about, seriously. Let's just get you ready, yeah?"

"I don't think this is a good idea," Dexter commented from the doorway. "Jonah, go home."

"No."

"Jonah, I don't think—"

"I'm going on," Jonah snapped, making Sherrie flinch as she finished dusting his face with powder. They didn't understand, no one could understand, because they could never know just how his mind worked. If he didn't perform, then he would only go home and dwell on what his mum said to him and dream of her wading out into the water until her head disappeared beneath the waves. And if he didn't perform, Colbie would have another reason to add to her list of reasons to not renew his contract.

Achilles may not be his for much longer, but there was no chance in hell he would let him go without a fight.

TWENTY-FIVE

"Do you remember your mother, Achilles?"

—"What Do We Fight For?" *The Wooden Horse*, Act One

Dexter's heart beat steadily beneath Jonah's cheek. They lay together in bed, the sun kissing their skin as it gently woke the residents of Castle Road. Dexter ran his fingers up and down Jonah's waist, his arm wrapped around him as Jonah rested his head on his chest. They didn't know the time, but Jonah guessed it must have been late morning from the way the sunlight seemed to be positioned in the sky. Yet it was Sunday, and he expected Dexter to flee at first light, like he usually did, but he stayed, his body a comforting presence, one Jonah didn't want to ever lose.

Jonah wished he could erase the week he had just endured. His mum's call on Tuesday night had made him lose his footing, and he could still feel himself free-falling. He'd missed the signs blaring out at him, the ones telling him his mum needed him, that she wasn't coping, that the book clubs and girls' nights were excuses to have a few glasses of wine, then a few more and a few more until . . . until she couldn't take it anymore.

The guilt possessed him. The show Tuesday was the absolute worst he'd ever performed onstage, and that was taking into account the nativity at school where he walked out dressed as a sheep then cried for five minutes before falling down the stairs in the wings. Only, this time he was in front of hundreds of people who paid a lot of money to see the show and he fumbled his lines, forgot his blocking, and accidentally hit Dexter in the face during their fight sequence, which resulted in a bloody nose and a lot of swearing offstage.

The rest of the week fared no better; his inability to brush himself off and get back on track resulted in him being taken off the Saturday evening show, and he spent the duration of it sobbing in his dressing room until Dexter finished and took him home. It was past midnight by the time Dexter ran a bath filled with decadent bubbles the scent of honey and lavender, and one part of Jonah just wanted to hide beneath his duvet, but the part of him completely smitten with Dexter appreciated his gesture and went along with it.

"Did you bring bubble bath with you?" Jonah asked as Dexter got into the tub with him.

"Yeah. I noticed you didn't have any, and baths should not be taken without bubbles."

Jonah relaxed against his chest as Dexter sat behind him, his legs on either side of Jonah as the hot water caressed their limbs and the lavender opened Jonah's chest, allowing him to breathe freely for the first time in days. Dexter kissed the back of his neck, then the side of his cheek, the action not sexual, but caring, deeply caring, and Jonah could have stayed there with him forever if the water didn't eventually get cold and force them to get out. Dexter took him to bed, where he held him, and they lay together in a beautiful, comfortable silence until they fell asleep.

Jonah dreamed of St. Ives and honeybees dancing through fields of flowers.

And now, as they lay together in the stark light of the morning, Jonah could finally sense the dark cloud obstructing his mind lifting. He pressed a chaste kiss to Dexter's collarbone and closed his eyes, basking in the contentment he felt and the way Dexter made him feel completely and utterly safe.

"Are you leaving soon?" Jonah asked, hoping the answer would be no, but also not expecting any more from him than he'd already given.

"No."

"But it's Sunday."

"And I want to be here with you."

Jonah rested his chin on Dexter's chest to look at him. "Because I'm a mess?"

"Well, yeah," Dexter said with brutal honesty. "I'm worried about you."

"I'm fine. I'm just worried about my mum."

Dexter pouted slightly and ran a hand through Jonah's hair as he leaned into Dexter's touch. "I know. But you're doing the best thing right now, talking to her and your aunt every day."

"I think I'm going to go to Cornwall next weekend, head up Sunday morning and come back Tuesday in time for the show in the evening."

"I'm sure she would appreciate that."

"You can come with me if you want."

Dexter's top lip twitched slightly. "Really?"

"She's been going on about me finding a boyfriend for ages. It might cheer her up if you came along."

"Boyfriend?"

Jonah groaned and rested his head back on Dexter's chest. "Don't start with the cockiness. I don't have the energy."

"I just didn't know that's what we were calling each other now."

"What else would we call each other? Non-casual sleeping partners? Man friends? Person I like but isn't my boyfriend?"

"Okay, okay." He laughed, his chest moving as he did. "You don't need to be so salty. I like it. Jonah Penrose is my boyfriend."

"Aren't you lucky?"

"The luckiest." His grip on Jonah's waist tightened. "I will come to Cornwall with you."

"Yeah?" Jonah tipped his head to look at him. "Really?"

"Really." The smile Dexter gave him could melt icebergs. He held the sun, Jonah was sure of it; he could light up any room with that smile of his. Jonah wanted to know how he did it, how he always looked so golden and beautiful.

"I love you," Jonah whispered, and he didn't regret saying it. He didn't feel the need to hide behind sarcasm or maybes anymore; he knew how Dexter made butterflies flutter in his chest, and he wanted him to know just what that meant to him.

"I love you too." Dexter kept his sunshine smile. "But only this much."

He held up his hand and pinched his fingers together, showing only about a centimeter of space between them.

"You're such a dick," Jonah said as he batted his hand away.

"But you love me."

"Yeah, I really do."

The Forge welcomed its guests with golden chandeliers and white-tiled floors polished to within an inch of their lives. The light from the crystals cascading from the fixtures above reflected on the flooring, creating a stunning kaleidoscope of colors Jonah focused on while he tried to stop his palms from sweating. Melanie sat opposite him, her phone in hand as she scrolled through her never-ending inbox. Jonah picked up the napkin neatly folded on the side plate in front of him and wiped his hands on it.

Melanie glanced up from her phone and raised an eyebrow. "What are you doing?"

"My hands are so bloody sweaty she's going to think I'm a tap."

Melanie gave a laugh, then sipped at the sparkling water she ordered. "Relax. She's not scary, Jonah."

"That's easy for you to say."

"Did you . . . did you tell Dexter about meeting Julianna today?" She fished the slice of lemon out of her drink with one of her nails, then squeezed it into the water before dropping the rind onto her napkin.

"Nope. I stayed hush-hush."

"That's good, for now at least. We don't want his agent getting wind of it."

"Stephen?"

Melanie nodded. "He's a savage son of a bitch. He doesn't care who he throws under the bus. And I've heard he's trying to get that little boyfriend of his a bigger role than the one he has now."

Jonah continued to wipe his palms on his napkin. "Boyfriend?"

"Henrik Larsson."

Henrik Larsson made my life a misery.

Jonah assumed, when Dexter told him about Henrik basically ousting him from his role in *West Side Story*, it was because of a fling they had. But no, Stephen was involved, *Stephen* broke his heart, and if Jonah was going to put two and two together, which he definitely was going to do, he guessed the breakup came from Stephen's eyes wandering to Henrik.

"He's not a leading man," Jonah said.

Melanie snorted and gave a nod. "You said it, not me. Ah." She nodded and waved to someone coming from behind Jonah, and when Jonah turned his head he saw Julianna Orwell, in all her fabulous glory, walking toward them.

He'd seen photographs of her, of course, but nothing compared to just how stunning she seemed in real life. He couldn't peg her age, not from just looking at her, but if memory served correctly, she was in her early fifties. Her shoulder-length, spiraled black hair shone beneath the chandeliers, and her cool brown skin showed absolutely no signs of aging. Jonah stood as she approached, as did Melanie, and he took her hand into his when she extended it with a dazzling smile bright enough to rival Dexter's.

"Wow, sweaty palms," she said with a thick Welsh accent and laughed, and oh God, why didn't he wipe his hands on the napkin some more? "Hey, Melanie." She leaned forward and kissed the other woman's cheeks before they all took their seats.

"Thank you both for meeting with me," she said, placing her phone on the table and dumping her handbag on the floor. "Jonah, I saw you in *The Wooden Horse*, and, wow." She placed her hand over her heart. "You were phenomenal. You took my breath away."

"Thank you," he said, overwhelmed by her; how on earth was Julianna Orwell giving him a compliment? "That means so much, honestly."

"It's a tough role, emotionally charged, and so much choreography. I'm in awe of the entire cast and crew."

"I think everyone was surprised at how well it's done here," Melanie said. "I've heard rumors about a Broadway transfer."

Julianna nodded and took a sip of her water. "Yes, I think it would translate well on Broadway." She narrowed her eyes at Jonah and smiled. "If they asked, do you think you would run away to New York to play Achilles?"

"No," he said with surprising confidence. "I mean, don't get me wrong, Broadway would be incredible. But not right now. My family's here."

"Of course. It would be a big move." Julianna tapped her finger on the menu in front of her. "Which is good news for me, because that means I don't have to compete with New York directors wanting you."

"Are we getting straight into business?" Melanie asked, picking up her own menu to study. "I've told Jonah you're doing the revival, but not much else."

"Well, we've secured a theatre. It's slightly bigger than the Persephone, but that's all I will say for now. I want it to be more immersive. I want some tables actually on the stage so the audience can be part of the show. But that's not really the interesting part, is it?" Julianna laughed. "You are both here to discuss casting with me."

"When will you be auditioning?" Jonah asked.

"We will put out casting calls soon for the ensemble roles. But for the main parts, we are reaching out to people we're interested in to see if it's something they would like to be involved with. For full transparency, I am meeting with a couple of other actors for the role of the Emcee. We've already cast our Sally, but I'm keeping that a secret from anyone who isn't signed to the show." She mimicked locking her mouth shut and throwing the imaginary key over her shoulder.

"I think I know who it might be," Melanie said, eyes twinkling.

"And I think you will be wrong." Julianna waved down a waitress. "Can we get some mixed starters to share, please? Then we will order the mains soon." The waitress nodded and scribbled on her notepad before scurrying away. Julianna opened her mouth to talk again but stopped and waved her hand in the air, her vibrant smile somehow getting even brighter. "Oh, look!" she said, raising her voice. "Stephen!"

Jonah turned his head in the direction she was waving, only to see Stephen Carrington at a table with Colbie and Dexter. Dexter's eyes caught his and the two of them stared, not really knowing the correct protocol for bumping into a partner when they were clearly at meetings they were keeping secret from each other. Stephen stood from his chair, crisp suit tailored perfectly to his body, and made his way over to their table, where he leaned down to kiss Julianna on the cheek. He'd slicked his dull gray hair away from his chiseled face, skin clear of stubble, eyes dark, reminiscent of a shark.

"Julianna, darling," he said, his voice dripping with money. "How truly wonderful to see you!"

"And you," Julianna said, placing a hand on his arm in a sign of familiarity. "Sorry, I didn't mean to interrupt your lunch."

"It's just business," Stephen said with a dismissive wave of his hand. "You know what it's like, signing contracts." He let his eyes linger on Jonah, the slight curl on his upper lip giving away his apparent distaste for him, which was rather ironic, seeing as Jonah thought he resembled a rat dressed as fake royalty.

Melanie cocked her head to the side as she gazed at Colbie and Dexter at the table across the room, then smiled as she turned her attention to Stephen. "You should probably get back to them. Colbie Paris isn't a woman who likes to be kept waiting."

"You're right," Stephen said, his words friendly but tone laced with poison. "Important changes happening over at the Persephone. Though, I'm sure you know about that already." He offered Jonah a pitying look. "Anyway, Julianna, it was lovely to see you. Give me a call and we can get dinner."

"Absolutely," Julianna agreed. Stephen excused himself and went back to his table, where Dexter looked at Jonah with wide eyes.

"Anyway, what were we saying," Julianna said, snapping her fingers together as she tried to recall her train of thought. "Ah, yes, casting. Jonah." She placed her hand over his on the table and he stopped caring about his sweaty hands and tore his eyes from Dexter. "I would love to have you come in and read for the Emcee. It's totally informal, not an audition, more of a compatibility exercise so we can see if you can work with my directing style."

She was practically handing him the Emcee on a plate and, if the paperwork sitting in the middle of the table across the room was what he thought it might be, then he needed to eat up whatever Julianna served.

"I would be honored to. It's literally my dream role."

"This production is going to be very dark, raw, fueled by the threat of war and raging emotions. But I want it to be more sexual than ever before, for it to really skirt the line of the darkest time in our history with carnal desire. I want to show a *Cabaret* no one's seen before, and I think, after seeing you perform, we could create something very special."

Jonah looked over his shoulder again only to see Colbie leaving the restaurant, Dexter following behind with Stephen's hand placed on the small of his back, his thumb moving in small circles.

"When are you hoping to open the show?" Jonah asked, giving Julianna his full attention again.

"Next June, so, not long at all."

"That would coincide well with Jonah's current contract," Melanie said.

"That's if you're ready to pass Achilles onto someone else," Julianna said, her tone playful, and Jonah simply smiled back at her, knowing it didn't matter if he was ready; Achilles had just been handed over to Dexter right in front of his eyes.

TWENTY-SIX

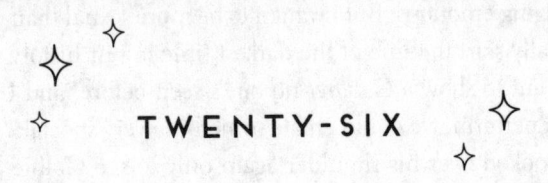

"I'll kill him, I'll drive my sword into his flesh and allow the Gods to feast on his blood. My gift to them before I give myself over to the underworld."

—"Answer Me," *The Wooden Horse,* Act Two

The atmosphere backstage at the Persephone could only be described as icy. It reflected the rain pouring outside onto the pavements as the headlights of cars bounced off the wet asphalt. Bastien stood in the wings, his own body language tense as he side-eyed Jonah, who gazed intently at Dexter waiting in the opposite wings. Jonah had avoided him from the moment they signed in, and it seemed Dexter was intent on avoiding him too; they didn't go to each other's dressing rooms as usual, they didn't stand near each other during warm-up, and Jonah could feel the vacant space by his side where Dexter should have been in the time leading up to the show growing larger by the second. Bastien clearly picked up on the sour note between them but didn't say a word, probably knowing by now that the best thing to do when it came to Dexter and Jonah's relationship was to stay well out of it.

As the orchestra played the opening notes of "The Road to Paradise" and the ensemble moved onto the stage, their bodies contorting as they weaved themselves together to the music and raised their voices to sing, Jonah tried to push all thoughts of the meeting earlier that day to one side. Out of the corner of his eye he could see Sherrie's bright hair in the wings, contrasting with Romana's darker features, but they were gesticulating wildly, an argument performed in whispers before Sherrie turned on her heel, wiping her eyes. Part of him wanted to go after her, to see if she was okay, but he couldn't, not now. The stage was calling. He stayed still as he watched the cast, the choreography precise and beautiful, and he could still see Dexter on the other side of the stage, his eyes on him. It strangely felt like lines were being drawn. Battle ready. Jonah didn't want to think of Dexter doing anything behind his back, but seeing him at a meeting with his agent and Colbie shouldn't have come as any surprise; Melanie warned him this was Colbie's intention. But actually seeing it happen left Jonah with a cavernous feeling in the pit of his stomach.

He trusted Dexter. He threw caution to the wind and put his trust in him and waited for Dexter to say something, anything, even a hint at what he must have known was going to happen. But then again, hadn't Dexter already told him months ago when drunk in the back of the Uber? *Achilles is mine.* The words fell from his mouth loud and clear. *Mine.* Jonah should have listened, he should have taken those words seriously. But he didn't; he allowed Dexter to become something else entirely, and now he loved him and the pain of being basically usurped hurt, like Dexter was driving a dagger directly between his shoulder blades.

Jonah channeled his warring emotions into his performance, determined to put the previous disastrous week behind him. He could feel the audience glued to him as he commanded the stage. When act two rolled round and he stepped on to perform "Answer Me" opposite Dexter, the tension between them reached a boiling point, and the audience witnessed what Jonah could only describe as a real fight. Their moves may have been rehearsed, the blows against each other planned and meticulously rehearsed, but Dexter put strength behind his actions, a strength Jonah couldn't contend with. And it suddenly dawned on Jonah that Dexter was angry with *him*. What for, he couldn't say. Yes, he'd seen him at a meeting with Melanie and Julianna, but meetings happened, and he wasn't going behind his back, he wasn't signing contracts that directly impacted Dexter. So, when they got to the part where Dexter pulled him closer and he would usually step to the left, the move Dexter messed up so many times back at rehearsals in June, Jonah moved out of his reach. Dexter faltered for a millisecond and stepped right, tripping over himself before falling to his knees with a loud thud.

Jonah heard the audience gasp, not knowing if the fall was intentional or part of the scene, and he saw Dexter look up at him, eyes wide, panicked, before he lunged forward and continued their routine seamlessly. God, Dexter was a professional, even after Jonah just did the most unprofessional thing he'd ever done in his entire career. As Jonah got him back onto the floor and straddled his hips, he raised the dagger over his head and braced himself for Dexter to stop it from plunging into his neck. But he didn't move. Instead, he looked up at Jonah, hands by his side as if in complete surrender. A tear rolled down his right cheek, away from the audience, the emotion entirely Dexter's and not part of Hector at all. Jonah hesitated, his own breaths pulling at his chest, and he wondered how the unspoken words between them could speak such volumes without really saying anything at all. He didn't know what Dexter could be thinking, why he felt anger toward him, because Jonah hadn't gone behind his back to steal a role from him. Yet, there he was, the perfect image of a man betrayed, and Jonah didn't understand it.

He brought the dagger down toward Dexter's neck, hitting the blood pack like usual, and watched as vibrant red spilled out over Dexter's skin. The stage revolved as they were plunged into darkness, and Jonah climbed off Dexter's lap and reached out to touch him, but Dexter flinched and moved away from the stage as fast as he could. Jonah stayed on his knees for a few seconds until he knew he couldn't stay there any longer, and he got up, positioning himself back in the wings, ready for his next song.

"Why did you do that?" Dexter's voice bounced off the walls in Jonah's dressing room. They'd remained professional until the end of the show, bowing together as usual, smiles plastered on their faces. But as soon as it finished Jonah could feel Dexter slipping away from him, moving so quickly there could be no words spoken. He watched Dexter slam his dressing room door closed before going to his own, then several minutes later Dexter appeared, face flushed, stage blood still staining the skin around his neck and cheeks, making his outburst seem all the more dramatic.

"You deliberately changed your move, knowing I would fall. Why?"

"I didn't—"

"Yes, you did!" Dexter exclaimed as he threw his hands in the air in defeat. "Why try to embarrass me? What have I done that's so wrong, Jonah? You've ignored me all night, then you do that, why?"

"Are you going to pretend I didn't see you today with Stephen and Colbie?" Jonah asked as he scrubbed the fake blood from his hands in the sink beside his mirror. "Or is this another case of selective amnesia like not knowing me at yoga?"

"You haven't let me say anything to you about it because you've not been near me tonight," Dexter snapped back, his voice trembling slightly. "Just like you didn't tell me about your meeting with fucking Julianna Orwell."

"I didn't realize I needed to tell you about every single thing I do, Dexter."

"Do you realize how hypocritical you sound right now?"

Jonah did, in fact, know how hypocritical he sounded, but he was already digging himself a hole, and he would be damned if he didn't finish the job. "*You* don't tell me your plans, Dexter. What do you do every Monday, huh?" He continued to scrub at his hands despite the blood being long gone.

"Is this why you're being like this? Because I don't spend every waking second with you? Get over yourself, Jonah."

Jonah turned then, water dripping from his hands as he looked at the man opposite him. "I don't want to spend every second with you. You're the one who needs to get over himself. The world doesn't revolve around you, despite what people have made you think."

"You're such an arsehole."

"*I'm* an arsehole? You just signed a contract to take my job from me, Dexter."

Silence filled the room. Outside, in the hallway, Jonah could hear the other cast and crew members leaving the building, and beyond that the sounds of Shaftesbury Avenue bubbling with life, which only made the room feel all the more vacant. Jonah could see a million things running through Dexter's mind; his eyes didn't seem to focus on any one thing, instead he looked down at his feet then finally back at Jonah, his brows furrowed and mouth set in a deep frown.

"What are you talking about?"

"Don't play that game with me." Jonah grabbed his coat from the back of his chair and pulled it on, shoving his arms through the sleeves aggressively. "I know why you were there with Colbie, I know she's pushing me out so you can take over as Achilles. I've known for ages, actually. I've just been waiting for you to tell me, but I guess signing the contract is the most important thing, huh? It doesn't matter about me at all." Jonah picked up his bag and rummaged about inside for his headphones. "I thought you might have the decency to say something rather than going behind my back."

"Is that why you were meeting with Julianna Orwell?" Dexter asked, his voice steady, remarkably calm in comparison to Jonah's shrill outbursts. "Because you're leaving the show?"

"I'm not leaving, I'm being ousted. And I had to sit there and see you take away something I've worked my arse off for. And then . . . and then you walk out with his hands on you, and I—"

"Stephen's hands on me?" Dexter asked. "Because the moment I realized he was touching me I told him to get off, but you didn't see that, did you? Because you were too busy already running away with the idea I'd do something to . . . what? Hurt you? Humiliate you?"

"You've done things to hurt me before. Intended to humiliate me too. Why not do it again?"

"Because I'm in love with you, Jonah."

Jonah gripped his headphones tightly in his hands as he looked at Dexter. His words sounded sincere, and it made Jonah's heart beat double time in his chest. *Thump. Thump. Thump.* But he couldn't believe him; Edward told him he loved him, he took him to bed and fucked him in the days leading up to leaving him for someone else. For seven months he made Jonah believe he was the only person in his life, and Jonah fell for it. So how could he believe Dexter when he stood there telling him he loved him when he was also betraying him? Was betrayal not the same when it came down to its core?

"Then why not tell me?" Jonah asked, his voice quieter now as he stepped closer to him. "Why not tell me?"

"You don't trust me." It wasn't a question. Dexter said it as a blanket statement, a fact, and Jonah hated the accusation, but couldn't turn away from it either.

"How can I?"

"I think the problem here is with you, not me," Dexter said, placing his hand on the door handle to open it. "And I think until you realize that, there's no point in us pretending we can make this work."

"Are you breaking up with me?"

"You can't be in a relationship with someone until you sort yourself out. Why would you want to be with me if you can't trust me?"

The question hung in the air between them and sucked all the hope out of the room. They looked at each other, brown eyes searching hazel, and Jonah couldn't think of the words to respond. If only someone gave him a script, he could recite the perfect thing to say in this situation, a way to salvage what could have been his best shot at finally finding happiness, but there were no playwrights with the answer he needed. For without words, he couldn't tell Dexter he loved him, he couldn't tell him it wasn't because he didn't trust *him*, he'd just been hurt and that meant he couldn't stop himself from dissecting every aspect of their relationship, even though he knew just how unfair that was on Dexter. And even though Jonah knew he could find something to fix the tear opening in the tapestry of their relationship, he decided instead to pull out a giant pair of fabric scissors and eradicate it altogether.

"How can I trust you when you've still not told me why you were at that lunch with them?" Jonah stepped past him and into the hallway, the cool air from outside hitting his skin as another cast member let themselves out of the stage door. He could sense Dexter behind him but didn't look to see if he was following him to say something else or leaving to get lost in the heart of London. Jonah picked up the pen by the sign-out sheet only to see Omari hurtle toward him with the theatre phone in hand.

"Jonah," he said breathlessly. "I don't know why I'm now your bloody

PA, but you've got a call. Polly? I think? They said you weren't answering your phone."

"Polly?" Jonah frowned and took the phone from him. "Hello?"

"Hey, love, it's Penny."

"Oh, hi." He stepped to the side to allow other people to leave through the door he was blocking and groped around in his bag for his phone, and there, on the screen, showed six missed calls from his mum and four from Penny. "Is everything okay?"

"Is there any way you can make your way home?" Penny spoke delicately, her voice soft as if trying to soothe a child to sleep. Jonah turned away from Omari and took the phone back to his dressing room, passing Dexter on the way, who looked at him skeptically.

"Why? Has Mum done something to herself?"

"No. No, she's . . . she's okay. It's your dad, love."

Jonah froze in the middle of the dressing room. "Dad? What's wrong with him?" He'd been doing well. His mum's photos showed him looking more like his old self, physically at least. "Has he had a fall?"

"He was taken into hospital earlier today, he was having some chest pains so they sent him there to be on the safe side. But since going in he's deteriorated rapidly."

"Deteriorated? Is he . . . is he going to be okay?"

"Jonah," she said with a deep inhalation of breath. "The doctor told us, if he has family, then it would be best for them to come and see him as soon as possible."

"He's dying?"

"We aren't sure how long he has left, love."

"I . . . I won't be able to get a train until the morning. I could . . . I'll have to get a taxi and beg one to take me out there," he blurted, his mind jumping over obstacles to find a solution. "But it's still going to take me about six hours, Pen."

"I know."

"Will I be too late?"

"I can't answer that," she said. "But we will be with him, me and your mum. Just get here when you can."

"Tell him I love him?"

"Of course."

"And I'll call when I'm on my way."

He held his phone in his hands, thumbs hovering over the screen as he tried to think about what company he could call to take him out there. It would cost a fortune, but it didn't matter. He would give his last penny if it meant getting to sit with his dad one last time. He didn't expect it to be so soon; he didn't expect it for years in fact. But this, now, it shocked him to his core. His dad. The man who carried him on his shoulders when they went on adventures in the park, the man who held his hand as they collected cockles along the shoreline, the man who read him stories about pirate ships and princesses locked away in castles before bed was dying.

"Jonah?"

He looked over his shoulder to see Dexter standing in the door frame. "Dexter, not now, I've got to—"

"Go home, I heard."

"Yeah, so, um, I'm sorry, I can't do this right now."

"Let me drive you."

"What?"

"I have a car," Dexter said, as if Jonah should have known that little morsel of information, which, to be fair, he really should have.

"Why do you have a car?" Jonah asked. "You live in London. Why bother?"

"I don't think that's really the concern here right now, is it?"

"How long have you had a car?"

Dexter made a small huffing sound. "Does it matter, Jonah? It's parked on my road. Let me take you."

"It's an almost six-hour drive, Dexter."

"Well, we will have to stop for coffee, then, won't we?"

Jonah blinked back some tears, then wiped his hand across his face. "But you just broke up with me."

"That doesn't matter right now. Let me help you." Dexter held out his hand to him, and Jonah looked at his palm, then took it into his own. "Good. Come on, we've got a long drive ahead."

TWENTY-SEVEN

"Father, please forgive me."

—"I Pray the Gods Forgive Me," *The Wooden Horse*, Act One

Jonah decided the reason Dexter never told him about the car came down to one very simple thing: he couldn't actually drive. He somehow managed to stall each time they came to a stop, didn't seem to understand the concept of lanes, and blamed the other drivers for the mistakes he was making. Jonah, however, remained quiet in the passenger seat, deciding instead to focus on the sounds of the radio rather than Dexter's incessant road rage.

They'd said barely more than ten words to each other since getting in the car apart from when Dexter asked Jonah for help with directions. Eventually Jonah fell asleep, his head resting against the window, neck at an uncomfortable angle when he woke to Dexter slamming his hands on the horn and swearing profusely at a little old lady who could barely see over the steering wheel of her car. He snuck a glance at the GPS; they were still two hours away from the hospital, but so far he'd not had any calls from his mum or Penny to say he was too late, which gave him hope he might get there to talk with his dad one last time.

Saying goodbye seemed like an odd concept; he'd said goodbye to his dad in so many ways since his diagnosis. He'd said goodbye to the memories his father could no longer recall and tried to keep them safe in a neat box he tucked away in the recesses of his own mind. He'd said goodbye to their conversations, the ones they had back on summer nights in the garden as the sea crashed against the bottoms of the cliffs. And he said goodbye to the fit man who once competed in the dad races on field days and always won, lifting Jonah up into the air and yelling in triumph as the other dads still attempted to cross the finish line.

Jonah sniffed and wiped some tears from his eyes, looking out the car window at the darkness whizzing past them.

"There's tissues in the glove compartment," Dexter said, jerking his head toward the handle in front of Jonah's knees.

"Thanks," Jonah mumbled. He opened it to fish out a brand-new packet of tissues and pulled one out to swipe across his nose. "Sorry. I know I look gross right now."

"You always look gross, so no change there."

Jonah narrowed his eyes at him but managed a smile. "I can always count on you to make sure I never forget just how shit I look."

"You sure can." Dexter kept his eyes on the road, tapping his fingers on the steering wheel and bobbing his head along to the music on the radio.

"You can stay at my mum's house and sleep once we get there," Jonah said, knowing they hadn't discussed any logistics with their middle-of-the-night expedition. "Not that I'm expecting you to stay or anything."

"Thanks. I'll probably need to get some rest before driving back. If . . . if you're okay with me heading back, that is."

"Dexter, I still can't believe you're actually driving me. Of course I don't expect you stay. Especially after . . . well . . . you know."

Dexter cleared his throat and clicked off the radio, the comfortable backdrop of the music suddenly gone. "I know now isn't the time for us to be talking about this, but I just need you to know I haven't gone behind your back. Not with anything. I'm not interested in messing around in relationships, Jonah."

Outside they passed a family of trees, all of them reaching out to each other, branches intertwined, bodies barren, the leaves already turned to brown and fallen away.

"You want to know what I do on Mondays?" he asked seriously. "Every morning at ten I have an hour session with my therapist. Then my mum calls me for our weekly check-in, which usually lasts about eight minutes on average as she fills me in on the lives of the half sisters I've never met." He kept his eyes focused on the road. "Then I have to clean the house because I need to do something after that call that doesn't make me feel like absolute shit because she ran away and left me. I thought maybe I could try something to calm me, which is why I went to yoga, but then you were there and I squashed your dick, so cleaning seemed the safer option."

Jonah wanted to reach out and place his hand on his knee, but he couldn't, not now, not now things were frozen between them.

"I think . . . maybe we both have some issues with trust, Dexter."

Dexter allowed his eyes to drift from the road for a second as he looked at Jonah. "What do you mean?" he asked, his eyes already back on the road.

"It's what it all boils down to, isn't it, because why not tell me that before?" Jonah asked carefully.

"Stephen said therapy was a waste of time. And he hated the cleaning, said I was neurotic."

"I'm not Stephen."

"And I'm not Edward."

Jonah tensed at the mention of his name, flashbacks of Wes walking toward him back at the Persephone, fingers curled in a fist, and the pain following shortly afterward. "I think maybe you're right."

"About what?"

"I can't be with someone until I sort myself out." Something inside of Jonah stung, a physical pain he didn't know he could experience. He watched as Dexter swallowed thickly, and he wanted to kiss him, he wanted to touch him and beg him to hold him until everything felt okay again. But once the storm passed, would there be trust? Dexter didn't deserve Jonah's insecurities forced on him, and Jonah didn't deserve it from Dexter either.

Dexter clicked the radio on again, and they listened to a woman drone on about illegal aircraft for twenty minutes until a song finally came on. "Afternoon Delight." At three forty-eight in the morning. Jonah looked at Dexter only to see him glance back at him with a smile. They fell back into a somewhat comfortable silence and watched the countryside pass them by.

The beeping of his dad's heart monitor reminded Jonah to stay awake. He'd never felt so exhausted, but he saw his mum asleep in the chair next to the hospital bed and knew one of them needed to stay awake to hold his dad's hand. He'd relieved Aunt Penny of her duties, and she left the hospital reluctantly, but he could see just how tired she was too. She took Dexter with her, instructing him to follow her back to the family house on the edge of the cliff where he would no doubt sleep in Jonah's old bedroom and wonder how the hell he ended up in Cornwall with a man he just broke up with.

Jonah held his dad's hand in his and looked down at the IV poking out from his skin, the surrounding area mottled and bruised, his hand skeletal, old, so terribly old. The selfish part of Jonah wished he would wake up so they could talk. It didn't matter what topic his dad chose, he would talk to him about anything for hours if it meant he could just hear his voice. But he knew he just needed to be grateful he made it in time, that he was there, by his side in case the worse thing really happened.

"The man you came here with is handsome," his mum said, pulling Jonah's attention away from his dad's peaceful, sleeping face.

"I thought you were asleep."

"I seem to only close my eyes for fifteen minutes before I remember where I am and I find my eyes are open again, looking at him, making sure he's still breathing." She sat forward and yawned, her own body frail. She seemed decades older than she really was. "How did we get to this point, hey, sausage?" She took his dad's other hand into hers and carefully stroked his fingers.

"I still can't understand how he's deteriorated so quickly."

"He's got fluid in his lungs. Pneumonia does that."

"I feel like I've failed him."

"No," she said sternly. "No, Jonah Penrose. You've failed no one."

Jonah sucked in a shaky breath. "I've failed you. I should have been here."

"Jonah." His mum sighed. "Your father and I, we watched you grow up here, we saw you develop passions we could never have imagined you would get into. And we saw how talented you were, no, *are*, and we wouldn't ever dream of holding you back. Things have been pretty bloody shit here recently, but that's not because you've been in London."

"But you've not been okay."

"You're right, I haven't," she admitted. "I'll hold my hands up and say I've been an absolute mess since your father got ill. But no one gives you a handbook and says this is exactly how you should act when your husband no longer remembers who you are." She stopped for a moment. "Actually, they gave me some pamphlets." She smiled and shook her head. "But a piece of paper doesn't hold all the answers. And neither does a bottle of wine."

Jonah sat back in his chair, letting go of his dad's hand now that his mum was awake and keeping up the contact. "I never thought this would happen," Jonah said. "I never thought about losing him. It just didn't seem like a possibility."

"No one likes to think about their parents no longer being about. I remember when your Nanna Rose passed away, I felt like someone took away my lungs, like I couldn't possibly go on without my mum living down the road. But, I did. I kept breathing, because I had you and your dad and people surrounding me who held my hand and let me remember her in different ways."

"You mean the rosebush you planted then killed?"

She let out a loud laugh, then clapped her hand over her mouth as his dad stirred. "Oh, shut it, you," she whispered. "Nanna Rose would have appreciated me trying. It wasn't my fault that bloody bush was intent on dying."

"Roses?" his dad mumbled, slowly opening his eyes, blinking up at the lights above him. "Someone plant a rose?"

"No, Mum killed the rosebush," Jonah said, leaning forward to take his hand again.

His dad turned his head slightly to look at him, and for a few seconds no expression settled on his face, before he finally smiled and squeezed his hand. "Oh, hello, boyo."

"Jonah came all the way from London to see you," Jonah's mum said, smiling as she looked at her husband fondly. "We had to tell him, what with you coming into hospital."

"That's a long way," his dad said solemnly, his voice hoarse. "I'm only being dramatic. No need for you to come up."

Jonah shook his head, his nose scrunching slightly as he tried not to cry. "It's fine, I got a ride because I'm so famous these days."

"Are you, now?"

"Oh, yeah, totally." Jonah laughed.

"A handsome man drove him here, Bill," his mum cooed, and Jonah could tell she was trying to lighten the atmosphere, because she, too, could hear how exhausted he sounded.

"A handsome man! What's his name then?"

"Dexter."

His dad's lips drooped as he considered the name. "Huh. Does he like maths?"

"Oh, I don't think so, not particularly. Why?"

"Dexter sounds like someone who enjoys an equation."

Jonah let out a snort and shook his head. "No. Well, not this Dexter, anyway."

"Is he your boyfriend?" his dad asked, something hopeful in his eyes, and Jonah couldn't say no. He couldn't say that, actually, they broke up several hours ago because they were both insecure idiots who couldn't separate past hurt from their present relationship. So Jonah nodded instead.

"Yeah."

"Good . . ." His dad hummed and licked his lips, though they remained dry. "My son, he needs to settle down, maybe you can talk to him and tell him to get his finger out his arse and find a nice man."

"Bill, what are you —" his mum started, but Jonah shook his head gently, and she stopped.

"I'll have a word," Jonah said. "Anything else you want me to tell him?"

"Yes," his father said, then coughed wetly, spittle clinging to the edges of his mouth. "Tell him I'll leave the landing light on for him so it's not dark when he gets home."

All the air left Jonah's lungs. The landing light. He left it on whenever Jonah went out with his friends like a lighthouse calling him home, and Dad remembered, he remembered the tiny little gesture and provided it to him again now, something Jonah had forgotten about finally falling back into place.

"Okay. I'll tell him."

"And tell him . . . tell him . . . tell him we can play the piano when I get home . . . the song . . . what's the song again?"

"'You Win Again.'"

"Yes. The Bee Gees."

"That's right." Jonah placed his other hand over the top of his dad's and closed his eyes for just a moment, pretending they were in the garden back home, the grill on the BBQ hot, sausages cooking beneath the blistering summer sun while the sprinkler watered the vegetable patch.

"How does it go?" his dad asked, his eyes heavy but focused on Jonah.

Jonah took a breath and quietly recited the song to him, the tune one he could never forget, and he was there—a child again, sitting at the piano with his dad, their fingers dancing along the keys, and laughing each time his dad got the lyrics wrong. He sang to him, and they strolled along the beach as the sun kissed the waves before hiding beyond the horizon; the sea tickled their ankles as they held their shoes in their hands, knitted jumpers covering their bodies as they talked about life and the dreams Jonah wished he might someday achieve. Dreams he *did* achieve. Dreams his father got to see him grasp and make his own. And as he reached the final chorus, his dad's hand in his, he was standing outside the Palace Theatre in London having just watched *Les Misérables* for the first time. And he knew his father would be there, alive in his memories, forever.

TWENTY-EIGHT

"I can still feel your hand in mine, just like the nights we danced beneath the stars, back when we were younger, when you were only mine."

—"The Melody of Achilles and Patroclus,"
The Wooden Horse, Act One

As the taxi pulled up the long gravel driveway, Jonah held his breath, realizing this would be his first time back in his old home now that his father had passed away. He and his mother stayed by his father's bedside as he drifted back to sleep, then, two hours later, he stopped breathing. Jonah kept hold of his hand, brushing his thumb over his dad's knuckles, telling him how much he loved him.

The hours since then passed in a blur; the day seemed to stretch on forever, and Jonah couldn't say he knew the time if someone asked him. But as they returned home, the sun still sat lazily in the autumn sky, orange and magnificent, bathing the ocean in shades of gold. Outside the house Dexter's car sat parked alongside Aunt Penny's, and Jonah couldn't quite believe he was still there, in his childhood home, waiting for him. He helped his mum out of the car, looping his arm around her waist, her body so small against his, and took her inside, where the heating had been put on and the smell of something aromatic wafted from the kitchen.

"Oh, Nancy," Penny said, greeting them in the cobblestoned hallway. She wrapped her arms around her sister, taking her from Jonah, and the two of them burst into tears. Jonah closed the front door and tried not to look at the family photo hanging on the wall beside it, his dad smiling at him, a reminder of happy days he could only hold onto now from within photographs. He left his mum and aunt in the hallway, Aunt Penny wiping away his mother's tears while she cried rivers of her own.

He heard movement inside the kitchen, pots and pans clanging together, and as he made his way to the hub of the house, he stopped in the doorway to see Dexter hunched over the stove stirring something in one of his mum's large cooking pans while Sally sat at the dining table nursing what he assumed could only be a glass of whiskey from his dad's liquor cabinet.

"Jonah," Sally said when she saw him. She rushed to pull him into a bone-crushing hug. "Oh, love, I'm so sorry."

"Thank you," Jonah said, still not fully comprehending the gravity of what had happened. It didn't feel real, his dad no longer being there, but he also felt a strange sense of relief knowing now his mind would be at rest and that there would be no more falls, no more confusion, no more pain.

"Jonah," Dexter said, tucking a tea towel into the belt loop of his trousers as he made his way over to them. "I don't know what to say."

"It's okay," Jonah said as Sally released him. "It's, um, it's okay."

"I wasn't sure if you and your mum would have eaten anything, or if you would even be hungry, but I made a curry . . . just in case." He gestured over to the pan on the oven, but immediately grimaced when he saw Jonah's blank expression. "Sorry, I shouldn't have—"

"What?" Jonah asked, snapping back into focus. "No, don't apologize, that's really lovely of you, thank you. I'm not sure mum will eat anything, but we can heat some up for her later if she wants to."

"I'm going to go speak to her," Sally said. She kissed Jonah's cheek, then made her way out to the hallway to where his mum and Aunt Penny still lingered.

"I'm surprised you're still here," Jonah said as he sat himself down at the dining table, his limbs suddenly heavy, the exhaustion from the day finally catching up with him. "I thought you might have gone back for the show."

"It didn't feel right to leave," Dexter said as he took the seat beside him. "But I can go. I realize this is a super-personal situation, and I'm not trying to insert myself into it."

"No, you're not doing that at all." Jonah didn't want to say how comforting it felt to have him there, even after their fight, even after the Dexah ship had sunk to the ocean floor.

Jonah looked around the kitchen, his eyes settling on several bottles of wine lined up along the edge of the counter. Dexter saw him looking and shook his head. "Apparently your mum and aunt rounded up all the wine in the house, and they're donating it to the local library for raffle prizes," he explained.

"Right," Jonah said, unsure, the bottles of wine almost threatening as they loomed in the room.

"Bastien and Sherrie both called me. I told them your phone was off. Omari then texted asking for your mum's address so he can send some flowers and herbal teas or something. I also spoke to Evie and told her what was happening and that you would contact her when you're able, but I told her not to expect to see you for a few days at the very least."

"Thank you."

"Bash asked if you could call him when you feel up to it too. He's worried about you."

Jonah nodded. "Sure."

"Jonah." Dexter went to reach for his hand then stopped himself. "I'm so sorry. If there's anything I can do, please just say."

"You've already done enough, Dex, seriously. You've done more than most people would do. Driving me here . . . I wouldn't have got here in time otherwise. Thank you."

"You don't need to thank me."

Jonah wiped his eyes as he tried to stifle a yawn. "I need to go lie down. I don't know if I'll be able to sleep but . . . fuck, my body hurts."

"I made the bed," Dexter said quickly. "So, it's all good for you up there . . . you don't want to try and eat something first?"

"It smells amazing, but I don't think I can stomach anything right now."

Dexter gave an understanding nod. "Well. I'm going to head back first thing in the morning. I'll sleep on the sofa tonight, if that's okay?"

"Oh, you can . . . you can share the bed with me, it's fine, honestly I—"

"I'll sleep on the sofa," Dexter said with a sad smile. "If you're still asleep by the time I have to leave I won't bother you, but please message me when you get up? Just because we . . . I'm still here for you."

Jonah nodded, then pushed out of the chair to stand. He felt wobbly on his feet, as if he'd been drinking for hours, but he knew it came from the emotional fatigue he'd slumped into. "I'm still here for you too," Jonah said as he left the room, looking back at Dexter one last time before heading up to bed.

Colbie Paris didn't possess a single compassionate bone in her body. She spoke to Jonah with nothing but contempt on the phone as she expressed a deep frustration at him for taking time off work, even though his dad just died, and told him just how difficult he was making things for her. After her last call he screamed into his pillow, covering his face with it entirely, willing the feathers inside the case to absorb all the animosity he felt toward her. He'd only just got home, and she somehow knew he'd arrived back in London and plagued his phone with calls and texts, asking if he would be on as Achilles the next day. He knew Colbie was crossing professional lines; the way she was operating could not be ethical under any circumstances, but she made him believe he had done something wrong, that his father's death was nothing but a major inconvenience.

"I'll sort it out," Melanie said when she called him to check in on how he was doing. "It's bloody unacceptable. If she has an issue, she can talk to me from now on. Don't answer any calls from her."

"I just," Jonah said between tears. "I thought I could take compassionate leave."

"You can."

"But she said—"

"I don't give a flying fuck what she said. This is why you have me, to handle situations like this." She sounded angry, but luckily not with him. "How was the funeral? Did you get my flowers?"

"Yes, they were lovely, you didn't have to do that."

"It was the least I could do, Jonah."

"And the funeral . . . well, it was a funeral, can you even say a funeral went well? It was nice, loads of people came, and we listened to his Phil Collins records afterward."

"I'm glad it went as well as it could. Look, I want you to take a few days and call me next week so we can discuss work, but until then don't give it another thought. I mean it, Jonah, turn your phone off if you have to, and if you're not up to talking next week, just drop me a message and we can figure it out from there."

"Thanks, Melanie... You're not mad I wasn't around for the follow-up with the people from *Crazy for You*?"

"No," she said with surety. "Family comes first. Other jobs will come along. Keep well. You've got this, okay?" Thank God for Melanie Cowperthwaite and her no-nonsense attitude. He would crumble without her, and he made a mental note to send her a thank-you card and a box of chocolates the next time he ventured out of the house.

He didn't want to turn his phone off, though. He could screen his calls from Colbie, especially as he'd now set Melanie on her, but he wanted to stay connected with everyone else; he'd never felt so lonely. He needed Bastien and Sherrie; he needed Omari to tell him to stop eating ice cream and cheese because his body was practically made of mucus at this point. And he needed Dexter, though he couldn't reach out to him, not now that he'd fucked everything up. Not long ago, he had been trying not to sing while walking down the street, a spring in his step as he danced through a rainstorm. Now there would be no singing in the rain; he didn't have anything left to sing about. His career was in a downward spiral, his family was broken, and his love life had disintegrated right in front of his eyes.

As he lay on his bed, he thought about his first night in London all those years ago. He didn't know anyone, he didn't have a job, an agent, a boyfriend, nothing to really call his own. But Castle Road took him in and he built his way up, and now he would have to do the same thing all over again. At least this time he had friends, he had an agent, and his career would hopefully survive the wrath of Colbie Paris. And as for his love life? Well, that could remain on the back burner.

"Hey, love," Bastien said as Jonah opened the door, and Jonah could see him trying not to judge the clothes he was wearing.

"Don't judge me," Jonah warned, stepping aside to let him in. "I feel like I've not slept in a year, and I got home to find I had barely any clean clothes, so it's the old tracksuit or nothing." He slammed his front door after Bastien let himself inside and closed out the gale force winds pummeling down the road.

"I don't care what you look like," Bastien said as he hugged him. "You smell gross, though, darling."

"I know," Jonah said, his voice muffled as he buried his face against Bastien's shoulder.

"When did you last shower?" Jonah paused as he thought about it, and Bastien groaned and pushed him away. "If you have to think about it that long, Jonah, it's time for a fucking bath."

"I know, I know," Jonah said, and he led the way to the kitchen. "But I didn't know you were coming until about ten minutes ago or I would have made myself pretty for you."

"You still look pretty," Bastien conceded. "And I can deal with your stench. I've really missed you." Bastien leaned against the countertop as he watched Jonah fill up the kettle. "How are you? Or is that a stupid question?"

"You know what, I'm actually okay? I think it's sunk in now that he's gone. I helped mum sort his stuff at the nursing home, and I brought some of his records back with me. I think it's just going to be a case of making sure Mum is okay now."

"Is she still drinking?" Bastien asked, trying to keep his voice light, but Jonah could see the concern in the way he twisted his mouth.

"My aunt is keeping an eye on her. Obviously, she can't be watched all the time, but I think she's doing okay, considering."

"And you're really doing okay?"

Jonah got two mugs from the cupboard and shrugged. "Yeah. I'm okay."

"You'll be back to work soon?"

"Why? Has Colbie sent you to get information out of me?"

Bastien made an unimpressed huffing noise and shook his head. "She's barely spoken to me in weeks, the cow. Who knew she would be so bitter about me leaving?"

Jonah scooped out two spoonfuls of sugar into Bastien's mug. "You didn't tell me you told her. She didn't take it well?"

"She's recast me already," Bastien said with a laugh. "I thought you of all people would know that."

"Why would I know that? You think Colbie shares anything important with me? I think she wants me to vanish into the ether so she doesn't have to think about me ever again."

Bastien scowled and grabbed the cup then tipped the sugar back into the sugar jar. "No. I'm on a strict wedding diet. Don't make me fat, Jonah."

"But you always have sugar in your tea."

"And I'm cutting down. Omari told me the other day I was looking saggy." He ran his hands down his sides to his hips to emphasize his physique. "Gotta keep all toned for my husband to be."

"Oh, he would love you no matter what," Jonah said and heaped three spoons of sugar into his own cup for good measure. "And you're not saggy. Ignore Omari."

"It's hard to ignore Omari, though, isn't it? And I didn't think Colbie would tell you about the person taking over my role, I thought Dexter would."

"Why?"

Bastien frowned, his brows furrowing as he looked at Jonah like he'd just said the most stupid thing in the world. "Because he's going to be Patroclus after I leave? I mean, it makes sense, it's a bigger role than Hector. And he came to talk to me about it first, which was sweet, and I said of course it's okay, because I'm gonna be in New York living my best married-man life."

"I thought Dexter was taking over Achilles?"

"You're Achilles," Bastien said slowly, as if someone had knocked Jonah over the head and he was now giving him all his life information. "Why would he be taking over your role? Are you leaving?"

"Wait. Is that official? He's going to be Patroclus?"

"Yeah, he said Colbie had been in touch with his agent. I think they signed contracts a couple of weeks ago. Why is that a problem? Surely, getting to make out with your boyfriend every night isn't a bad thing?"

"He's not . . . We broke up."

Bastien's expression changed from trepid concern to annoyance. "Nope." He shook his head. "I've had Sherrie wailing down the phone at me about breaking up with Romana. I'm not having the same shit with you. No. I'm not having all that back-and-forth between the two of you for months, which nearly broke me, by the way, just for it to end so quickly. Nope. No way. What's the problem and how do I fix it?"

"Oh God, I think I'm gonna throw up." Dexter hadn't gone behind his back. He hadn't tried taking Achilles. He was leaving behind Hector, sure, but taking on Patroclus, a role he played so perfectly back when Bastien was ill all those months ago. Patroclus. Not Achilles. And Jonah accused him, he shouted at him and told him he didn't trust him over his own Goddamned insecurities.

"Don't you dare throw up on me," Bastien said, backing away while pointing at the sink. "In the sink, babe, in the sink."

"I'm such a fucking idiot," Jonah whined, gripping the edge of the work surface as he groaned loudly. "This is my fault. It's all my fault."

"I'm sure you can fix it."

"I can't."

"Look, don't put pressure on yourself," Bastien said, daring to come closer again as he placed a comforting hand on Jonah's back and rubbed small circles there to comfort him. "You've got a lot going on right now. Give it some time. If it's meant to be, then it's meant to be, right?"

"I should have trusted him."

"What happened?"

"I saw him at a meeting with Colbie and his agent. And I thought they were signing contracts for him to take over as Achilles. And I thought that because Colbie had been dropping hints to *my* agent about not renewing my contract. I hate her, Colbie, I fucking hate her."

"She's an absolute idiot," Bastien fumed. "You know what? Fuck her. Fuck her. She doesn't deserve you. She doesn't deserve me. She doesn't deserve Dexter either." Bastien paused then rubbed a hand over Jonah's back again. "Let it all out, babe," Bastien said, and it only dawned on Jonah then he wasn't just shouting, but he was crying too. A weight lifted from his shoulders, and he could finally see the end of an endless dark tunnel. He could see light there, and he could run toward it, and hopefully find Dexter along the way.

TWENTY-NINE

"Come with me. We don't need their war. We can bathe in rivers and feast on the fruits of the vine."

—"Come with Me," *The Wooden Horse*, Act Two

Julianna kissed Jonah's cheeks before cupping her hands around his and smiling warmly at him. He knew he performed well, but he wasn't expecting such an emotional response from her. He had just finished singing "I Don't Care Much." He saw the way she watched him as he performed, her eyes following his every movement before she tried, and failed, to blink back tears.

"You were amazing," she said, leaning close to him before letting out a giddy laugh. "Isn't he just perfect?" she called over her shoulder to the rest of her team, who gave a whooping cheer and clapped their hands together. "I knew this role was made for you the moment I saw you onstage at the Persephone, but I needed to make sure, and I'm so glad you came here today and did what you just did up on that stage."

"Thank you," Jonah said, and she hugged him, then bobbed up and down on the balls of her feet in excitement.

"I'm going to be calling Melanie as soon as you leave. I really hope you take this part, Jonah. We are going to be making something truly magical, and you're going to be at the heart of it. And, on a completely personal level, thank you so much for coming here today. Melanie told me these past couple of weeks have been hard for you. I'm so sorry for your loss."

"Oh," Jonah said, flustered. "Thank you. It's been . . . I don't even know where to begin."

"I lost my mum last year," she said. "I understand how overwhelmed you must feel right now."

"It's an odd feeling more than anything."

"Melanie said you're back onstage tonight. Are you sure you're ready?" Julianna asked.

"Yeah. Dad wouldn't want me moping around. He'd probably be cross with me for taking any time off, actually."

"Well, break a leg, okay? We are all rooting for you."

Jonah felt like a broken record as he thanked her and the rest of the casting team again and again. He was still floating in a sort of daze. She loved him. They all did. He took the song, a song he once played on the piano with his father, and placed everything else to the back of his mind. He hadn't felt like this since his audition for Achilles. He left the room back then with a small glimmer of hope that he might get the role, and he did, and now . . . now Julianna Orwell was asking him to be part of one of her shows.

He kept his hands in his pockets as he walked, turning the month's events over and over in his head. His father's death, the funeral, breaking up with Dexter, and now, to finish it off, auditioning for Julianna. He stopped on Brick Lane and grabbed a coffee, balking at the cost of it but paying anyway. He walked down the street and sipped it as a small burst of rain splattered from the sky. The coffee tasted bitter and burned the back of his tongue, but he'd be damned if he didn't pretend to enjoy his five-pound cortado. As the rain gained momentum, he ducked down the metal stairs that led to the Brick Lane vintage market to avoid the downpour.

He'd been here a few times with Sherrie and stood by as she fawned over retro jackets and oversized sunglasses. He'd even been here once with Bastien when he insisted he needed a particular style of cowboy boots and got it in his head they would be waiting for him at the market. They weren't, and he left in a mood before buying some overpriced sliders at a pop-up fashion shop in Covent Garden. Jonah preferred regular stores; he didn't like having to search through racks upon racks to find something he liked only to be disappointed when it wasn't his size or cost more than his monthly rent. Today, however, the market wasn't as crowded as it usually was, and he meandered around without the pressure of Sherrie needing to find all the bargains or Bastien darting toward anything that resembled a cowboy.

He took little interest in the clothes, looking down at his phone rather than actively browsing, absently scrolling through Dexter's Instagram. He'd archived a lot of the photos of them together, the ones of them messing about backstage that the Dexah fans went wild over when he posted them. Now the gossip forums were filled with #RIPDexah hashtags, though neither of them confirmed a breakup. They had nothing to confirm, given they never made anything official on social media, but Dexter removing the photos spoke more than words ever could. He hadn't, however, deleted the photo he posted of Jonah the day after Wes attacked him, and Jonah read and reread the caption until he could see it even when he closed his eyes:

> @Itsjonahpenrose I promise to always make you smile like this, even on the days when smiling is the last thing you want to do.

He didn't know if Dexter left it there deliberately or if he'd forgotten to remove it when culling Jonah from his social media, but he hoped it was the former, that the promise still stood. Jonah just needed to sort himself out, which was exactly what he was going to do. As he slipped his phone into his pocket, deciding he'd had enough of Dexter's salad photos and pouting selfies, he stopped in his tracks and stared at the garment in front of him.

A jumper. Forest green with a Golden Labrador embroidered on the front. It truly was as hideous as Jonah remembered it. He ran his fingers along the collar then down the sleeves and turned it inside out to look at the label. Piniquo. And there, just beneath the label, was an ironed-on name tag reading *Dexter Ellis*. Because of course Dexter ironed his name into his atrocious items of clothing.

"What are the bloody chances?" Jonah muttered to himself as the woman behind the till craned her neck to look at him.

"That's a Piniquo. It's part of their limited collection. They didn't make many of those," she said with a smile.

"Thank God for that," Jonah said back, which earned him an unhappy look from her. Clearly the Labrador had more fans than just Dexter. "How much is it?"

"Well, it *is* Piniquo," she said, clicking her tongue against the back of her teeth. "I'll let it go for seventy."

"Seventy *pounds*?" Jonah almost choked on his own spit.

"It's Piniquo."

"Where did you even get this? It belongs to my friend. It's got his name in it." Jonah pointed to the name label.

The woman shrugged. "People bring stuff in all the time, and I buy it off them. Your friend must have brought it in."

Only, Jonah knew that definitely wasn't the case, but he wasn't about to argue with a stranger over an ugly Labrador jumper.

"Seventy seems a lot."

"They sell for over two hundred brand new. And that one's in mint condition."

Two hundred pounds. Dexter had spent over two hundred pounds on the ugliest jumper known to man. "Fine," Jonah said, and he almost wept as he handed over his debit card and the woman packed up the repulsive thing and popped it into a paper bag.

"Enjoy your new jumper," she said with a smile that said, *you're an absolute mug for paying that much.* And Jonah just nodded and walked away from the daylight robbery.

Dexter opened his dressing room door and smiled when he saw Jonah standing on the other side. Jonah wasn't quite sure of the reaction he would get from him. They had texted only once since Dexter left Cornwall, then they left each other alone like any normal people who had just broken up would do. But the smile he gave Jonah told him he'd missed him, and it made Jonah's heart yearn for him yet again, because Jonah missed him too. He really, really missed him.

"I got you a present," Jonah said, holding up the paper bag with a grin.

"What? Why?"

"As a thank you for driving me to Cornwall."

"Jonah, seriously, you didn't have to—"

"Open it," Jonah said, shoving the bag into Dexter's arms before moving past him to go into the dressing room where he sat himself down in Dexter's chair. "You're gonna bloody love it, trust me."

Dexter raised an eyebrow and opened the bag, peering inside. A brief flicker of confusion worked its way over his face before he pulled the jumper out of the bag, his mouth spreading into the brightest of smiles.

"You got me a new one," he said under his breath while running his fingers over the embroidery at the front. "Jonah, this is honestly too much, I know how much these things cost."

"Actually," Jonah said, standing up again to take the jumper from him and turn it inside out so he could point at the name ironed inside. "It's not new. It's yours."

Dexter stared for a moment, then an obscene pout formed on his lips. "So, you *did* steal it that night? I knew you swiped it from me, I just knew it."

"No." Jonah laughed. "No, I swear to God I didn't steal it. I hate it. I hate it even more now I had to buy it from an overpriced vintage stall. But I found it, and it had your name on it, so I couldn't just leave it there, could I?"

Dexter eyed him suspiciously. "You promise you haven't been hiding this for months to then look like the hero for bringing it back?"

"You could just say thank you, you know. Now I can't afford to eat for a week because of that thing."

Dexter's expression softened, and he rubbed the material between his fingers, acquainting himself with it again as if saying hello to an old friend. "Thank you," he said, then hesitantly made a move to hug Jonah, but stopped, only for Jonah to finish what he started. He wrapped his arms around him while Dexter did the same.

"I've really missed you," Dexter whispered. "I've had no one around messing up their blocking or fumbling their lines to gloat over at the end of the show."

"Fuck off." Jonah laughed, stepping back to smile at him fondly. "I've missed you too. Even missed those pesky little critiques."

"I've wanted to call, but I didn't want to intrude. But I've thought about you every day, Jonah. There's so much I've wanted to tell you."

The clock above Dexter's dressing table clicked loudly into the room, telling them they didn't have time, they didn't have the luxury of being able to just stop and talk to each other; Troy waited for them, their onstage deaths needed to be carried out before anything of importance could pass between them.

"Do you want to go for that drink we never went for?" Jonah asked. "Tomorrow morning, coffee?"

Dexter nodded right away. "Yeah." He clutched the jumper in his hands. "That would be nice."

"And I think I know what it is you need to talk to me about."

"You do?"

"Yes. It's about ironing name labels into your clothes, isn't it?"

Dexter chucked the jumper at him then, hitting Jonah square in the face as he laughed. "You need to shut your face, Jonah Penrose. I used to live with six other people when I first moved to London and had to label all my shit otherwise I'd never see it again. There's nothing wrong with being organized."

"I wasn't judging you."

"Yes, you were, you prick." Warmth spread through Dexter's voice. "Now leave me alone so I can get ready. I need to look perfect so I can upstage you."

Jonah watched as Dexter sat down and grabbed some of the powder by the side of his mirror to brush over his face. The ease with which they settled into each other again made him believe it might be okay. Even if their romantic relationship couldn't be salvaged, there would be a friendship left in the foundations, one Jonah would take and hold onto forever. He needed Dexter in his life.

THIRTY

*"We let them sleep tonight with a false sense of peace.
For tomorrow we rain fire down upon them."*

—"The Horse," *The Wooden Horse*, Act Two

Dexter stirred his green tea while Jonah dipped his finger into a large hot chocolate complete with whipped cream and marshmallows. A large dollop of cream coated his fingertip, and he raised it to his lips to lick it off and groaned all while Dexter focused on him intently.

"That's literally the best whipped cream in the world." He looked at Dexter. "You want some?"

Dexter cleared his throat and shook his head. "No, thanks."

"Right, can't spoil the delectable taste of green tea with something that has an actual flavor."

"Green tea does have a flavor."

"You're right," Jonah agreed. "It tastes like punishment."

Dexter smoothed his hands down his jumper, maroon with an embroidered pineapple just beneath the center of the collar, though Jonah admitted to himself it wasn't as bad as some of the others.

"If you're quite finished insulting my choice of drink, I think we should get to what I need to say to you."

Patroclus. Jonah knew the important announcement would be him taking over the role from Bastien, but he kept his expression neutral. "Sure. Go ahead."

"I fired Stephen."

Jonah froze with his finger in midair, piled high with whipped cream.

He stared at Dexter for several seconds until the cream flopped off his finger and splattered onto the table.

"You what?"

"I fired him. I don't know if that's the correct term for parting ways with an agent? I'm going with fired because it sounds more dramatic," Dexter said smugly and grabbed a napkin to wipe up Jonah's mess. "I guess I have you to thank for it. You told me I had issues with trust, too, and at first, I didn't want to admit that, but you were right. I do. And it's all down to him."

"Wow, Dex, that's huge."

"I know. And it wasn't until . . . okay, so, I have something else I need to tell you."

"Go on."

"I know you think I've been conspiring behind your back to take Achilles from you, but it's honestly not the case, because I've enjoyed playing Hector," he said as he wrapped his hands around his drink. "But after Bastien said he wouldn't be renewing for another year, Colbie offered me Patroclus."

Jonah nodded slowly, the truth finally being placed on the table in front of him. "Right."

"Which is what the meeting was about, the one you saw us at. They were both pushing for me to sign on, but something didn't feel right, so I didn't. Stephen basically screamed at me when we got back to his office. And . . . and he said some stuff that really bloody hurt."

"What did he say?"

"Did you know Henrik auditioned for Achilles?" Dexter asked, focusing on his tea rather than Jonah. "Because I didn't. I was doing *West Side Story*, as you know, and that's where Stephen met Henrik, and he signed him as a client." He took a deep breath. "Their affair started then. And I think I knew it at the time, but I didn't want to acknowledge it because I was so in love with Stephen, I would have done anything to keep him."

Jonah dipped his finger back into his cream and licked it again. "I get it. Sometimes pretending nothing's wrong is easier than accepting the truth."

"And that's not even the thing that's hurt me the most," Dexter said. "He told me he withdrew my name from consideration for Achilles. He called Colbie and said I was no longer interested, just so Henrik would be seen as a contender."

"Sorry, what? He did *what*?" Jonah leaned forward as he spoke, the anger he felt at stupid Stephen Carrington practically melting the marshmallows dotted on top of his drink.

"Of course, it backfired, because you then came along and blew Henrik out of the water."

"Dexter, I'm so sorry."

"He told me they didn't want me. He made me feel shunted, like I wasn't good enough, and he saw what that did for my self-esteem. Then he crushed me even further by leaving me to be with Henrik all while we were still in a show together." Dexter sniffed and quickly swiped his hand beneath his eyes, stilling any tears that threatened to fall. "And Henrik loved it. He loved seeing me feel like shit behind the scenes. I begged Stephen to get me an audition for something, anything else, and I think he only did it out of pity, but thank God he did."

"He's a bastard," Jonah said, trying hard not to grind his teeth out of sheer frustration. "You didn't deserve any of that."

"This all came out the day of the meeting, which is why I was angry that night. I was angry at what Stephen admitted to, angry at Colbie for trying to force me into another role to capitalize on my relationship with you, and angry at *you* for meeting with one of the biggest directors in the industry without telling me." He looked up from his drink. "Are you leaving the show?"

Melanie had called Jonah at nine thirty-two that morning and told him she'd just got off the phone with Julianna, and that they were officially offering him the role of the Emcee. Contracts would be sent over by the afternoon, and if Jonah was happy, then he could sign and Melanie could call Colbie and tell her where to stick her poor attitude. It should have been news Jonah shared with his partner, something he could scream about with Dexter the moment he got off the phone, if he didn't think of him as his enemy, even when he knew full well that's not what he was.

"Yeah. I'm leaving," Jonah said. "Colbie's been awful to me, Dex. I feel like I'm walking on eggshells around her, not knowing if my position is safe, and that's down to her hinting to my agent that I wouldn't be offered another year. So, yeah, I met with Julianna, and I'm going to be leaving at the end of my contract."

Dexter nodded slowly, then pushed his tea away from him. "What's the show?"

"*Cabaret*."

Something lit up behind Dexter's eyes, a recognition; he remembered their conversation in bed after spending the night together for the first time. "Please tell me it's the role you've dreamed of."

"It is."

"Jonah," he said, voice softening. "Jonah, that's amazing. I'm so happy for you."

"I'm sorry I didn't tell you. I'm sorry I didn't involve you in any of this. I should have, and it's my fault for being insecure."

"I don't blame you for being insecure. It's the way this industry works, isn't it? We have to exude confidence, but behind closed doors there's mountains of rejection and constant self-doubt. And working with Colbie Paris will shrink anyone's self-worth. She's treated Bastien terribly since he gave her notice, and now she's doing the same to me."

"Because you won't play Patroclus?"

"Because I'm not extending at the end of my contract either."

It took Jonah a moment to get his head around what Dexter just admitted. "But, Dex, you can be Achilles again. I'm leaving. The role's open, and you know it's yours. People want you to play him again."

"You know, I think I'm done with Achilles," Dexter said with a laugh that sounded more sad than joyful. "It's time to let go. I knew I needed to let him go the first time I saw you as him. You were beautiful, and still are. You've taken that role and made it your own."

"Dex—"

"Jonah." He smiled. "It's going to be okay. I got a new agent the moment I got back from Cornwall, and she set me up with an audition straight away. And I got it."

"You did?"

"Yeah. The paperwork's all signed. Which means we are both saying goodbye to *The Wooden Horse*."

"What role did you get?"

"Bobby Child"

"Wait." Jonah couldn't stop himself from laughing and put his hands over his face. "*Crazy for You?*" he asked as he lowered his hands, only to see Dexter looking royally pissed off at him.

"Why is that so funny?"

"I auditioned for Bobby," Jonah said, as he continued to laugh. "I was rubbish. Totally rubbish. Went left instead of right. You and your aversion to the right clearly rubbed off on me."

Dexter allowed himself to laugh as well. "Wait. Really? *You* auditioned for Bobby?"

"Yeah."

"I didn't know you could tap-dance."

"I can't. I mean, I can, but not to that standard." Jonah wiped a tear from his eye and took a deep breath to calm himself. "I'm so glad you got it. You're going to be amazing. I can't wait to come see you in it."

"You'll come watch?" Dexter asked, sounding surprised.

"Well, yeah, obviously?" Jonah's stomach dropped as he took in Dexter's suddenly subdued expression. "Would you not want me to?"

"I thought that maybe once *The Wooden Horse* is done for us, then that would be it, you know? Working with an ex is one thing, but continuing to be around that person when you no longer need to be might be seen as strange."

Jonah looked at his hot chocolate, the whipped cream dribbling down the glass in a sticky mess. "I don't want to be your ex, Dexter."

"I don't want you to be my ex, either, but I don't think you've somehow managed to overcome your distrust of me in a couple of weeks. We can't be together without trust, Jonah. It's not fair to either of us."

"Do you trust me?" Jonah asked.

"Yes."

"Then let me try this again. Please. I've let my past experiences have an impact on us, I know that, and I can't go back and change anything. And, honestly, I never thought I would be sitting here opposite you asking you to be patient with me, because, Dexter, you were a royal dick to me when we first met."

Dexter grimaced. "I know. I know this isn't all on you."

"But we've not come this far to let it slip through our fingers. I love you. I meant it when I said that, Dex, and I still mean it now."

"Is love enough?"

The hot chocolate suddenly turned Jonah's stomach. He didn't know what to expect from their conversation, but he hoped they might be able to move past the wall they'd built out of sheer stupidity. But Dexter couldn't see a way around it, and Jonah feared that no matter how many bricks he pulled from the foundations Dexter would keep putting them back in place. Jonah bit down on his bottom lip to stop it from trembling. He *did* trust Dexter. He trusted that Dexter loved him, that he would drive six hours in the middle of the night for him, that he'd walk by his side protectively to stop people from hurting him. He wanted to give Dexter his heart and trusted he wouldn't do anything to hurt it, but Dexter wouldn't take it.

"We should really be heading to the theatre," Jonah said, rising from his seat and grabbing his coat from the back of the chair. He looked past Dexter through the large window at the front of the café to see a torrential downpour of rain waiting for him outside.

"Should we get a taxi? We'll get soaked in that," Dexter said, picking up his own coat to shrug over his shoulders.

"I'm actually just gonna get the tube, but you get a taxi, seriously. I think I need to just clear my head for a bit."

"Oh. Okay, yeah, sure," Dexter said as Jonah's fight-or-flight mode kicked in again and he walked away, his heart pounding in his chest.

Jonah stepped out into the rain and shivered, the cold air wrapping itself around his body as he walked along the pavement, not caring that his hair was already sticking to his forehead. He thought to himself that if his life was a musical, then now would be the perfect time for a groundbreaking ballad where the orchestra soared as he choked back tears. Only, this wasn't a musical. There were no violins, no slow dances, and no lyrics to sing. But then again, that song in a musical would usually signify change, the place where the main character reflected on their journey and found the strength to go on before ending the show with the most outstanding symphony. Perhaps this was Jonah's turning point; he could easily look back to the beginning of the year and see he wasn't the same person he was back then; he had been in a relationship based on lies, performing night after night without realizing he could be more than just the role he thought he didn't deserve. Because he did deserve it. Even now, knowing Stephen pulled Dexter from the running, he knew he earned Achilles, and a part of him believed that even if Dexter hadn't been screwed over by his agent, he would have still beat him out for the role.

Because Jonah was bloody good at his job. He could sing the socks off most people, he could dance, though maybe tap wasn't his forte, and he could act; he knew he could make people laugh and cry with the way he delivered his lines, and he could sleep well knowing he excelled in those things. And maybe he really should have realized this before; maybe it would have saved his relationship, or maybe it wouldn't have. Maybe he and Dexter were always meant to crash and burn as quickly as their flame ignited. But, for now, love wasn't enough, and Jonah needed to accept that and move on, even if moving on from Dexter Ellis seemed like an impossible task. He needed to try.

THIRTY-ONE

"You are blinding, like the sun."
—"Eternity," *The Wooden Horse*, Act Two

Jonah woke to the sound of something tapping against his window. At first, he ignored it, figuring it could only be overly confident droplets of rain, and he allowed himself to drift back to sleep. Only, the tapping didn't stop. When the taps became harder and more frequent, he resigned himself to the fact someone was trying to break into his house and he was too tired to care or do anything about it. They could take whatever they wanted as long as they didn't take his duvet and they let him sleep. It wasn't as if his drawers were filled with Piniquo clothes and designer shoes. But whoever was trying to break into his house was clearly doing a terrible job of it; they didn't break into any doors, and the tapping continued relentlessly until Jonah let out an angry groan and got out of bed, plodding toward the window with his duvet wrapped around himself.

The streetlights on Castle Road were out, indicating the unsociable hour, but even in the darkness Jonah could see the heavy sheets of rain pounding onto the road below. And there, on the pavement outside his front door, stood his potential thief. Jonah cracked open the window as a stone flew up and just missed his face. He swore under his breath and leaned his head out, the rain flocking to dance in his curls, peering down at the person below who looked up at him with wide eyes.

Dexter.

"Jonah!" he called up, not keeping his voice quiet despite the sleepy state of Castle Road. "Jonah, I'm an idiot."

"Are you throwing stones at my window?" Jonah hissed, trying not to wake his neighbors, even if Dexter didn't have the same concern.

"You weren't answering your phone, so, yes."

"Why not knock on the door?"

"I did."

The rain had well and truly soaked every inch of him. As Jonah's eyes adjusted to the darkness, he could see the coat Dexter wore clinging to his body, his hair saturated and floppy across his forehead as his breath twirled in the air in front of his face. They had said little during the double show day at the Persephone; they didn't outright avoid each other, but they didn't spend any time together either. So, seeing Dexter beneath his window in the middle of the night, his palm filled with stones, was really not anything Jonah could have expected. But then again, he could never guess what Dexter Ellis might do next. The man was a mystery, endearingly so.

"Please let me in. It's cold," Dexter said.

Jonah looked down at him, knowing full well he was going to let him in, but he lingered there for a moment, taking in his face shining beneath the moon and glistening with raindrops. If it wasn't the most ridiculous thing in the world, it might have been romantic, the perfect moment from a film, the balcony scene from *Romeo and Juliet* without the mountains of death at the end. Jonah moved away from the window and shut it as quietly as possible before heading downstairs to let the not-burglar into his home. When he opened the door Dexter stepped closer, but he didn't attempt to come inside. He looked at Jonah in his pajamas, hair ruffled from sleep, eyes heavy, face confused, and opened his mouth to speak as a loud clap of thunder rumbled across the sky.

"Come in," Jonah said as he gripped the door, moving aside to let Dexter in, but he stayed where he was. "Dex, you're standing out in the middle of a thunderstorm, come in."

"No. Let me say this first." Dexter took a deep breath. "I'm stupid. I'm so fucking stupid, Jonah. Of course love is enough. It's more than enough. And it isn't even love, it's more than that. We don't have to rely on just love, because this, us, is so much more than love." He talked quickly, the words tumbling from his lips. "I don't know why I didn't just kiss you in the café and tell you I still want to make you smile every day, that I want to be that person for you. If you'll let me. Please let me, Jonah."

Dexter Ellis, the penis destroyer, the guy with an incomparable ego and questionable fashion sense, wanted him. He wanted to give himself to Jonah and make him *smile* for fuck's sake. Jonah stepped outside, his feet bare against the pavement, and he let the rain cover his body as he cupped Dexter's cheeks and pressed his lips to his. Dexter wrapped his arms around Jonah's waist and kissed him back. His skin was freezing, yet the way he kissed burned; the passion there, the intense need and tension they'd put aside for weeks suddenly pouring out between them. He tasted like mint plucked straight from the garden and a hint of butterscotch, sweet and smooth, like the ones from the candy shop back home in St. Ives. Jonah didn't know how long they stood out there in the rain in the dark. It could have been only a moment or an eternity, time stood still with Dexter; and he was there, with Jonah, where he always should have been.

"Come inside," Jonah whispered, pulling Dexter by the lapel of his coat into the hallway, where the rainwater dripped from them and created puddles on the floor. Jonah suspected Dexter might complain in the morning when his designer clothes were sopping wet, but there, in the moment, it didn't matter. A little drop of rain never hurt. But it made them both tremble from the cold, and Dexter slid the coat from his shoulders and let it fall to the floor before reaching forward to pull the pajama top over Jonah's head.

Jonah ran his hands over Dexter's shirt, the material clinging to his skin, and as he unbuttoned it, he let his fingers trail along Dexter's collarbone, skin damp, glistening, beautiful, like always. He guided the shirt from Dexter's shoulders and let it fall to the floor with the other items of clothing before he unbuttoned Dexter's jeans and watched as he stepped out of them. His underwear clung to his thighs, and they stood looking at each other, chests heaving as the silence of the night swirled around them. Dexter kissed him again, gathering him against the wall, their bodies flush against each other, and Jonah could feel just how hard Dexter was as he pressed his thigh against him. Dexter let out a moan, and he ran his fingers through Jonah's wet hair as he trailed kisses down his neck, nipping at the skin slightly, making Jonah shudder.

"I love you," he whispered against his skin, and Jonah's spine tingled as Dexter kissed down his abdomen. "I've missed you." Dexter dropped to his knees and wasted no time in removing the pajama bottoms from Jonah's body.

The heat from Dexter's mouth made the weather outside seem distant, and Jonah could have honestly stood there until fireworks lit up his world, but he needed more, he wanted more; he wanted Dexter in every way possible, and he reluctantly guided him from his knees back up his body to kiss his mouth again and again until Dexter was moaning against his lips indecently.

"Come upstairs," Jonah said between kisses, pulling Dexter to the staircase, their hands barely leaving each other as they made their way up to Jonah's bedroom. Dexter lay himself on the sheets, unmade and messy, his lips slightly swollen, cheeks flushed red, and God, Jonah wished he could keep that image of him. Beautiful and yearning to be touched. Jonah crawled between his thighs, and Dexter let him explore his body, his tongue tracing lines from his navel to his hips, tantalizingly slow. Dexter dropped his head back onto the pillow as he panted, words coming from his mouth but none of them audible, and Jonah loved that he could render him a mumbling mess with just his mouth.

"I've missed you," Jonah said as he kissed his thighs. "So. Fucking. Much."

"God, Jonah, please—"

"Please what?"

"I need you."

Jonah smirked and ran his fingers along the sensitive skin on Dexter's hip bones. "What do you need me to do?"

Dexter groaned in response and bucked his hips up, needy, his body tense, and Jonah could easily help him unwind, but he wanted this to last, to take the pace and slow it right down so he could remember each little moan and movement.

"I want you to fuck me," Dexter said, voice hoarse, full of want. His hazel eyes locked on Jonah's, and he reached for Jonah's hands, pulling him close to kiss him. "Please. Please fuck me."

"So polite," Jonah hummed before pulling away to grab the lube and a condom from his bedside drawer. They'd never done this, not Jonah fucking him; previously it had always been the other way round. It was just how they fell into things, and Jonah was more than happy with that. But he *had* thought about what it might be like ever since Dexter said, "What if I would rather be on top of you like that?" back in rehearsals months ago.

And, yeah, he'd definitely thought about Dexter on his lap, riding him, far more times than he would care to admit, because the thought of it drove Jonah wild. He reveled in taking his time, making the most delightful moans and gasps drop from Dexter's lips, until he writhed beneath him and even Jonah couldn't take it any longer, he wanted him, he wanted him so badly it hurt.

"Like this," Dexter said, placing his hands on Jonah's shoulders to keep him between his thighs. "Want to look at you." Dexter kissed him softly, the sudden desperation from only moments before gone, and they stayed like that for a couple of minutes, listening to the sounds of their breaths as they kissed slowly and Dexter allowed Jonah to move his legs, settling as Dexter nodded and placed his hands on the small of Jonah's back.

"Go slow," he said, and he gasped as Jonah pushed into him, and Jonah rested his forehead against Dexter's as he closed his eyes, losing himself in the feeling of him, of being inside him, and, fuck, he'd never felt this close to someone before.

The rain outside trickled down the windowpane, a constant and steady sound as they lost themselves in each other. Jonah's hands clutched the bedsheet on either side of Dexter's shoulders as he pushed into him, and he took in Dexter's features as the other man's eyes fluttered closed. Dark black eyelashes, pink lips, the little freckle just beneath his left eye, the miniscule scar on the edge of his jawline. He could write songs about him if only he possessed the talent to do him justice. Sex between them previously always came with an intense and passionate tension, but now, with it all stripped away, it felt all the more intimate. They found a rhythm together, Jonah finding just the right angle to position his thrusts to make Dexter cry out and gasp while muttering words beneath his breath. Jonah knew he wouldn't last long, not with Dexter beneath him like this. Not that endurance seemed to matter right then; it wasn't about the sex, not really, it was about them being together again, in the closest way they knew possible.

When Dexter came, he dug his fingers into Jonah's shoulders and moaned his name, arching his back and exposing his neck for Jonah to press more kisses against his skin. It didn't take long before Jonah came undone himself after that, the waves of his pleasure almost blinding, like seeing stars for the first time. Jonah practically collapsed next to him, his body utterly spent; sex after a two-show day was quite the feat, but he'd do it again and again if Dexter asked it of him. He wanted to feel like this with him always, close, closer than he'd ever been with someone, and content, happy, and safe.

"That was totally worth waiting out in the rain for," Dexter said as he tried to slow his breathing. "I feel like I need to sleep for a week."

Jonah rolled onto his side and kissed Dexter's cheek. "Maybe tomorrow you don't get up at the crack of dawn to go for a run, and you can stay in bed with me until we absolutely have to get up?"

"It's already past five," Dexter said, stifling a yawn.

"What? Seriously?"

"It was about four when I walked round here. So, definitely gone five by now."

"Why didn't you wait until morning to talk to me?" Jonah asked with a laugh. "I wasn't going anywhere."

"Because I lay wide awake in bed knowing I needed to see you and that I wouldn't be able to rest until I saw you. And, like I said, it was totally worth it. I regret nothing." He covered his hand with his mouth as he yawned. "I don't want you to think I'm rude by immediately going to sleep after sex."

"It's good to know I've worn you out."

"Well, it wasn't just you, though, was it? We did two shows yesterday, then I stayed awake until coming here, so don't big yourself up too much."

Jonah rolled his eyes and rested his head on the pillow. "Thank you, as always, for keeping me humble."

"You can always count on me, babe."

THIRTY-TWO

"The sun rises."

—"To Troy," *The Wooden Horse*, Act One

Colbie loomed in Evie's office, her hands flying over the keyboard on her laptop, eyes burning. Her red hair fell over her face, and if Jonah squinted his eyes, she looked like her head was made of flames, angry, always angry. He knocked on the door frame and her head snapped up toward him, unlit cigarette between her lips, and she pointed to the chair opposite her desk.

"Sit," she instructed, and Jonah hesitated, not wanting to take orders from her as if he were a dog, but he did as she said and sat awkwardly as she placed her cigarette down next to her laptop.

"Why the hell have I had your manager on the phone to me this morning informing me you will not be renewing your contract for another year?" Colbie asked, placing her hands flat on the wood of her desk and leaning forward to peer at him from behind wisps of red hair. "Don't you think this is something we should have been discussing ourselves? If you had talked to me, you would know we have planned to keep you on here for as long as possible."

He knew her words weren't fully honest; they only came from losing Bastien and Dexter, and now losing Jonah as well. Principal roles were often changed from year to year, it wasn't unusual to have an entirely new cast for a new season, but she was losing three powerhouses all in one fell swoop and it wasn't her choice to get rid of them.

"I thought it best to let Melanie deal with it, as she handles my contracts," Jonah said. "It's time for me to move on."

"You're making a huge mistake," she said, tapping her long fingernails against the desk. "This role is what's put your name on the map. You were nothing before coming here."

"Well, I know that's not true," he said, and noticed just how calm he felt talking with her. "I can't deny this role has been amazing for me, but to say I was nothing is a bit of a low blow, Colbie."

"You can't be going on to be doing something bigger than this. You're first billed, Jonah, it's your face on the promotional material, your name people recognize. I know what shows have been casting, and I know what shows are going to be opening. The only thing worth your time would have been *Crazy for You*, but we both know Dexter landed that." She couldn't have known about *Cabaret*; her comment only solidified that. Julianna kept the show on a strictly need-to-know basis, wanting to make the announcement as spectacular as possible.

"I'm not sure what the point you're trying to make here is?"

"I'm basically saying you're taking a step backward. Why do you want to leave for something that will no doubt only make you fade into the background?"

Jonah ran his tongue along his teeth as he thought of what to say. He didn't want to burn bridges with her, but at the same time, working with Colbie Paris again wasn't on his list of things to ever do again.

"I've not been happy with the way I've been treated here."

Colbie's eyebrows shot up in surprise. "What do you mean? Who's treated you badly?"

"You surely can't be that oblivious, Colbie."

She cocked her head slightly and rested against the back of her chair. "You've been unhappy with the way *I've* treated you? I'm sorry, Jonah, but I fail to see how anything I've ever done could be seen as mistreatment. I'm barely here."

"My dad died, and you called me repeatedly to tell me how me being off from the show was an inconvenience. You've constantly made me feel like I'm not good enough to be here. You told me I had to help ticket sales by forging a fake friendship with someone and tried to control my personal social media accounts. You're unprofessional, Colbie, and I don't want to work in this environment anymore."

Colbie's mouth twisted, and she crossed her arms over her chest. "I'm running a business here, Jonah. I need to know when my cast is going to be at work. I don't think calling you to ask that is unreasonable."

"I get that, but I didn't need the guilt trip to go along with it. It's why I have an agent, so you can talk to her when I'm not able to answer those questions. My dad had just died. I didn't care about this place. At all."

"Fine." She held her hands up in surrender. "But the other stuff? Social media is a tricky thing, people follow you because you're in the show and they want to know about your life. Plus, it's not like I asked you to lie, is it? You and Dexter seem perfectly happy to me."

"You're missing the point."

"What's the point, then, Jonah?"

"It's not right to make someone feel like they're constantly walking on eggshells. I've never felt so insecure in a position before. It's the weird mind games—"

"You really should choose your next words carefully if you want to ever work with me again, Jonah."

"I *don't* want to work with you again, Colbie." He knew admitting it to her face would blacklist him with her production company, CPTG, forever, but fuck it, he couldn't let himself be treated the same way ever again. Not by her. Not by anyone else. "You won't change. Why would you?" He waited for her to say something, but when she didn't, he sighed and pushed out the chair to stand. "I'm guessing we're done here, then?"

"I guess so."

"I still love this show," Jonah said seriously. "And I'm never going to look back on it with anything other than the best memories, because I've worked with some of the most talented and nicest people in the industry."

"Good for you, Jonah," Colbie said and waved her hand in the air, brushing away his words. "Get out of my sight and let's finish off these last few months so I can see the back of you."

Jonah let out a short, bitter laugh. She looked at him, her face unreadable. He thought he might have seen a flicker of regret there, but to expect any such emotion from Colbie was like finding the pot of gold at the end of the rainbow. Colbie Paris. The woman with fire for hair, who no longer dazzled Jonah like she used to, would now just be a shadow in the wings.

There must have been a time when Jonah didn't feel exhausted, when his body didn't cry out for sleep and his feet weren't covered in blisters. Going from rehearsals for *Cabaret* to the shows at the Persephone seemed fine in theory, but actually doing it for the past few months was absolutely not fine. It wasn't like he wasn't enjoying himself; he was, he loved the days in the studio with the people who were going to be his new theatre family; he loved working with Julianna, her professionalism and attention to detail beyond anything he could have imagined. He got to work long hours with Omari, who'd also secretly auditioned for the show and would be joining as one of the Kit Kat Club dancers. A beautiful ensemble role he would absolutely shine in. Which meant he received even more daily reminders to stay away from dairy and to cleanse his skin each and every second he wasn't rehearsing. His mind and body were exhausted. But he also loved going to the Persephone after rehearsals, putting on his costume for Achilles, and belting out song after song to sold-out audiences while sneaking in kisses with Dexter any moment he could.

Being at the theatre also meant he could comfort Sherrie, who seemed to burst into tears every time she saw him. She did the same to Bastien and Omari, her emotions surrounding them leaving far too great for her to handle. Jonah did his best to reassure her they'd still be friends, but he could see the uncertainty behind her eyes. Jonah knew theatre schedules could be notoriously unkind to friendships between shows. But they would make it work. At the very least, he knew he would be there to listen to her updates on her continuously baffling relationship with Romana. And in return, Sherrie promised to listen to Jonah talk about Dexter, though their romance contained far less drama than hers, which Jonah was eternally grateful for.

They somehow managed to settle back into their relationship quickly, invading each other's dressing rooms and heading back to Camden together after the shows. They split their nights between their homes, Jonah's clean but untidy place on Castle Road and Dexter's show-home level of organization and cleanliness over on Lawford. Some nights they said very little on their way home, both too tired; but just being together, palm to palm, created a deep sense of comfort. He craved more time with him, time to go on dates, time to run away and get lost in each other for hours on end, and time to talk into the early hours of the morning. Time they simply didn't have. For when Jonah was rehearsing for *Cabaret*, Dexter put in the hours for *Crazy for You*, and the blisters on his feet were even worse than Jonah's.

"I think . . . I think my toes might actually fall off," Dexter said one night after they got back home and he pried his shoes from his feet. "I can't feel them. Can they fall off, is that a thing?" Then, after spending ten minutes on Google and convincing himself he had the start of gangrene, Jonah talked him out of going to the hospital to request his toes be amputated. The two of them sat on the edge of the bathtub and bathed their feet until one in the morning while sipping on glasses of wine.

Now, though, as they took to the stage for *The Wooden Horse* for the final time, Jonah pushed aside the pain in his body and physical and emotional exhaustion; this would be his farewell to Achilles, to the role that made him an Olivier winner. The role that introduced him to the absolute whirlwind known as Dexter Ellis and gave him the confidence to know he was better than what Colbie Paris thought of him.

"I don't know if I'm ready for this," Bastien said from the wings as he dabbed the sleeve of his costume against his eyes. "Goddammit, I'm crying already."

"Stop it," Omari hissed as he started to cry. "You've set me off, you bastard."

"I'm right here with you, okay?" Jonah whispered and took Bastien's hand into his. "Patroclus and Achilles forever, right?"

Bastien's face crumpled as more tears fell from his eyes. "Don't say shit like that, Jonah. For God's sake, I'm an emotional mess, why are you making me cry more? You're such an arsehole."

Jonah laughed and pulled his friend into a hug. "Save the tears for later, okay? Let's go out there and give the best performance we've ever done, yeah?"

"Deal," Bastien mumbled, then pulled away to take a deep breath and fan his hand in front of his eyes. "Don't cry. Don't cry. Don't cry."

But he cried, he cried more than Jonah thought humanly possible. The moment Bastien stepped out onto the stage the audience erupted into applause, and he stood for a few seconds, not able to say his lines because of the deafening sound of cheers. Jonah smiled from the wings as he watched his friend try to subtly wipe the tears from his eyes, but the audience didn't care. They only clapped more until finally dying down to allow the show to continue. They offered the same respect for all the cast members who were due to take their final bows that night, and when Jonah made his entrance, the world stopped for a minute. He looked out at the crowd, their faces beaming, and for the briefest of moments, he thought he saw his dad in the same seat he sat in opening night. He could see his sea-blue eyes and wispy hair, the smile on his face showing nothing but pride for his son. He wanted to reach out to him, to tell him how much he missed him. But even though Jonah knew it wasn't him, he allowed himself to believe it until the cheering went quiet and he started to sing. His father remained in the seat until the song ended, then he turned back into just any other man. Jonah thanked him silently for being there, for always being there.

Performing Achilles for the last time wasn't as gut-wrenching as he expected, probably because he knew it wasn't just him leaving; most of the cast were moving on, leaving only a couple to stay for the next year. The next time the curtains opened at the Persephone there would be a new Achilles, and he would be played differently, with different movements and mannerisms. Jonah didn't mourn the Achilles he knew; he was part of him now, and the legacy Jonah left behind was not something to despair over, just the end of a chapter in a book, ready to be taken over by a new main character.

As the cast took to the stage for their final bows, Dexter smiled brightly at Jonah and he reached for his hand, so they bowed in unison with the rest of the cast. When they stood, every single member of the audience got to their feet, and Jonah tried to take in every one of their faces no matter how impossible that was. He saw his mum in the stalls with Aunt Penny and Sally, her hands clapping above her head as she whooped and cheered for him, the skeletal woman he knew her as a few months ago replaced by a beacon of health. He knew the path she walked would forever be a rocky one, but one she didn't walk alone. He waved at them, and they waved back, cheering even louder, and he laughed as Sally and Penny danced happily in the small space in front of their seats.

He turned his head to look at Dexter, to watch him reveling in the applause, but Dexter was looking at him, his eyes glassy, and he gently cupped Jonah's cheek and pulled him close to kiss him, center stage, in front of everyone. He first kissed him on this stage, not that he considered it their first real kiss, but this was where it started, Jonah knew it. The crowd cheered again, as did the cast, who were hugging and laughing around them, the happiness surrounding them beyond anything Jonah could have possibly imagined. He tried not to cry, but Dexter was there, his arm wrapped around him, and the lump in Jonah's throat grew until he was blinking back tears and trying his hardest to remember he needed to breathe.

At some point the backstage crew came out with flowers, handing them to the cast members leaving, and Jonah tried to juggle his massive bouquet as he pulled out a scrunched-up piece of paper from the belt of his costume, all while being handed a microphone to speak. He cleared his throat and the audience went quiet, as phones came out to take photos and videos of the speech he was about to give. He didn't actually want to give the speech; the graduating cast wrote it one night while hanging out late at The Roundhouse, and voted Jonah as their spokesperson despite his protests. And now, standing in front of his friends and the hundreds of people who came out to see them, he suddenly felt nervous, as if he were walking to the stage to collect his Olivier all over again.

"Thank you so much for the love you've shown us all tonight," he said as Bastien wrapped his arm behind his back and Dexter smiled fondly at them both from behind his own bouquet. "For a lot of us, this is our final night here at the Persephone performing *The Wooden Horse*. This show is special to so many people. It tells a story of love, betrayal, family, and hope. The message of everlasting love is still relevant today, and we can look at Helen and Paris, and Patroclus and Achilles and see ourselves in them, in the way they loved so fiercely that we still tell the story of the face that launched a thousand ships to this day. The characters we play are from Greek mythology, but their emotions and actions are as real as we are standing here up on this stage." The paper shook in his hands as he spoke, and he felt Bastien press closer to him, his anchor, as always. "So, thank you for being part of this journey with us. And thank you to everyone involved in the show. We will always hold our memories here at the Persephone close in our hearts, and we hope you remember our voices for years to come."

As they walked offstage, he saw Sherrie in the wings as she pulled Romana into a kiss, the two of them fitting together perfectly, almost like a harmony written just for them. If they could make it work, they could be beautiful together, and he hoped the Persephone would be kind to them. He looked over his shoulder one last time at the audience in the beautiful theatre. The red velvet, the sparkling chandeliers, and ornate coving and paintings on the ceiling all looked back and bowed to him, and there, in the wings, he bowed back and said his goodbye to the stage of the Persephone.

THIRTY-THREE

The Reprise

The Carmichael Theatre plunged into darkness. Jonah steadied himself and waited for the clicking noise of the table seats along the front row to rise to the stage level and the subsequent gasps from the audience sitting in them as they realized what was happening. Julianna Orwell certainly had a vision. A circular, rotating stage with audience members around the outer ring, making them part of the experience. Customers of the Kit Kat Club. Jonah didn't want to even think how much those seats must cost. When he first saw the layout of the stage, audience tables included, Jonah couldn't believe Julianna was actually going through with it, and thought the best thing to do was walk straight out the door and be unemployed for a while; you couldn't hide with the audience that close, any tiny mishap would be noticed and potentially pulled apart. But, after his brief moment of sheer panic, he relaxed with the idea; he trusted Julianna, and he trusted himself. *Cabaret* with stage rotation and moving tables for the audience? It would be something entirely new for the West End, and he couldn't wait to be part of it.

The orchestra played their first notes, and a spotlight shone down on him, center stage, alone. His costume would surely make his mother gasp, and he listened out for her, but heard nothing as he turned toward the audience, wearing only a tight corset with suspenders climbing up over his shoulders and leather shorts cut off to just above his knee. He wore black boots on his feet and white socks to his knees. Sparkling silver eyeshadow and deep red lipstick graced his skin, and his hair, parted to one side, his curls neat, pretty, playing on the fine line between masculine and feminine, finished the look, the perfect way to introduce the enigma of the Emcee to the audience. It was one of seven costumes he would wear throughout the show, the most changes he'd ever experienced, each one thought out with the tiniest details. Like this outfit for the opening number, with its not-so-subtle sexuality, black hearts stitched into the top part of the socks. Such a slight detail, not noticeable to the majority of the audience, but those who caught it would see the intricacies. Jonah fully expected Dexter to see it, what with his love for needlework.

Cabaret hit differently than *The Wooden Horse*. The shocks in the latter came from the in-your-face violence and realistic bloody deaths, but *Cabaret*? The shock came solely from the audience, seeing how someone like the Emcee contorted into something deadly and terrifying right before their eyes without them noticing until it was too late. Life in the cabaret was not beautiful, despite the Emcee's assurances; it was dark and deceitful, and so heart-wrenchingly stunning he could hear people sobbing when the actress who played Sally Bowles performed the titular song toward the end of act two. *The Wooden Horse* left people with a sense of hope, it told them Patroclus and Achilles found each other in the stars, and *Cabaret* left them reflecting on their life while shining an unapologetic torch on history. And, as much as Jonah loved *Cabaret*, he still loved the message of *The Wooden Horse* more, and he'd keep it with him as a beacon of light while pouring his soul into a character he knew would keep him awake at night.

Achilles would be the light on the landing, the thing showing him the way home, back to the house in St. Ives where his father played the piano and made jam sandwiches to eat in the garden. Achilles would lead him home to Dexter every night, where they would hang up Emcee and Bobby Child and become themselves again, two idiots in love whose feet still hurt so much they splurged on a foot spa massager because it made Dexter feel fancy.

The stage rotated as the final scene of *Cabaret* played out, Jonah facing opposite the actor playing Cliff, the role he once played, and he thought of how far he'd come, now leading one of the most anticipated West End revivals with Julianna Orwell at the helm. He could feel all eyes on him as he sang the finale song, and he looked out and saw Dexter sitting with Mum, the two of them hanging on his every word and movement, the ending one of the most striking no matter the direction. Jonah thought of the people who came before him, from Joel Grey and Alan Cumming to Neil Patrick Harris and Raúl Esparza, and fully acknowledged the honor of now adding his name to the list of those lucky enough to play such a rich and complex role.

He'd done it. From sitting at the piano playing the notes to "I Don't Care Much" slowly with his father, not understanding the meaning behind it, just feeling a deep connection to the tune and the way his father hummed it as they played, to now, standing on a stage in the West End in the role he always hoped might belong to him. He only wished his dad were there to see him, and in a way, Jonah knew he was there—not in a watching-over-him sense, but he could hear him in the music, in the way the pianist glided their fingers across the keys, and within his own voice as he sang his final notes. The stage descended into darkness, leaving the audience breathless, stunned, until they erupted into applause.

The warm June air greeted Jonah as he stepped out of the stage door at the Carmichael, and he smiled at the people waiting there for pictures and signatures. He felt a surge of anxiety strike him right in the chest, still not past the fear of someone marching forward and punching him in the face, which he thought was actually a pretty normal way to feel after being assaulted. But he saw Dexter and his mum standing close to the door, Dexter with the biggest bouquet of red roses Jonah had ever seen, and the panic quickly subsided. He was safe. He signed some programs and took photographs with the people who asked, then stopped when he came to a woman holding not only the new *Cabaret* program but also the program from *The Wooden Horse*, the old small one printed on recycled paper.

"I hope you don't mind," she said and tucked a strand of blond hair behind her ear. "I didn't catch you at stage door when I saw you when *The Wooden Horse* first opened, and yours is the only signature I'm missing."

Jonah smiled and took the pen she offered him, then signed both programs. "It's absolutely fine. Thanks for coming to the show tonight, did you enjoy it?"

"Oh, God, I was blown away." She smiled back at him. "I've never seen *Cabaret* before, not even the film. I only came because you were in it. I'm quite the fan." She blushed as she spoke and took the programs back from him. "Thank you for stopping to speak with me. I really appreciate it."

"Thank you for coming to see the show," Jonah said sincerely, and she stepped away to let him talk to the last few people remaining in line.

"Don't forget to use the steamer I got for you," Omari said before Jonah could walk away. "You were fabulous tonight."

Jonah blinked in surprise at the compliment. Omari wasn't one to talk about performances; he preferred to focus solely on skin and body care. "Thanks, so were you."

"Oh, I know." He smirked. "See you tomorrow when we can dazzle everyone all over again."

As Omari sauntered away, Jonah went to his mum and Dexter, waving at a few people who still lingered, perhaps too shy to come speak to him but happy to wave, so he did so with a smile.

"Will you sign my program, sausage?" his mum asked as she rummaged in her handbag and pulled out a sharpie.

"Mum," Jonah groaned, but took the pen and scrawled his name across the front of her booklet. "I'm your son. You don't need to me to sign every program from every show I do."

"You being my son is exactly why you should sign it for me!" she protested with a laugh as she slipped both the pen and program into her bag. "I'm proud of you, though seeing you in what I can only describe as frilly bloomers and not much else for the song about the threesomes was a bit eye-opening."

"That was my favorite part," Dexter said, and he kissed Jonah on the cheek, then handed him the flowers. "Hold these for me. Word must have leaked I was coming here tonight, because someone came and gave them to me, since I'm so famous and fabulous." He smirked as he spoke. "God, I love being adored."

Jonah raised an eyebrow at him, then looked at the flowers, the petals soft, as if made of velvet. He smiled. "Oh, right? Of course, I will hold them for you, love."

"I guess you can have them, though, seeing as you just had your opening night. It's only fair, after all."

"Is he always like this?" Jonah's mum asked.

"Yes," Jonah said swiftly before Dexter could protest.

"Well, whatever works for you both." She looked between them and smiled. "Now, I'm going to love you and leave you."

"What? Aren't you going to travel back with us?" Jonah asked, not liking the thought of his mother, who hardly ever left St. Ives, skipping off into the heart of London at eleven at night on her own.

"No, dear. Cathy—you remember Cathy, don't you? Her son got married to the girl he found on the internet? She sells the pickled onions at the market on the weekends? Well, she's also in London this weekend and told me there's a little late-night show we should go to, so she got us tickets and I'm going to meet her now."

"A late-night show?" Dexter asked, quirking a brow.

"Oh, yes, lots of men dancing on tables, so I've heard."

"Mum, are you going to a strip show?" Jonah asked, the sheer horror in his tone evident.

"A strip show makes it sound so uncouth, Jonah," she tutted. "But, yes, lots of abs and bums." She giggled. "Maybe even a willy."

Jonah lifted the roses to cover his face as he groaned. "Wow. Okay then, Mum, have fun."

"You don't want us to walk with you to the venue?" Dexter asked. "It's not a problem."

"No, no, don't be silly," she said, then stood on her tiptoes to kiss Dexter on the cheek before doing the same to Jonah. "I don't know why you're so mortified by penises, Jonah, honestly. It's not like you don't have one of your own, and I'm sure you've seen his plenty of times." She gestured at Dexter.

"Okay, Mum, that's enough, go, have a good time. But, um, well . . ." He struggled for words.

"I'm strictly on the orange juice, love," she said and hugged him again, crumpling the roses slightly, and cupped his cheek as she looked in his eyes. "I'm so proud of you, Jonah. Dad would be too."

"Thank you."

"Enjoy the rest of your night, boys. I'll see you for breakfast in the morning." And with that, she swung her handbag over her shoulder and sauntered off down the road toward Covent Garden.

"She'll be fine," Dexter said as they watched her go. "You've got to let her live her life, Jonah."

"I know. I just worry about her."

"That's normal. But from how she was today, I think she's really found her feet." He smiled. "She is quite the person to watch a show with," Dexter said. He put his arm around Jonah, and they started toward the bus stop; it was Dexter's turn to have his preferred method back to Camden. "She kept grabbing my knee and squeezing super tight."

"Any excuse to get her hands on you." Jonah laughed. "She always tells me how handsome you are."

"Sounds like she's going to have her hands full with a lot of other men tonight."

"Who knew leaving Cornwall would bring out the man-eating side of my mum?"

"I think it's kinda sweet, actually." Dexter smiled. "To see her so happy. She really is doing well."

"Yeah, I know," Jonah said as he ran his fingers over the petals of the roses. "Thank you for these. They're beautiful."

"You were outstanding tonight, you deserve them. Seriously, I think I had goosebumps throughout the entire show. It's quite possibly the best thing I've ever seen in the West End, and I'm not just saying that because my boyfriend is one of the leads."

"Wow, such a glowing review from the one-and-only Dexter Ellis." Jonah grinned at him. "No criticism to be found."

"Well, actually, you were behind—"

"Stop."

"You didn't—"

"Dexter."

"Only like, a millisecond behind in 'Two Ladies.'" He stopped to stand in front of Jonah and tucked a curl behind his ear before leaning forward to kiss him.

"Was I actually?"

"No, but I need to keep you on your toes, can't have you thinking you're going to win an Olivier for best actor in a musical *again* next year. We both know that award's mine."

Jonah smacked his hand against Dexter's chest with a groan before laughing. "Well, we'll see, huh? You've got a month before your opening night. Best polish those tap shoes if you even stand a chance of being nominated." He let Dexter hold his hand again as they meandered down the road, taking their time; they finally had time to take. Jonah listened as Dexter talked about the show, about the parts he liked the most, about the costumes he wished Jonah might bring back to the bedroom. As they waited at the bus stop, their bodies huddled together, the smell of red roses danced between them. Jonah took a deep breath and closed his eyes and let London carry them home.

ACKNOWLEDGMENTS

This book was inspired by the theatre, by a love of the arts and all aspects of it. Thank you to everyone who works so tirelessly in the industry to bring stories to life. You inspire generation after generation, and without the beautiful world of the theatre, this book wouldn't exist.

First, I must thank my agent, Nina Leon. I am so honored to have an agent who constantly inspires me, who works all hours under the sun to do the best for her clients and still manages to be hilarious and always there when you need her. Nina, there are no words for how much your support means to me. Thank you for your patience, for your calming words, and for believing in me and this book. This really has been such a wonderful adventure and I'm so glad you've been there by my side for all of it.

Special thanks must also go to my lovely editor, Jackie Quaranto, for taking a chance on this West End romance and for bringing your talent and passion to the project. It has been a truly amazing experience. To find an editor with the same love for the theatre as mine really was the icing on the cake. Working with you has been a dream come true. Thank you for championing this book and for picking up all the musical references; you really are a star.

Of course, huge thanks goes to team *Jonah* at Harper Perennial: Megan Looney, Stacey Fischkelta, Michael Fierro, Joanne O'Neill, Jen

Overstreet, and Stephanie Mendoza. And those thanks also extend to the wider HarperCollins team including Amy Baker, Doug Jones, Jonathan Burnham, Heather Drucker, Lisa Erickson, and Robin Bilardello; thank you all for making this book come to life. I must also thank the beautifully talented Jessica Cruickshank who created the gorgeous artwork for the cover.

Thank you to my beta readers, Allison and Kristen; you were there the moment Jonah became a little spark in my mind, and your encouragement and words of wisdom helped to shape him and his ridiculous thought processes. Extra special thanks to Allison for reading all the stories that came before this, from Charlie to Jonah and beyond. You've been there for them all. Thank you for being my friend, for always being at the end of a message to pick me up, and for teaching me so much over these years. Forever "safe keeping" buddies.

Thank you to Gavin. You are the strongest person I know, and I wouldn't be where I am today without you. Your own creativity inspires me, I love how you see the world, and you never fail to make me laugh. Thank you for all the cups of tea; you know you make the best ones. Big love. And to Arlo, my favorite person, thank you for being my duet partner. The Glinda to my Elphaba. The Hamilton to my Burr. You inspire me more than anything. Keep being yourself because you are amazing.

To my mum and dad, who encouraged their creative child to always shoot for the stars. Thank you for your encouragement and endless love. I'm very lucky to have you both, and please forgive the bad language in this book. I love you.

To Brittany, Laura, and Si, the best friends anyone could ever ask for. You've all had to endure me talking about the book world for hours on end; you've helped me work through plot holes and panics when writing sex scenes. Thank you for always letting me drag you to the theatre and for never complaining when I play show tunes on car journeys or constantly make musical references. You allow me to be myself, and I love you all for that. You really do make my life sparkle.

A huge thank you to my family, to Lita and Mick for their endless support, and to my lovely drama team for being totally fabulous humans.

Sharing this with you has been the best thing anyone could ever wish for. Thanks for believing in me, for being there for me to vent to and share ideas with and, more than anything, laugh with.

And last, but by no means least, thank you to you, wonderful readers. Jonah means so much to me; he came to me at a time in my life when I felt a little lost, and he reminded me the world was still full of magic. I loved every minute of writing this book, and I hope that you enjoy reading it. So much wonder and beauty can be found within literature and the theatre, the power and importance of the arts is something we must all treasure. Thank you for being along for the journey with me, for supporting queer voices and stories, which we need now more than ever. Please keep supporting diverse books and authors, keep the books on the shelves, and celebrate everything that makes diversity magical. Thank you, forever.

ABOUT THE AUTHOR

Robyn Green was born and raised in Suffolk, England. After falling in love with the theatre at a young age, she spent time performing onstage before moving her focus behind the scenes, where she now specializes in costume design and curation. Robyn's passion for the arts is the main source of inspiration for her writing. *The Dramatic Life of Jonah Penrose* is her debut novel and her love letter to the theatre.